Advance praise for
THE INTERCEPTOR

THE INTERCEPTOR

Richard Herschlag

BALLANTINE BOOKS • NEW YORK

To Sue, the love of my life.

A Ballantine Book
Published by The Ballantine Publishing Group
Copyright © 1998 by Richard Herschlag

All rights reserved under International and Pan-American Copyright Conventions. Published in the United States by The Ballantine Publishing Group, a division of Random House, Inc., New York, and simultaneously in Canada by Random House of Canada Limited, Toronto.

http://www.randomhouse.com

Library of Congress Catalog Card Number: 98-96257

ISBN: 0-345-41742-9

Manufactured in the United States of America

First Edition: September 1998

10   9   8   7   6   5   4   3   2   1

Author's Note

My years working as an engineer for the City of New York were extremely rewarding. While no one is perfect, the people I worked with were on the whole honest, concerned, and professional. In many cases, these people worked many extra hours with no additional compensation other than the satisfaction of a job well done. This was true both within the borough president's office, where I worked, and in city agencies such as the Departments of Environmental Protection, Transportation, and General Services—agencies that have performed remarkably well in building and managing infrastructure systems that in size and complexity rival those of a small nation's.

Though it is hoped that the characters and events portrayed herein feel genuine, this book is a work of fiction. As such, it draws on specific realities of the physical environment and general realities of the political environment. These ingredients are added, stirred in with the fictional elements, and brought to a boil to create a story that is technically and sociologically plausible. Nonetheless, that story is purely a figment of the author's imagination. And although some readers might imagine that a given character resembles a real person, none of the characters are intended to portray living persons, and none of the fictional events the characters engage in ever actually transpired.

MAP OF MANHATTAN

THE BRONX

HARLEM RIVER

George Washington Bridge

Riverside Park

North River Plant

135th St.

St. Clair Place

Morningside Park

352 W 110 St.

115th St.

Riverside Park

96th St.

HUDSON RIVER

81st St.

72nd St.

66th St.

Site of Hudson City

CENTRAL PARK

HELL GATE

QUEENS

Roosevelt Island

59th St.

49th St.

11th Ave.

Broadway

Joel Haney's Apartment

30th St.

EAST RIVER

NEWTOWN CREEK

18th St.

18th St.

Locations of Sewer Outfalls and Regulators

14th St.

Union Square

The Glass House

BROOKLYN

Bank St.

Washington Square Park

Tompkins Square Park

Canal St.

City Hall Park

Municipal Building

Brooklyn Bridge

South Street Seaport

N
W E
S

15/64"=1 mile

Chapter 1

Like the Chelsea piers, Joel Haney had seen better days and hoped to see better days ahead. Piers 59 through 62 on Manhattan's West Side had a distinguished history. When they were completed in 1910, New York City's mayor, George G. McClellan Jr., proudly proclaimed that the Chelsea piers provided a "waterfront with an architectural appearance worthy of the city." The piers were far more than four docks on wooden piles extending six hundred feet out into the Hudson River. They were enclosed by a single steel-framed structure with a facade of granite and concrete that spared no expense. Along Eleventh Avenue, where the piers faced Manhattan, the three-story structure looked as stately as a courthouse or a bank with its gargoyles, towering arched windows, and gable-roofed head houses.

Although you wouldn't have known it looking from Eleventh Avenue, each of the four head houses was aligned with one of the four piers and followed it all the way out to its end, offering immediate protection from nature to any passenger or cargo, coming or going. Inside, the naked framework of built-up, riveted steel plate girders and columns revealed the technology that not only held up the building, but had allowed New York and its harbor to become a world force in only a few short decades.

The Chelsea piers wasted no time making their mark. On April 20, 1912, thousands of people crammed onto the piers to await the arrival of the *Carpathia*, which carried the survivors of the *Titanic*. More than fifteen hundred people had lost their lives when the *Titanic* hit an iceberg and sank into the cold sea. Without television or radio, cramming onto the Chelsea piers was the closest most people could get to the sights and sounds of the disaster, not to mention the fastest way to see if their friends and relatives had survived.

The Chelsea piers stood at the beginning rather than at the end of another disastrous voyage one day in May 1915. This time the thousands of New Yorkers who crowded the piers wore happier faces as they waved bon voyage to the luxurious *Lusitania*. Days later, a German U-boat off the coast of Ireland torpedoed the *Lusitania*, sinking the ship and sending 1,198 people, including 124 Americans, to their deaths. That day effectively marked the beginning of America's entry into World War I, where millions of European soldiers drowned in poison gas and in trenches soaked with rainwater and blood.

Over the next several years, while the Chelsea piers launched sailors off to war, it also opened its arms to stars like Mary Pickford and John Barrymore, who made movies about battle, adventure, and romance only a few blocks away at the Chelsea Studios, on West Twenty-sixth Street. Commuting by private yacht to the Chelsea piers took only a few minutes from Hoboken, New Jersey, and only a little longer from a variety of other nearby points along both sides of the Hudson. Actors, directors, and materials for building sets came in, and finished movies went out, shipped not only up the Hudson but all over the world.

During the next few decades, as New York continued to thrive, everything under the sun came and went through the Chelsea piers. Longshoremen could be seen working at all hours of the day and night, loading and unloading beef, grain, fruit, leather, furniture, lumber, bricks, steel beams, and even the trucks that would help speed the decline of the docks.

But waterfront decline due to the growth of trucking and the U.S. highway system was still many years away. The golden age of the Chelsea piers was still going strong on August 24, 1936, the day crowds lined the shore to greet Jesse Owens, who had just shown up Hitler and the Nazis by winning four gold medals at the Olympics in Berlin. Just six years later American soldiers and sailors, both black and white, were leaving the Chelsea piers by the tens of thousands to fight the Nazis with tanks and shells rather than hurdles and javelins.

There wasn't anyone waiting to greet Joel Haney by the Chelsea piers on the cool, cloudy night of April 5, 1993, and there wasn't much glory in picking up hookers. Until recently, that was the best he could do to recapture his own heyday. Haney was now thirty-seven, somewhat portly, and losing his once bushy hair, to the point where the bare spots on the right and left temples were racing to get to the middle.

Like the Chelsea piers behind him, he still had the outlines of his imposing stature. At six-foot-three, with broad shoulders, a wide, squarish chin, a slightly flattened nose, and eyes set far apart, people throughout his life asked him if he played football, which he had. Playing for Canarsie High School, he made second team All-City as a middle linebacker his junior and senior years. But now, twenty years later, he did very little running, and when he walked, he hunched over marginally, not because he was getting ready to make a tackle, but because that was how his body expressed the depression that had taken hold of him the last few years. When he muttered, it wasn't defensive plays that came out of his mouth, but a series of encrypted laments about the bad turns his life had taken.

A more current and less obscure lament of Joel's concerned what he'd been smelling down by Eighteenth Street and Eleventh Avenue—raw sewage. Here, at the Eighteenth Street outfall, a six-foot-diameter trunk main was connected to an even larger interceptor. The two were linked by a large regulator valve. The valve was normally positioned to send millions of gallons per day of raw sewage from the Eighteenth Street trunk line straight to the interceptor, which carried it uptown to the sewage treatment plant in West Harlem.

The smell coming off of the river lately was a pungent odor of rotten eggs, with components of methane and ammonia. That smell wasn't normally supposed to be there, at least not nearly to the degree it had been of late. There hadn't been any severe storms during the past week, so there was no reason to send the sewage directly into the Hudson. It was possible, Joel thought, that the regulator had malfunctioned—that it had been "tripped" and was locked into the bypass position. If so, it should have been fixed by now. It was all speculation at this point anyway. Viewing the outfall involved climbing a shoreline fence and standing on a rickety pier. In addition, the outfall was below the water level in the Hudson that night, so Joel could not fully verify what was going on without going down below.

From what he could tell, the squad that had replaced his was working a night shift. There were yellow traffic cones surrounding the metal access plates to the valve chamber situated in the middle of the far right lane of the southbound side of Eleventh Avenue. Three nights before, from a hundred yards away, he had seen a couple of shadowy figures disappear into the chamber and then reemerge. Without thinking, he began to film them with the night setting on his camcorder. After two minutes he stopped filming and decided not to get involved or even to approach the valve chamber. If these guys were as incompetent as they seemed, it was better to let them hang themselves than to stick his nose in the middle of it. That tape was still in his flight jacket.

At 10:30 P.M., as Joel fixed his lens on the modest darkened sky-line of Hoboken on the Jersey side of the Hudson, the smell of raw sewage was now unbearable, even to his battle-scarred nose. He couldn't concentrate on his project this way. And he suddenly didn't care about the political consequences of interfering with the new squad. Someone was making a travesty of sewer mainte-nance. There was no substitute for doing your job the right way.

Joel looked through the lens as he walked toward the yellow traffic cones surrounding the open valve chamber. As he neared, a heavyset, broad-shouldered man in his mid-forties emerged from the hole and looked straight into the lens. He had a sallow com-plexion, weather-beaten skin, a black and gray goatee that was not well groomed, an upturned nose, and bushy dark eyebrows pushed oddly close to the bridge of his nose. His dark eyes looked out of equally dark, wrinkled pockets of loose skin. His thick, long gray hair was combed straight back, rising several inches over his forehead. He wore a threadbare flannel work shirt and gray wool jacket and clutched a foot-long wrench in his right hand.

"What the fuck are you doing?" he said.

"Actually, what the fuck are *you* doing," Joel replied, lowering the camera and looking directly at the man. "Smells like you got a tripped regulator down there. Either that or you guys need a shower."

"The only thing we need, asshole, is for you to pop that tape out right now and give it to me."

"I can't do that, chief, but I'll tell you what I *can* do. I can give you some advice. Find someone who knows what they're doing down there. Then follow him around for a few years and watch what he does. Then you might not have to embarrass yourself like this."

"Okay, now I'll take the camera too, asshole."

"Hey, you'll die trying," Joel said.

The sewer worker took three quick steps forward and lunged at

Joel with his head down like a bull's, his arms swinging. Joel felt the acute jolt of the wrench hitting his left hipbone and was aware that his camcorder had been launched when the guy's head hit his stomach. Joel's baseball cap had fallen to the ground as well.

With both his arms free, Joel was punching the sewer worker rapidly in the face—five, six, seven times—until the man stumbled backward, dazed from the blows. Joel now tackled him football-style, his right shoulder impacting just below the waist, bringing the man down hard on his back. No sooner had he flattened his adversary than Joel scrambled back toward the southbound side of Eleventh Avenue, where his camcorder sat relatively intact in the right lane. Joel hesitated as a brown Dodge Shadow rolled by, its right wheels missing the camera by inches.

"Shit!" he shouted as a speeding yellow cab followed right behind and crushed the camcorder under its right wheels, sending dozens of pieces flying like shrapnel in all directions. "Shit!" he shouted again.

Then, on the same pavement in front of him where the camera pieces were still coming to rest, Joel saw the long shadow of an arm and a wrench sweep across toward the shadow of his own head. There was no sound as he watched his own shadow collapse to the pavement. The shadow and his own body became one, and he was aware of bleeding from the head as he wriggled on the shoulder of the road. Several cars whipped by as Joel's body was dragged facedown by the ankles inside the circle of traffic cones surrounding the open valve chamber. The sewer worker, standing over the body, pulled a walkie-talkie out of the left pocket of his jacket and pressed it against the side of his face.

The worker and his own body now seemed much farther away in Joel's dreamlike field of vision. He heard sounds again, but not limited to those coming from the street. The sound of his father's voice was all around him, biting and sarcastic as ever. "Well, Joel, you finally got out of the sewer." Virtually at the same time, he heard a soothing female voice, "It's time to get out, Joel. It's time to get out."

"I got a problem over here," the sewer worker said into the walkie-talkie.

"What is it?" the voice on the other end replied. "Where are you?"

"I'm at the Eighteenth Street valve chamber," the sewer worker said. "I had a guy over here trying to get me on camera. I took him out. He's down."

"You fucking moron," the voice said. "I'll be there in a minute." Two minutes later, with cars still whizzing by, Max Mc-Cord emerged out of the darkness on the service road, a block north of his crew member and the body.

McCord was a wiry, ornery, forty-eight-year-old ex-con with wrinkles beyond his years and cold gray eyes that sat way back in his head. He had been moved around frequently from unit to unit after botching various assignments and being halfheartedly defended by the union. The city had initially blamed McCord for the 1985 sewer collapse at Eighty-fourth Street and East River Drive. Allegedly, McCord had repeatedly neglected to report and address a series of chronic leaks in the line. When push came to shove, the city had little more evidence against McCord than a low efficiency rating and a bad temper.

McCord was out of breath from running as he stopped inside the circle of cones.

"I asked him for the tape," the sewer worker explained, "but he tried to get smart with me."

"You think everyone's trying to get smart with you," McCord said. He kneeled alongside the body and placed his index and middle fingers against its neck. McCord looked up. "He's dead."

"It was an accident. I wasn't trying to kill him, but he could've turned that tape over to the cops . . ."

As the crew man argued, McCord paid no mind and walked three steps to where Joel's baseball cap lay, picked it up and looked at the Local 375 insignia on it. He glanced at the wrench and then looked over at the pieces of camera scattered along the southbound lane—pieces that cars rolled over every so often.

"What's wrong?" the crew man asked.

McCord had now walked back to the body, leaned down, and rolled it faceup. "You're even dumber that I thought, Paul," he said without raising his voice. "This is Joel Haney."

"Who the fuck is Joel Haney?"

"He works for DEP—Bureau of Sewers," McCord said. "That's where *you* work, remember? He has something like fifteen years on the job. He worked right here at Eighteenth Street until we got this gig. You really fucked up big-time." McCord shook his head.

"Maybe he knew," the crew man said. "Why was he down here with that camera?"

"He's making some kind of porno film," McCord said. "This is where he picked up hookers. Whatsamatter, you don't want your fat ass on film?"

"He asked me about the regulator."

"Of course he asked you about the regulator," McCord said. "It smells like shit down here. So you hit him with a wrench."

"Yeah . . ."

"Well, at least you didn't shoot him. But now I'm gonna have to think of something," McCord said, scratching his head.

"There's the fucking river. Let's just throw him in."

"Could you please just shut the fuck up?" McCord said, his fingers still touching his head. "That body will float back to the top in a week. And then we're dead meat. We have a hundred fucking possible witnesses as it is." McCord pointed briefly to the passing southbound cars on Eleventh Avenue.

"So we'll take him somewhere else . . ."

"Someone should hit *you* with a wrench."

A white Econoline van with a Department of Environmental Protection logo on the outside headed west along Fourteenth Street at 12:15 A.M. McCord drove and his crew man sat in the front passenger's seat. The body lay in the back, wrapped in thick tarpaulin from head to toe. The Local 375 cap was back on Haney's head.

"Will this really work?" Paul asked.

"Better than anything *you* were gonna think of," McCord said. "He works along Fourteenth Street. He drinks, he shoots porno flicks. When they find him, they'll think he was up to some bullshit on the job. Maybe they'll just get confused. But it's a long way back to what really went down."

"Are you gonna tell Fuckface about this?"

"I'm gonna *have* to tell Fuckface about this," McCord said. "Fuckface'll probably tell me to kill you, and I'll be glad to do it."

McCord pulled the van to a halt in the middle of Fourteenth Street, almost equidistant between Sixth and Seventh Avenues. Except for a small delicatessen on the north side of the street, all stores were closed, sealed with steel pull-down security gates. The large brick Salvation Army building on the south side of the street was darkened except for one light on the third floor and another on the eighth. The sidewalks appeared empty of pedestrians for two hundred feet in either direction. It had begun to drizzle.

McCord had made sure the back of the van was as close to the sewer manhole cover as possible without covering it. With the van's engine running but the headlights and emergency flashers off, he quickly opened the two rear doors. He hopped gently onto the pavement, inserted a three-foot-long set of steel prongs into two slots along the outside of the manhole cover, which read NYC SEWER across the middle and MADE IN INDIA across the bottom. Once he'd pulled the cover off its rim and slid it to the side, he lay the prongs on the pavement and reached into the back of the van for the body. At the other end, inside the van, Paul was lifting the tarpaulin-wrapped body around the head and shoving it toward McCord.

"Loosen that thing up," McCord said. "C'mon, damn it." Paul used one hand to begin unwrapping the body and continued pushing. Once the legs were over the open manhole, McCord steadied the body with one hand and began rapidly unfurling the tarpaulin with the other. "Let go now," McCord said. A second after his crew man had let go, McCord held tightly onto the tarpaulin and let the body, now halfway down the manhole, slide the rest of the way. The tarpaulin was now light in his hands and a thud was heard along with a small splash.

"They love it when you come to work early," McCord said.

Chapter 2

Jon Kessler sat comfortably on the toilet, newspaper in hand, and looked across and down at his two-year-old son Steven, who was sitting like a prince on a little toilet of his own. Jon contemplated what Steven would look like in twenty or thirty years. Most likely, his son would undergo the same transformation he had. His pug nose would elongate and widen. His wide smile would get a strong, prominent chin to match. His fine, penciled eyebrows would thicken to become heavy arches, sturdy enough to protect the clear, deep blue eyes below from most storms. Steven's eyes would be the only feature that would remain unchanged by time and the bad weather it brought. And even they would come to show shades of gray, losing their pure blueness. More dramatically, Steven's thin, straight blond hair would become thick, wavy, almost black, just as his life was likely to become more burdened, twisted, and dark.

For all he still wanted from life, Jon's wish list was headed by his absolute desire for privacy when he was on the pot. Some things were sacred, like his fundamental right to seal himself off from the overly intrusive outer world while he cleaned out his inner one. But now even this basic privilege was in jeopardy as his son came with his own wish list and a series of surefire lobbying tactics, including screaming, crying, and thrashing.

That was all right, though, Jon had originally thought. Steven was largely oblivious to what he was doing on the pot, how he was doing it, and what he was thinking while doing it. But after slowly eroding over the past several months, what was left of that illusion came crashing down when Steven started imitating him. He would "squeeze" by squinting his eyes, scrunching up his face, and groaning with a half giggle. As an added attraction he occasionally flailed his fists.

At least his thinking still remained private, Jon thought. No one could take that from him. As Jon looked around at the neatly tiled blue and white floor and walls, he saw more than a modern Long Island bathroom. This was a room he had largely designed and built himself, along with the rest of the two-story house in Rocky Point, a small town on the north shore, about sixty miles east of Manhattan. The streamlined, low-flow, tank-type toilet; the use of rainwater collected on the roof; the tiles made from recycled glass—they were all his doing. When all else failed, he could sit here and find refuge in the knowledge that he knew how things were put together and could put them together himself if he chose to.

Now as Jon wiped, stood, and pulled up his pants, Steven insisted on being the one to flush. "Daddy, Stevie do it." He reached carefully for the compact metal handle and pulled.

"Good job, Stevie."

Steven's face studied his father's residue as it went round and round the bowl: "Daddy, where it go?"

"Down the drain, Stevie, down the drain."

"Down the drain," Steven repeated, knowing somehow that he had gotten as good a response as most people of any age who ever ask the same question.

Jon was a civil engineer who came from a long line of people who wanted and needed to understand how things worked. His father was a retired aerospace engineer who had worked on a series of top secret projects for the defense industry. He survived the massive layoffs at Grumman in Bethpage, Long Island, in the early 1970s and took an early retirement ten years later, before the plant closed its doors for good. Jon's grandfather had been a subway car mechanic for the New York City Transit Authority. Accountant, patent lawyer, apparel designer—these were the professions that inhabited his family tree. For the Kesslers, knowing how things worked—knowing the guts of something—was an end in itself, something like a religion. And like a religion, it had several purposes and benefits as well. With such a mind-set, you were more likely than not to become gainfully employed in some way, shape, or form, and eventually be seen by yourself and others as an expert in one or more areas of interest. You were also more likely than not to make mental and emotional adjustments when times got rough, and thereby maintain both sanity and personal relationships. You had an anchor during rough weather.

But Jon, like the people from whom he descended—and even the people out there who didn't try so hard to understand the way things worked—frequently reached the end of reasoning's line. When someone or something close to the essence of your being was challenged, peeling away layers of cause and effect eventually reached a dead end. Behind that barrier lay the Supreme Being and the sometimes very private ideas He held about why you needed to be running around on this troubled planet in the first place. Without some kind of faith, optimism, or even resignation, despair was always just around the corner or in your face, no matter how many damn good questions you asked.

Jon had some of that faith, and it led him back to doing his share of good things and asking his share of insightful questions, fulfilling his end of the cosmic bargain. Civil engineering became for him a primary path to achieving this purpose. When designing a road, drainage ditch, or filtration system, the answers were virtually all there if you looked hard enough. On a good day you could go home with your work rolled up neatly in a cardboard tube.

Jon was now thirty-four. Two and a half years earlier, he had been appointed chief engineer for the office of the Manhattan borough president. He didn't get to spend billions on highways, bridges, and sludge treatment plants. Those responsibilities were spread out among the commissioners of various huge city agencies. He wasn't the one who designed these projects either. That fell to engineers within those specific agencies or, more likely, the outside consultants those agencies hired. But in his position, Jon had the opportunity to review and analyze virtually anything the borough president considered worth reviewing or analyzing.

Whether it was called budget analysis, capital review, or value engineering, Jon was very good at it. He had developed a knack for taking a large, seemingly complex dilemma, translating it into one, two, or three concisely stated questions, gathering the relevant data, and answering the questions in straightforward English, understood easily by the public and the politicians they elected. Over the past year or so, he had come to see this ability, in this job description, as a calling in life. It was a nice plateau to arrive at. But like so many Americans recently, he had seen plateaus grow smaller, more slippery, and less stable. No engineer could seem to fix that.

At 2:35 on a Tuesday afternoon, April 6, 1993, the phone rang in Jon's tiny office located in the rear of the larger office, room 2035. He knew he had four rings to play with until the voice mail system kicked in, and he was compelled to use up every second of that time. He scanned the eight-by-eight-foot room crammed with file cabinets, tubes of rolled-up plans, and piles of overflowing manila folders. Like the rest of room 2035, this smaller room was not part of the original configuration. His solid metal door did not match the ornate wooden door that still remained at the front. His bulky, gray metal vintage 1960s desk at the center of the small, packed space provided a less than adequate eye for this hurricane. Jon tried to keep the desk clear, but marked-up drawings, urgent memos from supervisors, requests for information, and technical reports always seemed to be closing in on him. The best he could do was create neat stacks and arrange them in terms of priority. Even the computer on the desk did not provide an escape, as it added to rather than replaced the storm of information around him. For genuine refuge, Jon had to look at the off-white plaster walls, where he had framed and hung more than a dozen survey maps showing how Manhattan had existed decades and even hundreds of years ago—complete with farmland, streams, and strangely shaped city blocks with only the beginnings of a grid system.

When those wouldn't do the trick, he could look at the framed photos of famous baseball players he had hung on the same walls—Mickey Mantle, Duke Snider, Ted Williams, Willie Mays, the '61 Yankees. When he was feeling overwhelmed, these men all looked back at him and told him to hang in there and do the best he could . . . that he could still get a hit with an 0-and-2 count.

When even his wall of fame couldn't help him, Jon would look up. Though the room was only eight by eight, the ceiling was eleven feet high. For a few moments, he could get lost up there among thoughts of a Higher Power and cheap white acoustic tiles. If truly inspired, he could move the plants away from the narrow windowsill and catch a sliver of New York: the brick fortress of One Police Plaza, the randomly developed Lower East Side, the half-reconstructed Manhattan Bridge. It wasn't quite worthy of a postcard, but it was all he had.

Now, during the third ring, Jon caught his own reflection in the glass from the Sandy Koufax frame. Jon looked a little like the photo of Koufax—a strong forehead, large chiseled features, but with a boyish grin and a little baby fat to offset those features. Unlike Koufax, however, he wasn't smiling much today and he hadn't shaved in the past forty-eight hours.

He picked up the phone and felt a small lump form in his stomach when he recognized the voice on the other end. It was Paula Derbin, the attorney who more or less ran the show for Manhattan borough president Arthur Shuler. Officially, she was responsible for the legal ramifications of every move the borough president made. Officially, her title was chief counsel. Unofficially, her title was chief. After she and Art Shuler decided what to do, Paula Derbin knew how to justify it—politically, economically, and, of course, legally. Her aggressive, disciplined mind was dense with facts, codes, and realities pertaining to the city and the people who ran it. She was feared for her tendency to verbally bludgeon without warning, coupled with the implicit support she enjoyed from Art Shuler. She had a license to kill, and used it both for political advantage and personal whim. When those two objectives coincided, it was time to run. That was the grim reality in which most of the office lived. One hundred three people each cowered before Paula Derbin when their turn came. None of them would normally permit anyone to speak to them the way Paula did, yet she got away with it day in, day out, because of who she knew and how similar her approach was to a guerrilla assault.

Jon Kessler, however, represented a multiple threat to Paula Derbin. Like only two or three others in the office, he wouldn't quite take "the treatment." He dared to argue with Paula at times, albeit in much more self-restrained and polite tones than he would have preferred. She returned the fire twice as hard every time, causing her short black hair to flap like a mop head over a beet-red face and a neck of popping veins. Her thick framed glasses would struggle to stay in place while her fury boiled over like gang members at a rumble. Rumor had it that life as a corporate lawyer could not satisfy her lust for power, influence, and glory, so she quit a major New York firm several years earlier and got on the government track. Now, at forty-one, she was speeding down the rails.

While Paula Derbin exercised the advantage of her power to hire and fire, she resented the use of Jon Kessler's tiny shield—the knowledge that finding an articulate, policy-oriented, licensed civil engineer to work for an unimpressive city salary was not easy. She had discovered that problem with Jon's predecessor and Jon's predecessor's predecessor.

"Hello," Jon said, speaking carefully into the receiver, "Jon Kessler, Borough President's Office."

"It's Paula," came the disturbed voice on the other end, virtually quivering. "You need to get down here right away and see me."

"Regarding . . . ?" Jon asked as calmly as his throat muscles would allow him.

"We will discuss that when you get down here. If I wanted to have this conversation over the phone, I wouldn't have told you to come down!"

"Okay," he replied, maintaining his composure, "I'll catch the next elevator."

"You do that."

As he did several times every working day, Jon now waited on the twentieth floor by the elevator bank, just to go down one flight. The stairwell had been closed since the rape that occurred between the fourteenth and fifteenth floors ten years earlier. Jon wondered what the city's response would be should a rape ever occur on the elevator. Would they close all of them or only that one shaft? As he continued waiting, he marveled at how these management types consistently did not want you knowing what it was about until the last possible moment, lest they lose their advantage. But Jon already knew, more or less. Two weeks earlier he had handed in a thorough report on the North River Sewage Treatment Plant. Located along the Hudson River in West Harlem, the twenty-eight-acre plant treated all the raw sewage for the west half of Manhattan—sometimes as much as 300 million gallons in a single day. Since the plant's opening in 1986, the residents of West Harlem had been complaining about the rotten egg odor emanating from North River and sweeping over their community, invading playground and bedroom alike with an unbearable, eye-irritating, stomach-turning stench.

Those complaints had fallen largely on deaf ears until about two years earlier, when the city was forced by state and federal authorities to acknowledge that the plant was in violation of its permit for a variety of reasons. To many powerful figures both inside and outside New York City government, without a legally viable sewage plant to hook up to, new land development in Manhattan was dead.

The highest profile development of such kind was the recently approved Hudson City, a massive residential and commercial venture proposed by Ronald Arlen. By design, Hudson City would rise up out of the old semi-abandoned rail yard on the extreme west side, between Fifty-ninth and Seventy-second Streets—the single largest unbuilt parcel of land left in Manhattan. There, sparkling new luxury high-rises would look out over the Hudson and New Jersey in one direction, and down on Manhattan's West Side on the other.

According to Ronald Arlen—originally from Brooklyn and dubbed ironically by the tabloid press as "the Dodger"—Hudson City would become, de facto, the cultural and commercial center of the area, bring billions into the local economy, and even include a waterfront park as a throw-in. For those who believed, as the Dodger did, that Manhattan was the capital of the world, Hudson

City would be the capital of Manhattan. And while the project would cost Arlen and his backers an estimated three to four *billion* dollars, its resale value was estimated to reach more than twice that by the end of the century. Add in the hundreds of millions in property and other taxes the city could potentially take in, and it was plain why such a sense of urgency surrounded Hudson City.

Of course there were problems, massive problems, with the Hudson City proposal, as detractors frequently pointed out. Manhattan was already overcrowded and environmentally overburdened. Automobile traffic on the West Side was horrendous, and so was the air quality that came with the traffic. During morning and evening rush hours—and the eight hours they sandwiched—the intersection of Seventy-second, Broadway, and Amsterdam became a poster child for gridlock. A realistic driver allowed ten minutes just to pass through this hellish bottleneck, thereby making himself less likely to become merely another brick in the wall of honking and hatred. Stay cool. Count to five hundred and repeat your mantra. Or listen to Mike and the Mad Dog yell about why the Knicks lost.

Meanwhile, the public transit situation on the West Side was no better. Commuters suspended their sense of distance and privacy and packed like M&M's onto the subway platforms and into the cars. As was the case aboveground, Seventy-second Street seemed to serve as the focal point of the problem, with the staircases and platforms at the station on Broadway often becoming unbearable. Stairways built for 1904's demand were coping with present reality, so crammed that there was motion in only one direction at a time, and that motion almost undetectable. Looking down at the narrow, teeming platform gave you the impression of a fire drill on a balance beam, but it was merely another day on the IRT Broadway line.

Meanwhile, the view of the Hudson that so many thousands of West Side apartment dwellers enjoyed would be taken away and later resold in tiny parcels to those who could afford a small piece of the Hudson City dream. And even many of those lucky people would have that view partially obscured by an old elevated highway, known to some as Route 9A, to others as the Henry Hudson, to others as the West Side Highway, and still others as the Miller Highway. The federal government had recently finished rehabilitating the Fifty-ninth to Seventy-second Street section of this highway to the tune of $65 million. Like the Hudson River itself, it seemed here to stay. The elevated highway would slice the proposed public park in half, raining down carbon monoxide, soot, and diesel exhaust on sunbathers, obscuring the sound of kids' laughter with the roar of stretch limos, Chevy vans, and Mack trucks, and placing a large, plated steel column where second base might have been.

But the Dodger had a plan. Move the highway. Tuck it beneath a platform that would be built to support most of the new buildings, right where the elevation of the West Side plummeted naturally twenty-five feet or so down toward the river. Surely the federal government would pay $300 million to enhance the Capital of the Planet, even if they would be negating the purpose of the $65 million already spent. Even if there was a massive federal budget crisis. Even if the country's entire political landscape had shifted away from public funding of big projects in big, Democratic-leaning cities.

Then there was the issue of water usage. Hudson City would demand several million gallons of water a day. In the context of New York City's current water dilemma, that was seen by critics as a problem. The reservoir system, mostly constructed between 1870 and 1929, was feeling the strain of modern times as well. Water demand for the city as a whole had long ago surpassed 1.5 billion gallons per day, causing second and third degree drought warnings to become more and more frequent. Water, captured in the Catskill and Delaware River basins roughly a hundred miles north and delivered to the five boroughs by two enormous tunnels, was the lifeblood of New York City. Now, near the close of the twentieth century, the patient needed a transfusion.

As subterranean workers—or sandhogs—raced to finish the third water tunnel, elected officials and federal regulators on the surface debated about whether to construct a five-billion-dollar filtration plant to deal with the deteriorating quality of the water supply. As upstate New York became more populated and developed, pollution and runoff into the reservoir system became a significant problem. New York's drinking water, once considered the best in the nation, was now only on the cusp of acceptability as far as the EPA was concerned. Each year, to avoid having to build the five-billion-dollar plant, the city would file a stack of documents thick enough to be divided up several times and still give Jon Kessler's two-year-old son the benefit of a good position in the barber's chair.

Yet somehow, through a series of promises, deals, and manipulations that several local newspapers were still investigating, Ronald Arlen had steered his way around all these objections. One by one they fell like dominoes—the borough president, the City Planning Commission, the City Council, the mayor—giving the Dodger a zoning variance of gargantuan proportions and apparently ending one of the most hard-fought, controversial, not-in-my-backyard struggles in the city's history. The Dodger could finally gloat at the victory over his rival, Donald Trump. He had purchased the derelict rail yard for a mere $275 million. With each approval, the potential resale value skyrocketed. The thought of Trump kicking himself made Ronald Arlen smile with glee.

But the gloating was premature. One of these objections absolutely refused to die. There were still serious doubts that North River could handle the additional two, three, or four million gallons of raw sewage that Hudson City was likely to produce each day, let alone that of any subsequent large developments. As a way of sidestepping the issue, the agreement signed by the Dodger and Borough President Shuler mandated the creation of a special committee to rule on whether Hudson City would be issued a permit to hook up.

So even with the overall approval, there was still one missing piece in the puzzle—a piece large enough to keep billions of dollars of financing on hold. After all, a World Capital drowning in its own sewage wasn't much good to anyone. And even the Dodger, having rarely financed anything out of his own pocket other than engagement rings for a series of international models, was in no position to go it alone on this risky venture, especially after watching his fortunes take a nosedive in the late 1980s.

Jon Kessler knew his own work underlined and highlighted that already bold question mark. He was neither a proponent nor an opponent of Hudson City, but was there simply to get the technical facts and let the politicians thrash it out. He knew he had gotten the facts straight this time, perhaps more thoroughly, more concisely, and more relevantly than ever before in his life. The results were in. In spite of ongoing city efforts, the North River plant would continue to stink up West Harlem right through the turn of the century and perhaps well beyond. In addition, the 170-million-gallon-a-day established limit for the plant would continue to be violated on a frequent basis and lead to various water quality violations.

Jon's stomach muscles tightened as he entered Paula Derbin's fairly large and well-appointed office. The glass-topped, chrome-legged desk, mahogany bookcases, and high-quality, deep pile blue carpet all shouted privilege.

"Have a seat," Paula said, motioning to a leather sofa-chair against the wall and sounding calmer and more restrained than she had on the phone just a few minutes earlier.

"Sure," Jon answered. He hesitated, then sat in the sofa chair, sinking as the sound of moving air whistled around him. Jon knew the old sofa-chair ploy. The chair was low and mushy, causing the user to fall in and spend the entire conversation looking up to the boss as if she were the international tribunal and you the war criminal. He obliged anyway and looked up at Paula Derbin. "So what's up?"

"A lot is up," Paula replied. "I've looked over your report, and there are some serious implications in it. Are you aware of them?"

"Well, look, that represents a year of objective research—"

"I didn't *ask* you whether the research was objective," Paula asserted, "I asked you if you were aware of the *implications*."

"Yes. I'm aware of the implications."

"Clearly we have two options," Paula said. "The first option is for you to take the report home and spend more time fine-tuning it before we take the next step."

"We can skip that," Jon said, "because that report already *is* fine-tuned. I wouldn't have wasted your time on something where the methodology was unsound or the data was insufficient. It's done now." Jon combated the slight shakiness in his voice.

"Fine, then," Paula continued. "We can submit it for review . . . formally."

"What do you mean, 'formally'?"

"I mean sending it to an environmental consultant who's done some work for Art from time to time, pro bono," Paula explained somewhat breathlessly.

"Yeah, well send it to anyone you'd like," Jon stated, "but I don't see the point of having yet another person duplicate Pat Truitt and Jay Gonzalez's efforts. They've both reviewed it and both praised it, with only a few comments regarding a couple of things that need to be explained or tightened up. They both liked it."

"*And* they both work here."

"What's wrong with working here?" Jon returned. "You and I do too."

"What's wrong with it is a lack of independence," Paula said. "Having our office stand behind your work is only part of the picture. You have no idea what kind of attack your report might be subject to once it's released. Both you and this office, at such a time, will be in a much better position if we can tell the critics: 'It's already been reviewed formally by a respected environmental consultant.' "

"As I said, I have no problem with sending it out," Jon reiterated. "My only concern is time."

"What's your rush?"

"My report makes predictions with regard to various improvements being made to the plant as of certain dates in the not-too-distant future. For instance, to what degree will the covers being installed over the primary settling tanks reduce odors? Those covers are supposed to be completed by late 1994. That's barely a year and a half from now. I don't want the report coming out in January 1995, making a 'prediction' about something that one hundred thousand noses in West Harlem are already well aware of."

"It *won't* be coming out in January 1995." Paula groaned at what to her was the utter ridiculousness of Jon's projection. Her eyes rolled and her hands flailed as if she were conducting the pitifully undisciplined Civil Service Symphony Orchestra, always holding her back from being the maestro she was truly born to be. "You are overreacting again."

"How much time are we talking about?"

"A month. Can you wait a month?" Paula asked somewhat rhetorically.

"A month is fine. Can you tell me the name of the consultant?"

"That information is confidential."

"Since when?"

"Since I said so. I don't want you, or anyone else for that matter, pestering them for the next month. Remember what happened with your report on the lead paint chipping off of the Williamsburg Bridge? Just let them do their job."

"Okay, a month," Jon said.

"Give or take."

"Hopefully give . . . or is that take? I'll mark it down on my calendar."

"Whatever you'd like."

"You know, I'm not in a hurry just for the sake of leaving some room for my projections," Jon explained. "The conclusions in that report point the way to policy decisions that should be made sooner rather than later."

"I know all about the policy implications," Paula steamed, "which is exactly why we just went through this whole exercise. The borough president is the one who ultimately has to make policy decisions and then take flak for them. That's why he was elected. *You* were not elected to *anything*. You need to be more of a team player and perform your duties more in the context of *this office* and its overall political function. This is not about your glory." Paula always made a point of pronouncing "borough president" in its entirety, as if to recapture the power stripped from the office in the charter reform of 1990. The "BP," used by the tabloids, wouldn't do.

Jon now pulled himself up from the quicksand chair to a standing position. "I'm not looking for glory. I'm looking for a little environmental justice. Isn't that what Art Shuler stands for?"

"You don't know Art Shuler, so don't you dare imply *anything* about him."

"I'm not. Is that all?"

"That's all."

Jon walked quickly down the hall to the elevators and tried to commune with the ball of nerves in his stomach. The ball had many meanings. It meant because of his financial circumstance he had to hold in his rage. It meant in spite of a degree from Columbia's School of Engineering and twelve years of intense work, he was ultimately a pawn for a bunch of political hacks. The ball meant he was on the outside, not on the inside. It meant he somehow had to get better at playing a game he despised.

At least when he got back to the twentieth floor he'd be closer to home in a sense, taking refuge in his tiny office, separated from the main floor of the Borough President's Office by the sealed-off building stairwell, but connected to the world by a phone line. He also had Larry Golick and Al Gibbs, the only two civil service veterans who remained of his engineering staff. There had been a housecleaning three years earlier, in which four longtime engineers were transferred to other agencies in order to leave more of the borough president's budget for political appointees. Jon's predecessor resigned in reaction to the move, and Jon was brought in from Hazen & Sawyer—a prestigious private firm—to head up this streamlined engineering staff.

Now in his late forties, Larry Golick came to work in a T-shirt every day—usually one with the New York Mets logo on it. At five-foot-ten, he still retained a suggestion of the athletic build developed playing stickball in the 1950s and 'sixties, but his gut perpetually pushed the T-shirt back out of his pants. His large, round eyes and puffy cheeks made him appear cuddly, like a teddy bear. But this teddy bear combed what was left of his straight, gray hair from left to right over a large bare tract of scalp. Seven gray hairs stuck oddly out of his temple, a constant reminder of a failed transplant operation performed seventeen years earlier. His voice had a soothing quality, suggesting a cross between a trusted friend and a grandfather.

Normally gentle-spirited, Larry Golick had for twenty years handled requests for detailed block-by-block maps of Manhattan. Since the streamlining, however, he only handled requests to see the *Racing Form*, and those requests all came from himself. His single-handed work slowdown was intended as a protest against an uncaring administration and resulted in more work for Jon, who couldn't stand the idea of the taxpaying public's requests going unfilled, especially when he could be indirectly implicated. Meanwhile, Larry hid safely behind his civil service status, which made firing him next to impossible. It was a hopeless stalemate, because the borough president would never hire back Larry's friends, Larry would never stop reading the *Racing Form*, the public would never stop coming in for maps, and Jon would never stop being inclined to plug the holes in the dike.

Al Gibbs was a black engineer in his early fifties. The story went that he had cracked sometime around 1970. Until that time, legend had it, Gibbs was one of the most brilliant engineers in the city. At age thirty he had already risen to deputy chief engineer of the Bureau of Sewers. When the breakdown came—for reasons still discussed and debated by veteran city workers—he was transferred to a cardboard job in the Borough President's Office, where he could alternately sleep and fantasize aloud. For over twenty years he had served in this capacity with distinction.

A few feet away, an attractive young woman leaned back in her chair and peered around the partition wall of the cubicle where she sat. She watched as Jon attempted to sneak past Larry Golick, but Larry quickly looked up from the racing pages of the *Daily News* and spoke.

"It's the King! How is the King?"

"The King sucks," Jon replied. "The King is tired of commuting back and forth to Long Island. The King is tired of waking up in the morning and not knowing if he's in his own bed or on his friend's floor on the Upper West Side. The King is frustrated that it took eight months of painstaking research to produce something of extremely high value only to see it sat on by a political hatchet lady. The King is depressed that his staff consists of a permanent one-man labor strike and an escapee from Bellevue. The King is bitter that as a result, he's the only member of his graduating class doing twenty hours a week of clerical work. The King is unhappy about the fact that the Queen has gained thirty pounds since the Prince was born. The King is irate that George Steinbrenner still owns the Yankees."

"You must have just come from Paula's office."

"You bet your harness-racing ass I did," Jon said.

"What's happening with your report?" Larry asked.

"It's being handed over to some consultant," Jon replied. "We may never see it again. If it were anyone else but Paula handling this thing, I wouldn't think twice about losing another month. What's another month? But I don't trust her."

"I don't trust her either," Larry agreed. "She fucked me, and she fucked my friends."

"I hope you were wearing protection."

"This never would have happened when Andy Stein was borough president."

At that moment Al Gibbs rose abruptly from his seat several feet away and struck a fierce tai chi pose. His words rang out in a clear, steady, focused baritone.

"I am deadly force. I am two hundred and five pounds of rock-solid, shipshape muscle licensed to kill on behalf of the United States Army. Trained to snuff out the life of the overmatched enemy, I strike without warning . . . *yaaa!!*"

The young woman watching from the cubicle dropped her jaw, raised her eyebrows, and quickly went back into hiding.

Al Gibbs kicked his right foot into the air with less than lightning speed and resumed his ready position. "That's what we did in Grenada. Took 'em by surprise. I had to kill a man with my bare hands."

Just as quickly as he had risen, Al Gibbs collapsed back into his seat and slumped over the surface of his desk, his forehead supported by his palms and fingers. Now he spoke softly, bemused and dejected: "You put your life on the line for your country, get that Purple Heart, come back home, and whaddaya get? A bunch of ignorant civilians who think we was just jerking off over there. I'm tellin' ya . . ."

Larry steered the focus back to Jon. "So, tell me, why do you think Paula's against your report?"

"It's got to be Hudson City, Larry. Hudson City is practically a done deal. Arlen got his approval to build, the rezoning of the old railroad yards, all of it. The borough president gave his approval and now is essentially out of the picture. The only things the Dodger really needs at this point are financing and a permit to hook up to the sewer. So it's *not* really a done deal. Beyond that, your guess is as good as mine."

"Well, I wouldn't trust Paula to tie my shoes."

"I know," Jon reasoned, "but Art Shuler himself has a long political history of *fighting* things like environmental racism. He fought the siting of the North River plant in West Harlem in the first place. He was outspoken about the issue in the eighties. The way I see it, he should be dying to put out a study like mine. And he does still run things around here."

"Well, you know how much power Paula has in this office," Larry countered. "And you know who gave it to her."

"Art did," Jon said, finishing Larry's train of thought. "But you should never rule out going over someone's head as a last resort. I'll wait the thirty days, like she said. After that, I'm going right back into motion."

"It's a shame you have to go through this."

"I'll make good use of the waiting time. Starting right now. I'm going into my office, locking the door, curling up on the floor, and taking a meganap. Could you keep people away for about forty-five minutes, O Royal Gatekeeper?"

"Oh, wait a minute," Larry said. "I forgot to tell you. Your intern is here." Larry pointed to the adjoining cubicle and waggled his eyebrows just enough to let him know an attractive woman was sitting on the other side of the partition. "I gave her a seat and told her you'd be back in ten minutes."

"What happened to the guy they sent me last year?" Jon said. "The Russian guy who spoke three words of English and tried to steal my computer." Jon walked toward the cubicle.

For the first time since he'd stepped into the office on the twentieth floor, he saw a streak of long brown hair with red highlights. He tried to compose himself and recalled that he already was fairly composed. Of course, he'd been married for seven years and it didn't matter anyway. Those scoping days were over.

"Hi," Jon said as he put one foot into the cubicle and looked down. The woman looked up from her chair, wheeled around, smiled, and lifted herself slightly to shake his extended hand. She was about twenty-four, slender, five-foot-five, with engaging brown eyes and attire that was a cross between professional and grunge. Beneath a faded, worn denim overshirt was a businesslike white blouse. Peering out from under her carefully groomed, layered brown hair was a set of silver skull and crossbones earrings. She appeared slightly shaken.

"Hi, I'm Naomi Pierce. I'm glad I finally got to meet you."

"Me too," Jon acknowledged. "I hope I didn't keep you waiting too long in that cubby."

"Not at all," Naomi replied, "I was having a ball looking at some of the old maps on the desk."

"That's nothing compared to what's inside." Jon unlocked his office door and led Naomi inside, closing the door behind him.

"Hey, who is that guy?" Naomi asked.

"Who, Al? He's a basket case. I know this might be quite a culture shock. Hey, check out *this* map." Jon pointed to a three-foot-long hand-drawn map of Manhattan framed and hanging on the wall directly behind his desk.

"That's an original, isn't it? It must be something like two hundred years old."

"Excellent guess," Jon confirmed. "The grid plan. It was, in fact, drawn in 1811. The state legislature commissioned it as part of an early planning effort. This is the plan that made most blocks short from north to south and wide from east to west. But a lot of other aspects shown look strange if you know Manhattan today. One of the most amazing things about it, if you notice, is that it shows a grid system of streets and blocks right where Central Park is today."

"Were those blocks constructed and removed," Naomi inquired, "or were they never built in the first place?"

"They were planned for but never built," Jon explained. "And thank God, or thank Olmsted, right? Can you imagine how congested Manhattan would be today if you could have an address like Sixty-eighth and Sixth?"

"Some homeless people have that address," Naomi said with a grin.

"But at least they're in the park. So tell me about yourself."

"I'm going for a master's at NYU in public policy," Naomi said, sitting in the chair facing Jon's desk, "and I'm doing a two-part independent research project on New York's sewage policy."

"Well, I'm Dr. Sewage, so you've come to the right place," Jon replied, taking the seat behind his desk. "Are you looking to cover a specific subtopic, or are you looking to just go with the flow, Ralphie boy?"

"Well, Norton . . ." she said with a grin, "I'm proposing to do a couple of papers on how New York City plans to meet its anticipated need for treatment capacity."

"That's going to be a very short paper or two," Jon quipped. "New York's idea of planning for sewage is waiting . . . waiting patiently to be sued. The city is being sued right now by several civic groups, and would rather hire a few lawyers and pay out a few settlements than fix the problem itself."

"What is the problem itself?" Naomi asked.

"As a for instance, okay, I'm working on North River, up in West Harlem. For all its problems, don't get me wrong, it's far better that a plant was built than not built. But ever since it opened in 1986, it's been stinking up the neighborhood and handling a hell of a lot more than the hundred seventy million gallons a day it was designed to handle."

"Let me ask you something," Naomi said, moving her chair a few inches closer to Jon and straightening her back, "where did the sewage go before 1986?"

"Right into the Hudson. It's one of New York's dirty little secrets."

"That's hard to believe."

"Believe it," Jon said. "Think of it this way. Because sewage is typically not pumped, the sewers normally lead continuously downhill. To a degree, they parallel the natural terrain, but eventually they wind up at a low point—meaning a stream, river, or ocean, often well beneath the surface. That's the way it was for the better part of a hundred years—straight in. And that represented a vast improvement over what existed before."

"Originally, they had open sewers, didn't they?" Naomi asked.

"Right. Or none at all. In the 1840s or 'fifties—before the Civil War—if you walked around Manhattan, you'd see a combination of gutters flowing with sewage, taking it to a pond or something, and a bunch of outhouses in people's courtyards, which were really nothing more than holes in the ground. Building an intricate system to bring it all to the rivers was an enormous relief. People generally don't realize it, but without a real sewer system, you can't have a city as we know it. Parisians realize it, though. They even have a sewer museum over there, in homage. Can you imagine the disease and smell that went before?"

"Only if I really concentrate," Naomi said. "People probably considered the Hudson and East rivers to be endless resources."

"Exactly," Jon said. "Once the stuff goes in, it's gone—forget about it. The rivers might as well have been outer space. But after a few decades of population explosion, the rivers were rancid and the fish were disappearing. The city started building the first couple of treatment plants as early as the 1930s. At least they had the convenience of being able to locate the plants right at an existing outfall, since the sewer system had already been built for them."

"But North River wasn't one of those treatment plants," Naomi said.

"No, the plants on Coney Island, Ward's Island, and later Newtown Creek were built by the city at its own behest and were pretty rudimentary in design, though they were incredibly large. There were no substantial federal requirements for treating sewage until the Clean Water Act of 1972, which required primary and secondary treatment for all municipal sewage going into open bodies of water. But it took years for all the funding to come through and all the design and construction to occur. Plants like North River were part of that wave."

"And now one hundred percent of New York's sewage is treated?" Naomi conjectured.

"Actually, no. That's another dirty little secret. You know those catch basins in the street?"

"Yeah . . ."

"They collect storm water, right? Well, as brilliant as the folks were who originally built the sewer system, they made one huge oversight. That storm water and the waste water from all the buildings go right into the same lines—a combined sewer. That's a very efficient arrangement if it's all going into the sea, but those planners never anticipated that eventually waste water would need to be treated at the end of the line."

"So the relatively clean rainwater winds up being treated along with the waste water," Naomi said.

"Exactly. And when its rains, that can double or triple the load on a plant."

"But since it's essentially diluted sewage, isn't it easier for the plant to handle?"

"The strange thing is, no," Jon explained. "The strain on the pumps is roughly the same per gallon no matter how dirty the water is. With other areas of the plant, like the huge settling tanks, the waste water just sits for a couple of hours while the heavy waste matter settles and the light stuff—like grease and scum—rises to the surface. It takes a couple of hours in that state, again, regardless of the waste content of the water. The bottom line is, the plant is not built to handle that much water. So you know what they do?"

"Dump some of it into the Hudson?"

"Bingo," Jon said. "They have a few different options, but they all reduce to the same thing . . ."

A knock came on the door, followed without pause by the door's opening. Larry poked his head through and spoke obsequiously. "King, I'm really sorry to bother you, I know you're very busy right now, but there's a gentleman up front who needs a map of part of Canal Street for a moving violation he's fighting. I told him he'd have to speak with the chief engineer."

"Thanks a fucking lot. Tell him I'll be busy for at least another five minutes. And tell him it used to be your job to get maps until they decided to give it to an engineer with a professional license. And tell him we're fifty-three orders behind and counting. And tell him New York's political and civil service systems are irrevocably screwed up."

"Yes, King, whatever you say, King," Larry said, slipping back out the door and closing it behind him.

"So," Naomi said with a coquettish smirk, "you wear many different hats in this office."

"Including a dunce cap for taking this job in the first place. Anyway, where were we?"

"You were talking about dumping water into the Hudson . . ."

"Right, they have a few options. In a severe storm situation, they can run the sewage through the plant real fast and have a substantially smaller percentage of the pollutants removed than the normally required eighty-five percent. Or they can bypass entire sections of the plant and dump the sewage straight in at the end of the line. Or they can open any of what they call the regulator valves along the main interceptor to the plant and divert the sewage into the river well before it even gets to the plant."

"But the result is always the same," Naomi followed, "diluted raw sewage dumped into navigable waters."

"Yup. There's even a fancy name for the whole syndrome," Jon said, "combined sewage overflow—or CSO."

"Is that legal?"

"Not really. The city is under a state and federal order to correct the problem by building these huge holding tanks. They have to be complete within the next several years or massive fines will be imposed. They can't arrest the whole city. Where would they put us? Anyway, that's today's crash course in human waste. I hate to throw all of this at you at once, but we'll have time when I'm not rushed to go through these things more in detail."

"No, sure . . . great, this is exactly the kind of stuff I'm interested in. So . . . I hear you just did a report on odor control."

"Yes I did," Jon said, "but that's an entirely separate conversation. The politics of this office have the report on hold right now. But there's a whole lot of great things you can research and do before discovering the dark side of the Borough President's Office. I don't wanna bring you down on your first day."

"I can take it," Naomi said.

"I'm not sure I can. But if you can, let's start you with something small and you can work your way up from there. I'm gonna set you up with a desk right outside, right where you were sitting.

That means you'll have to listen to the ranting and raving of Old Al Gibbs. If you can take that, you may be ready for the big time."

"Yes, I heard some of it before," Naomi said, implying with her eyes that she had heard every last word. "Something about Grenada and deadly force . . ."

"And that's just the beginning," Jon revealed. "In the coming weeks, you'll hear about the Tet Offensive, napalming Cambodia, going undercover against Castro for the CIA, doing reconnaissance behind Iraqi borders, doing drug interdiction in Colombia . . . and all of it total bullshit."

"I can't wait."

"I'll give you the key to my office. If it gets to the point where you can't concentrate and I'm not around, you can let yourself in."

"Thanks."

As Jon led Naomi to an unoccupied cubicle just outside his office, he understood that his routine would probably change with her in proximity. And even if the routine didn't change that much, the comfort level with which he experienced the routine would change dramatically. He already considered skipping that nap he'd told Larry he was going to take. Perhaps he would modify it by simply putting his head down on his desk. He barely gave a damn how he appeared to Larry or Old Al Gibbs and the droves of map-seeking citizens they palmed off on him. But his earnest intern was another story. Even though he had a solid metal door and a lock to protect him, she seemed like Superwoman to him. What if Superwoman could see through the door and observe him in a fetal position near the base of his file cabinet? The thought was too much to bear right now.

"Okay, I'll help you clear some of this mess away," Jon offered. "This is mostly some junk a bunch of engineers who were transferred out left all over the place. They were pretty pissed off, I understand."

"You rarely see anger expressed by the breaking of a drafting compass," Naomi remarked.

"Or four of them."

With his peripheral vision Jon saw the "gentleman" who wanted a map of Canal Street. He was short, about forty-five, over 300 pounds, and bellicose. Larry could no longer contain him, even with a large Formica counter as a barrier. Now things got worse. Jon understood that he had accidentally made a microsecond's worth of eye contact with the man, thereby, according to the un-written laws of life in New York, establishing more than enough fa-miliarity to be accosted and assaulted.

"Hey," the big man explained. "I just need a minute of your time. I gotta fight a ticket in court tomorrow at two-thirty."

"Look, hang on," Jon said, "I'll be with you in a couple of minutes."

"You don' unnerstand," the big man let out, flustered, "I had to cut the corner like that because of the angle of the curb. Dis guy over here is of no help to me whatsoever."

"I'm sorry," Larry said flatly, "I can't work out of title. I'm an attendant. You see, they told me I'm only qualified to write things down and deliver things. So they're gonna get what they paid for. I talked to my union representative."

"Hey," the big man called back to Jon, "I'm really in a hurry here. I have to see my lawyer—"

"Hey, my man went to Columbia," Old Al Gibbs shouted as he leaped up to face the big man from across the counter. "He don't have to take your shit. He hung out with professors and Nobel prize winners who worked on the damn particle gun. You ever play with one of them particle guns? Phitew . . . phitew . . . phitew . . ." Al fashioned an imaginary particle accelerator out of his thumb and index finger and shot apocryphal molecules around the room. "Hoo, he blows a hole clear through the enemy's thorax . . . phitew . . . phitew . . ."

"Al," Jon said, "sit down. You're an embarrassment."

"I'm sorry," Larry apologized to the big man, "he's a little shell-shocked."

"Hey, I could care less," the big man replied. "If he can get me a map of Canal Street, he's still better than all of you bozos put to-gether."

"Me, get a map?" Al asked while rotating slowly and omi-nously. "Ol' Al Gibbs go fetch a fucking map? You got the wrong dude, boy. I ain't no map fetcher. I am death. I am the grim reaper incarnate. I am the awful dusk for those who would raise a hand against this great nation. I am a precision machine trained to kill on sight."

"Okay," Jon said, turning to Naomi. "Good luck."

Chapter 3

Detectives James Mercado and Janine O'Connel of the Tenth Precinct in Manhattan drove an unmarked blue '87 Plymouth Fury west along Fourteenth Street at 9:40 A.M., Tuesday, April 6. Mercado slowed the vehicle as they neared the cordoned-off area just east of the intersection of Fourteenth and Hudson Streets. As he yanked his head around for the parallel park, he caught a quick, refreshing glance of O'Connel's thick, flowing, shoulder-length orange hair. Her full lips and thin, gently curved eyebrows appeared almost as orange in the bright morning sun. If you looked straight into her soulful green eyes and ignored the dark blue suit, you were surrounded for a moment by rolling green fields in Ireland. But when she spoke, you were back in New York.

"Jimmy, you almost clipped that pole."

"Almost doesn't count," Mercado replied, looking directly at O'Connel now for another moment with suave, expressive brown eyes and a wide, irresistible Spanish smile. He finished parking and turned off the engine. Running his right hand through his short, thick black hair while his left hand fingered through the pocket-sized notebook on his lap, he glanced momentarily through the window at the cordoned-off area.

"Are we gonna have to go down there?"

"Hey," O'Connel said, "my uncle used to work in the sewer."

"Then let's get your uncle to do it."

As Mercado and O'Connel got out of the car and stepped over a large puddle that had formed along the curb, a young, tall, black-uniformed officer stepped up to them. "Officer Davis," he said. "Detective Mercado?"

"This is Detective O'Connel," Mercado said, clutching Davis's extended hand. "What've we got?"

"We've got a male, white, mid-to-late thirties, discovered dead in the sewer about an hour ago by one of his crew. The victim's

31

name is Joel Haney. He was the foreman of the Fourteenth Street
sewer crew."

"Is he still down there?" Mercado said.

"Yes he is, Detective," Davis said. "We preserved the scene."

"Thanks a lot," Mercado said, rolling his eyes. In no rush to go
down below, he took a small satisfaction in being able to take his
time interviewing the witness first and begin collecting forensic
evidence a little later.

"Any chance of getting boots and flashlights?" O'Connel
asked.

"The crew member is gonna have to help you with that," Davis
said. "His name is Charlie Sharpe. He's right over there. He's still
a little shaken up." Davis pointed to a stout black man in his early
fifties kneeling about fifteen feet from the open manhole, and led
the two detectives toward him. As the three shadows surrounded
Charlie Sharpe, he looked up, his face round and deep, oval eyes
sincere and prepared for the strain of getting back on his feet.

"Mr. Sharpe," Davis said, "Detectives Mercado and O'Connel
are here from the Tenth Precinct. They'd like to talk to you."

"Fine, fine," Sharpe said, lifting himself up with what seemed
like sheer will. "I sure as hell wanna talk to them."

"Let me know when you want to go down," Davis said to the
detectives, pointing toward a tall white officer standing guard over
the open manhole.

"Charlie Sharpe, Bureau of Sewers . . . Fourteenth Street . . ."
Sharpe extended his hand. Mercado shook it firmly and let go.
O'Connel stepped forward and did the same.

"Can you tell us what happened this morning?" Mercado said.

"Joel was late, but that wasn't so unusual, so the rest of us went
about doing what we were supposed to do, which was check the
catch basins along Fourteenth and check down inside the sewer
for any cracking after that big storm."

"It rained that much last night?" Mercado said.

"For a couple of hours in the middle of the night," O'Connel
said. "It woke me up twice."

"Woke me up too," Sharpe said. "You wouldn't know it by
looking in the sewer now, though. The flow in the mains goes up
within the hour or so and goes back down the same way after the
heaviest part of the storm. You go down there now and it's calm,

compared to when it was raining. You know how you know there was a storm if you didn't wake up from it?"

"How?" O'Connel asked.

"Puddles on the sidewalk," Sharpe said, "and in the gutter. There shouldn't even be any along Fourteenth, but they did such a shitty job here when they rebuilt everything. Sidewalks with low points in the middle, sidewalks draining back into the stores, watered down concrete that cracks right away. I'll tell ya, somebody got a kickback on this job. The only person I know who stepped in was a young guy from the Borough President's Office—an engineer. He did a report on it and got the *Post* down here. They did a big story on it. Now it's being investigated."

"What happened this morning, Mr. Sharpe?" O'Connel said. "You were checking the sewers . . ."

"I opened up that hole over there off of Hudson, put my flashlight down, and there's someone lying down there. I get closer and I see it's Joel's flight jacket and I'm saying 'What the hell are you doing down there?' Then I get down there . . ." Sharpe's voice trailed off as his breath shortened and his eyes swelled up with tears.

"I'm sorry, Mr. Sharpe," Mercado said, placing his right hand on Sharpe's shoulder for a moment.

"My flashlight's on him and he's white as a sheet, and I know right then that he's dead, goddamnit. He's almost facedown, I put my hand on his cheek and it's cold, and I try to pull him up and he's stiff. Then I realize his arm is stuck between the ladder and the wall, and I figure what the hell can I do besides get on the walkie-talkie. I get a hold of Sal from my crew and tell him to call 911."

"Can you tell me anything else?" O'Connel said. "Did you know him well? Was he having any problems on the job? Did he drink? Could he have slipped and fallen?"

"He quit drinking over a year ago," Sharpe answered, raising his voice defensively. "When he made up his mind to do something, he did it, man. And no way Joel slipped. He never lost his footing. He was a linebacker. And he was good underground. He wasn't crazy about it, but he was good underground. He could even work out of trade and fix electrical components when he had to."

"Was he having any problems with anyone that you know about?" Mercado said. "Someone on the job? Off the job?"

"Everybody liked Joel," Sharpe said. "He was a good man to be around. I worked out of the same yard with him for something like ten years. We worked together for a while on the East Side, then for years together at Eighteenth Street. That was a better assignment than this shit. We were responsible for a regulator and a tidal gate and all that. What we have on Fourteenth Street is a newly lined, gunited sewer, with not a whole lot to do. Just your run-of-the-mill sags and obstructions on some side streets."

"You were transferred to Fourteenth Street?" Mercado asked.

"Yeah," Sharpe replied, "a few months ago."

"Any reason?" Mercado asked.

"Nothing they ever explained to us," Sharpe said. "Our area supervisor told us it was a permit problem. The city has state permits for all its sewage treatment plants, and a few of those plants are over their limit. But that didn't have nothin' to do with us. We were a good squad. Eight years without a complaint. When they sent us here, you couldn't get them to answer a thing. Falcone, that's our area supervisor, nobody—"

"Was Joel Haney upset about this?" O'Connel asked.

"A little," Sharpe said. "I mean, not much. He was our foreman, but he was gonna be out of here by the end of the year anyway. Like me, man: He was just doin' time."

"Why was he gonna be out of here?" O'Connel asked.

"Not because anybody wanted him out," Sharpe said. "*He* wanted out. He was going to film school. He was shooting a movie . . . a documentary. He had backers and everything."

"Can you tell us who these backers were?" O'Connel asked.

"Look, I have no idea," Sharpe said. "He met them over at the New School, over that way on Fifth Avenue. You can ask them. He was very private about this stuff. He explained it to me once and then never mentioned it again."

"What was the documentary about?" Mercado asked. "Did it have anything to do with the sewer?"

"No, nothin' to do with the sewer," Sharpe said. "If I tell you what it was about, you're gonna think he brought this down on himself somehow, but he was a good man. . . ."

"We're not here to judge anybody," O'Connel said. "If this was not an accident, we wanna find that out and find out who did this to him. The more information you give us, the better our chances are of doing that, even if you feel embarrassed for him."

"Okay," Sharpe said, wiping his sweaty forehead with his open right palm. "It was a film about hookers down by the docks. It was about their lives. Joel wasn't sleeping with any of them either, . . . well, not for a long time. You don't have to believe me if you don't want to. But when he was all done with that, he actually wanted to help them. That's the kind of guy he was."

"Can you give us any of their names?" Mercado asked, readying his pen against his notebook.

"You know what kind of names those girls have?" Sharpe said. "A first name and that's it. And that's usually a nickname. Let's see, what do I remember? Nicole, Tiffany, Cashmere, Lizard . . . and a girl named Barbara. She was his favorite, but she got killed last year."

"Yeah, I know about that one," O'Connel said. "We still haven't solved it. Maybe we should've talked to Joel Haney."

"He wanted to know worse than you do," Sharpe said. "It ate him up inside. I think he loved her. That's half the reason he was doing this film. I'll tell you, I can't remember the names, though. Most of them hung out along Eleventh Avenue and the docks . . . Nineteenth Street, Twentieth, Twenty-first . . ."

"Any trouble you can recall with any of these prostitutes?" O'Connel asked. "Any trouble with their pimps?"

"None that I know of," Sharpe said. "He paid the girls extra, and he paid the pimps if he had to. I guess a couple of them didn't want any part of it, and Joel tried to avoid the ones with pimps just the same. But there wasn't any incident that I know about. Not one. But like I said, he was very private."

"But you think *somebody* did this to him," Mercado said, looking up from his notebook and looking Sharpe straight in the eye.

"Yeah . . . I do," Sharpe said, looking over toward the open manhole, then staring back at Mercado. "Someone put him in there. Joel never came to work early. Forget that. I mean, he was good, like I told you, once he was here. But he had other things going on."

"Let me ask you something," O'Connel said. "Remember you mentioned that the flow goes up in the sewer after a storm? How high can it go?"

"Depends on the storm," Sharpe said. "It could go two feet high, three feet, four feet. It depends on how much rain fell, how fast, what size the pipe is—"

"Hey!" It was Officer Davis's voice as one man, then another, emerged from the open manhole.

"Don't worry about us," said the first one to emerge. "We work here." He was in his early thirties with slightly wavy, short, light brown hair which was receding in the front. With his thick but carefully manicured mustache, wire-rimmed glasses strapped onto his head, and fair, reddish complexion, he appeared almost too academically inclined to have just emerged from a sewer. The man who emerged behind him was closer to forty, with long side-burns, dense black eyebrows, and a tall, white forehead capped by a high stack of curly black hair.

"This part of the sewer is off limits right now," Officer Davis snarled. "It's part of an investigation."

"That's what we were doing," said the one with the glasses, "investigating. And I don't happen to see any of New York's finest down there." Now he looked over at Sharpe. "Nothing, Charlie . . . nothing."

"All right, Sal," Charlie said. Now glancing at Mercado and O'Connel each for a moment, he addressed them. "These guys are part of our crew. This is Sal Perelli." Charlie pointed to the one with glasses and then pointed to the other crew member. "This is Mike Kovenich." Sharpe led the two detectives toward Perelli and Kovenich, so that the detectives, the crew members, and Davis were all in a circle, with the tall white officer five feet away, still guarding the open manhole like it was Buckingham Palace.

"I'm Detective Mercado, and this is Detective O'Connel," Mercado said to Perelli and Kovenich with as much cheer as he could muster. "We're from the Tenth Precinct. We'd like you to work *with* us on this."

"Hey, sorry if we ruffled any feathers," Perelli said unapologetically. "When Charlie told us what happened, we figured the best way to help was to see if there was anyone else or anything else down there."

"And there wasn't?" O'Connel said.

"Just the usual shit," Perelli said, deadpan.

"Did you touch or move the body?" Mercado asked.

"Don't worry," Perelli said. "We both stepped over him very carefully. Maybe we touched it slightly with a boot or something, but he's still hooked into the ladder by his arm. If you want, I'll take you down right now for a look."

"Well," Mercado said, "we'd better get it over with, before someone else down there gets to it first. I paid two hundred dollars for these shoes. Can someone get us a pair of boots?"

"I have an extra pair in the truck," Sharpe said, raising his right hand to eye level, pointing. Mercado followed Sharpe to the back of the parked DEP van. Sharpe opened the doors, reached in, rummaged around, and came up with a pair of knee-high black rubber waders that appeared large enough for Mercado to slip into without removing his shoes. Mercado spoke as he accepted the boots from Sharpe.

"Was Haney married or single?"

"Divorced," Sharpe said. "Two kids. His wife left him three years ago. He saw the kids on weekends or whenever. Joel got a raw deal."

"Was there any bad blood there?" Mercado asked.

"For something like this to happen?" Sharpe said. "No way. She left him. Left him behind is more like it. He didn't like it, but he dealt with it. It's not like I found *her* in the sewer." Sharpe looked up into the sky now as Mercado steadied himself against the truck with one hand while trying to slip into the first boot. "It's a shame, man," Sharpe said. "Joel was gettin' out and I was gettin' out, too. I'm still planning on taking that early retirement. Eighteen months to go."

"Good for you," Mercado said, now struggling to get into the second boot.

"Right now I don't feel like I can last another eighteen *hours*," Sharpe said.

"I understand," Mercado said. "We don't have to do this all today. Detective O'Connel and I will be getting in touch with you as the investigation proceeds. Same with the guys in your crew."

"Everything goes in circles," Sharpe said. "In 'seventy, when I was still pretty new, I lost a good friend. A real good friend. We were digging the interceptor tunnel for the whole west side of Manhattan. Fucking thing collapsed, crushed him just like that. After watching that, I was a basket case for a year."

"I'm sorry," Mercado said.

Three minutes later Mercado gently kicked the manhole cover and read the MADE IN INDIA inscription across the bottom. He had read recently how international trade agreements were changing the face of everything from shoe manufacturing to computer hardware. Apparently, foreign competition had reached the sewers too. Mercado now followed Sal Perelli down the ladder of the open manhole. Perelli's flashlight illuminated the lowest visible rung of the ladder and the back of the body's head and neck. Mercado's fingers accidentally traced the smooth, cool, damp concrete walls. From below he heard the steady rush of raw sewage passing into one side of the manhole and out the other.

"My God," Mercado said, "does sewage usually smell like a dead body?"

"I dunno," Perelli replied, "does a dead body usually smell like sewage?"

Perelli avoided the lowest rungs of the ladder by taking a long stride to the concrete bottom of the manhole. Mercado followed, avoiding the lowest rungs, the body, and Perelli. Both Perelli's and Mercado's flashlights now shined on the body, which was face-down and clothed in a flight jacket, Wrangler jeans, and brown leather cowboy boots. While the right arm was hooked at the inside of the elbow between the ladder and the wall, the left arm fluttered and bobbed slightly in the shallow current. Mercado shined his flashlight on the gash at the back of the corpse's head.

"You don't get that from falling," Mercado said. "Unless you fall from ten stories onto a crowbar." His voice echoed within the narrow chamber.

"You're definitely calling this a homicide, then?" Perelli said.

"Unless he wakes up and tells me otherwise," Mercado replied. He paused and then aimed his beam down the tunnel, first toward the east and then toward the west. "Does anyone else roam around down here?"

"Outside of our crew?" Perelli responded. "I doubt it. Sure, it's city right-of-way only. But in reality, anyone who can get the cover off of a manhole is free to do it. It's not like people are dying to get in here."

"They are now," Mercado said. He used his beam to trace the body. "Wait a second—Janine has the camera."

"Is that your partner?"

"Yeah."

"I can take her back down when we get back up," Perelli said. "Or I can take you back down and you take the pictures."

"Ah . . . no," Mercado said. "I'll let Detective O'Connel get a whiff of this. I've had about all I can take."

"Are there any more questions you'd like to ask me?" Perelli said.

"Not down here," Mercado said. "I wanna get up and make sure EMS can pull this body out. This is horrendous."

Mercado pulled a piece of yellow chalk from his pants pocket and scratched a horizontal line along the concrete wall, just above the level of the body. "I'm trying to outline this thing," he said, "but it's next to impossible."

Chapter 4

At 5:35 P.M. on April 6, in the elevator on the way down, Jon Kessler ran into Jay Gonzalez, the environmental analyst for the land use division of the Borough President's Office. The elevator was crowded, and from one corner to the other, Jay motioned with his eyes to Jon that they should talk discreetly outside. Once on the street, they were protected from a slight drizzle by the huge glazed terra-cotta tiled arches of the Municipal Building, a tall, ornate Romanesque office building with columns, built shortly before World War I as a testament to the growing power of New York City. Also protected from the drizzle were clusters of smokers, city workers flushed out of the building by the city's tough antismoking law passed two years earlier. The desire to smoke had built up during the afternoon, and now, whether they were headed home via subway or back upstairs for overtime, they had some catching up to do. Jon found a spot beneath the arches just barely out of the way of both the smoke and the rain. Jay tested the water with one foot.

"I heard your new intern's cute. Smart too."

"If she's as smart as I think she is, she won't be back tomorrow."

"Well, hang on to her," Jay cautioned, 'cause you'll probably need all the help you can get over the next few weeks. I heard through the grapevine that someone from Ronald Arlen's organization is coming to see Paula on Friday. It may just be the Dodger himself."

"What for?"

"Your report, buddy," Jay replied. "It's got them all nervous. Hey, proving that the plant everybody wants to hook up to is going to continue to be a health hazard to West Harlem? You know what kind of money is on the line?"

"Yeah, but Hudson City is a done deal as far as the borough president is concerned, right?" Jon conjectured. "He approved it with conditions attached, and now it's up to a mayoral committee as to whether Hudson City can eventually hook up to the city sewer system. Art Shuler is out of the loop right now."

"Yeah, technically speaking," Jay argued. "Mayor Gianetta worries about whether to grant the hookup and the borough president quietly goes back to being the citizen's advocate. But you know it's really not as simple as that. Paula and the Dodger got tight during those negotiations. She went to lunch with him, sometimes one-on-one, sometimes with Art, sometimes with Arlen's fiancée along."

"So what? They're entitled to negotiate anywhere they want to. Theoretically, they can negotiate in a hot tub."

"Maybe they did," Jay remarked. "Look, I've been around a lot of these meetings, and I know they got very chummy during the process. And maybe they were that way before the process too. I don't know. But the bottom line is, they're still that way now. They still hang out. And more importantly, Art Shuler staked his whole political career on that deal. He pissed off all his old West Side liberal constituents in exchange for a bunch of high-rises and a new image of deal maker, creator of sensible development and new jobs. Next stop—City Hall."

"Yeah, that's what I've heard. Charter reform. Just being borough president isn't good enough anymore. And what you're telling me is I'm standing in the way."

"Potentially," Jay continued. "Art has to see Hudson City come to fruition to reap the benefits, now that he's past the point of no return. If for some reason—like rotting sewage, for instance—the project dies, Art looks like shit, and believe me, he never gets his old constituency back. So it's go for broke now—you know that."

"So point-blank, what are you telling me? That Art is friends with the Dodger? That Art is halfway down a political slippery slope? That there's the promise of some sort of payoff in the future? That perhaps there's already been a payoff of some sort? Maybe Art is another Donald Manes in the making?"

"Anything is possible," Jay explained, almost defensively. "I don't even know for sure yet. I'm gonna keep checking it out for you. I'll be talking to Pat. I'll talk to a lot of people, discreetly or indiscreetly, as the situation calls for. Hey, I'm in this too. You know how I feel about dumping environmental problems into black and Latino neighborhoods. I just want you to lay low a little. I definitely have to lay low a little right now. I have a couple of bambinos at home."

"You mean Babe Ruth *and* his identical twin?"

"That's it, Jon, you gotta keep laughing."

"What eats me up inside," Jon lamented, "is that I remember sitting in Paula's office two years ago and being told: 'If you can get to the bottom of the problem at North River . . . you'll be knighted . . . canonized.' That was her political goal, and Art Shuler's too."

"Hey, things change," Jay said. "This is the way I see your situation. Somebody throws you up in the air and says: 'Don't worry, I'll catch you.' But two years later, when you land, they're not there anymore."

"And in their place is a long spike, upon which I'm impaled."

"Exactly. Okay, I gotta run. I know you got that long train ride. Just hang loose."

"Hey, we've gotta have another one of those three-hour Stink Tank lunches with Pat and Laura soon."

"Yeah, sure," Jay shouted just before disappearing into the IRT stairwell. "Shoot for sometime next week."

Jon awoke at 2:10 A.M., Wednesday, April 7, and understood within a minute or so that he was in his own bed, in his own home in Rocky Point. His right hand lay upon the pouch of flesh that was once his wife's firm stomach. Bearing two children in the space of four years while working as a computer consultant had taken a physical toll on Elaine. But her laments regarding the supreme sacrifice of being a working mother had fallen on virtually deaf ears as of late. Jon didn't like being outdone. As he saw it, he had no way to match her and little way to help her. The best he could do was work harder at his job and try to remember her as she had appeared when they'd met eight years earlier.

Elaine Martz had blond hair with autumny streaks of brown, usually kept long and pulled back into a healthy ponytail. Her high cheekbones, fair skin, and squarish English jaw along with her long, elegant nose, gave her a somewhat royal look. That air, however, was offset by a smattering of freckles, smallish cute ears, and a slight mischievous crookedness to her broad, toothy smile. Her wide-set green eyes penetrated all forms of thought and matter. At five-foot-four and usually more slender, she still made a strong athletic appearance with shoulders strengthened by years of throwing clay and legs firmed by years of chasing racquet balls.

However, Elaine hadn't made a pot in three years or hit a racquet ball in five. The supreme sacrifice showed in her eyes, which seemed less focused lately and often appeared bloodshot; in her skin, which was a bit blotchy; and in her brown streaks of hair, which now had their own streaks of premature gray. Her degree in fine arts from Swarthmore College was now shelved along with hundreds of plates and mugs around the house. A little over five years ago she had made the difficult transition to computer technology largely for the sake of money. She now worked in Patchogue for the Long Island Lighting Company's in-house computer help desk. There, she fielded seven and a half hours a day of phoned-in, panic-stricken questions about crashed hard drives, corrupted files, and unretrievable backups. The atmosphere of crisis intervention seemed to spill over into the house in Rocky Point, where Elaine paced and complained in high-pitched tones about financial and personal problems Jon considered nonexistent. "Quit your stupid job tomorrow," Jon would say. "We can live off my salary."

"We need to pay off this house," Elaine would respond, "and start saving for college for Stacy and Steven before it's too late." To Jon, Elaine always seemed to be planning for some cataclysmic event that would leave them living underground in a reinforced concrete bomb shelter. If so, he thought, who needs a house and college? He felt burdened by the void in Elaine's life, and felt worse that he couldn't do anything about it. What Elaine did about it was to dabble in New Age fads—tarot cards, crystals, the I Ching, palmistry. She'd spooked him on their first date by telling him correctly he was a frustrated athlete and what their first child would look like. She spooked him again four years later when she spent the evening calling everyone they knew in California to ask if they were all right. The next night, as Jon sat in a bar with two friends, he watched an earthquake disrupt the second game of the World Series between the Oakland A's and the San Francisco Giants.

For all of his reliance on empirical data and scientific formula, Jon recognized that Elaine had a kind of sixth sense beyond simple intuition. But rather than pour it into gimmicks for a few minutes a day, he wished she'd return to being that carefree artist he could sneak up on from behind as she leaned over a wheel, so he could slip his hands beneath her stained denim work shirt and lick off the earthy taste of clay and sweat.

Jon now remembered that in his tiredness upon returning home, he'd undressed and left various items of dirty clothing and work-related material scattered throughout the house. Just as in his office, that lack of order bothered him. Until shortly after Stacy was born, he had been uncompromisingly neat. But now that he was responsible for two small children and one enormous borough, compromise was here in a big way, especially for high but less than vital standards like neatness.

It was the first considerably warm night of the spring, and the heat was turned down. For the first time in a long time, fresh air curled in from an open window and crawled gently over the bed. As he lay there, Jon recalled a piece of the dream he'd just had. In it, he was thrashing around in an open tank of sewage, similar to the ones in the North River plant. As he begged for help, Paula stood nearby along the deck and told him repeatedly: "You're overreacting." This scene had recurred in his dreams several times over the past month. At the moment, he felt and heard Elaine shifting position and adjusting the blanket, of which she now controlled two-thirds. He thought she might be awake, and he anticipated feeling guilty over it, not because he'd done anything to wake her, but because she seemed oddly in tune with his occasional insomnia.

"Are you awake?" Elaine spoke loudly enough for him to hear if he was awake, but softly enough not to rouse him if he was asleep.

"You bet I am."

"I can't sleep," Elaine announced. "What time is it?"

"It's after two," Jon said. "You want one of my Excedrin PMs?"

"I don't believe in those," she replied.

"You don't have to believe in them. You just have to take them."

"Jon, can I talk to you about something?"

"Now's the time. A couple of days from now I might be asleep." He sat up in bed.

"I did a tarot card reading on you this evening," Elaine said. "Some dangerous cards came up."

"Oh, please, not again," Jon said. "What the hell does my future have to do with how you cut a deck of cards?"

"It doesn't cause anything—it's more like an effect . . . a sign."

"Screw the cards," he said.

Now Elaine sat up. "Okay, fine. I did the reading for your benefit."

"Thanks, but you're better off listening closely to your own thoughts," Jon mused. "I believe that when something bad is about to happen, little explosions go off in your head. Those explosions are like a Morse code telling your unconscious mind exactly what's going to be happening, blow by blow. And the strange thing is, you get the emotional impact of it without consciously understanding any of it. When the events themselves start happening, you're less upset than you might have thought you'd be. You're just standing there saying: 'Oh . . . oh . . . uh-huh . . .' "

"That's true," Elaine agreed. "It's like a natural process that spreads the pain out more evenly."

"But why? Why not let us know the moment the information is available?"

"Maybe it's all been available the whole time," Elaine proposed. "Maybe God needs to keep some partial secrets from us to see how we react at certain times."

"Like laboratory rats? Am I supposed to be thrilled at the thought of being a laboratory rat? If God is such a great scientist, can't He accurately theorize all reactions without creating a tiny, helpless being to experience the suffering?"

"I guess not," Elaine conjectured. "Or I guess we're somehow benefiting from the suffering."

"Well, I'm a rare and selfless person. I want my benefits cut— so there's more to go around for everyone else."

"Jon, I have no idea. I don't even know what we're doing half the time."

"Make that all the time," Jon emphasized. "If you told me ten years ago that I would live in a big house with a beautiful woman as my lifelong playmate and enough money to indulge in any of the basic pleasures and yet still find a way to be miserable, I would have laughed in your face."

"Well, look what we have to do to maintain it and put a little something away," she stated. "We're both answering to crazy people all day. You have to travel two hours each way. I have to get up with Steven and Stacy at six in the morning. It sucks."

"Exactly. That's why we should get out of the system as soon as we can. We're letting ourselves be used as fuel for a big machine that may harvest the fields a little better or faster than we could ourselves, but leaves atrocious fumes and enormous tire tracks in its wake. I say, the deal's off. We'll harvest our own fields."

"And hump like bunnies?"

"You got it, kid," Jon said. "We'll sock away twenty or thirty thousand dollars, buy an acre even farther out than we are now, upstate, in the mountains somewhere, plunk a trailer home on it, and spend all our time doing the things we now spend all our time struggling to get to."

"I'll quilt and make pots all day and play games with Stevie and Stacy," Elaine said. "And you'll play baseball."

"And play with Stevie and Stacy. She's gonna be the best baseball player in her school. She may look like a miniature version of you, but she's got my swing. Have you seen her hit the ball off the batting tee lately? I couldn't do that when I was four. I wouldn't mind spending an hour or two a day hitting ground balls to both of them when they're a little older."

Elaine looked straight up at the ceiling. "It sounds nice, but I don't know if I'd have the guts to do it if I was face-to-face with the decision. I mean, we have certain financial goals. . . ."

"*You* have certain financial goals."

"I've worked hard to get where I am," Elaine continued. "I don't know if I could just walk away. Could you drop engineering completely? I thought you enjoyed it."

"I do," Jon said, "but not on these terms. I mean, this is a nice wall," Jon continued, pounding on the wall at the head of the bed, "but is it so nice that I want to spend the rest of my life taking a two-hour train ride to petition a politically motivated hatchet lady to acknowledge my work—which was hard enough to do in its own right—just to pay interest to a bank that bought from a bank that bought from a bank that bought the wall from the contractor who paid the carpenter who actually built it? I'll build the wall myself, for Chrissakes, and cut out all the middlemen. I tried to do that with this house, but I ran out of time."

"Well, you'd better build those walls thicker next time," Elaine advised.

"Why's that?"

"You just woke up Stevie."

At 6:45 on Thursday evening, April 8, Jon sat in a folding chair nine rows deep in the community room of the high-rise apartment building at 626 Riverside Drive and waited for the meeting of the West Harlem Environmental Review Board (WHERB) to begin. This was practically ground zero for the war between the North River plant and the people of West Harlem. The mammoth plant was situated just on the other side of the Henry Hudson Parkway.

In the 1960s, the plan was to locate the facility in the Seventy-second to Seventy-ninth Street vicinity along the Hudson due to the convenient location of existing sewer lines and the minimal dredging of the riverbed that would need to be done. But the combined political muscle of wealthy West Siders and nasty long-shoremen prompted the city, and Mayor Lindsay, to shift the location uptown. The new facility would sit on a twenty-eight-acre platform extending partially into the Hudson. In addition, the plant would be completely enclosed, the air filtered to ensure that no airborne pollutants would make their way into the surrounding neighborhood. As an added layer of insurance against those same airborne pollutants, the construction of a huge park was promised, to be located directly above the plant—on a platform over the first platform. In effect, the city and state were saying: "We're so confident of the environmental safety of this plant, we're going to let your kids play on top of it."

However, in the early 1980s when the plant was still under construction, federal budget cuts led to the scaling down of these plans, limiting the enclosure to only a very small portion of the plant. Unbelievably, the plans to construct the park on top remained intact, with New York City and State saying, in effect: "We're so confident of your kids' need for a place to play, we bet they'll play nine feet above huge, open vats of sewage."

When the North River plant actually went on line in 1986, the nervous speculation and abstract debate turned into angry rallies and bitter recriminations. From roughly 125th Street to 155th Street, along Riverside Drive, Broadway, and Amsterdam Avenue, the odors ranged from mildly annoying to overwhelming, depending upon where you were standing and which way the wind was blowing. On one particularly foul-smelling day in mid-July of that summer, a forty-five-year-old black schoolteacher by the name of Clarissa Marbles led a sit-down protest smack in the middle of the elevated Henry Hudson Parkway. That action brought attention to the problem, but not the tens of millions of dollars it would take to enclose the plant.

Now, almost seven years later, Clarissa Marbles got ready to address the committee she had formed that summer for the sole purpose of fixing the plant across the street. Since then, WHERB had added a half-dozen other issues of environmental concern to West Harlem, but North River remained the focal point. The situation had improved somewhat over those seven years, thanks in no small part to the brazen Ms. Marbles. Millions had been dedicated recently to enclosing particularly foul areas of the plant, while the park was scheduled to be opened in less than two months—well before the improvements below would take place.

Right across the street, the ultimate civic boondoggle was evolving in strange ways even the most cynical satirists couldn't have predicted. And in the community room of 626 Riverside Drive, you could catch a powerful whiff of hydrogen sulfide every now and then. Clarissa Marbles cleared her throat and called the meeting to order.

"I am Clarissa Marbles, for those of you who don't know me. I am the chairperson of the West Harlem Environmental Review Board. I want to welcome all of you to our monthly meeting. Now I want to get right on with it, because we have a lot of ground to cover. We've got a park opening up in a few weeks and that plant is still smellin' . . ."

Clarissa snarled for emphasis when she arrived at a key word in a gripe, and she sometimes launched without warning into a flurry of inner-city slang when something angered her. Just as easily, she would slip right back into the smooth, educated speech pattern that commanded respect from visiting government officials. Together, the one-two punch of academia and the street put fear into the hearts of her opponents. She continued with fervor.

"Those repairs they're makin' are not gonna be ready in time for the park opening up, so we have to tell our children about it and explain it to them. And speaking of explaining, I am pleased to call up to address us Mr. Edward H. Connor, area engineer for DEP. You all know Mr. Connor—he's here just about every month—and he'll be reporting on the odor monitoring devices they've installed in our neighborhood."

Clarissa Marbles motioned to Edward Connor, who straightened his shoulders behind the makeshift dais before addressing a predominantly black and Latino audience of about two hundred. He was in his middle forties, with prematurely white hair, and he related facts in the manner of both an engineer and a police sergeant.

"Thank you, Ms. Marbles . . ."

"*Chairperson* Marbles."

"Chairperson Marbles," he amended, and proceeded. "Now, as you know, we've installed seven air pollutant monitors at different locations in the neighborhood. You've probably noticed these units at one location or more. They're approximately four feet by four feet, and seven feet high, with the steel casing housing an actual unit inside. These units will be giving hourly readings of several pollutants, including hydrogen sulfide, methane, sulfur dioxide, carbon monoxide —"

"I have a question," an Hispanic woman of about fifty sitting in the fifth row let out. "When can we get the readings from these monitors?"

"Fairly soon," Connor responded. "The units are up and running, but right now they're still in shakedown—"

"You been telling us that for months now," Clarissa Marbles interjected with a vengeance. "Month after month, no readings. You ought to be ashamed of yourself, comin' to this community and tellin' us a team of thirty engineers can't get one reading out of a machine designed to do precisely that—after a whole damn year? *Shakedown?* The only shakedown is what y'all been doin' to us for seven years!"

This brought thunderous applause and hoots of moral indignation from the packed room. Connor, having gone through an almost identical ritual every month for the past year, lowered his head meekly, knowing that within twenty to thirty seconds he could lift it again and resume.

"I can understand your frustration, and I want to assure you that we are currently doing everything within our power to get those monitors on line, and by next meeting we should have some kind of hard numbers for you."

"Well, I hope for your sake you do," Clarissa admonished. "Thank you very much then, Mr. Connor. Next on our agenda, we have Mr. Jon Kessler, chief engineer from the Borough President's Office. Mr. Kessler has been regularly reporting to this community his independent findings on North River and has been very hard at work with a major study on the plant. Mr. Kessler . . ."

As Jon approached the dais, his stomach tightened, not because he had a problem with public speaking, but because he was barred by Paula Derbin from discussing the results of his study until it was cleared. Therefore, while babbling about whatever came to mind, he had to bottle up the knowledge that these people were going to be living with their problem for years to come. He recalled how two and a half years ago, upon attending his first couple of meetings here, he was skeptical of Clarissa Marbles's rage and that of her audience. While he believed the rage had validity, he viewed it as a general frustration with the state of their lives, and that this monthly meeting served as a kind of group therapy where innocent city employees took unwarranted abuse. But within a few months of nonanswers and evasions from the city, he began to see how legitimate the anger really was. Now, ironically, he was being paid to fan those same flames, not entirely unlike Connor.

"I've always been straight with you," Jon began, "and this is no time to stop. About a year ago, I set out to get the hard, cold facts on odors coming from the plant. The North River plant superintendent has staff members who take hydrogen sulfide readings all over the plant, inside and out, four times a day. I was allowed to see those numbers, and I used them to come up with a very sound mathematical model of the air space in and around the plant. I can tell you how I constructed that model, but I can't tell you the results at this time. The borough president has an outside consultant reviewing my findings to establish certainty, and I must respect his wishes." Jon knew that because of the good faith he had demonstrated over the past two and a half years, he would not be eaten for lunch. Nevertheless, hands went up all over the place.

"When *will* you be able to tell us what you found?" a sharp-looking black man in his twenties demanded.

"Hopefully in one month." Just then, a powerful rotten egg scent of hydrogen sulfide wafted into the room.

On Friday afternoon, April 9, at one-thirty, Jon exited the small mail room on the nineteenth floor of the Municipal Building and stepped into the spacious marble hallway clutching a handful of envelopes. There was an atmospheric electricity present that could not be felt with the five senses but was powerful nonetheless. Within ten seconds the senses themselves filled in the rest of the picture.

The elevator door opened and out stepped Ronald Arlen with his entourage. Jon understood that regardless of what anyone thought of the Dodger's ethics, some people carried with them a highly charged force field that sucked you in. Though detractors mockingly referred to Arlen as the poor man's Donald Trump, right now he was a force in his own right. As the five men and two women, all in expensive, dark business attire, walked by, the Dodger—at six-one and 220 pounds—did not physically dwarf Jon's own six-foot, 180-pound frame. Yet for that short time, the difference seemed as big as one run seems late in the seventh game of the World Series.

As the elevator doors closed behind him, Jon made a deliberate attempt to squelch from his own brain the last hint of awe. When the doors opened onto the twentieth floor, he marched into room 2035, past the map counter, and saw that both Larry and Old Al Gibbs were gone, probably out to lunch. Naomi Pierce, however, sat quietly at her new desk—which was now cleared except for a stack of documents and a black leather handbag—absorbing a brochure on the dissolved air flotation method of sewage treatment.

"Hey, I thought we scared you off," Jon remarked.

"I don't scare that easily," Naomi returned. "But I did use your room for a while this morning. Al was talking about how he had to snap the neck of a Soviet informant."

"You should have stuck around for that one," Jon said. "He dumps the body in the Volga River. It's one of my personal favorites. I'll be in my office if you need me."

"Okay."

As Jon sat down at his desk, he noticed on his message pad a well-articulated pen doodle of a peeled banana. The phone rang before he could dwell on its meaning.

"Hello . . . Jon Kessler . . ."

"Miss Know-It-All has an account with First Fidelity," came a deep, sonorous voice.

"Who is this?"

"Miss Know-It-All has an account with First Fidelity."

"I really don't have time for this shit," Jon shouted into the receiver. "If you have something to tell me, tell me who the hell you are and what the fuck it is!"

"It's only me," the voice resumed. "And I told you: Miss Know-It-All . . . First Fidelity . . . check it out."

"Is that it?"

"Yes."

"Have a nice day," Jon said, slamming down the receiver.

Chapter 5

At two-twenty Friday afternoon, April 9, James Mercado stood in front of the Tenth Precinct building on the south side of Twentieth Street, between Seventh and Eighth Avenues, and pulled a cigarette from a pack of Camels. Other detectives, as well as patrol officers and civilian department employees, walked in and out of the five-story, white, masonry-faced building and acknowledged Mercado with a hello or a nod, as he acknowledged them in return.

Mercado was not in top form today and came close to believing these innocuous greetings were indictments of the smoking habit he could not seem to kick. He knew better, but felt resentment over how he was forced to compartmentalize his few pleasures in life just to sustain them. Now, as he drew and released his first drag of the afternoon, smoking represented that problem. Until two years ago he was allowed to smoke at his own desk while calmly putting together puzzle pieces in his mind. It was a ritual that had helped get him through twelve years as a detective. Out of conscious consideration for those around him, he never went through more than half a dozen or so cigarettes in a day. As much sense as the new city law made, he often wound up feeling banished.

Even Twentieth Street, which he now viewed from the sidewalk, fed his sense of being encumbered. The precinct building was sandwiched by small brick apartment buildings with fire escapes and old curtains in the windows. While the personal matters of Twentieth Street residents often spilled right out in front of the precinct—complete with noisy marital squabbles and rent strikes—he had a duty to keep his own personal life far from the building, not merely walled off. Meanwhile, because of the premium on parking, cars were parked diagonally, making an already narrow street even narrower. While driving on Twentieth Street was slow, pulling in and out of a space was painstaking. There was always the possibility of scraping another car, especially the vehicle of a resident, who would make a federal case out of it.

In the same way that precinct problems encroached upon the street, police problems seemed to invade his personal time. As much as he loved to sit back and enjoy a movie, either at the theater or at home, he found it harder and harder to do with each passing year. Mercado had tempered himself into a blade that could cut through a situation's window dressing. His mind had become a machine for making logical and probable connections that most others would pass over.

When Mercado came home, it was difficult to dull the blade or unplug the machine. The writers, actors, and directors of the movies in which he once could lose himself were now all suspects in the crime of creating implausible stories. He knew how many digits had to be hit to dial Trenton from East Rutherford, New Jersey, how long it took a strangling victim to die, and what steps were involved in hot-wiring a '78 Oldsmobile Cutlass.

Those and a million other obscure details that he knew—some without thinking, some with—jumped out at him, whether from a movie where minute detail had been neglected or from a small fib his wife or daughter hadn't thought through thoroughly before telling. He could not turn it off. He tried hard to suspend his disbelief, but his disbelief was even stronger than his will.

Lately, Mercado had gotten to thinking that this problem was the cumulative result of the dozens of murder cases over the years he had not been able to solve. Even as a nine-year-old he was plagued for months when an 1888 Morgan silver dollar disappeared from his strongbox. Who took the coin, how they did it, and where they were hiding it were more important than the twelve-dollar value of the coin itself, even though it was the most valuable one he owned. His father, who had fought against Francisco Franco's army and then fled Spain for New York in 1939, was a resilient, determined man and Jimmy Mercado's role model. He told his son Jimmy that if he didn't learn to put things aside, he would be plagued. Now, more than three decades later, Detective Mercado often found himself thinking about current unsolved homicides, eight-year-old unsolved homicides, and the 1888 silver dollar, all interchangeably.

"Jimmy . . ." It was Janine O'Connel's feminine yet raspy voice coming from three feet behind him.

Still puffing on a Camel, Mercado didn't even bother to turn around. "Yeah . . ."

"Whatsamatter, Jimmy? Having a bad day?"

"Having a bad year," Mercado said, now wheeling around to face O'Connel, who, wearing only a tight pink crew-neck sweater above the belt this brisk April morning, unintentionally showed off her robust chest. She seemed unaware of how radiant her whole body had become in the sun.

"Well, it's gonna get a little worse," O'Connel said. "Reinhart wants to see us. It's about the Haney case. He's got some big shot from DEP up in his office."

"Does this guy work in the sewer too?" Mercado asked.

Mercado put out his cigarette as he and O'Connel walked into the small, decoratively arched front entrance of the Tenth Precinct building. Inside, cops, clerks, and victims milled about on a wooden floor beaten down and dulled by ninety years of traffic generated by everything from public lewdness to multiple homicide. The only people cheered by the pea-green painted walls were suspects who had just been released. The asbestos ceiling tiles, classified as hazardous and yellowed from the decades prior to the smoking ban, had been cited eleven years earlier by the Department of Buildings, but who could force the police into correcting an open violation? When Mercado and O'Connel stepped into Captain Eugene Reinhart's second-floor, translucent-windowed, metal-partitioned office a minute later, they were greeted by two unpleasant sights—one familiar and one not.

Though Reinhart's entire gut could not be seen from behind his desk, people sensed how big and repulsive it was and kept their distance. Fifty-five, but physically old beyond his years, his sad brown hound-dog eyes rested in fleshy saddle bags, which themselves rested in another set of saddle bags. His complexion was as sallow as the asbestos ceiling tiles and, if you included his jowls and the scalp easily seen through several strands of gray hair, almost as vast in area.

Standing to the right of Reinhart's desk and bracing himself against the back of a chair was a thin-boned man in his late thirties, about five-foot-ten with a neat, slicked-back lid of black hair that looked like it could be peeled off in one piece. Large black round-framed glasses drew attention away from his slitlike eyes, which tended to look directly at you for a moment then dart around wildly. Below, a large nose and slightly bucked teeth dominated the lower portion of his head like the rest of a cheap disguise from a novelty store.

"This is Lee Sarnow, DEP assistant commissioner," Reinhart began. By the time O'Connel closed the door behind them, Mercado had already taken a seat in front of Reinhart's desk. O'Connel remained standing for a moment to shake Sarnow's hand before taking the other seat, near Mercado.

"I'm Detective O'Connel . . . glad to meet you . . ."

"Mercado . . ." O'Connel's partner was less enthusiastic.

"Lee came down here to try to make our lives a little easier," Reinhart continued. "We talked it over before you came in, and we agreed we can do a little better on this one if we work together." Reinhart turned and fixed his gaze on Sarnow for a moment. "Mercado and O'Connel are two of my best detectives. Why don't you tell them what you'd like to do, and they'll tell you what they need."

"Okay, thank you, Captain Reinhart," Sarnow said, clearing his throat but proceeding to speak predominantly through his nasal passages. "I'll level with you all. This is obviously an embarrassing situation for my agency, and it's really an embarrassing situation for all city agencies."

"Why's that?" Mercado asked.

"Well, I don't know how much you already know," Sarnow said, "but I'm going to come clean right here. Joel Haney was into a lot of not-so-wonderful things. Now this stuff is eventually all going to be aired out in public, and it's going to be egg on everybody's face—mine, his, yours, everyone who works for the city. Now I'm not saying Joel Haney brought this down on himself. It's your job to figure out exactly what went on down there. I mean, as problematic an employee as he was, he was one of our own, and if in fact he was killed, we'd like to see the guilty party brought to justice as much as anyone.

"But what I'm proposing is that we be very up-front about what this guy was into, right from the beginning. I'll tell you everything there is to know, open up all our files, and we can do the same with anyone you want. And that includes the media too . . . whatever. It's better we get this out in the open now, up front, than look like we were holding something back later on down the road."

"What is it you think the media will be so interested in?" Mercado asked.

"Well, where do I begin?" Sarnow said, throwing his hands apart to indicate a huge body of information. "He made porno films. Joel Haney made porno films. He ran around Chelsea, the docks, with a camcorder, getting hookers for his porno films."

"I heard he was making a documentary," Mercado said.

"Who told you that, one of the girls?" Sarnow said. "Give me a break. My six-year-old nephew could come up with a better excuse than that."

"How'd you find out about these . . . porno films?" Mercado said. "You didn't happen to rent one, did you?"

"Sources inside the department—and out—have come forward," Sarnow said.

"Could you give us their names?" O'Connel asked. "We'd like to talk to them."

"Well, I'm sorry," Sarnow said. "We've accepted this information on a confidential basis."

"What about getting this whole thing out in the open?" Mercado said. "Airing it in public . . . ?"

"Look, I can provide you with actual tapes," Sarnow barked, slapping the padded back of the chair he was still using to prop himself up and momentarily raising his eyebrows up over his large-framed glasses. "When you see a tape of Joel Haney himself having sex with some blond hooker, you're not going to care *who* gave me those tapes."

"Yes I am," Mercado said.

"So Haney was going to star in his own porno videos?" O'Connel asked.

"What can I tell you?" Sarnow said. "He was a vain guy."

"I think that's true of most sewer workers," Mercado said, winking at Reinhart.

"Look, I'll see if I can get them to come forward," Sarnow said in a more withdrawn tone, now removing his glasses and looking closely at the lenses.

"I don't want us to get off track," Reinhart said, looking right at Mercado. "We can get into all these details later on. Raise these questions as they come up . . ."

"Sure," Mercado said, rolling his eyes.

"We're only here now to establish a game plan and open up the lines of communication," Reinhart said. "What Assistant Commissioner Sarnow is offering can make your life a lot easier."

"It already has," Mercado said.

"Look," Sarnow said, putting the glasses back on, "this isn't easy for me. I just wanna be honest as possible and cut our losses. Some of Haney's extracurricular activities he was apparently doing on the job. We're supposed to be running a tight ship here, especially with the mayor's layoffs, downsizing, fiscal responsibility. They're gonna be asking us how long we knew about what this guy was up to, and we're gonna have to say . . . *too* long."

"How long is that?" O'Connel asked.

"A year," Sarnow said. "Something like that. Maybe more. We're gonna have to answer to the fact that we had a renegade employee and did next to nothing about it. I mean, we're trying to figure out what to do with hundreds of tons of sludge that we can't dump into the ocean anymore. We're trying to avoid having to build filtration plants for drinking water because we're not sure how to raise five billion dollars without breaking the taxpayer's back. With all this going on, I'll admit it—it's hard not to let one guy slip through the cracks. And you know what the union is like . . ."

"Then you have a disciplinary file on Haney," O'Connel said.

"A file . . . right, yes, we can get you that," Sarnow said. "Here's my card." He reached into his pocket, pulled out his wallet, handed Mercado and O'Connel a card each. "We'll get you something. If you don't hear from me in a couple of days or haven't gotten anything in the mail, call me. Call me anytime. I want to hear how the case is going. I want to get to the bottom of it and move on. Maybe Haney slipped and fell. He was an alcoholic— did you know that? He was known to pick a fight."

"Yeah, I heard they really know how to tie one on down in the sewer," Mercado said.

"I'm just offering it up in case it leads somewhere," Sarnow said. "He was a gambler too. I don't know if he owed any serious money. If I hear anything I'll let you know."

"Sounds like everyone in the world was after Joel Haney," Mercado said. "Bookies, black market video distributors, bartenders . . ."

"Your guess is as good as mine," Sarnow said.

"I want to thank you for taking time out of your busy schedule to come down here," Reinhart said, reaching over to shake Sarnow's hand. Mercado had taken out his black notebook and was now wiping off the smooth plastic front and back covers with the sleeve of his gray suit jacket.

"Yeah, thanks," Mercado said, for the first time sustaining eye contact with Sarnow for more than two seconds. "I appreciate what you must be going through with all the work on your plate. I have the same problem." Mercado handed the notebook to Sarnow, who reached for it with his right hand.

"What's this?" Sarnow asked.

"My notebook," Mercado said. "Take a look inside." Sarnow opened the book and glanced at Mercado's tiny, neatly organized yet chaotically crammed handwriting as he flipped through the pages.

"What am I supposed to be looking at?" Sarnow asked.

"This is *our* busy schedule," Mercado said. "Three new cases in the past week, eleven in the past month, eight of them still open. So thanks for your help, but this may take longer than you want."

"I understand fully," Sarnow said. "That's why I'll do whatever it takes." Mercado reached forward, and Sarnow returned the notebook.

"Of course once in a while, the answer just falls into our lap," Mercado said, gingerly returning the notebook to the right pocket of his jacket.

"That's always nice," Sarnow said, fumbling with the lower button on his own suit jacket and taking a step toward the door.

"Thanks for dropping by," O'Connel said, lifting herself partially out of her seat and extending her right hand to Sarnow, who shook it quickly.

"Sure, no problem," Sarnow said, opening the door. "We'll work together. We'll be in touch." Sarnow exited and closed the door gently behind him. Mercado, O'Connel, and Reinhart stared at each other silently for five seconds.

"That was fucking pitiful," Mercado said.

"What a dipshit," O'Connel said.

"I happen to need that dipshit right now," Reinhart replied. "You didn't have to needle him like that, Jimmy."

"Yes I did," Mercado said.

"C'mon, Gene, you can see he's all wrong," O'Connel said. "He was so desperate to smear Haney, you'd think *he* killed him."

"Is that what you think?" Reinhart asked. "That this up-and-coming politico—not even forty, and second in command of the biggest agency in the city—spends his time putting his own sewer rats out of their misery?"

"When people lie to me, I like them to be consistent," Mercado said. "That's all I ask."

"And I'm asking you to cut me some slack," Reinhart said, slapping his desktop with an open palm. "I cut the two of you slack every day just by letting you work together."

O'Connel blushed and rolled her eyes.

"Can't you think of something new to stick up my ass, Gene?" Mercado said. "That one's as old as your clip-on tie."

"I'll ask you nicely once," Reinhart said, "then I'll order you. Work with that little son of a bitch. *Pretend* to work with him. I don't care how, just make him believe he's in the loop. How hard can that be? Call him once in a while with something that sounds good. Make it up if you want to. Pretend to be interested in what he says. Go with it. Who knows? You might even get something out of it. And if not, just go where the investigation takes you. Just keep me posted on the real stuff. I'll take care of the rest and make that son of a bitch feel real good about himself."

"Why bother?" Mercado asked.

"Why bother?" Reinhart said. "You know that mobile crime unit we got last year—the mobile command post with Special Operations Division capabilities and a hundred thousand dollars' worth of surveillance equipment? You know the forty new bullet-proof vests our patrol officers got? All that came from the Borough President's Office. That little son of a bitch is married to a woman lawyer who runs that office. I hear she's a psycho. All I need to do is piss off her wuss husband and we can kiss the next two hundred thousand dollars of discretionary contributions to this precinct good-bye."

"Is that what this is about?" Mercado said. "A few new toys for the squad? Sure. I can deal with that."

"*That's* where the mobile unit came from?" O'Connel said. "I'm surprised. I thought Art Shuler was a liberal—soft on crime."

"Things change," Reinhart said. "Shuler's looking at a mayoral run this year. The outer boroughs love two things—jobs and safe streets."

"So that's what this is *really* about," Mercado said, smiling widely, "your pipe dream of becoming the next police commissioner. You know, you have to get a real tie for that job."

"You give me too much credit," Reinhart said, fighting off a smile. "I can't look that far ahead. I have trouble looking ahead to next week."

"No, no," Mercado said, "you're entitled to your fantasy. Just like Joel Haney."

"All right, get the fuck out of here," Reinhart said. "Go solve a murder."

Mercado and O'Connel exited Reinhart's office and walked down an aisle of metal desks on the second floor until they got to their own—two desks several feet apart, each near its own window and both served by the same dinosaur-age fluorescent light fixture hanging tenuously from the ceiling. Like his notebook and his memory, Mercado's desk was overrun with files and messages, aside from the occasional Dunkin' Donuts box.

"What are we gonna do about the routine stuff?" O'Connel asked. "Like canvassing Fourteenth and Hudson, going door to door . . ."

"Ah," Mercado said, sitting and putting his head in his hand, "that's going to be a nightmare. Looks like we're married to this case—and all the others. Let's see if we can get some uniforms to help out on that. It would be nice to have the coroner's report back in a couple of days, but the way they're jammed up, we'll be lucky to get it back next week. In the meantime, we have a lot of people to talk to, and we'll be real lucky if we get even one that's anything close to a material witness. We ought to get a list of hookers together and see what we can find out about them. I'll start on that."

"I'm sure you will," O'Connel said. "What about Sarnow?"

"He's yours for now," Mercado said. "I want you to find out everything you can on him. Who his friends are, how he got his job, where he worked before. Just try not to get too attached to him while you're at it."

"Hey, after you, there could be no other," O'Connel said with a smirk. "I'm surprised you gave him that little vote of sympathy at the end. And that you let him see your notebook."

"Look at it this way," Mercado said, holding the notebook carefully along its edges and slipping it into an envelope, "at least we have his fingerprints now."

Chapter 6

On a cloudy Tuesday, April 13, just past two-thirty in the afternoon, Mercado and O'Connel stepped out of the Country Kitchen Restaurant onto the sidewalk at the intersection of Fourteenth and Hudson Streets. Because this was where both Greenwich and Hudson Streets funneled into Ninth Avenue, it was an unusually broad intersection, especially for typically dense lower Manhattan. You looked out and saw a large, paved tract of urban land with no clear guidelines. To cross on foot from the east corner of Fourteenth and Hudson to the west corner of Fourteenth and Ninth involved venturing across a pedestrian no-man's-land with the width of two major New York avenues and no island between them. Pavement markings were scarce since the Fourteenth Street reconstruction was just being wrapped up, and painting them was the final item in the contract.

The Hudson Street reconstruction project, meanwhile, delayed repeatedly by stalemates between the general contractor and the city, was still very much ongoing. A block south along Hudson

Street, open trenches could be seen, meaning not only pavement markings were missing, but also the pavement itself. If you were feeling lucky, you could try to jaywalk from where Mercado and O'Connel stood to the small, triangular block formed by the Hudson and Ninth merge.

If you were feeling suicidal, you could try the full jaywalk, clear across to the rectangular block at the west corner of Fourteenth and Ninth. That meant not only challenging cars hostile to pedestrians, but cars also hostile to each other. While New Yorkers were often bad at taking direction, sometimes they were even worse at improvising. Cars changing imaginary lanes and responding to yellow traffic lights by accelerating talked to each other with blaring horns.

The sound of these horns permeated the intersection and traveled to its outskirts, where they bounced off a variety of buildings with no clear theme connecting them. There were three-story brick and wood structures, each with a small store or tavern on the ground floor and two stories of apartments overhead. Right next to them were large warehouses used for anything from pharmacy supplies to meatpacking. Now, looking out at this confluence of chaos and confusion, Mercado stopped in his tracks and gripped his forehead with his thumb and two opposing fingers.

"Where are we going with this?" he asked.

"Nowhere," O'Connel said.

"Today's one of those days when I'm wondering why I became a detective," Mercado said. "If I have to ask one more person if they saw anything occur the night of April fifth or the morning of April sixth by that manhole over there, I'm going to jump in the sewer myself."

"The people in these bars don't remember what time they had their first shot today," O'Connel said, "much less something they saw last week."

"The people upstairs in the apartments aren't much better," Mercado said. "They don't look out their windows anymore. They all have cable."

"I have something that might cheer you up, Jimmy," O'Connel said. "I dug up some dirt on Sarnow."

"Let's hear it."

"My college friend Jane Myers works at the Parks Department, over in the Olmsted Center across from Shea Stadium. She's a landscape architect. She's worked there for eight years."

"She's the one who decides where to put the trees?" Mercado quipped.

"There's a lot more to it than that," O'Connel said.

"Right. I forgot about the benches . . . where to put the benches."

"Sarnow was chief of staff at the Olmsted Center for about three years," O'Connel said.

"No kidding?"

"Apparently he made life over there miserable for everybody."

"How did you even know to call your friend?"

"She used to tell me these incredible stories about this guy, and I thought his name was Sarnow or something like that. And sure enough, this is the same guy. It seems like this guy's personal mission in life was to break the back of civil service. He used to stand by the sign-in book every morning and at 9:05 sharp he would draw a red line. Anyone who signed in below that red line, even three minutes later, was in trouble. Two incidents and something would be entered into your personnel file. When your review came up—bang, no raise, no promotion. Technically, there was nothing the union could do. And to add insult to injury, if you were late, you'd find something ridiculous like two dollars and forty-nine cents—your prorated salary—taken out of your paycheck."

"Way to go, Sarnow," Mercado said.

"Wait, it gets better," O'Connel said. "He was obsessed with people using Parks vehicles for personal use. You know those green GMC Jimmy vans? He would follow people around in an unmarked car when they went out to the field."

"Isn't that the Inspector General's job?"

"Jane told me Sarnow used to follow *them* around too," O'Connel said. "Anyway, he caught a friend of Jane's on her way back from inspecting a swimming pool up in the Bronx. She got chlorine on her, which burned a hole through her shirt, so on her way back to Queens she stopped at her apartment in Manhattan to change."

"Uh-oh."

"Bang, that was that," O'Connel said. "Sarnow took pictures, everything. She was fired the next day. He made an example of her. Wrote a memo to the entire staff warning about 'the epidemic of stealing time from the city.' And she was one of the best field engineers they had."

"Of course . . ."

"Then someone tipped off the *Voice* to the fact that Sarnow was using a Parks vehicle every weekend to go upstate—Saugerties, I think—to a cabin he was renting. The *Voice* asks Sarnow for his side of the story and he has the arrogance to say: 'Well, my car was in the shop.'"

"Gotta hand it to this guy . . ."

"The *Voice* prints the article," O'Connel said, "and nothing happens to Sarnow."

"Of course not. He's the chief of staff."

"While all this is going on," O'Connel said, "he has a little thing going on the side with the secretary for the electrical engineer's unit."

"Sarnow? Ooooh . . . that's hard to swallow."

"She was a biker chick," O'Connel said. "She came in dressed in super tight jeans, leather biker boots, a leather vest with tassels and studs. Rumor had it she had a skull and crossbones tattoo on the inside of her thigh."

"Let me get this straight," Mercado said. "Our little weasel could handle *that*?"

"She used him," O'Connel said. "She got a raise. She never got red-lined. This went on for something like six months. Then one day she walks into work with a ring on her finger, marches up to Sarnow and says it's over. She got married over the weekend to her real boyfriend on some kind of bikers' trip . . . spur of the moment."

"What? You mean Sarnow wasn't good enough?"

"He took back the biker chick's raise," O'Connel said. "Wrote her up for typos, made sure she got tons of extra work. Then he tried to have her dismissed for violating the city's dress code."

"I didn't even know the city *had* a dress code," Mercado said.

"Sarnow dug up some obscure rule from the 1940s," O'Connel said. "And then the biker chick threatened to sue Sarnow for sexual harassment. But one day, in the middle of this whole mess, the biker chick's three-hundred-pound biker husband walks into the Olmsted Center, finds Sarnow in the cafeteria, lifts him up by his shirt collar in front of everybody and says: 'I don't care who you are or who you know. If you ever bother my wife again, I will come back here and rip your head right off that skinny little body.'"

"So they settled it out of court."

"Basically," O'Connel said.

"So who *did* Sarnow know?" Mercado asked.

"Art Shuler," O'Connel said. "The first time Gianetta ran for mayor, Art Shuler gave him the Upper West Side and Liberal party endorsements."

"I thought Gianetta and Shuler didn't like each other."

"They don't," O'Connel said. "Shuler ran for borough president instead. They both won the Democratic primaries and their elections. Shuler's reward was he got to appoint a whole bunch of his friends into high positions. One of them was Sarnow, who was Shuler's page when Shuler was a city councilman. He got him the chief of staff job at the Olmsted Center with Parks. Knowing absolutely nothing about parks didn't count against him."

"So how did he wind up at DEP—Bureau of Sewers?" Mercado asked.

"Sarnow went too far," O'Connel said. "While he was busy harassing the biker chick one day, he walked into the office of the electrical squad and there she was, flirting with one of the younger engineers."

"Ooooh, I'll bet the little weasel didn't like that."

"No he didn't," O'Connel said. "Just for kicks, he wrote up the whole electrical squad. Put disciplinary notes in the engineers' files and docked their pay. One of the guys in the electrical squad had enough. This guy's brother was big in DC37—you know, the technician's union—and they got a lot of sympathy from all the other unions on this. That Christmas, when they had the annual Christmas tree lighting ceremony at City Hall, the mayor pulled the switch in front of five thousand people and not one bulb went on."

"Wait a second," Mercado said, "I heard about this."

"Joe Rodriguez, the head of DC37, walks up to the podium and says to the mayor: 'Your honor, we have to talk.' They settled it inside City Hall in five minutes. Rodriguez said they could not live with Sarnow. So the electricians had pulled out the main wires on the tree. Rodriguez said either get rid of Sarnow or no lights. The mayor took the lights."

"I remember that," Mercado said. "That was our little weasel?"

"That was Sarnow. But a few months later the mayor asks

Shuler to run for Manhattan borough president again instead of running against him in the primaries, and Shuler agrees. So by the following year, they found Lee Sarnow a new job—at DEP."

"So if Art Shuler makes it through the primaries and the general election," Mercado said, "a schmuck like Lee Sarnow will be deputy mayor."

"Scary thought, isn't it?" O'Connel said.

"Shuler'll get killed in the outer boroughs anyway."

"Don't bet on it," O'Connel said. "I read he's building up quite a war chest."

"And Gianetta can't change his mind and run again because of term limits."

"Actually, Gianetta's grandfathered," O'Connel said. "But don't hold your breath. Eight years is enough for anyone."

"Could you imagine Reinhart doing those press conferences after a drug ring arrest?"

"He'd need a complete makeover," O'Connel said, "and a personal etiquette trainer."

Mercado looked at the manhole from which Joel Haney was pulled the week before. "You know, I don't think Haney was killed in the sewer, or even on this block . . ."

"Right," O'Connel said. "I tend to agree with you."

"Someone, for some reason, who knew where he worked, killed him and dumped him in the sewer somewhere upstream. The rain came, filled up the sewer, and washed Haney westward. His arm got stuck in the ladder, and that's where Sharpe found him. Now first of all, I don't even like having this theory, because if I'm right, we have to go door-to-door for a mile east of here. Like I said, I'd rather jump in the sewer. But unfortunately I think I'm right."

"Hey," O'Connel said, "I don't know what to do with this thing. I've called DEP a dozen times asking for maps of the sewer and for someone who can tell us whether there was enough rain to drag that body. These people, whether it's a secretary or an engineer, sound like they're ready to crawl under a rock. They won't return calls. They tell me that kind of information is hard to get. That it wouldn't be accurate. They tell me they have to clear it with the Assistant Commissioner's Office. The Assistant Commissioner's Office tells me they'll look into it. What the hell am I supposed to do?"

"Thanks again for the open investigation, Sarnow," Mercado said. "And that's what concerns me. You know Jack?"

"Detective Dunleavy?"

"Yeah," Mercado said. "He told me if we want maps of the sewer and technical advice we should call Jon Kessler, the chief borough engineer. Jack said this guy turns things around in one day."

"Great, then call him," O'Connel said. "What's the problem?"

"The problem is, can we trust this guy?" Mercado said. "He works for the Borough President's Office. Remember what Gene said about Sarnow's wife at the Borough President's Office? Since we're ninety-nine percent sure there's some kind of cover-up going on, how do we know Kessler and everybody else in that office isn't getting the same kind of pressure the people at DEP are getting? Kessler might be a dead end too. Worse—he might tell his boss to tell Sarnow what we're up to. Who knows? They could use him to throw us further off the track."

"Go ahead and call him," O'Connel said. "The way I see it, we don't have much to lose. Sarnow probably already knows what we're up to since we already asked DEP for the same stuff. If Kessler won't help us, we've wasted a phone call. If he steers us off the track, so what? I don't feel we're on a track to begin with. Lost is lost."

"You're right, Janine. It can't get much worse. And something else comes to mind. Remember when Sharpe told us some engineer in the BP's office was the only one willing to expose Fourteenth Street?"

"Right . . ."

"That's mob territory," Mercado said. "If this is the same guy, and he's the kind of guy who would stick his neck out like that, maybe he's okay. But I'm not going to leave it up to guesswork. The hell with the phone call. I'm going to go over there in person and meet him. I wanna know who I'm dealing with."

"I remember when you looked *me* over for the first time," O'Connel said. "I feel sorry for Kessler."

"Well," Mercado said, "at least you passed. And another thing. I'm going to ask him for the maps first and not fully explain why. Let's see if he even gets me those before I ask him for anything else or explain anything else."

"So I can stop calling DEP?"

"You can stop—but don't." Mercado pulled out his notebook and flipped through it. "I want Sarnow thinking we're lost." Mercado paused. "It's funny. After everything he did, Sarnow got nailed at Parks for sexual-harassment-related stuff. I was smart. I stopped hitting on you *way* before you got married."

"Yeah," O'Connel said, "but way after *you* got married."

Chapter 7

Jon Kessler tended to suffer through long periods of waiting for anything that was of great importance to him. He wasn't comfortable with the notion that something into which he'd poured his mind and heart was floating about somewhere in the wild blue yonder, outside the grasp of his direct influence or control. Though he considered himself someone who believed in God, he found small consolation in the notion that the results of his efforts were in God's hands.

First, he didn't understand how God did what He did. The physical laws upon which Jon based his livelihood—static equilibrium, conservation of momentum, conservation of energy—seemed to leave little room for this other Entity. Second, if the matter was in God's hands, then there was some additional burden on him to utter the right prayers, to think the right thoughts at odd moments. To Jon, that was guesswork, and you couldn't design a safe bridge using guesswork. Third, and most important, he didn't believe the matter—in this case, his report—was really *in* God's hands. It was in the hands of a bunch of New York City bureaucrats, and though God had been known to bring certain people back from the dead, some things were asking too much.

It was Wednesday morning, April 14. Eight days had passed since Paula Derbin decreed a month until the report—entitled "An Assessment of Odor Control Measures at the North River Water Pollution Control Plant"—would be returned from review. That left twenty-two days to fill with something else. Jon wondered whether Paula's clock started ticking when his did or if her clock was ticking at all. His mind had seized the number "thirty." For all he knew, the term "a month" had flown into her head randomly and left the same way. Nevertheless, he would be counting down, like Times Square revelers on New Year's Eve.

He looked through the opening of his office door and saw Naomi hunched quietly over the *Consent Order on the North River Water Pollution Control Plant*—a fifty-eight-page document describing what the city had to do with the plant to avoid massive fines by New York State. He observed Naomi's concentration and was impressed. He recalled how long it had taken him to get the big picture regarding sewage—the federal, state, and local laws, the hodgepodge of technologies applied, the complex physical layouts of the massive treatment plants.

Jon had found that the best way to get the big picture—after perhaps someone in the know had mercifully spent an hour or two giving you a rough but viable framework—was to start anywhere and simply not panic. It took a special person to turn confusion into meaningful questions, especially in the beginning, when they tended to pile up quickly, like greasy dishes at a delicatessen. Beyond raw intelligence, it required a subtle confidence that at some point the questions could be cleaned and put away one by one.

Jon perceived that Naomi possessed that confidence, and for that alone he automatically felt some kinship with her. He knew also that she was experiencing the frustration of waiting as well. Although not as helpless as the form his own waiting now took, no matter how hard she pushed it would still be a while before the big picture would begin to come together and she could contribute something. He decided to make the best of his waiting and hers.

"How would you like to take a break and see something amazing?" he asked, walking up on Naomi from behind.

"That depends entirely on what it is," she replied, rolling her head back to make eye contact with him.

Jon smiled and stepped closer to Naomi's desk to make further eye contact easier. "The reconstruction of Sixth Avenue, in progress," he explained. "Up till now, you've probably experienced it only as a traffic jam. Here's your opportunity to experience it as an engineering marvel."

"Sure," Naomi said enthusiastically. "I need a break from this legalese."

"Not that I understand everything about it," Jon added. "Not that anyone does. Reconstructing a street like that is like twenty-four months of exploratory surgery."

"Don't they have the equivalent of a CAT scan?"

"Yes and no," he replied. "I'll tell you on the ride up. Let me get my coat."

As Jon slipped on a tweed sport jacket, Old Al Gibbs started in, talking loudly to himself. "What kind of first date is that? He takes her to a hole in the ground? That's the best my boy can do?"

"Drop it, Al," Jon said flatly. He noticed a blush on Naomi's face before she quickly regained her composure. A sharply dressed Spanish-looking man, about forty, with a head of short, thick black hair stood on the other side of the counter. Except for the fact that he was clean-shaven, he looked a lot like Keith Hernandez, the former New York Mets all-star first baseman. But this one seemed more interested in grabbing a map than a ground ball. Jon knew that look anywhere, especially here. And now the dreaded eye contact followed.

"Sir, are you the chief engineer?"

"You know, it's funny you ask," Jon replied as he bolted for the door. "I just resigned three or four minutes ago. Al Gibbs over here is in charge now."

Twenty minutes later Jon and Naomi emerged from the F train just north of the intersection of Twenty-third Street and Sixth Avenue, officially known as the Avenue of the Americas. Renamed in 1945 as part of an image-sprucing program devised by the president of the Sixth Avenue Association, Jon considered anyone who actually called it "Avenue of the Americas" to be an out-of-towner. Now, as they walked, he and Naomi were quickly surrounded by heavy equipment—a crane, a backhoe, a derrick, and NYNEX and Con Edison supply trucks. The west half of the street was enclosed by waist-high concrete barriers—known as Jersey barriers—inside which all the construction activity took place. While the uptown traffic flowed along sluggishly in the two remaining open lanes, within the barriers, trenches and holes lay open, surrounded by various crews poking, sifting, digging, and jackhammering around bits and pieces of utility lines exposed for the first time in decades in their beds of rock, concrete, and soil.

Jon directed Naomi's attention first to the naked cylinder of bricks extending six feet below the surface. Ironically, the heavy steel manhole cover still sat on top, so the vision was the exact opposite of what one typically saw at a work site. Surrounding the manhole cylinder was a mesh of pipes, conduits, and cables, with only a few of the pipes actually connected to its walls.

"There it is," Jon said, "the guts of New York. Not too glamorous, but then again neither are my small intestines."

"They have to replace all this, then?" Naomi asked.

"No, just some of it, while keeping the rest functional during construction. That's part of what makes the process so tedious. The first question is, why rebuild Sixth Avenue at all? I mean, it worked the last time *I* drove over it. It's still the commercial capital of the Western Hemisphere."

"Well, obviously because it was in poor condition," Naomi replied.

"Actually, that's the secondary reason," Jon said. "The primary reason is that the federal money is there to do so. Every couple of years, Washington appropriates billions and billions for these types of 'infrastructure rebuilding' projects. The money comes with a time limit, so there's a window of opportunity for the city to use it. You can bet they're gonna find a way to use it with the kind of money it brings into the local economy. The funding formula is eighty-five percent federal, ten percent state, and five percent local for one of these jobs. So for one buck, New York City gets a twenty-buck bang, plus whatever additional ripple effect that money has as it works its way through—jobs, income tax, real estate investment . . ."

"But what was actually wrong with Sixth Avenue," Naomi asked, "other than the usual potholes?"

"Well, once the city has its hot little hands on the money, the politicians have to decide which streets need it the most. If it's just a matter of potholes, DOT can send a patching crew to pour some hot asphalt in. Or if the potholes and cracks are too numerous, they can repave the whole street in literally a few nights. That's all highly superficial work by comparison to what they call roadway reconstruction. Beneath four or five inches of asphalt is a concrete bed that may be another ten inches deep. Once that goes, you can patch and repave a dozen times a year and it won't matter. The potholes and cracks will be back by next winter like a bad flu."

"So how do the engineers know if it's the concrete bed beneath that's deteriorating?" Naomi asked.

"The workmen drill cores, all the way down, even past the roadway bed, into the soil or bedrock below. They pick a spot where they think there are no utility lines—there *are* still a few, you know—and they drill this hollow six-inch-diameter cylinder straight down. What they get out is a thin column that shows the engineers the degree of deterioration, or erosion, or the soil type at each level. They drill a bunch of these cores, scattered all over the street for a few blocks, and then try to draw a meaningful conclusion."

"What about the sewers and other utilities then?" Naomi asked.

"That's all factored in too. The engineers look at records of how old the sewers are, what they're made of, whether there's infiltration at the joints, how old the water mains are. You realize they're doing this for streets all over New York and establishing a priority list. It's a huge, interagency task. DEP—Bureau of Sewers and Bureau of Water Supply—will tell DOT about its own lines, Con Ed will tell DOT about its stuff—which is electric, gas, and steam. If a sewer line is more than forty-eight inches in diameter, it gets a human walk-through . . ."

"Or would that be a human *crawl*-through?" Naomi conjectured.

"Yeah, for the ones forty-eight inches or just over, they send the seven sewer dwarfs: Slimy, Stinky, Sludgy, Smelly . . ."

"Hi-ho, hi-ho, it's down the drain we go . . ."

"Hey, that's pretty good. I'm gonna steal that one," Jon said with a grin of surprise, "and tell my friends down at the Bureau of Sewers I thought of it. Anyway, do you know what they do to inspect the inside of sewers that are less than forty-eight inches? They do a videotape inspection. They open up a couple of manholes and slip in a waterproof video camera on wheels attached to a pulley system. All this is done on a dry day, of course—on a rainy day, the sewers might be running too full."

"Then on a dry day, they're fairly empty?" Naomi asked.

"Yes, relatively speaking," Jon replied. "Though the sewage treatment plants in New York were underbuilt, the sewers themselves are generally not. On a dry day, a five-footer might be running six inches to a foot deep. I'll have to show you one of the videos. I mean, talk about dirty movies. When you watch one of them, you don't have much of a perspective other than the sewer walls, so you tend to feel like you're going straight down through a pipe yourself, rather than at a one percent horizontal slope. Or if you're moving against the flow, you feel you're traveling straight up the pipe. Your peripheral vision sees the brick or concrete or cast iron the sewer is made of . . . whipping from the foreground and then out of view behind you like some kind of weird subterranean *Star Wars* clip. And along the bottom of your screen, say you're traveling against the current—the murky water is coming right at you, then disappearing beneath you at maybe four to five miles an hour."

"And you see human . . . waste matter in that flow? You don't have to answer that."

"Dr. Sewage tells all! Actually, you can't make out much of that. Between the murkiness of the water, the speed, and the fact that most waste matter has been broken up and diluted by that point, it doesn't look that different from floating down the muddy Mississippi. But every once in a while something white and lumpy comes whipping right at you."

Naomi winced, then grinned in anticipation.

"That's right," Jon confirmed. "It's a piece of toilet paper. They tend not to decompose for a while. Okay, ready for lunch?"

"I'll be skipping the next several meals," Naomi replied.

"The funniest part, though, isn't gross at all. This thing is narrated! You see a number running the whole time at the lower right-hand corner of the screen, telling you how many feet you've logged, and then the voice comes on." Jon launched into a blue collar Brooklyn accent reminiscent of TV sewer worker Ed Norton: "Yeah, right over here along the east wall, around foot number thoity-three, we got some crackin' and some spallin' along them walls."

"Not exactly *National Geographic*," Naomi remarked.

"Not exactly," Jon agreed. "The only wildlife you've got is an occasional rat."

"No alligators?"

"The last time that was documented was 1935. The biggest ones were about two feet long. Kids in those days bought small imported alligators from pet stores. Some of them got flushed down the toilet and some might have been tossed into the sewer by disgusted parents. The ones that survived kept growing."

"Are there any still down there?" Naomi asked.

"I doubt it," Jon replied. "Back in 1935, Teddy May, this weird old guy who ran the sewers for most of the first half of the twentieth century, told his workers to go down there and get rid of them. They shot the alligators with .22s. In some cases they forced the alligators into trunk mains where the flow was strong and would eventually flush them out to sea. No, they're long gone as far as I know. But the legend lives on."

"That's absolutely fascinating."

"Just listen to Dr. Sewage," Jon said. "This is rough stuff. Jacques Cousteau wouldn't last a minute down here."

"So they make these sewer videos all over the city, and review them?" Naomi asked.

"That's right. I once saw, over at DEP, a whole library of them . . . 125th Street, Columbus Avenue, Riverside Drive . . . all labeled . . . just bizarre."

"Tapes I probably won't find at Blockbuster," Naomi quipped.

"Maybe in the adult section—"

The sound of a jackhammer from a trench only several feet away overtook them, pushing beyond the aural threshold and penetrating their skeletons. Naomi grabbed the inside of Jon's right elbow in order to move them both farther away from the trench. By then the jackhammering had paused.

"They're trying to lay a new twenty-inch steel water main to replace that eighty-year-old, cast-iron twelve-inch water main," Jon said. "But the new line has to be completely laid in place for blocks before they can take the old one out of service, or else a few thousand people will go without water for weeks. So these guys have the problem of having to establish an entirely new lane, and as you know, there is no such thing as a clear lane in lower Manhattan."

"Above *or* below ground," Naomi said.

"Right. And sitting in the way over here is a concrete support holding up a steam pipe crossing this section of the street. These three guys may spend the whole afternoon solving this one little problem. They can't just blast through the concrete, or they may break the steam line. So first they make a temporary support out of wood for the steam pipe and then they carefully chip away at the old concrete support."

"Who uses the steam?" Naomi asked. "Where does it go?"

"It goes into buildings for heating and cooling purposes, both residential and office buildings, and commercial facilities like laundries or restaurants. All sorts of places. You're probably wondering why one building uses gas and the one right next to it uses steam, both sold to it by the same company—Con Edison."

"Yeah, why do they need both, especially since all of it's so hard to maintain and reconstruct?"

"Well," Jon said, "very little of it was planned out, at least in the beginning. A lot of these lines were put here by various private companies competing with each other. Until late last century, virtually every building was heated by coal stoves. There was typically one in every kitchen. It was really a mess. There was soot all over the place. There was, in that sense, a hell of a lot more air pollution in New York in those days than today. And the ashes that remained were put right out into the street in cans. Before they were collected, the ashes usually blew around for a while.

"Then the New York Steam Company was formed privately in 1880 along with at least one other competing firm, and they started laying down steam pipes all over the place and selling steam to buildings, quite a few of them on Wall Street in the early days. This was based on who would buy it, not on some grand plan for the island of Manhattan. They were in this to make money. And then the gas companies got into the act. There were a bunch of privately owned gas companies laying down lines as far back as the 1820s and all through the mid- and late 1800s, mostly for street lighting purposes before electric lines were put in. And some gas lines were installed to be hooked up to gas kitchen ranges. By the end of the 1800s the Consolidated Gas Company of New York had absorbed its competitors, but electricity was already starting to take over street lighting. In the early 1900s, Consolidated Gas absorbed the electric companies too.

"So the gas company went into competition with the New York Steam Company over supplying buildings for heating purposes. By around World War Two the lion's share of the battle to put lines in the ground was over. So the picture you see today when they open up the street is a sort of freeze frame of how that battle ended almost six decades ago. Steam heats maybe fifteen percent of the buildings, gas and oil heats the rest."

"And now Con Edison controls the steam, gas, and electric lines," Naomi concluded.

"Right," Jon said. "Consolidated Gas became Consolidated Edison in 1936."

"And I suppose that allowed them to consolidate all their maps and records too," Naomi said.

"Actually, no one knows exactly what's underground until they open it up, and sometimes not even then. You would think, given the resources and sophistication of New York City, that you could walk up to me and say: 'Okay, Forty-eighth Street between Fifth and Madison,' and I could say: 'Okay, here's a map of that street showing everything underground there.' But no such map exists, not one that's up-to-date anyway."

"You're kidding me," Naomi said.

"I wish I was," Jon replied. "The last time there was even an attempt made to compile a complete utility map was the 1930s, under the Work Projects Administration. They call those the WPA maps. During the Depression, the city had unemployed engineers, architects, and draftsmen up the wazoo, and they were put to work for minimal wages on all sorts of interesting projects that would never have been undertaken in a good economy. Like all the huge public swimming pools in New York. But even those maps—and I'll show them to you sometime, they're gorgeous—were not truly complete the day they were drawn."

"What do you mean?"

"For example," Jon explained, "when they drew a sewer, they didn't show the spurs. The spurs are the connections to each building or house. They might be four or six inches in diameter and there could be more than a dozen on one block. These pipes are weaving their way from the building basement or below, down into the street and in between the other utility lines until they meet the sewer or the sewer manhole. The same is true of all the other lines too. What you don't see on these maps are the lines connecting individual buildings to the main electric, gas, steam, water, or telephone lines. Maybe that's a good thing because the maps are unbelievably cluttered as they are. But all these connection lines are as real as the main lines shown when you're digging and trying to navigate your way through the mess."

"Then how do they proceed when they dig," Naomi asked, "working with an imperfect map?"

"Wait, it gets worse," Jon said. "These maps are not based entirely on as-built drawings, meaning the draftsmen may have drawn a water main two feet in from the curb where it was designed to go, while the construction crew, on the day they installed it, may for one reason or another have laid it down *four* feet from the curb. On top of that, these maps are over fifty years old. Many utility lines have been replaced or added since then."

"How do you handle this monstrosity?"

"Here's what we do," Jon said. "When the Department of Transportation is ready to design a street reconstruction job, the engineers there try to put together an up-to-date utility map exclusively for that project. They *start* with the WPA maps, because it's as good a starting point as any, and it shows things that are still in the ground and that you won't find on any other map—like mail tubes."

"Mail tubes?"

"The post office used to send mail all over town and under the river with pneumatic tubes. I'm not kidding. Paris stopped doing that only a few years ago. Anyway, after they've got the WPA maps, they go to each utility and request the most up-to-date map for those streets for just their specific utility. Each company or agency has a pretty accurate record of its own lines, though not necessarily including connections to individual buildings. DOT or its consultant gathers as much of the information as possible and plots it out on a plan drawing. And that includes any physical information they can get ahold of pertaining to the street. The location of existing streetlights, trees, traffic lights, curbs . . . You know, there are vaults under the sidewalks."

"Like where jewelry is kept," Naomi said.

"Maybe on Forty-seventh Street, the diamond district," Jon remarked. "The vaults I'm talking about are hollow spaces directly below the sidewalk, where a store or building may use that space for storage or mechanical equipment. Steel beams support the sidewalk. We definitely want to know that before we start breaking up a given sidewalk. The Department of Buildings has records of most of the vaults, but the only sure way to get that information is to go door-to-door, building-to-building, and do a vault survey."

"What's the bottom line, then?" Naomi asked. "Once you have all this information plotted out, with what level of confidence can a crew dig?"

"A moderate one. Sometimes they hit a surprise. Last year on this job, they hit the concrete footings for the Sixth Avenue elevated train line that was torn down in 1938. Back then, when workmen took out the columns, they left the footings buried, not far from the surface. No one bothered to make a record of that fact. When these guys hit the concrete blocks last year, they're like: 'What the hell is this?' And they were sitting right on top of the subway roof, so they had to remove the footings by hand instead of with backhoes. The whole fiasco cost four million dollars and delayed them almost a year.

"These projects are like crime scenes after a murder. A crew takes the drawings, they take colored paint or chalk and draw right on the pavement to indicate certain lines—if you walk along Riverside Drive tomorrow and see the letter G or the letter E with an arrow, you'll know that's gas and electric, not the outline of a dead body. They use whatever they can. If they see a couple of gas valves three feet from the curb, they know there's probably a gas line connecting them. They use sonar equipment to help establish location and depth of water lines and other lines. And finally, they dig slowly and carefully and pray. And you'll only hear about it if something goes wrong. Like if they break a water line and flood the subway. Or if they break a steam line and asbestos shoots into nearby apartment windows."

"Like crime scenes after a murder, huh?"

"What's the matter?" Jon said. "You look skeptical. People have this stereotype in their heads about engineers sitting at a desk all day with a pocket protector and hair that hasn't been washed in a month. But a lot more goes into this job than meets the eye. You have to not only know the laws of physics, but how to apply them in the real world. That means piecing things together when you're solving a problem. You rarely have all the information you need or want, so you go by experience and reasonable assumptions. When you're working with other people, you have to communicate to them, clearly, exactly, what your thought process is without getting bogged down in minutiae. Sometimes I've had to explain why a certain building collapsed even though I wasn't actually there when it happened or maybe never before, to see why it was predisposed. In that kind of situation, you're gathering clues patiently, painstakingly, like a sleuth, until you can make a pronouncement with reasonable yet not absolute certainty. Your professional license is on the line. I've always thought a good engineer could solve a murder case if he had to."

"You think you'll ever have to?" Naomi asked.

"Only if Larry sends me any more map seekers," Jon replied.

The foreman of the water main crew now motioned for Jon and Naomi to move a few feet back of the concrete barrier to provide some additional clearance for a twenty-inch main being lowered into place by a crane and steadied at either end by highly alert crew members. The crew members strained to listen through the noise to the barking of the foreman, a large, potbellied middle-aged white man with a cigar butt in his mouth whose massive shoulders bulged from his gray sleeveless T-shirt.

"That's good, Jon," the foreman shouted. "Right there."

"Thanks, Frank," Jon shouted back.

As the two stepped back up to the sidewalk, Naomi turned to Jon and made eye contact. "Do they know who you are?"

"Frank does. A lot of them don't, but they must assume I have something to do with the city if I'm wearing a tie and carrying a clipboard. I mean, either I'm getting paid to do this or I'm crazier than that guy who comes around here on in-line skates wearing a wedding dress."

"If you don't mind my asking," Naomi said, "what exactly *do* you do when you come out here?"

"Somebody has to serve as a sort of interface between these huge construction projects and a public official like the borough president. You might say, well, doesn't the Department of Transportation employ liaisons for that same purpose? Why can't the borough president's liaisons talk to the Department of Transportation's liaisons and discuss why a given project is running three months behind schedule? Because he'll get DOT's company line as an answer. He might tell the borough president, 'Oh, we hit a lot of bedrock,' instead of the real answer, which might be: 'The sub-contractors refuse to work until they get their money.' There's no way I can catch everything, but at least I can't be outsmarted very easily about the technical issues. I try to give Art Shuler a public policy on infrastructure . . . that's based on reality."

"Okay," Naomi said, "so *that's* what you do out here."

"Well, actually I come out here to get away from Al."

When Jon got back to his office, he sat down and went right for the *New York Post* he'd saved from the previous Wednesday. During his superficial flip through the paper that morning, he had passed right by an article neither the headline nor substance of which he could remember right now. The article troubled him for a full week nonetheless. He had a habit of putting away unpleasant things for when he was better able to reckon with them, whether that time was minutes, hours, or even days later.

There it was on page eight, occupying only a third of the page and stating the news matter-of-factly: DEP WORKER FOUND DEAD IN FOURTEENTH STREET SEWER. The body was identified as that of Joel Haney, thirty-seven, a white male and seventeen-year veteran of DEP's Bureau of Sewers. The cause of death was believed to be a blow to the head, but an autopsy had not yet been performed. Mr. Haney had been assigned for the past month to maintenance detail along the Fourteenth Street sewer, one of the larger mains in the borough. The case was being investigated by the Tenth Precinct as a possible homicide. Possible witnesses and suspects were being questioned.

Jon now cut out the article and held it in his hand for almost a minute. Having cut it out, he was past the point of denying to himself the article's importance. Now the question was what to do with it. If he stuck it on his wall or bulletin board, it would be a constant unpleasant reminder of something he dreaded but did not yet fully grasp. In addition, its presence might prompt visitors to bring it up in conversation, forcing him to explain what he did not yet understand, and perhaps to appear paranoid as well.

If he shoved the article in a desk drawer, the public-viewing dilemma was eliminated, but he still might be reminded of it at important times. If he filed it under "North River," someone else in the future, sifting through this much accessed folder might ask him what he thought it had to do with that particular sewage treatment plant. The solution, then, was clear. Create a new file folder: "North River Related." The folder now held one item. Jon remembered something else now and stepped outside his office. He walked over to Larry, who was hunched over and circling with a pen the name of a horse in the *Racing Form*.

"Larry," he said, "did you get a map request today from a guy around ten-thirty in the morning? Or did Al give you one from around that time? I don't think you were around when I saw this guy."

"Oh yeah, King," Larry replied, as if remembering something from a past life upon being woken from a trance. "Are you talking about a tall guy in a nice suit?"

"That's right."

"He was a detective from the Tenth Precinct."

"Oh shit, great . . ." Jon exclaimed.

"I saw him on my way out to the bathroom," Larry continued, "right at the door. He said he needed a map of Fourteenth Street."

"And what did you tell him?"

"I told him to see the chief engineer," Larry replied.

"That was very thoughtful of you," Jon quipped.

"You know my situation, King," Larry said apologetically, "I don't do maps. It has nothing to do with you. It's because of that piece of work, Paula. She fucked me."

"It's got something to do with me *now*," Jon said. "You know what I told that guy on my way out? I told him I had quit three minutes earlier. Then I dumped him off on fucking *Al*. I had no idea he was a detective."

"Yeah, I know. He was very upset when I came back from the bathroom," Larry said innocently, as if describing a situation entirely thrust upon him. "He said you were insulting to him and Al was a nut job . . ." Larry started to laugh uncontrollably.

"What's so funny?"

"He . . . he says: 'This guy quit three minutes ago, and this nut is telling me, "I'm the grim reaper, I am death." What kind of psycho ward are you running here? I just want a map of Fourteenth Street, for Chrissakes.' "

"So you look like the good guy," Jon said, visibly upset, only marginally succumbing to Larry's laughter. "Did you get him his maps?"

"No, King, I told him I'm only an attendant. I'm not qualified to retrieve maps. I had him fill out a map request form, and I told him you'd get back to him. I told him you were the best chief engineer in the city, and you probably just had a bad day."

"My bad day is just beginning," Jon said. "Can I see the form?"

Larry handed him a single sheet of paper off the top of a pile on his cluttered desk. This particular pile was an eighteen-inch-high stack of chaos and unanswered prayers.

Jon read aloud from the sheet. " 'Detective James Mercado, Tenth Precinct. Needs any survey maps of Fourteenth Street area on west side, from Fifth Avenue to Eleventh Avenue. Also any available maps of the sewer in same area.' Do you know what this is about, Larry? This is part of a murder investigation."

"A murder investigation?"

"Yeah, a DEP worker was found dead in the Fourteenth Street sewer. I read it in last week's *Post*."

"Oh my God," Larry said, "if I'd have known, I would have called you on your beeper. He didn't say anything."

"Well, our little rinky-dink operation was just exposed for what it is," Jon said. "We go along thinking we're doing a disservice to the city just in the areas of parking tickets and architects developing plans and students doing term papers. Well, now we're holding up a murder investigation! And you know my policy toward cops and firemen. I drop everything for them out of respect for what they do, regardless of our stupid situation here. Now I've ruined all that goodwill."

"You haven't ruined anything, King," Larry said. "Call him back. I told him you were very busy. They have you doing a million things here. I'll go downstairs and get the maps for you. As long as you don't say anything to that bitch."

"What would I say?" Jon asked. "Get me everything you can find on West Fourteenth Street, Larry. Get me the sectional maps, get me the individual accession maps, the survey map, the 1874 Viele map. I think I have the new Fourteenth Street reconstruction plans rolled up inside. Hey, you know what else? Go upstairs and ask those guys at the Department of General Services for the WPA map."

"Yes, King. Whatever you say, King." As Larry made his way to the front door, Old Al Gibbs's muttering, which seemed to have been going on for quite some time, moved into the audible range.

"I don't give a shit that you some big jackass cop with a gun. Ain't no bullet gonna hurt Ol' Al Gibbs. I seen all kinda guns over in Grenada. I caught a bullet in my teeth. You gotta bite down at just the right time. Ain't no two-bit cop gonna intimidate Ol' Al Gibbs on his home turf. I got home field advantage. I got the crowd. I got the momentum. Big Mo . . ." Al got up and took a tai chi stance. "And I don't care if that gun *is* a nine-millimeter. I got a Glock in my *sock*, baby." Al's unintentional rhyme now worked its way up the conscious ladder of his cerebral cortex and inspired him to begin a dance reminiscent of both Native American rituals and early sixties Motown. "I got a Glock in my sock, got a Glock in my sock, got a Glock in my sock . . ."

"Your Glock is a crock," Larry lamented. "When was Grenada,

1983? In 1983, he was right here, doing that same fucking routine. Except then it was about Vietnam." The door slammed behind him.

As Jon paced the few steps back to his office, he saw one side of a suppressed smirk on Naomi's face, which was buried both in her hands and a sheaf of technical documents. He recalled that she'd lifted her head only two or three times in the last several minutes, at only the most outrageous or intriguing points of the discussion and Al's monologue, as she tried to stay out of the line of fire.

"Feel free to tell us to shut up if we're bothering you," Jon said to her.

"You're not bothering me," Naomi replied.

Jon collapsed into his chair in his office, picked up the receiver, and punched in the code to hear his voice mail messages.

"Hello, Mr. Kessler," came the first message, "this is Detective Mercado of the Tenth Precinct. I was in to see you this morning, but you seemed to be in a bit of a hurry." The words were measured, in a deep, thoughtful baritone with a New York edge. "I left you a request form, and I spoke to a Larry Golick, who suggested I give you a call when you weren't so busy. I'm looking for maps of the Fourteenth Street area on the west side. I'd appreciate if you could give me a call at the precinct. Thank you." He left his phone number at the end of the message.

Jon called Mercado without hesitation, skipping the other voice mails, and plotted out his appeal for leniency as the phone rang on the other end.

"Tenth, O'Connel speaking," said the young, slightly gruff female voice on the other end.

"Detective Mercado, please. This is Jon Kessler from the Borough President's Office."

"Jimmy, it's the guy from the Borough President's Office," O'Connel shouted at what sounded like arm's distance from the receiver. There was a five-second pause before Jon heard the next voice.

"Tenth, Mercado speaking . . ."

"Hi, this is Jon Kessler."

"Thanks for getting back to me," Mercado said.

"I want to apologize for this morning," Jon said. "I've got a staff of two—one's crazy and the other's on strike, and as a result virtually all the map work gets thrown at me, which is not supposed to happen."

"Okay, that's all right," Detective Mercado said.

"No, it's not all right," Jon replied. "It's not all right that I act that way toward anyone, but especially not an officer or a detective. I want you to know that I have a policy of helping you guys out in any way I can."

"I know that," Mercado said. "I spoke to Detective Dunleavy at my precinct before I went over this morning, and he told me you've gone out of your way for him a number of times."

"Just like I'm gonna do for you. Your maps are being located as we speak. Larry and I are both right on it. I'll have them copied and messengered over to you by the end of the day."

"Thanks, that's great." Detective Mercado said. "Can you get me a sewer map as well as the aboveground maps?"

"Yeah," Jon replied. "I'm getting you two sewer maps—the WPA map from the thirties, which, believe it or not, is still fairly accurate, and the Fourteenth Street reconstruction plans. That project is still being completed and may have affected the sewer anywhere east of Hudson Street."

"Excellent, thank you," Mercado said. "I've put in a call to DEP just to make sure I have everything that's available."

"Good idea," Jon replied. "They might have something we don't have. By the way, does this have something to do with the guy found murdered in the sewer?"

"Yeah," Mercado affirmed, "it's my case as of now."

"Do you mind if I ask you if you have any suspects yet?"

"We're questioning a few people, but I'm not really at liberty to say much right now. We're also waiting for the results of an autopsy."

"Well, if I can be of any help to you along the way, please let me know," Jon offered. "You might have some logistical questions come up, and I've recently spent a lot of time studying the sewer system . . . flow conditions, how heavy the manhole covers are . . ."

"I appreciate that, Mr. Kessler," Detective Mercado said, "but we're just not at that point yet. I have your number in my book, and I'll call you as soon as you may be able to help. Right now, I just need those maps."

"If you don't have them by five today, call me," Jon said. "I'm just a little rattled by this. As borough engineer, this is part of my domain. I kind of feel . . . invaded by this murder."

"I'll tell you something off the record," Mercado said, "but this is *strictly* off the record."

"No problem."

"We don't think he was murdered in the sewer."

"Uh-huh. Well, have you questioned his partner? Usually these guys work at least in pairs."

"That's if he was on duty at the time of the incident," Detective Mercado said.

"You mean he might have been killed off-duty and tossed into the same sewer where he usually works?"

"I really can't comment. Just get me those maps, okay?"

"You got it. I'll be speaking with you."

Chapter 8

Jon Kessler sat at his desk at ten-fifteen Monday morning, April 19, and tried to corral the energy necessary to get through another week, or at least to get to Tuesday in one piece. Thirteen days had passed since Paula's clock started running. During weekends in Rocky Point, Jon tried to soak up the freedom and fresh air he was deprived of during the week. As a result, he stayed up later each weekend night as his body and mind revived themselves and his capacity to enjoy life's essentials was replenished. By Sunday night he was usually up till 2:00 A.M., having run, lifted weights, hit baseballs off a tee into a net in the backyard, sifted through American history books, and channel-surfed, trying to extend his two-day minivacation as far as possible.

Like trying to enlarge an island by hauling out dirt from the middle and landfilling around the edges, you soon began to lose more ground than you gained. Awareness that the bill would come due Monday morning was of little consequence on Sunday night. Jon knew he'd dig his way out of the hole Monday morning just as he was doing now—by mapping out the week ahead, with an emphasis on tangible things he could accomplish and enjoyable things to do.

First, he congratulated himself for getting almost to the halfway point. It was thirteen days down, seventeen days to go in the thirty-day waiting period Paula had established. Jon had taken care to minimize his interactions with Paula, speaking when spoken to, appearing courteous and respectful as the day he was first hired. Pretending not to care about North River and the report was a game, one in which Jon believed he had only to match Paula to win.

Next, Jon reminded himself that he did have a lot to look forward to this week. The Stink Tank was having lunch today for the first time in almost a month, at the Panda Garden, a Chinese restaurant on Chambers Street between Hudson and Church streets that let them stay all afternoon as long as at least one person ordered dessert and played with it for a while. Although the group neither met regularly nor had a formal membership, it had certain unwritten bylaws. Many people in the office—in fact, most people in the office—were not Stink Tank members. The four core members of the Stink Tank—Jon, Jay Gonzalez, Pat Truitt, and Laura Ober—all had two crucial things in common other than working in the Borough President's Office.

For one, they all had a sharp interest in environmental policy. For another, they each had a severe case of idealism that kept them to various degrees from being inside players in the office. That notion was embedded in the very name they gave themselves. About a year earlier Paula Derbin had announced to the entire office through a long-winded but politically correct two-sided intraoffice memo that she and several other high-level advisers to Art Shuler were forming a Think Tank, which would meet biweekly to discuss policy issues of core importance and to shape the middle and long term approach to Manhattan's future.

Art Shuler himself would sit in some of the time. Why the entire office had to be notified via memo of the Think Tank's inception, when it was nothing more than a new moniker for business as usual, was the butt of a month's worth of office jokes. The popular assumption was that this was Paula's way of reminding everyone for the umpteenth time where the power lay without narcissistically referring to herself alone.

Within days of the memo, Pat Truitt dubbed his own little group the "Stink Tank." Since most of the conversations wound up leading back to North River, it seemed fitting. Pat even discreetly circulated a memo mocking Paula's: "The group will meet biweekly, or whenever Jay Gonzalez can scrape up lunch money from his bottom desk drawer. While the group will discuss a variety of key environmental issues, the focus will be on whether or not to call in sick the rest of the day. Proceedings will be kept confidential . . . since no one else cares anyway."

In reality, Art Shuler, Paula Derbin, and some of the other top dogs in the office would have cared a great deal to listen in on some of the Stink Tank meetings. As time marched on, the four members diverged more and more from the party line on crucial issues and became increasingly outspoken about it, at least around each other. The sincere but wisecracking Jon Kessler, the dry-witted and mildly alcoholic Pat Truitt, the upbeat but cautious Jay Gonzalez, and the idealistic-bordering-on-militant Laura Ober came to trust each other to the point where the presence of virtually any fifth person at lunch made it something other than the Stink Tank.

The week would continue to improve. On Wednesday, the Dodger himself was giving a tour of the seventy-two-acre Hudson City site to an assemblage of business people, elected officials, staff members, and media people. The ostensible purpose was to build up a positive head of steam for Hudson City going into the upcoming committee hearings on North River and whether Hudson City would be allowed to hook up. Ronald Arlen lived to hear himself talk. Paula had sent a memo "to all staff" encouraging anyone who had the inclination to attend, though it would involve not even a marginal work effort. Every last person in the Borough President's Office had heard it all before—the vision, the teamwork, the economic magnet. What both amused and annoyed the Stink Tank members, and others as well, was the constant cheerleading from the sidelines by Paula for every move the Dodger and the Hudson City team made. But an event was an event, and Jon had already decided to go.

The week would continue to improve on Thursday, when Jon and Naomi had agreed to have lunch and then do a tour of the North River plant. The order of lunch first and then the tour was not subject to change. People had been known to lose their appetite after a visit to North River, an effect that floating, reeking sludge had a tendency to create. Having some kind of platonic female companionship to anticipate, beyond that of his wife, appealed to Jon at this point. Jon and Elaine's responsibilities had many months ago eclipsed the sum total of their physical and spiritual pleasures, together or apart. They had decided long ago that concepts like the seven-year itch were pure cliché. Still, their conversations had been more strained and riddled with sarcasm lately, and Jon no longer felt compelled to call Elaine every night he stayed with a recently divorced friend in Manhattan. He believed firmly that this state was circumstantial and temporary. But he couldn't deny the appeal of having a woman to talk to whose consciousness wasn't dominated by several dozen easy and uneasy compromises made between the two of them.

By Friday, he would be solidly past the halfway point of the thirty-day waiting period. By Sunday he'd have played in the season opener of his adult semipro baseball league out on Long Island. In spite of the practices, the opener always seemed to signal that spring was here for real, and that beach weather wasn't far away. Now he simply had to review plans for the Columbus Avenue reconstruction for an hour and a half, and the worst of the week would be behind him. At this moment, the phone rang.

"Hello?" Jon listened as a man on the other end explained his need for a topographical map of the Union Square area. "You'll have to come in for that," Jon replied. ". . . Yeah, we have it. We're understaffed, and we've determined that taking phone orders pushes us over the edge. Do you know where we are? One Centre Street, across from City Hall, twentieth floor . . . Yeah, any time nine-to-five . . . Okay, you're welcome, sir."

At twelve-fifteen Jon manually dimmed the screen of his computer, even though the "I love you, babe" customized screen saver installed by Elaine during a rare visit to the office would kick in soon anyway. He grabbed his windbreaker and headed for the door. Larry, who was listening to New York's only country radio station, flagged Jon down.

"King, did you hear what happened with that sewer murder?"

"No, what?" Jon realized he had shut out the world for the past couple of days and hadn't even bothered to buy the paper this morning.

"Yeah, it was on page three of the *Post* this morning," Larry said. "The autopsy came back. That guy was killed somewhere else and then tossed into the sewer."

"That's what Detective Mercado implied," Jon noted.

"Yeah," Larry continued, "it says the dead guy was found by the guys from the morning shift. The autopsy showed that he was partially underwater for maybe seven hours, and that the wound on his head was as much as eight or nine hours old."

"Was he off-duty when he was killed?"

"Yeah," Larry replied. "He would have been on the morning shift, at the same sewer where he was found."

"So the people who killed him knew where he worked," Jon observed, "and maybe when he worked. How many people would know that? Probably not too many. Either someone who worked for DEP or someone who knew him pretty well. And they dragged him back to the Fourteenth Street sewer for one of two reasons. Either they wanted to make it look like he died on the job—if that's what they wanted, they blew it—or they were trying to send a message to somebody. Maybe to the other guys who work down in the sewer."

"King, *you are good*. That's a lot like what they said in this article. They didn't go into it much more than that. But they're gonna be probing the hell out of it. It's like one of their own, you know? There was also something in the article about Joel Haney—that's the guy who was killed—making porno films. He had some kind of racket going on the side. Maybe that's what got him killed."

"I wouldn't doubt it," Jon said. "That's a big underground industry."

"The DEP assistant commissioner announced it," Larry said. "He says he probably should have suspended this guy. He's gonna overhaul disciplinary policy. Hey, did that detective get those maps? I left them at the front desk of the Tenth Precinct for him last week."

"Then you went home early, right from there?"

"Well," Larry said defensively, "there was nothing left to do. . . ."

"Forget about it," Jon said. "I would have heard from him by now if he didn't get them. He hasn't called me back, but I think I'm going to give *him* a call."

"That's right, King, you could probably be a big help to him."

"Tell you what," Jon said. "I'm in a bit of a rush now. Could you leave the article on my desk, or slip it under my door?"

"King, your wish is my command."

Several minutes later, as he walked with Jay, Pat, and Laura westward along crowded Chambers Street, Jon believed that if he tripped, he'd be trampled. Between the throngs moving briskly in both directions, the clothing racks in front of the stores, and the hired guns guarding those racks with their lives, there was no room for error on the sidewalks. He often wondered if the outdoors existed in Manhattan for any reason other than to serve the indoors. There was much more indoor volume than outdoor volume near ground level. The indoors were typically equipped for convenience—carpeted, chock-full of beds, chairs, desks, phones, cable jacks, refrigerators, houseplants, bathrooms. All those items got there via the streets and sidewalks, but the streets and sidewalks themselves were unlivable.

There was not a single tree on Chambers Street between Broadway and Hudson. Why? It cost the city only about $350 to plant a tree complete with sidewalk tree pit. Jon often thought of donating the money himself or just showing up in the middle of the night with a sapling in the back of his minivan, breaking up one square of concrete sidewalk with a rented jackhammer, and letting nature take its course.

Nature took its course daily and nightly on Chambers Street and hundreds of other Manhattan streets when it came to relieving the bladder. The homeless and the drunk urinated freely on buildings, mailboxes, and parked cars, giving the street a perpetual stench. New York City's policy of not providing public rest rooms combined with New Yorkers' policy of impatience—or a condition of destitution—produced one huge public rest room everywhere.

One day on the corner of Chambers and Centre Streets, a public rest room miraculously appeared in the form of a green kiosk. A French manufacturer had installed about a dozen of them around Manhattan at no charge to the city as part of a three-month trial period. As far as Jon was concerned, the trial was a success, at least in the area immediately surrounding the kiosk. For a quarter, the glossy semicircular door would slide open and present a sparkling clear interior environment, inviting even in an age of deadly transmittable viruses.

The plastic molding of the seat and the walls were one. As the door closed around you, the lights came on and a powerful ventilation system sucked out foul odors faster than an intestinally challenged New Yorker could produce them. Upon leaving and closing the door, all became clear, like the answer to the bonus question on a game show. The sound of a pressurized flush was heard and felt, making it known that the whole compartment was being hosed down from the inside. This was followed by the sound of a powerful air blower, signifying that the interior would soon be dry.

There was plenty of room for error inside—big, New York–size errors. The French had taken care of it. Any extra surprises would be whisked away to the same sewers as everything else. Unlike giving out free needles to heroin addicts, having a private company take over the handling of parking violations, and having extra prisoners in a floating jail on the East River, the kiosks were the one experiment in recent memory that worked. Therefore, after three months, they were taken away.

The members of the Stink Tank entered the Panda Garden and were shown to their usual circular table near the back by an attractive young Oriental woman. Jon liked the high ceiling for the sense of openness it gave him and the ceiling fans for the way they kept the air moving. Pat Truitt looked edgy, as if he couldn't wait for the first martini to arrive. Only want of alcohol and red tape seemed to have that effect on Pat, whose fair-skinned, beefy face, wide mischievous smile, and big blue eyes gave the impression of an aging frat boy trying to find his way back to the party. But he never had found his way back, and had grown cynical as a result. Now he took a swipe at his short blond hair with one hand as he spoke, and at the extra-hot mustard with a fried noodle in his other hand.

"... even the sewers aren't safe anymore."

"Didn't you read the paper this morning, Pat?" Jay Gonzalez said. "That guy was killed somewhere else and *dragged* to the sewer."

"Thank God, then the sewers *are* still safe," Pat responded.

"Well, what's up with that?" Jay insisted. "Any idea on what happened?"

"How would we even be able to guess?" Laura Ober asked. "It could have been absolutely anything." Laura's clear, light black skin and neatly pulled-back hair provided a stabilizing counter-force to her agitated brown eyes.

With a combination of sultry and aristocratic looks provided by three African American grandparents and one Italian one, Laura Ober had the appearance that might have landed her work as a VJ on MTV if she cared. Instead, at age thirty-three, she cared about public policy. The past ten years had taken her from a degree in history at Yale to several positions working for elected officials in New York, back to school to get a master's degree in political science from Rutgers, back to work as an administrator for the Parks Department, and back to school once more at NYU for a Ph.D. in political science. To put herself through school this one last time, she took a job as community board liaison with the Manhattan Borough President's Office. She worked a flexible thirty-hour week and was assigned to Community Boards Seven and Nine, the former comprising the highly variegated, progressive Upper West Side, and the latter West Harlem, with its combination of educated, hardworking minorities and typical inner-city problems.

Sometimes, in a foul mood, Laura Ober cursed the day she was assigned these two chronically conflicting boards concurrently. With different economic, social, and cultural forces driving them, these two areas—contiguous along 110th Street—were often at odds. Whether it was a question of where to put the next homeless shelter, which board got more money for sprucing up its parks, or which got its subway stations remodeled, she seemed to be in the middle of it, even though she had little if any power over the decisions. Laura found herself not only having to defend various policies or verdicts she didn't like—something that every liaison had to do—but also defend herself against subtle and not-so-subtle accusations of playing favorites.

Making matters worse was the fact that the sewage produced on the Upper West Side was sent north to West Harlem to be treated. By the end of her first year on the job, this was the straw Laura believed would break her back. She had even put in for a transfer off either board to another one—*any* one—with Sandra Jackson, who headed the liaison staff. But before the transfer had a chance to come through, something happened—the Dodger came along. Single-handedly and unwittingly, Ronald Arlen did what Laura, the Borough President's Office, the mayor, and the entire City Council had been unable to do for years—provide the two boards with strong common ground. Arlen wanted to build a huge development on the Upper West Side and send its sewage to West Harlem. The Upper West Side didn't want his development, and West Harlem didn't want his sewage.

For months both communities lobbied, fought, and argued to block Hudson City, making Laura Ober's life livable again. She withdrew her transfer request, resumed going to the formerly boring board subcommittee meetings she had steadily been blowing off, and became a galvanizing force against Hudson City. To boot, she got a topic for her doctoral thesis: "Environmental Common Ground for Politically Opposed Communities: A Case Study." She stayed up an extra hour each night to review the day and make notes.

Much of this sense of purpose came crashing down when Art Shuler decided to back Hudson City and Ronald Arlen and to distance himself from the outrage over the North River sewage treatment plant. After the deal, Laura spent weeks publicly explaining her boss's decision while privately gagging on her own words. The innuendos returned with a vengeance—for some she was too white, for others too black. She stopped working on her thesis. She put in for a transfer again, but so far there was no response. At least once a week she considered quitting.

"*I* don't think a dead guy in the sewer could be just anything," Jay announced.

"*I* do," Laura shot back.

"*I* don't," Jay restated. "Sewage is a big issue now. North River is an issue. The street reconstruction and sewer reconstruction projects are issues. There's big money involved, and money plus construction means the mob, which is sometimes just a euphemism for big business."

"Oh, give me a break, Jay," Laura said, "that's all pure speculation. The murder wasn't anywhere near North River. As far as the mob is concerned, you probably still think the mob killed JFK."

"Uh, the mob *did* kill JFK," Pat said.

"This could have been some fairly random act of violence," Laura insisted. "Anyway, the guy made porn films. If you want to concoct a theory, concoct it around that."

"I don't think so," Jay said, shaking his head. "You're just afraid of what this implies."

"Well, she does have a point," Pat stated. "Conspiracy theories are often empty. Maybe this guy was smuggling his porn films through the sewer."

"That's where they belong," Laura said.

"In the *sewer*?" Jay asked rhetorically. "Smuggling in the sewer?"

"It's possible," Pat said. "I have a cousin who planned to use the sewer to smuggle drugs. I'm not kidding. He was stoned during the entire eighties and used to muse about how the sewer was the one place he could move a kilo of coke unimpeded."

"That's very impressive, Pat," Jay said, pointing a fried noodle first at Pat, then at Jon. "What do you think?"

"About what?" Jon asked.

"About the sewer murder?"

"I think his cousin did it," Jon replied, pointing at Pat, "then watched a skin flick."

"Exactly," Pat said. "Should we order?"

"I'll have whatever Pat's cousin was on," Laura remarked as she tossed her menu onto the table. "Anything that'll help me think clearly. I told myself by the end of the week I'd make the decision. I'm thinking of quitting. Work on my thesis more."

"What?" Pat said. "No more taping Paula lambasting you in her office? What the hell are we going to do for entertainment?"

"That's the way it goes, Pat," Laura said. "Anyway, it's time you made your own tapes."

"Before you quit, Laura, could you do me a favor?" Jon said, slamming his menu shut as if he finally knew what he wanted. "You're on reasonably good terms with Ron Alexander, who is the only other top adviser Art seems to listen to anymore other than Paula. Could you put in a good word for my report with Ron? Talk to him, write him a memo, have him mention to Art that Paula's dragging her feet by having this report endlessly reviewed. Tell him that as far as the public is concerned right now, Art Shuler doesn't give a shit about the environment anymore and needs to throw Manhattan a bone."

"I'm afraid Dr. Jay has a second opinion," Jay said, "and it entails complications. Remember I told you I would check some things out for you regarding the permitting committee?"

"Yeah," Jon said.

"Well, while I was busy checking out everything under the sun, the answer hit me over the head. Remember that Memorandum of Understanding that Art and the Dodger signed last summer?"

"*Remember* it?" Pat replied. "I *wrote* half of it. And *rewrote* ninety percent of that. And then rewrote ninety percent of *that*. Every time one of those two sons of bitches so much as farted I had to go back and reword something." Pat now looked up and smiled mostly with his eyes as the waitress gingerly lowered the martini she knew to bring without being asked. He took a sip, looked down, and looked back at Jay. "I don't ever want to see that thing again."

"Yes you do."

"No I don't."

"Yes you do," Jay said. "What makes you think that your last cycle of technical, environmental rewording was the last cycle of revision?"

"To tell you the truth, I haven't thought about it that much."

"I hadn't either," Jay said, "but I decided to take a look at the final, *final* MOU, the one with Art Shuler's and Ronald Arlen's signatures on it. I got it from Melissa, Art's assistant, when Art was out of the office for a couple of days. I got myself a bagel and coffee, sat down at my desk, and read it carefully. And guess what it says? It says the permitting committee to review Hudson City's application to hook up to North River shall be composed of seven members, *three* of whom are appointed by the borough president."

"Holy shit, that changes everything," Jon said.

"That's still not a majority," Laura said.

"Trust me, it still changes everything," Jon said. "They'll get that fourth vote somehow. It's a lot different than Art's having one vote. Who gets the other four votes?"

"One each to two citizens groups, one to the mayor, and one to the City Council's environmental committee. They'll get the fourth vote, no problem."

"How do you know 'no problem'?" Laura asked. "Jon, a minute ago you were saying Art Shuler hasn't done anything wrong. Now you're entirely certain the borough president is an integral part of some kind of plot to fix what will probably be the most important special committee vote to come along in the last twenty-five years."

"Maybe I changed my mind in the last few minutes," Jon

replied. "You of all people should be glad about this turn of events. *You're* the one who makes tapes of Paula. I might join the club. Just the fact that they would alter that document at the last second before it was signed and then not publicize that fact to the very people who helped put that document together *shows* me there's willful deception and a strong motive behind it. Now we've got a problem."

"*Thank* you," Laura said, smiling for the first time in a while. "I'm just testing you to see if you know what's going down."

Pat stared into his glass with a look of focused anger and looked back up. "Damn, even for someone like me who lost faith in the system half a liver ago, it blows my mind to think that sometime between when I fell asleep on the couch near the nineteenth floor front desk and sunrise—maybe two hours, total—those pricks went into the document and changed something so fundamental without telling anyone. It makes me want to kick their asses. It's funny—during the two or three hours that hot summer night that I slept out there on the couch, I vaguely remember having bad dreams. Like I was being violated."

"That was the other half of your liver," Laura said.

"What made you even think of looking at the final MOU?" Jon asked.

"I saw a tiny notice in the city *Record*," Jay explained, "saying that the city's Law Department had completed its review of the MOU and found nothing that wasn't consistent with the Charter or the Administrative Code. And the City Council, therefore, went ahead and gave it final approval. This is all something done seven months after the thing was signed and all the fanfare had died down. My sixth sense told me I'd better take a look."

"This is what I mean," Laura said. "We're working in a hostile environment."

"Who are the citizens groups' members?" Jon asked.

"Well, you're in luck," Jay said. "I don't know who the other is yet, but one of them is your girlfriend."

"My girlfriend?"

"Clarissa Marbles!" Jay said.

"Hey, is everyone going to the Dodger's tour on Wednesday?" Laura asked.

"Sure," Jon replied, "it's like getting an extra half day off from school."

"Laura," Pat asked, "are you still quitting?"

"No," Laura replied, "I'm gonna stay around and cause trouble."

"What about the thesis?" Jay asked.

"I'll let it write itself," Laura replied.

Coming back from lunch, as Jon walked toward the front door of room 2035, Old Al Gibbs's two-hundred-pound frame knocked into Jon's, throwing him a few inches to his right. As the door closed automatically and slowly behind him, Jon heard the beginnings of Old Al's soliloquy out in the hallway.

"I don't believe in autopsies, baby. When a man's dead, respect him. That body was his soul's temple. The time to do an autopsy is when the dude's still alive. That's what I did to Charlie over in Hanoi." Al assumed his exaggerated tai chi ready position. "I went 'Ya!' reached in, pulled out his heart and showed it to him." Al thrust his fist forward, quickly turned his wrist as if it were opening a doorknob, and pulled his arm back just as fast. He dangled the imaginary heart like a pocket watch in front of his own eyes while in a deep, ominous voice simulating the sound of the still-beating vital organ: "Booomp-booomp, booomp-booomp, booomp-booomp . . ."

Chapter 9

On a sunny Tuesday morning, 9:45, April 20, Detectives Mercado and O'Connel walked up to a four-story brick apartment building on the south side of Nineteenth Street just east of Eleventh Avenue. The building was three windows wide, revealed missing chunks of mortar between the bricks, and leaned about three degrees to the west at the top two stories, which were not braced by the shorter adjacent building. Mercado stepped up to the single metal-framed glass door, looked at the intercom, and stopped his index finger at the button that read SUP.

"Who is it?" said a growling male voice.

"It's the police," Mercado said. "Could you let us in?" A sharp buzzer sounded and Mercado pushed open the door. A heavyset white man of about sixty with a double chin, gray razor stubble, and bifocals emerged in slippers and a plaid bathrobe and walked toward the detectives. The hallway smelled of fried eggs, and the small dose of much needed fresh air was cut short when the door closed automatically behind O'Connel.

"I'm Detective Mercado and this is Detective O'Connel, Tenth Precinct."

"You here about Haney?" the superintendent said, jingling keys inside his right bathrobe pocket.

"That's right," O'Connel said.

"I guess you wanna see the apartment," the superintendent said.

"If you could," O'Connel replied.

"Uh-huh," the superintendent said. "Four A."

Mercado and O'Connel followed the superintendent up the steps, which sloped slightly to the right and were worn toward the middle from a century and a half of use.

"Don't worry about the stairs," the superintendent said. "They ain't gonna fall. This building's been leanin' for years and years. These stairs are leanin' with it, but they're solid. Building's solid too. It ain't goin' nowhere."

"If you say so," Mercado said.

The superintendent jiggled the key in the lower lock of apartment 4A and pushed the door open. As Mercado and O'Connel followed him in, they saw a single large room that ran all the way up to two front windows. Immediately to the left of the detectives were a kitchen area and a small bathroom. Farther along the left interior wall was a doorway to what appeared to be a bedroom. The floors of the main room were smooth and stained a light brown, with an Oriental rug covering most of the area. The couch and chairs had frames of exposed wood matching the floors. Hanging from the walls were several framed, full-size movie posters: De Niro in *Raging Bull*, Jack Nicholson in *Chinatown*, Kirk Douglas in *Spartacus*, Marilyn Monroe, Jack Lemmon, and Tony Curtis in *Some Like It Hot*.

"It's a shame about Haney," the superintendent said. "Nice guy, never bothered no one. Had a coupla good-looking girlfriends, I'll tell ya that."

"It's hot in here," Mercado said, walking toward the windows.

"Top floor apartment," the superintendent said. "Roof heats up."

"Mister . . . Mister . . ." O'Connel began, looking at the superintendent.

"George," the superintendent said. "George Fazekas."

"Mr. Fazekas," O'Connel said, "did you notice anyone visiting Joel Haney in the days or weeks before he died? In particular anyone unusual?"

"When did he die, a coupla weeks ago?" Fazekas said. "Nah, just those girls once in a while. You shoulda seen one a them—legs up to my face, boobs out ta here . . ." Fazekas cupped his hands and held them a foot away from his chest. "She looked like a hooker." Fazekas noticed Mercado having trouble opening one of the two living room windows. "Those are a pain in the ass 'cause of the building leaning. Try the other one."

Mercado pushed upward on the other window and got it to move about one-third of the way up.

"That's probably as good as you're gonna get it," Fazekas said.

"Better than nothing," Mercado said, now turning toward Fazekas. "Are you gonna be around later?"

"Yeah," Fazekas said. "I'll be downstairs. Knock on my door when you're done. If I'm not in, I just went around the corner for a minute."

"We might have a few questions for you then," Mercado said.

"However I can help you," Fazekas said. "I ain't the doorman, ya know. He mighta had someone up I don't know about."

"That's okay," Mercado said.

"All right," Fazekas said, "I'll leave you two alone. If you're gonna come back again, let me know. I want to get this place cleaned out. Maybe you can call someone from Haney's family to get his stuff."

"No problem," Mercado said. Fazekas closed the door gently behind him. Mercado pulled out two pairs of rubber surgical gloves. He tossed one pair to O'Connel and began putting on the other.

"Not bad for a guy who worked in the sewer," O'Connel said, stretching the gloves onto her hands, looking around, and then staring at a small abstract glass sculpture sitting on the top shelf of an oak breakfront. Alongside the sculpture sat a framed photo of a teenage girl and a younger boy, presumably Haney's children. Now, with the gloves on, O'Connel lifted the sculpture and admired it. "The whole place is nicely decorated. Except for . . ."

"All these porno films?" Mercado said, picking up one from

among a dozen scattered on the glass coffee table. "How 'bout this one . . . *Raiders of the Lost Cock?*"

"Personally, I prefer *The Day of the Jack-Off*," O'Connel said, lifting another VHS cassette off the coffee table.

"A guy with this great taste in movies has this crap lying around all over the place," Mercado said. "Go figure."

"Maybe they stimulated his creative juices," O'Connel said with a smirk. "You know, for that documentary."

"We might be watching a lot of X-rated movies over the next few days," Mercado said, thumbing through a long row of VHS tapes on the second shelf from the top of the breakfront. "It looks like these are the ones he shot for the film he was making. They're all dated." Mercado pulled one dated November 15, 1989, and popped it into the VCR sitting atop a twenty-five-inch color TV, itself sitting on a knee-high wooden cabinet. He hit the power button on the TV, fast-forwarded the tape in the VCR, then hit the play button.

The sounds of male and female moans came first. Then the blackness of the screen gave way to the image of Joel Haney and a young woman with long blond hair copulating in the missionary position. The lighting on the tape was not ideal, but good enough to reveal some peeling wall paint and a crack in the window. On the bed, the woman held Haney's head at a distance and cried out, "Yes, yes, yes . . ." in synchronization with the squeak of the bed. Joel Haney's hairy buttocks moved in rhythm as well.

"Oh my God," O'Connel said, "that's Barbara Sadowski, the prostitute who was killed last year."

"That's her all right," Mercado said. "You wouldn't think she was being paid for this if you didn't know better."

"It's called acting," O'Connel said, "and that's no documentary."

Mercado fast-forwarded the tape for roughly fifteen seconds and put the machine back on play. It was more of the same.

"No editing so far," Mercado said, "and really poor production values, even for a home skin flick."

"How would *you* know?" O'Connel asked.

"I'm a student of *all* types of film," Mercado said. He ejected the tape and replaced it with another one, this one dated July 8, 1990. Within a few seconds Haney's hairy buttocks filled the screen again, this time hovering over a thin white woman with short black hair and a butterfly tattoo on her shoulder.

"You really lucked out getting this case, didn't you?" O'Connel said.

"Hey," Mercado said, "I'll do whatever it takes to solve it. Even if it means sitting here and watching every minute of every one of these things."

"Still think Haney was shooting for an Oscar?" O'Connel asked.

"I don't know yet," Mercado said. "Sharpe didn't come off as a liar."

"Maybe Haney lied to Sharpe," O'Connel said. "Maybe he wanted to build himself up."

"I don't get the impression that there are too many secrets in the sewer," Mercado said. "To tell you the truth, I'm feeling bad about this whole investigation. We don't know for sure where the murder took place. We don't have anything remotely resembling a witness. We haven't had time to follow up on leads like the New School—they could tell us in two seconds whether he was enrolled as a film student and if this documentary exists. And we should have come here the day after Haney was murdered, not two weeks later."

"Jimmy, what can we do? Our case load is ridiculous. We're juggling everything right now. When was the last time we had the luxury of working on one case for a week solid? For even two full days uninterrupted?"

"Nice try," Mercado said, "but I still feel bad." Mercado now paced toward the windows, back again, and toward the windows a second time. He disappeared into the bedroom for a moment and spoke to O'Connel from there. "Okay, here's a tape editing machine, but where's his camera?" Mercado emerged from the bedroom and continued pacing. "I don't see things I expect to see, and I see things I don't expect to see, and it bothers me. I feel like someone got here before us."

"Someone did," O'Connel said. "Officers Akins and Nardo. They were taking inventory and photos a couple days after the murder. We have those back at the Tenth. We'll do a comparison and see if you're right."

"What if I am right and it *is* too late?" Mercado said, looking over the tapes on the second shelf from the top of the breakfront once more.

"Then I guess we're screwed," O'Connel said. A long female orgasmic moan emanated from the TV, which was still running the tape Mercado had put in several minutes earlier. "Damn that guy's good. I think that was real."

"At least as real as what we're looking at all around us," Mercado said. "Look at the dates on these tapes. They stop at November 'ninety-one. After that—nothing. If he was shooting some kind of documentary when he died, there should be all sorts of tapes dated right up through March or April 'ninety-three. Even if he wasn't shooting one, there should still be more recent tapes around. More homemade triple-X tapes or whatever. Why would he stop cold in November 'ninety-one?"

"He ran out of hookers?"

"In New York?" Mercado said. "No, the dates just don't make sense."

"You're right, Jimmy, they don't. Unless we find another batch before we leave. There was a date on this one." O'Connel reached down to the coffee table and picked up *The Day of the Jack-Off* tape. Holding it in front of her face, she looked at the small yellow purchase sticker stuck to the cassette cover. "Wait a second, this is dated 4-7-93. That's at least a day after Haney died."

"I knew he was horny, but this is ridiculous," Mercado said. "Lemme see that." Mercado took the tape from O'Connel's extended hand and looked at the sticker. "Sure, after he died, he crawled out of the morgue and bought one last porno tape, just for old times' sake."

"Tainted," O'Connel said.

"You bet it is," Mercado said. "Someone came in here shortly after the murder, went through all Haney's tapes, took away all his documentary tapes, left their own skin flicks, added some store-bought porn tapes to bolster the image, and hoped we'd draw the desired conclusions when we searched the place. Who could have flaked this shit? Personally, I like Sarnow."

"Sounds like Sarnow to me too," O'Connel said. "We'd better have that tape dusted."

"I'm taking half the stuff in this apartment down to the lab," Mercado said. "I wonder what other stuff he planted around here. I can't wait to find out."

"You think he flaked it himself?" O'Connel asked.

"Sarnow is a take-charge kind of guy," Mercado said. "And he's a little slow upstairs. It wouldn't surprise me. Do me a favor.

Run downstairs and get the super up here. Let's ask him who's been up here since the murder."

"Okay, Jimmy. I'll be right back."

Eight minutes later, when O'Connel returned to apartment 4A with Fazekas, Mercado emerged from the bedroom.

"Jimmy, listen to this," O'Connel said. "He says this is the third time he's let someone in since the murder."

"Yeah," Fazekas said. "Each time you guys send someone different. One time you send a tall black guy and a white guy with a gut like mine—"

"That's Akins and Nardo," Mercado said.

"Then you send me a guy with a long nose and glasses who tells me if I don't let him in he'll have a warrant for my arrest," Fazekas said. "Him and a tough-looking guy—not big, kind of skinny, but hard and tough."

"Tell me more about the guy with the long nose and glasses," Mercado said.

"Yeah, long nose, glasses," Fazekas said, "teeth like a horse. A nervous guy, your age, maybe a little younger."

"Sarnow," O'Connel said. "Who did he say he was with?"

"You guys . . . the police," Fazekas said. "You mean they wasn't?"

"Not exactly," Mercado said. "You've been very helpful. We'll have some more questions for you in a little while." Fazekas was now transfixed by the screen, which showed Haney going at it with a frizzy-haired woman partially clad in spandex and still wearing her spiked heels.

"Hey, I got no problem stayin' around and answering them questions now," Fazekas said, still transfixed.

"No, no," Mercado said, shoving Fazekas gently by the shoulder toward the door, "I really have to talk to my partner in private for a few minutes."

"You let me know—"

"We'll come and get you," Mercado said.

Fazekas shuffled off through the open door and down the stairway, muttering to himself. "Son of a bitch . . ."

"How do you like that?" O'Connel said, closing the door behind her. "Sarnow does his own dirty work."

"And there's more where that came from." Mercado held up a small plastic bag filled with white powder. "While you were gone, I found this in his top dresser drawer. Cocaine."

"Are we sure that wasn't Haney's?" O'Connel said.

"The autopsy found no drugs in his system, so it's not likely. You don't make money dealing a couple of ounces. Maybe he gave it to the hookers, but I doubt it."

"Off to the lab it goes," O'Connel said.

"My money's on Sarnow," Mercado asked. "The only question is, how did he keep from snorting it himself with that nose?"

"What have you got there?" O'Connel asked, pointing to the VHS cassette tape in Mercado's other hand.

"A tape with a recent date on it," Mercado said. "February seventeenth, 1993. Sarnow must have missed this one. It was in the drawer of his night table." Mercado stopped and ejected the tape running in the VCR and replaced it with the one he just found. A second after he hit play, the image on the screen came clear. A waiflike white woman in her early twenties sat cross-legged at the edge of a bed and faced the camera. A blue terry-cloth bathrobe partially covered a leather bra and a G-string. The peeling wall paint and crack in the window were the same as seen in the Barbara Sadowski tape. What must have been Haney's voice came from off camera.

"What do you think about when you're having sex with a customer?"

"How much I was just paid," the woman replied.

"And how much is that?"

"Twenty to go down, fifty straight, seventy-five anal. Extra things are negotiable."

"Do you ever worry about not getting Johns?"

"Worry?" the woman said. "We have a saying about that. Wanna hear it?"

"Yeah."

"You know why when you walk into a convenience store in the middle of the night you can't find lightbulbs, but there are eight brands of condoms?"

"Why?"

"Because fucking is more important than seeing."

"Hang on!" Mercado said, hitting the pause button. "That's Tiffany Kline, Barbara Sadowski's roommate. Joel Haney really got around."

"In this case," O'Connel said, "he got around the apartment."

"Now wait a second," Mercado said. "This was shot two months ago, about ten months after Barbara Sadowski was found dead. So first of all, we can probably still find Tiffany Kline at the same apartment."

"Barbara Sadowski's dead," O'Connel said, "but Haney's making a film in the same apartment with her roommate."

"But not a porn film," Mercado said.

"Understood," O'Connel said. "But it still makes you wonder if Haney had something to do with Barbara Sadowski's murder."

"You got a point," Mercado said. "Tiffany Kline didn't even mention Haney's name when we interviewed her last year. Like she's covering for him. Then he's over there again nonchalantly after Sadowski's found dead."

"Makes you wonder," O'Connel said. "Chances are he was having relations with both of them at some point."

"We're gonna have to pay her a visit," Mercado said. "One way or another, Tiffany Kline can clear some things up for us. Maybe Haney was tied up in this little ring somehow. He could even have been mixed up with Sarnow at some point. Hey, we might kill two birds with one stone."

"Or maybe one thing has nothing to do with the other," O'Connel said. "And maybe we find out that Haney really is clean."

"Could be this guy was the real thing," Mercado said. "Who knows—maybe he had noble ambitions. And Sarnow wants us to think he's just a whoring, coke-snorting lowlife."

"We are getting somewhere," O'Connel said. "Throw in the coroner's report, and you might have cause to stop complaining all the time."

"Well, let's not get carried away," Mercado said.

"Sarnow probably had this place staked out, just in case the real police showed up."

"That plan worked out great," Mercado said. "Good thing we didn't get here sooner."

"We have a lot more than we did a day ago."

"Whatever Haney's deal was, let's let that weasel keep making as many mistakes as his shriveled up little heart desires," Mercado said. "When he goes down, I want him going down big-time."

"That reminds me, Jimmy," O'Connel said, snapping her fingers once sharply. "I did that search of Sarnow's credit history on the Web."

"I gotta learn how to surf the Web one of these days," Mercado said, "right after I quit smoking."

"Check this out, Jimmy. His TRW history—it shows him with bad credit up to his ears right till March 'ninety-two. Thousands and thousands of dollars of late or missed payments. Then, poof—it all goes away."

"It must be the moonlighting at 7-Eleven," Mercado said, pulling a cigarette from a pack of Camels and lighting up. "See if you can pull his latest tax returns. Tax day just passed."

"It's on its way, Jimmy. Now Forensics tells us Haney was killed by a blow to the head sometime around midnight or a little earlier on the night of April fifth," O'Connel said, waving smoke away from her face. "Plus we got back from the coroner a video-tape found in the pocket of Haney's flight jacket."

"Waterlogged for eight hours?" Mercado said. "How good could that be?"

"We'll see," O'Connel said. "And we have a nice stack of maps showing us every manhole cover on or near Fourteenth Street. It's time to call Kessler back."

"Yeah, yeah," Mercado said, flicking ashes out the partially open living room window.

"Why put it off any longer?"

"Because once he tells us, 'Yeah, that body floated down-stream,' we're looking at enough canvassing to win a City Council seat."

"Let's get it over with," O'Connel said. "Call Kessler. By to-morrow. If you don't, I will."

"I'll do it, I'll do it . . . right after you teach me to surf the Web." Mercado paused and looked out the window. "Janine, I'm no slouch in bed. I'm right up there with Haney. What was the problem?"

"It was the smoking, Jimmy."

Chapter 10

It was hard for most people to believe that Manhattan isle ended as unceremoniously as it did here on the West Side between Fifty-ninth and Seventy-second Streets. Just as even the greatest individuals eventually had to die somehow, even the greatest, most celebrated bodies of land had to meet the water. People expected a great general to die overseas in battle and were disappointed to learn that he died not with his boots on of a gunshot wound during a ground assault but with his slippers on of a coronary during "Wheel of Fortune." Those same people would have been disappointed with Manhattan's frontier at the abandoned West Side Rail Yard. There was no promenade or overlook or platform. There was no real beach either. Instead, for a few hundred feet, brackish Hudson River water lapped up along a muddy, overgrown, uneven shore littered with cans, bottles, used condoms, and old railroad ties. Only the crying Indian from the 1970 TV ad that ushered in the environmental age was missing.

Then, for a few hundred more feet there was the remains of a concrete pile cap which at some point in the distant past served as a mooring for small boats. The pile cap rested on a few hundred feet of steel sheet piling, driven thirty or forty feet straight down into the soil to establish a "legitimate" shoreline—a bulkhead. There was a drop of a few feet to the water and a few more feet to the bottom, where the river had been dredged many years before. Unseen were the long metal tie rods several feet belowground anchoring the sheet piling, keeping the ancient, angry island from pushing out the piling and reestablishing its original slope to the water.

Seen clearly, however, was the spalling and cracking along the concrete pile cap and the dirt, weeds, and debris creeping over the top as if to keep pace with its overgrown pile-cap-less counterpart immediately to the south. The bulkhead had survived and done the job. But Manhattan wasn't giving up without a fight.

Breaking up the landscape were several wooden piers in various states of disrepair. The longest of these, known as Pier 1, reached out nine hundred feet toward Weehawken, New Jersey. In a borough where many blocks were only two hundred feet long, a walk toward the end of the pier made Manhattan fall away surprisingly quickly. The buildings receded and lined up in an orderly fashion. The sound of traffic receded as well and was replaced by the sound of water lapping up against the piles only a few feet below.

It took an experience like this to make the water real rather than just a blue-grayish extension of the island's concrete. From the island, the water was off limits, like a marble coffee table your grandmother had just bought. But nine hundred feet offshore and several feet above the surface, it was the same water you could find off the coast of Florida, Georgia, or the Carolinas. It was the same water that made its way to the Atlantic through thousands of streams and inlets.

Below, through one of the many missing or broken planks in the deck—a hazard making the water still more real—a phenomenon could be seen, as on piers virtually anywhere. The only rotted section of the piles was between the high and low water marks, where air and water took their turns. Above, the air alone, and below, the sea alone, left the piles more or less intact, even after a hundred years.

To the south, sticking out of the water, were the remains of two four-hundred-sixty-foot-long steel-framed piers once used for transfering freight cars across the Hudson by barge. The victim of a severe fire in 1971, the beams and columns were bent and twisted almost beyond recognition, like a roller coaster in an Escher drawing. There was talk by the Hudson City planners and by the New York Arts Council of leaving it as a testament to the city's past. So in a sense, part of Hudson City had already been designed and constructed.

As you walked along the pier back toward the shore, Manhattan reemerged as quickly as it had receded. If you were lucky, you returned a little wiser, a little more detached, the added reality of the water complemented by the diminished reality of the land. But in an hour or two, the old feeling of all land, no water was back with a vengeance.

In the West Side Rail Yards, symmetry evaporated quickly. The Henry Hudson elevated highway cut the huge lot crudely in half. East of it was the rail line now used by Amtrak trains. A variety of walls and fences separated the seventy-two-acre lot from every other lot in the borough, but it was unclear who was being fenced in and who was being fenced out. At the south end was a paved lot used by sanitation vehicles. Slightly north was a concrete wall and metal fence, behind which was a parking lot owned by ABC–Capital Cities.

A few hundred feet north was a thirty-foot-high wall built from schist rock and traveling all the way north to Seventy-second Street. Few people knew there was a street running atop this wall, and even fewer knew it was called Freedom Place. Freedom Place and the West Side Rail Yard were also separated by a fence, which sat atop the stone wall. Seventy-first Street, however, was not connected to Freedom Place, so a few hundred cars a day found a strange dead end overlooking the yard.

Back down in the rail yard, the ground was covered with a layer of weeds and debris that suggested homelessness and disease. The topsoil was soaked in creosote and dioxin. Ironically, only two or three feet down, the soil was relatively virginal, penetrated by few pipes and conduits, unlike the spaghetti beneath the paved streets. Still, it was hard to believe that with only a modest amount of excavation and planting of grass, this land would not somehow rebel against its new users.

At the foot of Pier I, at the gateway between reality and fantasy, stood Ronald Arlen. A platform and lectern had been set up along with a temporary public address system, which now pounded out the sound of Arlen's middle finger drumming a test pattern on a microphone. A crowd of about four hundred surrounded the Dodger in concentric semicircles about ten rows deep. The sky was overcast this Wednesday afternoon, April 21. Jon and his friends from the office looked on from the eighth row on what was the fifteenth day since Paula's decree. Ronald Arlen's layered, boyish hair was almost perfectly still in the moderate wind. His wide, unforced smile suggested a high level of comfort with public speaking.

"They said you couldn't build anything in New York anymore," he began. "Too much red tape, too much bureaucracy, overly high taxes. But to me, New York has always been and always will be the greatest city on Earth. The people of this city have an energy like no one else you'll ever find. That's the energy that comes from a thirst for life, from a desire to make things happen, and from knowing that you can and will get the job done. So when *I* have trouble, when I feel *I'm* not getting the job done . . ."

"I buy myself a politician," a middle-aged male voice boomed from the crowd. Amidst scattered laughter, Arlen's three bodyguards straightened their ties, folded their arms across their chests, and jerked their heads around to survey the various regions of the audience. The Dodger continued, hardly missing a beat.

" . . . I look at the people of this city, at New Yorkers, and ask myself if they would give up. I put myself in their shoes and realize how tough *they* have it."

"Yeah," Jay said under his breath, "they have to listen to *you*."

"Then I know the answer," Arlen continued. "They would never give up. They would find a way to get the job done. And that's what we've done. You wanted a park, so we're giving you a park . . . twenty-one acres of park. . . ."

"Right under a fucking highway," a ruddy-complected man of about fifty blurted out. Arlen continued, apparently buoyed by each combative remark.

"Twenty-one acres of public park, where our kids can play and grow up to be the athletes and responsible citizens of tomorrow. Soccer fields, baseball fields, basketball courts. A gift from one generation to the next. You wanted a place for the arts, a place for culture, so we're giving you an amphitheater." Arlen pointed south and slightly uphill along the property. "Three thousand seats, with a stage, lights, and a magnificent view of the Hudson. A place to share our unique and diverse culture. . . ."

"While you laugh all the way to the bank!" an older woman's voice rang out.

"This abandoned lot will be transformed before your eyes," the Dodger proceeded. "You see, this city has given me a lot, and I want to give something back. . . ."

"How 'bout my money!" let out the same ruddy-complected man who had spoken a minute earlier. Even though the hecklers were scattered, he seemed to be their ringleader. The bodyguards seemed more restless now, virtually aching for a confrontation.

"That's right," Arlen said, with a studied look of determination, "I want to give something back. Not just because of my financial success, but because I've been lucky enough to have people who *believe* in me. And foremost among those people is Donna."

"Yeah, Donna believes in silicone," Jon remarked quietly. Four years earlier, Arlen had dumped the thirty-nine-year-old ex-model Romanian mother of his two children for a twenty-six-year-old struggling actress. The break was anything but clean, with spurned wife and new girlfriend clawing it out at Arlen's sprawling Tampa estate, frequent newspaper photos of the voluptuous Donna Barlow emerging from a hotel suite known to be the Dodger's playpen, and legions of high-powered attorneys haggling over the legalities of a prenuptial agreement made between

Arlen and his bride back in 1976. Ex-wife Sophia Rakovnia Arlen had even written, with the help of a ghostwriter, a romance-glitz novel that was a thinly veiled account of her fourteen-year marriage to the Dodger.

"Donna gave me the strength and the courage to stand here before you today," Arlen continued. "I remember one day in 'eighty-nine when things for me had hit rock bottom. The bottom had dropped out of the real estate market and I was selling off things left and right just to keep paying a couple of big mortgages. The shuttle went, the yacht went . . ."

"Sophia went," a voice shouted, coming from the same middle-aged man who had earlier remarked about Arlen's fondness for buying political influence. A surge of laughter made its way through the crowd.

" . . . if it wasn't nailed down, it went," Arlen continued, "and even if it was nailed down, it probably went anyway. Even the casinos stopped making money for a while, and they were my bread and butter. And the Arlen Armada was sitting there, three-quarters built on Pacific and North Carolina avenues in Atlantic City, draining what little liquidity I had. Yes, the Armada was sinking, and I had to go into Chapter Eleven. The banks wouldn't cut me an even break. I was in debt—big debt. The kind that few of you could even conceive of . . ."

"Or would be stupid and privileged enough to incur," Pat sneered to those around him.

"This was the kind of debt," Arlen continued, "the kind of financial trouble, that eats you for lunch—the kind that breaks your spirit. I remember one day when I had just finished a meeting with the banks. They shot down my idea for refinancing three of my biggest properties—shot it down big-time. I'm feeling low right then, and I'm walking with Donna up Fifth Avenue and we see a homeless guy. I say to Donna: 'See that guy? He's worth nine hundred million dollars more than me.'"

"What a crock of shit," Jay muttered. "Where did you sleep that night, asshole? In a cardboard box next to his?"

"That's right," Arlen continued. "'He's worth nine hundred million dollars more than me.' How's that for a humbling experience? And you know what Donna does? She turns to me, looks me square in the eye and says: 'You know what the difference is, Ronald? He's never gonna turn things around. You *are*.'"

"Okay, that's it," Pat said, "give me a gun."

"And you know what?" Arlen said. "Starting the very next day, I did. I pulled myself up by my bootstraps and decided to stop feeling sorry for myself. Soon, the banks started seeing things my way. The economy started to recover, a few of my properties started to recover, and most important, *I* recovered. Today, I'm worth about a billion dollars more than that guy on the street."

"You're *still* worth nothing," the voice of the cantankerous older woman cried out in utter disdain.

"After all," the Dodger said, "*I'm* the guy who wrote *Making a Mountain out of a Molehill* . . . ."

"Worst book ever written," the ringleader boomed.

"And now I'm the guy who's written *Rebuilding the Mountain.* . . ."

"Second worst book ever written," the ringleader wailed. The three bodyguards had become increasingly agitated and now were homed in on the ringleader's exact location, four rows in on Arlen's left side and near a fortyish man many people recognized as a reporter for the *New York Times.*

"Hey, you must have thought a lot of the first one to go out and buy the second one," Arlen quipped, for the first time verbally acknowledging any of the hecklers.

"Don't flatter yourself," the ringleader replied full blast, "I found it on the train . . . and I left it on the train."

"Well, that just goes to show you," Arlen said, brushing off the ringleader in the most gracious way he knew how. "New York is a city of critics—eight million of them. And if you can't take the critics, you have no business doing business here. The timid run from critics. You see, it's all about vision—"

"Tunnel vision," the ringleader shouted. "The only thing you're trying to do is make money at other people's expense." The audience, looking more alert than it had throughout the entire speech, now split its focus between Arlen and the ringleader. They positioned their feet to allow a view of each debater with a minimum of body movement between exchanges. Television camera crews pointed their cameras at the ringleader, making the debate an official event.

"It's apparent that you don't know the first thing about economics," Arlen replied vigorously. "When I make money, everyone makes money. The bottom line, sir, is this: Can you take some union guy with a wife and kids who's aching to work, aching to put food on the table . . . can you look that guy straight in the eye and say you want to stop this project?"

"How *dare* you give me that crock of shit," the ringleader yelled, standing up, now visibly and audibly enraged. "Don't you know who I *am*?"

"No. Do you know who *I* am?"

"I'm Steve Sykes, former partner of Fastbinder and Sykes. I was the main sub on the Arlen Armada—remember me? I built the hull of your goddamned Armada, you son of a bitch. Then you went into Chapter Eleven, stiffed me, and went back into business under a different name two weeks later. *That's a half-million dollars of my hard-earned money sitting there decorating the front of your fucking casino, you prick!* I couldn't pay my men, I lost my business, I lost my wife, and you stand there in a two-thousand-dollar suit telling me about the working man?"

"Take it up with the bank and the courts," the Dodger replied.

"I'll take it up with *you*, you cocksucker!" Sykes now pushed his way up toward the lectern while uttering obscenities. He easily cleared out unwitting members of the crowd with his sizable arms and shoulders. Arlen's three bodyguards seized their long-awaited opportunity and met Sykes forcefully at the front row of the audience, well before he could reach the lectern.

The first bodyguard put his right shoulder down for a tackle as onlookers scattered and shrieked. Sykes's first punch connected with the side of the lead bodyguard's head, but Sykes was soon overwhelmed by the second bodyguard, who came straight over the top and got him in a headlock. The three, now all interlocked, fell as one top-heavy municipal project to the hard, untamed ground of the old rail yard. The third bodyguard stood back a few feet and spoke urgently into his walkie-talkie. Within a half minute Steve Sykes was subdued.

"Okay, folks," Arlen boomed through the P.A. system, "you've had enough of both of us by now. You know I've always talked about opening up a small arena for boxing like the old days, but this is not what I had in mind. I'll be happy to talk to you and take your questions individually."

The Dodger now stepped down from the podium and began milling about. Pat, Jon, Jay, Laura, and Naomi had drifted toward the scene of the altercation.

"Well, at least that guy got a couple of good punches in," Laura observed.

"Yeah, to Arlen's hired hands," Jay complained. "That's like kissing your sister. I woulda paid to see just one punch land in his face."

"No, a gun," Pat observed, shaking his head. "He needed a gun."

"Do you believe that guy's story?" Naomi asked.

"Yeah, I believe his story," Jon said. "All the details are there. I know for a fact that the Dodger filed for Chapter Eleven when the Armada casino was three-fourths complete."

"Actually," Jay said, "the Armada, Inc., filed for Chapter Eleven in 'eighty-nine, not Arlen himself. Then he opened it right back up under the name Carolina-Atlantic, Inc. I know he fucked over a bunch of subcontractors—like he always does."

"There's no way that guy was lying or just some psycho," Jon agreed. "I liked him. He was articulate . . . pretty funny too." As Jon spoke, Steve Sykes kicked at the bodyguards in futility as they dragged him to the edge of Arlen's property and tossed him out of the gate at Fifty-ninth Street. "Poor guy. Did you see the rage in his face? I tell you, I feel sorry for him. Have you ever seen that thing he built? I was down there last summer with Elaine. It's an exact replica of a sixteenth-century Spanish warship."

"People walk right past it, go inside, and promptly lose their Social Security check," Laura said.

"Not me," Jon said. "I stopped and took a good long look at it last time I went *before* I lost my paycheck. The detail on that thing is amazing. It's a work of art. And the poor schmuck gets burned for it. He's probably living with relatives. That's the way it works these days."

"A gun . . . a gun," Pat mused.

"Of course when the Dodger went broke," Jay remarked, "things were a little different. The banks actually put him on an allowance. A hundred thousand dollars a month personal spending money —not a penny more. Imagine seeing a car you liked and only being able to buy one of them."

"He shoulda shot him," Pat sighed.

Jon ambled off. He walked toward the shoreline, down the overgrown, debris-strewn slope. When he got to the water, he reached down and touched it with his right hand. He judged it was about sixty degrees—cold, but warm enough to sustain a swimmer for a while. At a depth of only a few inches, it was still clear enough to see the bottom. Like the cars roaring over the Henry Hudson above, the water molecules below were replaced every moment by new ones floating downriver. He felt the overwhelming desire to jump in and let someone replace him.

Instead he walked back up the slope as the cold river water evaporated off his right hand. He wandered over toward the podium area, where a crowd still lingered about the Dodger. There, Jon spotted a man about his own age talking to Arlen and taking notes. He seemed familiar to Jon, although he wasn't sure from where. Jon narrowed it down to high school or college, which wasn't narrowing it down much at all. It was strange to finally be old enough so that different parts of his life—at least on the fringes—occasionally merged into a murky whole. This, multiplied by a factor of twenty, is what he envisioned senility to be, and even a glimpse of it scared him.

Now, as if waking up from a short dream, he found that he'd drifted unconsciously to within three feet of Ronald Arlen. Then, as if reentering the dream, he found that the Dodger was speaking directly to him.

"Hey, I know you. You cost me five million dollars." Arlen smiled overtly and extended his right hand. As if part of the same dream, Jon shook it.

"Five million dollars? How'd I do that?"

"The estimate for constructing this magnificent waterfront park. We put in an estimate for sixty million bucks and your estimate was seventy."

"And we split the difference," Jon added.

"At that point, I needed to get Art's John Hancock," Arlen said, "whatever the price. I still disagree with you on those numbers. I think they're inflated. But what the hell—a deal's a deal."

"I probably could have found another ten million dollars of hidden costs necessary to build this park," Jon replied, "but there was pressure on me to scale it down. The items I found are legitimate."

"They are, huh?" Arlen replied playfully.

"Absolutely," Jon said. "First of all, the concrete pile cap is going to be very expensive. Jacketing the existing timber piles is also very expensive. I consulted with one of the best marine engineers on the East Coast about these sorts of issues."

"So did I."

"Then, looking at the excavation and fill operation," Jon continued, undaunted, "the environmental impact statement indicated that dioxin and other toxic chemicals are sitting in the soil since it was used as a rail yard for so many years. If the area was all going to be paved over, that would be one thing. But a lot of it is going to be seeded, with kids rolling in it. I recommended that the earth be excavated to a depth of three feet, hauled off, and disposed of properly. There were a dozen things like that that your engineer's estimate didn't take into account."

"Well, I still feel you owe me an apology," Arlen said.

"I have to call 'em the way I see 'em," Jon replied, a hint of defensiveness in his voice.

"Ah, I'm just fucking with you," Arlen said. "We need people like you who don't back down. It makes the city a better place." The Dodger extended his hand, and Jon shook it a second time. "Besides, five million is chump change. Tell Art I said hello."

"Will do," Jon said, pulling away slightly.

"Kessler, right?" Arlen asked.

"That's right."

Chapter 11

Later that Wednesday afternoon, in the elevator on the way up to the twentieth floor of the Municipal Building, doing his best to shut out of his mind the overwhelming smell of corned beef and greasy fried chicken leaking through a delivery boy's white paper bag, Jon was certain there were a bunch of messages waiting for him on his voice mail and that at least one of them was of great importance. He was usually right about such things. Meanwhile, he kicked himself for not insisting on eighty million for the park.

Jon walked briskly past a murmuring Al Gibbs, a sleeping Larry Golick, and the desk of the absent Naomi Pierce. He could just barely decipher what Old Al was saying: "Rubs elbows with the big shots, then comes in here like he's hot shit, all in a rush. . . ."

"Are you talking about me, Al?" Jon said to him in a loud voice. "Because if you are, you need to speak directly to me."

"I ain't talkin' *to* you or *about* you," Old Al responded just as deliberately, momentarily, breaking out of his bubble while looking briefly back over his shoulder, annoyed. Larry's snoring, meanwhile, reached an oblivious crescendo only a few feet away, his mouth now wide open, with his head supported from behind by a partition wall.

"Well, I know you weren't talking to me, since that would signify respect for me you don't even seem to have for yourself," Jon said. "But it sure as hell sounded like you were talking *about* me, since I just had an unpleasant conversation with Ronald Arlen. I don't know how you know these things. Are you psychic, Al?"

"Just go back to what you was doing," Al replied, still distressed at being probed, and now returning his head to the tender embrace of his own palms.

"You too," Jon said. "You go back to what you were doing. By the way, what is it you do?"

"Girlfriend comes in here tellin' me about him and the Dodger hanging out," Al muttered. "Now he thinks I'm runnin' one of them psychic fuckin' hot lines. . . ."

"She's *not* my girlfriend . . ." On "girl," the door to room 2035 opened and Naomi walked in looking blank and pale. Jon and Naomi had split up at the downstairs elevators when he stopped to talk briefly with the newspaper stand attendant. Apparently, she had arrived here first, spoken to Al through his bubble, left to go to the bathroom, and now come back.

"Hi, Naomi," Jon said with an exaggerated hand gesture.

"Hi," she replied with little enthusiasm.

Jon quickly turned and opened the door to his office. The message light on the phone was flashing. It flashed the same way for one message or for twenty, but he just knew this was a multiple flash. He picked up the receiver and dialed in his code. The computerized male voice, sounding as inert as Naomi a minute earlier, announced: "You have seven messages." Each word existed in its own pocket, undisturbed by the surrounding words. The word "seven" sat in a special double-stitched, silk-lined pocket. Now the messages themselves played, in real flowing voices.

"This is Detective James Mercado, Tenth Precinct. I wanna thank you for all those maps; they really have been helpful in our investigation. What I'd like to do is take you up on your offer. I could use your help figuring something out. So could you give me a call at your convenience at the precinct . . . Thank you. . . ."

" . . . Hello, I hope I have the right place. I need a map showing the Morningside Park area . . . the name is Elizabeth Weiser. I was referred to you. Could you call me back at . . ."

" . . . Jon, it's Elaine . . . I miss you, and I wish you were coming home tonight. I want to sit on your long, hard cock. Think about that while you're inspecting water mains . . . 'bye."

" . . . This is Paula, and I need to speak to you this afternoon when you get the chance."

" . . . Hello, Mr. Kessler, I was given your card by someone at DOT. He said you could get me a street map of the Times Square area showing survey markers. Do you have something like that? The name's Simon . . . Bob Simon . . . I'd appreciate a call at . . ."

" . . . Watch the girl. The girl is bad news. Watch what you say to the girl. . . ." It was the deep, sonorous voice that had called before with another cryptic message.

" . . . Hi, Fran Cassel, Parks Department . . . Could you give me a call please . . . thanks a lot."

Jon decided to wing it with Paula today. No phone call, no pondering the angles, just go in there and get it over with. Other than breathe, he couldn't recall doing anything overt in the past couple of weeks that could have conceivably rattled Paula, so he doubted his treatment would be much worse than normal. Perhaps the review of his report had come in early. If so, whatever the result, he could face it and defend his work if necessary. In any case, he had a couple of phone calls to look forward to should he leave the meeting feeling run over.

He walked past the desk of Melissa, Paula's long-legged, dark-haired, svelte twenty-fiveish secretary, and got a quick friendly stare before her eyes returned to the page she was reading. Jon wanted to dangle his toes a little before taking the cold plunge, but the opportunity had disappeared. Paula was unoccupied except for the folders she was sifting through, and motioned him with her right hand to step inside.

"You wanted to see me?"

"Yes, have a seat," Paula said pleasantly. Jon sat on the front edge of the quicksand sofa chair and tightened his leg muscles in

order to remain as even with Paula's eye level as possible—
essentially a losing battle.

"I've been talking to Evelyn," Paula continued, referring to
Deputy Borough President Evelyn Webb. "We know you have a
killer commute and you've been doing it for quite some time now,
and we have an idea."

"What's that?"

"Why don't you work at home one day a week?"

"No change in salary?"

"None at all. It'll make life easier. There's no reason you can't
take some of this work home. You have a fax machine, right?"
Paula was so glib and carefree that Jon speculated she was on
some kind of mood-altering drug.

"Can I pick the day I want?" Jon asked.

"Sure, take the day you want. I mean, I'd assume you'd take a
Monday or a Friday."

"Believe it or not," Jon explained, "I think I'll take Wednesday."

"Whatever suits you," Paula replied, raising both her hands and
tilting her head as a sign of joyful capitulation. "As long as you
can still perform the work and come in on an emergency basis that
day if I need you."

"No problem."

"Okay, then, what I'll need you to do is write a short letter to
Evelyn requesting the four-day workweek, and you'll be set."

"Sure," Jon said, "I'll get that out today. By the way, when can
I start taking that day?"

"Next Wednesday would be fine."

"Okay, thanks a lot," Jon said as he stood up.

"Sure, Jon."

He walked out and seemed to float down the nineteenth floor
hallway. He was getting one-fifth of his life back, apparently with
no strings attached. The work he would do at home on Wednesdays could be light, involving punching out a few short memos,
each of which he would fax immediately to one or more of his su-
periors at the office to give the impression of a little steam engine
off somewhere in the boonies grinding it out. Those memos could
even be done the day before and simply faxed on the Wednesday,
thereby allowing him to punch the clock the modern, long distance way. Meanwhile, he could sleep late, pump new life into his
marriage and family, and hit some baseballs in the backyard. Once

in a while, when a huge report really was due, he would actually use his full Wednesday to produce it, fax it in, and then experience an "instantaneous" commute home when it was done. He had it all figured out by the time the elevator doors opened to the twentieth floor.

Larry's eyes were open and still as Jon passed by his desk, indicating that Larry was either awake or dead.

"Larry," Jon said, "are you there?"

"Yes, King," Larry responded with a yawn, "I'm just waking up."

"Well go back to sleep. I was having great luck while you were out cold."

"Why, what happened?" Larry asked.

"Paula called me down to talk to me about something," Jon explained, "and as usual, I was ready for the worst. But guess what? It turns out she wants to give me a four-day week. Why, I don't know."

"King, that's great. Now you can be home with your family more and work on that house."

"But who's gonna watch *you*?" Jon replied. "You know, I hate to look a gift horse in the mouth. A bunch of other people in this office have special arrangements—to work around school or teaching positions, or their kids' needs."

"I have a special arrangement," Larry said.

"Yeah, a four-minute workweek—consciousness optional," Jon continued. "My question is not so much 'Why' as 'Why me *now*?' I was on reasonably good terms with Paula when I came to this office two and a half years ago, but that state of affairs has steadily deteriorated ever since, and right now it's pretty low. Not that I'd want it to be so great considering what I know about her."

"You *know* she's got something up her sleeve," Larry observed. "I wouldn't trust that bitch if you paid me. But what the hell. Take the day anyway. Life is short, and no matter what she's up to, at least you'll be away from here and away from that bitch."

"Continue that train of thought for a minute," Jon said. "Specifically *what* do you think she has up her sleeve? Just take wild guesses."

"I don't know, King," Larry replied. "Maybe she wants you out of the office at times, when she's meeting with certain people. Maybe she's gonna go through your files when you're not here. Maybe she just wants to keep you off guard while she plans her next move. Whatever it is, I'm sure it's something."

"It's not possible, then," Jon mused, "that she saw me working real hard week in, week out for two and a half years, commuting back and forth like a lunatic, and said to herself: 'Maybe that guy will be a little more productive if we take some of the stress out of his life'?"

"No. No way, King," Larry stated.

"Just asking. You don't trust anybody, do you?"

"Not in this administration," Larry said. "Maybe a few people who got their jobs through civil service or a fluke, like you. Otherwise, no. Look who their leader is. Let me tell you something about Art Shuler. Remember the homeless shelter scandal?"

"Yeah," Jon said, "he exposed that whole thing."

"He knew about it for years," Larry said. "You know Mort Zinstein, who had a long-term city contract to run those filthy places and who was indicted? That was Art's father's best friend."

"Yeah," Jon said. "The judge gave Zinstein the choice of two years in prison or one year in one of his own shelters."

"And he took jail," Larry said. "You see, Art was coming toward the end of his first term as borough president and realized he hadn't really done anything other than give a bunch of speeches and spend some money. So he said, 'What can I do that people will remember?' Then he turned in Zinstein."

"Just like that?"

"Just like that," Larry said. "Forget about the fact that he could have and should have done it fifteen years earlier when he was on the City Council. Forget about the fact that he had it in his back pocket the whole time, while the city paid two hundred fifty dollars a head per day so homeless people could get a Dixie cup of water and two crackers. Bottom line—it made Art look like a hero. But let me tell you, he's no Andy Stein."

"What about Shuler's father?" Jon asked.

"Art's father?" Larry said. "Art's father won't talk to him. He's eighty-something, he's loaded, from the tool and die business. He always gave his son a million bucks or more for each election. Even Zinstein gave him a hundred thousand once. From now on, Art's on his own. I don't know where he's gonna get the money to run for mayor. He never saved much on his own. His father made him."

"I guess his big accomplishment for this term was the anti-smoking law," Jon said. "I liked it personally."

"Even that's got something else behind it," Larry said. "You know Art was a big smoker for thirty-five years. Two packs a day. Then three years ago, his doctor told him he was precancerous. Unless he quit right away, he'd probably have lung cancer in a year or two. He was a complete neurotic asshole when he was quitting. I spoke to Melissa about it. He'd be in his office throwing things, breaking things, calling everyone a shithead or a cunt. Then one day he said 'You know what? If I can't smoke, nobody can smoke. Fuck 'em!' That's when he pushed that antismoking law through the City Council."

"And I voted for this nut," Jon said. "Okay, I gotta do some work."

"King, tell me you're not actually gonna work on your day at home too," Larry begged.

"Actually, I'm gonna call you every hour on the hour to wake you up so you can do some work."

"Thanks for warning me, King. I'll take the phone off the hook on those days."

"Tell you what," Jon said. "I won't call you if you promise on those days to sleep with your head propped up against my door. You know, like a sort of watchdog."

"It's a deal, King."

Old Al Gibbs's mumbling, which had begun over a minute earlier, was now finally cutting through the warm spring office air in room 2035.

"Son of a bitch has a four-day workweek. We didn't get no four-day workweek. Over in 'Nam, we had ourselves a fuckin' *seven*-day workweek. Twenty-four fuckin' hours a day, man. You go to sleep out there in the jungle, Charlie'll blow your fuckin' head off."

"Yeah," Larry said, "and he's been catching up on sleep ever since—here at the Borough President's Office."

"What's your excuse, Larry?" Jon asked. "Just get back from 'Nam too?"

"No, King. I was up late watching the Ranger game."

On the way back to his office, Jon leaned over to Naomi, who was hunched over a spread of books and papers. "So are we still set for tomorrow?" he asked. "Lunch . . . then sewage for dessert?"

"Oh, that's right," she said, craning her neck to look up at him and wincing to express a combination of apology and recollection. "Can we possibly do that some other time, maybe the end of next week? I have three finals coming up. In fact, I'm going to have to head home in a few minutes and just lock myself away for the weekend."

"Sure," Jon said. "Let's not even schedule anything until you're done."

"Thanks a lot."

"No problem."

When Jon opened the door to his office and looked at his phone, he saw that there were no new messages. He sat down, lifted the receiver, and dialed.

"Tenth, Mercado speaking."

"This is Jon Kessler, returning your call."

"Thanks for getting back to me," Detective Mercado said. "I was wondering if you could figure something out for me."

"I'll give it my best shot."

"Okay," Mercado continued. "Is there any way you could tell me what the flow was like around the time of the murder we're investigating . . . the one in the Fourteenth Street sewer? Like how fast the sewage was going?"

"Well, what I can do," Jon explained, "is give you a range of probable conditions based on whatever data is available. But let me ask you something first. What's your goal here? Do you have to know the velocity or are you more interested in how full the sewer was flowing?"

"Both, I guess," Mercado explained. "Haney's body was found right near the manhole at the corner of Hudson and Fourteenth Street. But what we're looking into is whether it's possible that the body was dumped somewhere east of there—like Eighth Avenue—and then carried west by the current."

"Okay," Jon said, "then you'll be more interested in how full the sewer was. Once the sewer is somewhat full, even a fairly low velocity can carry a floatable object."

"I understand," Mercado said. "Just get me as much information as you can—velocity and how full it was, and anything else you can think of that might be relevant. And put it in writing if you could, in layman's terms."

"How soon do you need this?"

"As soon as possible."

"My mouth wants to tell you I'll have it for you tomorrow," Jon said, "but my head is saying give it a week."

"Whatever you can do will be appreciated," Mercado said. "My partner and I tried getting this information from DEP, and it was a nightmare. They told me that kind of information wasn't available, and even if it was, it would be too approximate to help me. Basically, they gave me the runaround."

"That's DEP for you," Jon agreed. "Unfortunately, I'm going to have to approach them too. They get the printouts from the trunk meters—I don't. In fact, I've never even seen a printout. But I know they exist. From what I understand, they should give not only daily flow totals but also flow totals at hourly intervals. The trick is getting my hands on them."

"I hope it's not too much trouble . . ."

"It's some trouble, but not too much," Jon said. "In fact, as recently as a year ago I would have told you only a very rough guess was possible. But recently, DEP installed a few meters in some of the larger sewer lines—the ones they call 'trunk' mains."

"Okay then, that sounds good."

"Well, here's the problem," Jon continued. "There isn't a meter directly corresponding to the Fourteenth Street main we're dealing with. As big as that sewer is, it isn't one of the trunk mains. The Fourteenth Street sewer feeds into the Eighteenth Street trunk main by making a right turn uptown at Tenth Avenue. But I'll make a few realistic assumptions about the proportion of flow coming from the Fourteenth Street main versus whatever other mains feed into the Eighteenth Street trunk."

"Thanks a lot."

"Forget about it," Jon continued. "I get a kick out of it. Anyway, I have an idea. When I was doing my big report on North River, a couple of people at DEP went out of their way to help me. I'm gonna hit them up for information. Don't worry about it."

"It's always like that, isn't it?" Mercado observed. "You deal with these huge agencies, and you feel like a kid lost in a department store. Then, out of the blue, someone takes pity on you."

"Exactly."

"But it shouldn't be like that," Mercado said. "You'd think that if you worked for the city—I don't care which agency—when you reached out to someone in another agency, they'd automatically go out of their way to help you."

"Something like esprit de corps?"

"Yeah."

"In our dreams," Jon said.

"You got it. Listen, thanks a lot."

"Talk to you maybe middle of next week, then," Jon said.

"So long."

Jon stepped quickly out of his office into the main area and walked over to Larry, who was hunched over the *Racing Form*.

"Guess what?" he said. "That detective I had you deliver all those maps to called me back. He wants me to use my engineering knowledge to help him with that Fourteenth Street sewer murder. Isn't that cool?"

"King, you are truly great. Now you're solving murders."

"*Attempting* to . . . we'll see how far I get."

At 8:30 P.M. later that same Wednesday, Jon sat in the sleek, wood-framed, soft leather chair in Keith Richman's living room and looked out the open window and down at West Eighty-seventh Street just off West End Avenue. A subtle breeze carried in cool but moist air, sweetened by nearby Riverside Park, but at the same time slightly sooted by nearby Broadway. Spring in New York had become abbreviated over the past several years, some said because of a hole in the ozone layer, global warming, the greenhouse effect, general moral corruption—whatever came to mind. For some undetermined reason, spring was now just a pit stop for a brutal winter racing to transform itself into a merciless summer.

The seventeen-inch color television in the corner was muted and showed a revamped Yankee team playing under the lights in the Bronx. Jon's shoes were off. In his lap was a notepad on which he was doing some preliminary calculations for the detective. This exercise would yield nothing resembling an answer to the central questions of velocity and height of flow, since Jon did not yet have the trunk meter information from DEP. But he did have the Fourteenth Street sewer's inside diameters—which ranged from three and a half to five and a half feet—and enough additional information to go through the motions. By assuming various trunk main flows, he could establish a range of results—albeit a broad one—and organize the analysis to the point where, when he received the missing flow data, the final answer would take only a few more minutes to derive.

Keith emerged from the bathroom wearing tight racing shorts and a plastic helmet. He yanked at the handlebars of his three-thousand-dollar titanium racing bike and perfunctorily pumped the hand brakes.

"You sure you don't want to ride with me?" Keith offered. "You could take the other bike."

"Thanks, but I'll pass," Jon said. "I think I'll stay here and watch other people play sports."

"That's exactly the point," Keith contended. "Don't you need to get out and get some fresh air in your lungs?"

"I got plenty of fresh air today in the rail yards where Hudson City's going up. How far north are you riding tonight?"

"Yonkers and back."

"I *hope* 'and back.' "

"It's a piece of cake."

"You're a nut," Jon said.

"Hey," Keith explained, "if I stayed here all night, I'd probably start punching holes in the walls."

"I got *that* covered while you're gone," Jon said. "Where would you like 'em?"

"Start with the kitchen. Then work your way into the living room and finish up with the main bedroom."

"You got it."

Keith leaned his compact, muscular, five-seven frame into the titanium bike and wheeled it toward the door. As he opened the door to the ninth-floor hallway, he gave it one last try. "You sure you don't want to go?"

"Yeah," Jon replied. "I might lift weights for half an hour, but that's it. But that'll be right here in your living room. I don't need to go to Yonkers for that." Then Jon heard the door close and the lock turn.

There were real holes in the walls. They were made by real fists—most of them Keith's, some of them his ex-wife's, and none of them Jon's . . . so far. Less than two years ago, Jon had been an usher at Keith's wedding at a nondenominational church on the East Side. The legal union between Jewish Keith Richman and Irish Catholic Allison McCarty seemed based on a solid foundation of love, trust, careerism, and an occasional broken dish or centerpiece thrown when a college-level vocabulary wasn't enough. Having worked out almost everything humanly possible to work out during four years of living together, their marriage prospects seemed as sound as Keith's job on Wall Street and Allison's acceptance into NYU Medical School.

But within a few months of the honeymoon in Australia, the plaster started giving way. Allison complained that their lives were too separate. She was right, even though she had helped make it that way. The week they got back from Australia, she stopped biking in Central Park with Keith and joined a local running club. Keith kept biking. The next week, classes started and thirty-year-old Allison was determined to make up for the bulk of her lost twenties with a running start. She was out of bed by five-thirty in the morning and out of the house by six. Two hours and ten road miles later, she was back for a quick shower, nonchalantly bumping into Keith as he fixed his suspenders in the mirror. Hi. How was running? Have a nice day.

When Keith got home at seven or eight at night, Allison had already been home, studied for two hours, and gone back out for leg two with the running club. Only a year earlier, when she worked nine-to-five at a research lab and Keith made sure to be home most nights by six-thirty, they would often have sex right on the parquet living room floor before biking together up to the Cloisters near the northern tip of Manhattan.

But eight weeks into the marriage, the only intercourse they had was verbal—a chance meeting every few evenings in Central Park, Keith on bike, Allison on foot. They weren't entirely chance meetings, though. Keith knew Allison and her coed pack would be looping the reservoir between 8:20 and 8:40 P.M., so making sure their paths crossed wasn't too difficult.

The problem was knowing what to say once they were together in that situation. Keith could feel the ice form as he rolled up behind the pack. Hi. How many miles have you done? See you at home. Keith wasn't supposed to be there. Each time he would speed away faster. Eventually, he stopped circling the reservoir altogether. He found his own pack and experimented with riding over the George Washington Bridge and twenty-five miles or more up Route 9W, along the Hudson, reaching, Nyack, Haverstraw and other towns north of the city.

This was all supposed to end on November fourth of that fall.

On their own personal D-Day, Allison skipped running and announced that she wanted to have a baby as soon as possible. Keith's reaction was that the marriage was on shaky ground and that the two of them had a lot to work out before they could even consider having a baby. Waiting a minimum of a year made sense.

The November fourth hole started it all. It wasn't the largest of holes. In fact, it wasn't even made by a fist. Allison whipped open the bedroom door with her 109 pounds of runner's hard body. The metal doorknob drilled a deep hole in the Sheetrock. Keith did little but watch in amazement as Allison followed it up by returning to the living room a minute later and throwing a stack of color photos from Australia straight across the airspace, scattering them like the Sunday *Times* in an empty stadium.

The hole that Keith made on November fifth blew the November fourth hole away, in diameter, depth, and drama. It was made by his fist a foot and a half to the left of the living room mirror. It proved that he could make a hole too, and that he didn't need a fucking doorknob. He didn't need a pack of admirers. He didn't need to keep going to school to prove he was young while someone else paid the tuition. And he didn't need a baby to make him feel worthy. What he did need, however, was fourteen stitches across his knuckles.

Allison disappeared to her mom's for a week right after that. Although she returned to the apartment physically for a few weeks, she never came back emotionally or spiritually. By early December she was gone in every sense of the word. One of the coldest winters in recorded history immediately followed. The jet stream seemed to sweep right through apartment 91 of 302 West Eighty-seventh Street.

Jon, can you come over? My life doesn't make sense anymore. Why did this happen? Maybe we should have just kept on living together and not gotten married. Was she seeing someone else? Women are evil. I'll never marry again. My hand hurts.

From that winter on, Jon slept at Keith's apartment two to three nights a week, usually in a sleeping bag on the floor of the tiny spare bedroom, sandwiched between Keith's spare tenspeed and his mountain bike. During the brutal winter, he paid what was essentially one long house call to help get Keith back to something resembling mental health. It's not your fault. She was insecure.

She was always insecure. She wanted a marriage of convenience. She had an agenda, and you fell off the pace.

By the following spring, physical therapy had largely taken the place of psychotherapy. Keith's seventy-mile-plus bike rides to points increasingly north showed him he was master of his own destiny once again. Jon wasn't needed quite as much anymore, but was still on call for the occasional all-night counseling session. At the same time, Jon had found that when he couldn't make it home, he liked sacking out at Keith's bachelor pad with the holes in the walls.

Yet as Jon now flipped through sixty-seven cable channels, propped his feet up on the coffee table, and waited for the Mexican food delivery guy to ring the buzzer, he knew that the bachelor pad and its luxuries came with a price. The price was the tenuousness of relations between man and woman, and how the rope could snap under much less tension than anyone might have guessed. Keith had paid that price directly. Jon had escaped unblemished from Keith's misfortune other than the temporary blotchy skin caused by six-hour crisis-prevention talks lasting till 4:00 A.M. on worknights. But Jon feared he would have to pick up some direct costs himself one of these days—that the "process" wasn't through with him yet. In precisely the same wave of thought, he remembered he hadn't returned Elaine's call from the afternoon. He now picked up the portable phone and did so.

"Hello?"

"Hi, it's me. I'm sorry I didn't return your call earlier."

"I was worried about you," Elaine said. "I was just about to beep you."

"Well, if it's any consolation," Jon said, "I'd still like to take you up on that offer."

"Where are you, Keith's apartment?"

"Where else? Are you okay, Elaine? You sound . . . exasperated."

"I had a hard day at work and Stacy was a little maniac when we got home. And I just feel like I never get to see you."

"Well," Jon said, "the extent to which that may be true is about to diminish. I spoke to Paula today. She's going to give me a four-day week, starting next week."

"You're kidding me. That's great."

"Yeah. I'm gonna take Wednesdays to break up the week. I'll come home Tuesday nights on the train, relax, get up in the morning, run a couple of miles, have breakfast, bang out a few memos, fax them in, and be home free the rest of the day."

"And guess what?" Elaine said. "I'm going to be able to get some days off during the week because Barbara's coming back from maternity leave. We'll actually be able to spend time together, maybe hit the beach once it gets warmer. Who cares if a few thousand electric bills go out late?"

"Now you're talking. Why don't you run with me?"

"Someone has to watch Steven," Elaine said.

"Barney'll watch him. That fat purple bastard's gotta be good for something. Hey, why don't we get your wheel out and you can make some pots. Fix up the kiln . . ."

"We'll see," Elaine said. "I don't want to get too excited about this. Not until you've at least spent one Wednesday at home, or we've spent it together . . . you know how I am."

"Yeah . . . I know how you are."

"Why did Paula give you this?" Elaine asked. "She's usually a bitch."

"Look, I don't know, and I don't *wanna* know. Elaine, do you know what a gift horse is?"

"Okay, Jon. You'll call me at work tomorrow. Promise?"

"Yeah, yeah, I promise. Don't worry. Things'll be better starting next week. I love you."

"Okay, 'bye. I love you too."

Jon looked back down at the page of sewer calculations and decided to let it go for the evening. Toward the end of the day he had called Fred Barrow, engineer at the DEP central office in Corona, Queens. Jon and Fred had helped each other on a number of occasions, to the point where both of them had stopped keeping score. But according to Fred's outgoing message, he'd be on vacation till next week. In addition, Jon still needed information on the slope of the Fourteenth Street sewer, the friction factor of its lining, and an hourly report of rainfall on the night of the murder. This last item would require a call to the National Weather Service. Since it couldn't possibly all come together this week, and since he was now deluged with the urge to sleep, there was no reason to push it anymore tonight. Besides, Bernie Williams had just hit a two-run double to tie the game.

Chapter 12

It was the morning of Thursday, April 22. Upon being buzzed in, Detectives Mercado and O'Connel stepped out of a light drizzle and into the walk-up apartment building at 540 West Twenty-fourth Street. The detectives knew they had the best chance of finding Tiffany Kline at home early in the day, but they waited till about eleven in order to let her get some sleep. Nonetheless, when she opened her apartment door, she was still getting oriented to the light.

"Wait a second. You're the DTs from the Tenth, right?"

"That's right."

"Did you find him yet?" The twelve-inch opening in the door-way revealed Tiffany Kline's five-five, 100-pound frame with an oversized brown angora sweater hanging from her shoulders as if from a rack. Her legs were wrapped in tight gray sweat pants. She sniffled and rubbed her nose.

"Whoever killed Barbara is still out there," O'Connel said. "But we might have a lead. Could we come in for a minute?"

"Yeah, all right," Tiffany said. Quickly, she closed the door to release the chain lock before reopening the door all the way. The detectives followed her a few feet toward a wooden table near the kitchen, where she sat in a steel-framed chair and put her feet on the padding so her knees were stuffed up near her chin. She had a delicately narrow face, pale skin, slightly flared nostrils, and long straight brown hair. From beneath long, thin arched brows, her deep, doelike blue eyes revealed scrutiny and mistrust—the look of being permanently wounded and having held the whole world responsible instead of one evil man.

"I'd offer you something," Tiffany said, "but that's how I got into trouble last time I got booked." Her voice was sultry and ancient, like that of an old lounge singer.

"Do you know Joel Haney?" Mercado asked.

"Is that your lead?" Tiffany said, practically laughing. "That's what you came up with in a year? Not only is Joel the last person on earth who would've killed Barbara—he's dead too."

"We know that," O'Connel said. "We're looking for Haney's killer also. That and anything else about Haney, including his connection to Barbara."

"What do I know?" Tiffany said. "I told you everything I knew last year."

"We have a videotape of Barbara engaging in sexual activity with Joel Haney in this apartment from three and a half years ago," O'Connel said. "We have another tape of Haney and you, here, from only a couple of months ago."

"Okay, I'm a hooker," Tiffany said, holding out her wrists, "arrest me."

"That's not what we're here for," O'Connel said. "The uniforms are taking care of the mayor's crackdown."

"It was an interview tape," Mercado said, "that's all. We just want to know anything that you know about Joel Haney and who he might have been involved with."

"Okay, okay," Tiffany said, throwing up her hands. "I saw Joel three nights before he was found dead."

"As a client or for an interview?" O'Connel asked.

"Neither," Tiffany replied. "I passed him down by the river, around Eighteenth Street."

"Eighteenth Street, huh?" Mercado said.

"Where they're building that mall," Tiffany said. "That's where he used to pick up girls for his film. His documentary. I ran into him down there at night when he was filming. I was looking for tricks, and he was looking for a new subject."

"What happened?" O'Connel asked.

"Nothing happened," Tiffany replied. "He had already interviewed me. And he didn't pay for sex anymore. So he went his way, and I went mine. But he did give me some money."

"What for?" Mercado asked.

"Just like that," Tiffany said. "I'm trying to tell you, that's the kind of guy he was. Look, this gets messy."

"The mess is what we want," Mercado said.

"Joel wasn't the kind of guy who was going to be paying hookers all his life," Tiffany said. "It's more like we were here when he needed us. His wife left him like four years ago. They lived in Queens. He put her through law school, and she wound up with a whole different set of friends. I think she had a boyfriend. That's when Joel started coming around. He moved into this neighborhood because it was right near his job. He had a bad drinking problem for a while."

"Did he ever get violent?" Mercado asked.

"Nope. Not with us," Tiffany said. "He was a good guy. He got his girlfriend pregnant in college and married her, okay? That's how he wound up with his father's old job, to support his family. He did everything for her and got shafted. That's how he felt. That's how he got obsessed with Barbara."

"Obsessed?" O'Connel said.

"Not like a stalker or anything," Tiffany said. "Look, here's what happened, okay? I picked Joel up. This was like late 'eighty-nine, when his wife left him. I took him back here, and he paid for sex. It was weird, though. He was nervous. He couldn't look me in the eye, like he was embarrassed or something. He told me it was his first time with a prostitute, and he said he kept thinking about where we would be if there wasn't this money between us, and if there was any possibility of a relationship without it."

"Was there?" O'Connel asked.

"There might have been," Tiffany said, looking down for a moment. "I didn't want to discuss it, because it was too weird. I said, 'Just fuck me, okay?' And right after that was when things got really strange."

"In what way?" O'Connel said.

"He met Barbara up here one night," Tiffany said. "It turned out she looked a lot like his wife, Felicia. He called her the Felicia-like."

"Then what happened?" Mercado asked.

"He was up here every night."

"Paying for sex?" O'Connel said.

"That's right. With Barbara," Tiffany said. "It went on for about six months like that."

"He must have gone through his savings," Mercado said.

"He took a small loan out against his pension," Tiffany said. "He got a discount from Barbara too."

"What happened after six months?" O'Connel said.

"A lot of stuff. Joel was paying Barbara extra so he could film them. He became very possessive of her. He wanted some kind of commitment. He wanted Barbara . . . to kiss him on the mouth. And, you know, at some point, you have to clarify the relationship."

"Did he hit her?"

"I told you no," Tiffany said. "He just walked out and stayed away after that. But we heard about him all the time. He raised hell up and down this strip for a while. His divorce became final around the same time. I think it really hit him all at once. He went drinking, whoring, and filming for months. Didn't sell the videos. Just made them for fun. Then, after that, nobody saw him at all for a while, and around early last year he came by here out of the blue for a minute."

"To do what?" O'Connel asked.

"He stood out there in the hallway," Tiffany said. "Didn't even come in. He just wanted to tell us he was in AA, he was straightened out for good, and that we should be doing the same. That I should open up my lingerie store."

"What did Barbara say?" Mercado asked.

"Not much. 'Good for you. Good luck.' I asked him in, but he wasn't interested."

"Did you like him?" O'Connel said.

"Yeah," Tiffany said. "But what am I going to do?" She looked up at the ceiling. "Then, a few months later, I called the police when Barbara disappeared. And then she was found in the river. I didn't see Joel that whole time. A couple of times at his job, by chance. He never came up here again. Until this February, for his documentary. I already knew about it from the street, and he told me he was dedicating it to Barbara and to getting us all the hell out of here—once he got a distributor."

"Is it possible one of the pimps killed him?" O'Connel asked.

"Most of us are independent," Tiffany said. "I mean, yeah, it's possible. But I doubt it. Joel paid for the interviews. If there was a pimp around, he paid him too. No one got pissed as long as they were paid."

Mercado lit up a cigarette and looked back toward the bedroom, where there were still cracks in the paint and a cracked window, now with masking tape over it. He looked back down at Tiffany Kline, who had partially rolled up a sleeve of her sweater and was scratching a track mark.

Mercado held up his cigarette. "Do you mind?" he asked.

"No, go ahead," Tiffany said.

"Did Joel Haney ever bring anyone else up here," Mercado asked, "or mention anyone else who may have worked for the city? Anyone who might have been financing him in some way?"

"No," Tiffany said. "As far as I know, when he needed money, he took it out of his pension. Like I told you."

"And what about what you told us last year?" O'Connel said. "That Barbara was with someone who worked for the city just before she disappeared."

"Not Joel Haney," Tiffany said. "Barbara would have mentioned it. Some weirdo with a powerful job. I told you to check it out back then."

"You didn't give us much to go on," O'Connel said.

"What do you want from me?" Tiffany complained. "I never met him, never saw him. She didn't go into a lot of details with everybody. I think he picked her up in a car the first time. A car with city plates. She mentioned that he was rough with her. I wish I knew more. Anyone could have done it, though. There's a lot of sick people out there."

"Okay, Ms. Kline," Mercado said, "thanks for your time. You've been helpful. We may have to talk to you again if something comes up. Here's my card again. Good luck with the lingerie store." Mercado placed his card gently on the kitchen table.

"Thanks, Tiffany," O'Connel said. She and Mercado took a few steps back toward the door.

"There is one more thing I remember Barbara saying about that nut," Tiffany said. "I forgot if I already told you."

"What's that?" Mercado said.

"He forced her to urinate on him."

"I don't know what it is," Mercado said, "but this investigation keeps leading us right back to the sewer."

Chapter 13

The rain fell hard at the Rocky Point baseball field at one o'clock, Sunday afternoon, April 25. Jon Kessler and twelve over-thirty teammates from the Rocky Point White Sox watched from the dugout and used their cleats to play with dirt beneath the bench. Rainouts were heartbreaking enough as it was. A rainout on opening day felt like a wedding being called off. While it was true that the first practice in late March, especially if it was a fluky warm day, was always memorable for the reacquaintance it brought of horsehide with wood and fresh air with skin, opening day took that feeling of rebirth to another level.

Once everything counted, the big-time was back, even if only in one's mind. Whether a line-drive single past a diving shortstop, a ground ball smothered by the first baseman, or even a strikeout looking at a curveball that just caught the outside corner, you were "in the books" once again and the *real* new year had begun.

For Jon Kessler, playing baseball again was a rebirth of sorts. During most of his twenties he had shied away from the myriad softball leagues all over the five boroughs and the Island. He considered himself too busy with work, with Elaine, with building the house in Rocky Point, and with the arrival of two kids. Besides, after proving himself to be better than average at a competitive high school and college level, he wasn't ready to accept being merely much better than average in a local beer league using a ball the size of a grapefruit, nor accept the passing youth that went with it.

Then one day he was filling his Dodge Caravan with gas at the Rocky Point Sunoco station off Route 25A. Sucking gas out of the other side of the same pump area was a tall, lean fellow with a beard and a shorter, stockier man who was clean shaven. They were dressed in tight-fitting black pin-striped White Sox uniforms and engaged in an animated conversation about curveballs, sliders, and forkballs. Jon stuck his head between the pumps.

"Excuse me. Do you guys play *hardball*?"

"That's right, chief," the tall, lean one replied. "Real pitching, real stealing, the whole nine yards."

"I still play softball Wednesday nights," the stocky one added.

"Yeah, that's why you can't hit a curveball on the weekend," the taller one remarked.

"Hey," Jon said, "can you tell me how I can swing and miss at curveballs on the weekends too?"

"Are you over thirty?" the stocky one asked.

"Thirty-two," Jon replied. "And I plan to stay that way as long as humanly possible."

"Well, when you realize that's impossible," the taller one said, "give us a call. We play over-thirty baseball."

"It's a good league," the stocky one said. "Most of the guys played high school ball, some played college, and we even have a few ex-minor leaguers. It's pretty competitive. But no one there's breakin' your balls."

"Yeah, if you make an error," the taller one said, "you just shake it off. We have too much shit going on in the rest of our lives to let the game eat away at us."

"When you see some of my errors, you may feel differently," Jon said.

"Charlie Murdock," the shorter one said, extending his hand. "Glad to meet you."

Jon took down their phone numbers, and later in the season drove out to watch a couple of games. The following March he was thirty-three and came down to a local field for a tryout. He completely missed the first three pitches he swung at, one of which wasn't even close to the strike zone. But once he reminded himself to calm down and concentrate, contact started coming.

Jon was drafted by the Rocky Point White Sox that day. Over the course of eighteen games that season, he platooned in left and at third base and hit .390 with a home run and 14 RBI. The White Sox went 6–12 that season, which his teammates told him was an improvement from the previous season. There were other benefits. He made a few friends, which he hadn't had the opportunity to do in his newly adopted hometown on the north shore of Suffolk County. In addition, the three hours or so of baseball on Sunday gave him somewhere else to funnel his natural energy. He had just begun to feel thwarted at the borough president's office.

Now, as he and his teammates continued to look glumly from the dugout, the chances of playing had dropped to nil. The individual puddles that had formed where the second baseman usually stood were now one huge puddle. There was a lot of clay in the soil, so the field wouldn't drain anytime soon. "Hey, why don't we challenge 'em to steal the flag?" Charlie Murdock yelled from the far end of the White Sox bench.

"Why don't you shove a Louisville Slugger up your ass?" catcher Ed Lorenzo replied, to the laughter of an entire bench begging for its monotony to be broken. Charlie Murdock represented a possible escape hatch to Jon Kessler. Charlie's family owned Murdock Engineers, one of the largest consulting firms in Suffolk County. The firm designed everything from apartment complexes to golf courses to sewage treatment plants, and had even done some work for the city of New York.

Charlie Murdock had said half a dozen times that when Jon was sick, once and for all, of making the deadly commute and dealing with New York City politics, he could hit Murdock Engineers up for a job. While other jobs would certainly be worth looking into as well, you rarely knew the truth until you called someone's bluff. The Murdock option was one more soothing notion to play with when things got bad at the office.

Jon looked now to the rear of the dugout, to the Rocky Point High School parking lot. Water swept in broad streams across the asphalt pavement, rose and crested just before the two catch basins. From there, unseen, the water would run into a metal culvert, under Route 25A, into a small stream, and into a larger stream that eventually emptied into the Long Island Sound. This contrasted with the water percolating down through the playing field, most of which went to recharge underground aquifers—the ones that supplied drinking water pumped up through municipal wells into gravity tanks for storage, and supplied the assortment of private wells that still remained behind many individual homes. Whether the water ran to the Sound, an aquifer, or was simply evaporated back into the atmosphere, every cubic foot of water had to go somewhere, and all or most of it could be accounted for if you knew what you were doing. For Jon, this principle was yet another soothing notion.

Paula's clock had started running twenty-one days earlier. It was Tuesday morning, April 27, at eleven o'clock, and Jon picked up the phone in his office on the first ring. "Jon Kessler," he said. "Borough President's Office."

"Jon . . . how are you? Clarissa Marbles."

"Hey, how are you?" Jon asked with pleasant surprise in his voice.

"Fine. The reason I'm calling is regarding Laura Ober. I would like to thank her from the bottom of my heart, coming up here and finally having the courage to be so honest with all of us." Clarissa

Marbles was at her most regal, speaking in a careful, soothing, reserved, diplomatic tone.

"Why don't you thank her directly?" Jon asked. "You know the extension? Eight-three-two-oh."

"Laura and I are not on speaking terms at the moment," Clarissa confided. "Not for a few months now. I've been very hard on her this past year. I expect a lot from her. And now she's delivered."

"What did she do?"

"She told the entire Community Board Nine exactly what you got goin' on down there," Clarissa said. "That ol' Memorandum of Understanding was changed at the last minute after everyone went to sleep. How do you like that? And now the borough president's got three out of seven votes on that committee . . . *tchu, tchu, tchu* . . ." Clarissa sucked her teeth in disapproval.

"She told you that?" Jon asked.

"Is it true?"

"It's true," Jon said. "And now heads are gonna roll."

"Well, I believe what we have here is a fix," Clarissa asserted. "*You* know where Art Shuler stands on all of this. He stands with Ronald Arlen's wallet. And now that he's got that little hatchet lady runnin' everything down there, there's no chance he's gonna come to his senses."

"You're talking about Paula Derbin?" Jon asked.

"Uh-huh, Paula Derbin," Clarissa confirmed. "The worst mistake Shuler ever made. You can bet she arranged that whole switcheroo thing."

"She just gave me a four-day week," Jon said. "I have most Wednesdays off. Starting tomorrow."

"Why do you think she did that?"

"I don't know and I don't wanna know," Jon said. "I just need the time away from the office so bad I can't think about it too much."

"Keep your eyes open, honey," Clarissa warned like a stern church lady discussing the evils of alcohol. "She told me to my face in January of 1988, the first month Art Shuler took office, 'People like you are trying to keep Art Shuler down.' Imagine the nerve of that bitch! Who she think got Art Shuler elected in the first place?"

"I'm glad somebody finally said something . . . in public, that is . . ." There was a knock on Jon's closed door. It was followed by two sets of three quick knocks, gentle and virtually apologetic.

"Hold on a second . . . Yeah, who is it?"

"King," Larry said, poking just his head through as he opened the door, "someone's here for a street map of the Grand Central Station area. I told him he had to see the chief engineer."

"Tell him to see the mayor," Jon spit back. "The mayor's waiting for him right now, at the corner of Forty-second and Vanderbilt with a map in his hand."

"King, he says this is the third time he's been here . . ."

"Look, I'm on the phone. It's important. Tell him to hang in there. I understand Al'll be coming out of his coma any minute now . . ." Larry's head disappeared and the door closed. Jon continued with Clarissa. "Sorry about that. I was just saying that I was glad somebody from this office said something."

"It took guts," Clarissa said, "and we do appreciate it."

"I have guts too," Jon said, "but I have to keep them under wraps right now for my family's sake."

"I understand."

"That report I did will answer two-thirds of the questions ever asked about North River. I just have to wait a few more days for the thirty-day review period to end. I'm almost there now. In fact, day thirty happens to be the same day as the meeting next Thursday. Maybe I'll have some good news. You don't know how it kills me to sit there month after month and hear the same legitimate questions about air pollution and everything, again and again, and know that I could simply get up and tell you the answers."

"I appreciate your telling *me* your results, privately the way you did," Clarissa said, "the way that plant is going to continue to smell up our neighborhood right past the year 2000 . . ."

"And *I* appreciate your keeping it to yourself as we agreed," Jon said, "until I can make it public. And let me tell you, I'm sure you haven't told people, because it would have come back around to hit me like a ton of bricks by now."

"I can keep a secret even if it hurts me too . . ." Another quick series of knocks on the door came—gentle, apologetic.

"Damn it," Jon shouted, "I told you I was on the fucking phone and it was important!"

"I'm really sorry," Laura Ober said, poking her head through the door. "It won't take long."

"Oh, Jesus, I'm sorry," Jon said. "C'mon in here and sit down. I thought you were Larry." Jon continued into the receiver. "Our heroine just walked in. Can I call you back?"

"That's fine," Clarissa said. "And I'll see you next Thursday evening. Tell Laura thank you."

"Absolutely." Laura took the lone seat facing the desk and closed the door behind her as Jon put down the receiver.

"I just had it out with Paula," Laura said stoically. Her face appeared pale and puffy, as if she'd taken a ten-minute pit stop on her way upstairs to cry in the bathroom.

"She found out already? She must have informants everywhere. That's impressive."

"I'm not impressed," Laura said.

"I don't mean to sound amused," Jon said, "but it's weird when I see someone else getting nailed by her. It's like looking in a mirror."

"I nailed her right back," Laura said.

"Do you still work here?" Jon asked.

"Yes, I still work here," Laura replied. "What I got was a 'warning.'" Laura's face scrunched up in mockery of Paula Derbin as she said the word. "But I nailed her too. I said: 'Look, that MOU is a public document. I looked at it and read it in public. Is that a crime?'"

"But of course you told them a lot more than that," Jon speculated. "You told them the circumstances that surrounded it. The way it was slipped in at the last minute and why. Right?"

"That's correct," Laura confirmed. "They have a right to know. Someone also asked whether I knew anything about your report, and I said it was being held up indefinitely by the borough president's office."

"How do you know that?" Jon said, annoyed. "I'm coming up on the thirty-day mark as we speak. Paula said—"

"Why do you believe *anything* she said?" Laura interjected. "Because she gave you Wednesdays off?"

"Look, I'm a skeptical person," Jon said, "but is *everything* a lie?"

"Yes, *everything is a lie,*" Laura barked, revealing shades of anger she had likely shown Paula. "I've been hearing things the last couple of days about your report."

"Thanks for telling me so soon."

"I'm telling you *now*. I didn't want to bother you with it until I had more information. I spoke to Ron Alexander on Friday, and he said he doesn't know whether the report will ever see the light of day. He says that Paula has grave political doubts about it and is just using the peer review thing to stall it indefinitely."

"Great. Just fucking great. He's the deputy borough president. Can't he do anything?"

"He tells me he's pretty much out of the loop these days," Laura said. "He told me Art and Paula are intent on pushing Hudson City all the way through, no matter what."

"So I don't have a single advocate."

"Jon, I brought it up with Paula myself," Laura said, "just now, while we were having it out. I said, 'What about Jon's report? These people are breathing stuff that's killing them, and you're just sitting on the report. You don't go to these meetings. You just sit here and pontificate. We have to go to these meetings and face these people!' "

"Well, you're dead meat now," Jon said. "Congratulations. Clarissa was right. You *do* have guts."

"Clarissa 'Lost Her' Marbles? What the hell do I care *what* she thinks?"

"She's not as bad as you make her out to be," Jon said. "You have to remember that half the stuff she says in public is for effect. It's an act. You should make more of an effort to talk to her in private."

"Jon, that's the last thing I need right now. *You* go talk to her in private. I don't need any more of her polemic. I've had a lifetime supply of it in the last two years. The whole routine of calling somebody 'racist, racist' when they're of a different color and you don't happen to agree with them is an outrage."

"Okay, okay, I get it," Jon said. "I'm just saying she was this schoolteacher with no financial resources and no technical knowledge about sewage treatment and she almost single-handedly got the city to fork over fifty-five million dollars' worth of odor control improvements."

"I understand that some credit is due," Laura said. "Believe me, I understand."

"So Paula was pretty pissed, huh?"

"In a word, yes."

"Sounds like she'll be calling me down to chat soon," Jon said. "I can't wait." He rolled his eyes.

"Hey, if she wants war, she'll get war," Laura said. "This was the defining issue of Art Shuler's borough presidency—and we picked the wrong side. On one side we have a hundred thousand working class people trying to eke out an existence surrounded by high drug use and a high crime rate and an overflowing sewage treatment plant. On the other political side, we have a megalomaniac womanizing developer trying to build a small city as a monument to himself with borrowed money. That's not a ship I plan to go down with."

"You must have quite a collection of tapes by now," Jon mused. "Do you ever sit around on a Sunday putting them in chronological order? Did you ever think of putting together a Paula's Greatest Hits collection for CD release?"

"I've thought of doing a lot of things with those tapes, Jon. But I'm waiting for the right time. I sleep a little easier at night knowing I have those tapes. They're my insurance policy for when I leave here."

"I'd like to come over sometime and check them out."

"Sounds like fun. Four and a half hours of Paula Derbin, live, uncut. This tape is my twenty-third."

"I feel like a wimp compared to you," Jon confided. "But I feel I have to save my fire. Next Thursday marks thirty days since my report was sent out, supposedly. That's what I'm saving it for. I'll be in Paula's office that day, whether she wants me there or not. And I don't care what else is going on at that time. I'll have sweated out the thirty days, and I'll expect results. You know, it's really been a lot more than thirty days. I had a decent draft of that report circulating in this office as far back as December, but I had to force the issue just to get the powers that be to acknowledge it and get this thirty-day waiting period. That's five months of getting up in front of WHERB and trying to hold in an explosion. I don't know if I can—"

There were four forceful knocks on the door. Laura reached behind her before Jon could question the knocker. Jay Gonzalez stood in the doorway, took two quick steps into the tiny, crowded office, and abruptly closed the door behind him.

"Hi, Jay," Laura said.

"I thought I would find you here," Jay said, looking down at Laura. "Melissa told me you were pretty upset when you went in there."

"Not too upset to remember to hit 'record,' " Jon said.

"So you figured I'd cry on Jon's shoulder before yours?" Laura asked.

"There's no privacy down there anymore," Jay observed. "At least up here you can say whatever you want."

"You can even take a nap and get paid for it," Jon said.

"You won't be able to sleep when I tell you what I have to tell you," Jay said. "First of all, there's going to be a reorganization."

"Another one?" Laura said with a groan.

"That's right," Jay said. "Friday. They're going to haul us into Conference Room A and put on a show. But it's not going to be the usual musical chairs with raises for the heads of staff. This is going to slap us with a pile of new rules on what we can and can't say to whom, when, and where."

"Paula thrives on this shit," Laura said. "She's probably in her cell right now drawing up rules and regulations . . . having a multiple orgasm."

"I didn't know attorneys *had* orgasms," Jon said.

"So get ready for the new Ice Age," Jay continued. "But that's not even the main news I came up here to tell you. It looks like they found a seventh member for their sewer hookup committee."

"Let me guess . . . Paula Derbin," Jon said.

"Ted Santorini," Jay revealed.

"Ted Santorini from Queens?" Laura blurted. "That's it. We can pack it in now. He's voted against every environmental measure that's come up for vote in the City Council in the last dozen years. He thinks Reagan's still President."

"He thinks trees cause pollution," Jon added.

"And he's the swing vote on that committee?" Laura said. "When the Hudson City vote finally came to the City Council last year, Ted Santorini stood up and said he'd like to personally thank Art Shuler for bringing the spirit of economic development back to New York."

"I know," Jay said. "He'd vote to put a Kmart in the middle of the Great Lawn if you gave him the chance."

"We might as well put money down on a Hudson City co-op *now*," Laura said, "because that vote's going to be four to three in favor even if you stick Jesse Jackson, Al Sharpton, and Ralph Nader in as the other three committee members."

"I'm not any less cynical than you, Laura," Jon said, "but no matter how fixed it is, that committee will still have to grapple with the fact that that plant is up around 190 million gallons a day and is only permitted for 170. State DEC is considering removing North River's permit outright. How can a city committee rule that the plant is fit to accept an additional three to five million gallons when the state that oversees the plant doesn't even consider it fit to handle what it's treating now?"

"Details, details . . ." Laura said.

Chapter 14

Rocky Point was almost all forest when Elaine's paternal grandparents had bought their cleared one-acre lot with a bungalow in 1931. It was strictly a vacation spot near the beach in those days, easily affordable to anyone who wasn't wiped out by the Crash of '29. The only realistic way to get to Rocky Point then was to drive all the way along Route 25A, a two-lane road that started in Queens as Northern Boulevard and seemed to meander its way through every small town on the north shore of Long Island. In the Martz family's Model-T Ford, the trip was about four hours from their house in Flushing. Once you got to Rocky Point, enclosed by the woods and surrounded by salt air, you could convince yourself you were somewhere way down the Atlantic coast, or in another country for that matter.

During World War II the U.S. War Department used Rocky Point as an intercontinental radio base. Scientists had determined that the geological interference with radio signals was at a minimum in Rocky Point by comparison with hundreds of other towns along the coast. Suddenly, a dozen or so signal towers appeared along a paved strip that became known as Radio Road.

By the early 1960s the Long Island Expressway had pushed its way out into Suffolk County. By the late sixties it had reached sparsely populated towns with names like Ronkonkoma, Patchogue, and Yaphank. If you drove to exit 68, an hour from the Queens border, got off and headed north for a few miles on the William Floyd Parkway, you were in Rocky Point. Many families did just that, not only with cars, but with moving vans. By the 1970s the Martz shack was one of the last structures sitting on blocks, rather than winterized with a full basement. The signal towers had been torn down to build Rocky Point High School. A block or two both north and south of Route 25A, the town retained a somewhat rural feel, with no sidewalks or sewers, and some homes still using well water. But 25A itself had become a typical suburban strip, lined with Burger Kings, 7-Elevens, and Dairy Queens. Route 25A was currently being widened to accommodate still more development, which meant only one lane open in each direction for the foreseeable future. Sections of a four-foot-diameter concrete sewer were strewn all along the shoulder. But the smell of the ocean was still present.

Wednesday morning, April 28, at ten, Jon set the wooden form work for the fifth of six concrete footings to be poured in his backyard. Wearing only tight, faded jeans and Nikes, he was shirtless in sunny, 65-degree weather that felt more like 85 with his perspiration trapping the heat. He wasn't as quick to remove his shirt as he had been in his twenties, since there was now less bulk and definition to show off. Nonetheless, he found that like his mind, his body had a memory. A half hour of swinging the hammer or moving around bags of concrete pumped blood back to those dormant muscles like a blow-up doll reinflated. Who cared if the doll lost air quickly?

In any case, there was nothing to be embarrassed about, because this was not a public display—except for Elaine, whom he noticed staring at him from the kitchen window for quite some time. Three minutes later she was standing over him. Jon worked his way up her body with his eyes. The tights she wore highlighted athletic legs, and a musky smell told him she'd been on the Nordic-Track earlier in the morning. The white cotton knit shirt and denim overalls were old favorites of his. Her long hair had been untied from its ponytail. She stared at the form work for a minute before speaking.

"Will we ever be able to take it down?"

"No, Elaine, it'll be here long after we're dead and buried. I plan to be buried right under home plate. Of *course* we can take it down—in under twenty minutes whenever we want to. I designed it that way. It's all brackets and screws—only the concrete footings are permanent. Okay?"

"Okay."

"Can I go back to working on it now?"

"Can I ask you one more question?" Elaine asked.

"Yeah."

"Do you want to make love?"

"Yeah."

Six minutes later Elaine tightly clutched two wooden posts from the headboard and stared at the ceiling as Jon entered her. Four-year-old Stacy was eight miles away fitting puzzle pieces together to form a big whale. Two-year-old Steven was thirty feet down the hall dreaming about Winnie-the-Pooh and drooling. Their father meanwhile pressed his teeth into the tight exposed skin of his wife's left shoulder and pushed so there was nowhere left to go. As he pulled back and lifted his head for a moment, his eyes captured a vision that had driven him wild eight years earlier. It was a sight whose significance he could never fully verbalize. There, where her long blond hair met the shoulder strap of the denim overalls, where that met the collar of the white cotton knit shirt, where that met the fair, tight skin at the nape of her neck. He focused on that spot as he steered by her thighs toward a place they hadn't visited for a long time.

Eight years earlier, in the shack that still stood at the east end of the property, he had seen Elaine in almost the exact same way. On a fourth date, in the late spring, with no one else around, this young woman with schoolgirl looks had chosen to let him see heaven from the inside, and he found that heaven was not a dreamlike place where hollow angels floated in the distance, but rather a place where hard flesh and muscle let you get right up close. While seeing the same confluence of hair, denim, cotton, and skin from outside, and feeling it from within for the first time, he wondered how a life he considered to be hard could suddenly seem so easy.

The thing he had coveted most at age twenty-six was now his at age thirty-four. Why he could reach and touch this now and not before, maybe never again, was a mystery, but one that did not hold a candle to the sheer force and ecstasy of the experience itself. Where he had been before and where he might be later fell away. That day, the pine-scented breeze mixed with North Shore salt air, the feeling of the old bedsprings yielding to his knees, and the sound of this woman moaning to the rafters all etched a permanent space in his brain.

Now, part of the ecstasy was in the present, and part of it was in the past. But sandwiched between was a kind of hollowness. At twenty-six there had been the promise that nothing would be the same anymore. That the anxiety over what to do with your life, the anger over being disregarded, and the fear of being forgotten, might never return. Now, it was a fact that the best orgasm in the world could not make even a dent in those forces. Those forces were here to stay, and only decades of reverence, review, and reflection could begin to tame them.

"I may be able to get next Wednesday off too," Elaine said, lying on her side now and propping up her head in her right palm. "Won't that be great?"

"Great," Jon said.

"I had a feeling this was going to happen," Elaine said. "I did our tarot card reading this morning. Some very romantic cards came up."

"Yeah, that's not the only thing that came up," Jon said, looking away from Elaine. "Time flies, huh?"

"Are you okay?" she asked.

"Of course I'm okay," he replied. "I've just gotta get myself psyched to go into the other room and do some work."

"No you don't."

"Unfortunately I do. I have to refine the estimate for the reconstruction of the Audubon Ballroom. You know, where Malcolm X was killed? Our office contributed a million dollars toward its preservation. Then I want to do an analysis of North River flow trends. I've been putting it off for two months."

"Well, put it off again. Do it tomorrow. For two and a half years, Jon, you've put in sixty-hour weeks. It's time to take a little of it back."

"I *intend* to take a little of it back," Jon said. "What we just did was a start. And the North River stuff is my own stuff. It's not like Paula even *wants* me doing that. I think she'd rather see me having sex."

"Okay, suit yourself . . ."

"I want to do some work on these Wednesdays," Jon explained. "It would be too easy to let it all slip away. I want to show them that this system works."

"What about the batting cage?" Elaine asked.

"I'll get back to that around four o'clock, after the cement sets."

"What about playing with Steven?"

"I'll do that too," he promised. "He can watch me build the cage. As long as he doesn't get too close to the power saw."

"About the batting cage . . . ? I know work is terrible right now and you need to create your own little world where you can't be bothered by Paula Derbin or Art Shuler—"

"I haven't even *seen* Art Shuler in six weeks. Not even passed him in the hallway. I've seen Ronald Arlen more in that time. Art Shuler's like the parents in a Charlie Brown cartoon. You never see them, and when you hear them, it sounds like a trombone with a plunger on the end—'wah-wah-wah-wah-wah . . .' "

"C'mon, you can't tell me you don't feel the pressure every day," Elaine said. "I feel it coming off of you. You get up in the middle of the night, go into the TV room, and I find you there in the morning asleep on the couch, with your books and papers all over the place and the TV on."

"It's hard for me to sleep in a bed," Jon said. "I'm not used to it. Give me a floor, a train seat—something!"

"Why don't you just quit and work with Charlie Murdock from your baseball team? You won't have the commute and all this political crap to deal with, and you'll make just as much money."

"More."

"Okay, more," Elaine said. "Why suffer?"

"It's not suffering like stubbing my toe on a piece of furniture," Jon said. "This suffering has a purpose. My parents and my family and teachers all pushed me into engineering because it's safe and it pays. You sit there and draw lines and someone pays you a thousand dollars or more a week. No moral conflicts to worry about. You're more or less executing something someone else already conceived and funded. It doesn't matter if the world really needs another high-rise or another parking lot—as long as someone thinks it does, is willing to pay for it, and thinks they can make money off it. Then the engineer is brought in strictly as a hired gun. And they call it a noble profession—give me a break. Making sure that this unneeded monstrosity doesn't fall down and is built cost-effectively is a noble profession? Hey—*bombs* need to be structurally stable and cost-effective too."

"Okay, Jon, you made your point, but you could be here on Long Island designing sewage treatment plants. Would that be frivolous? Would that be prostituting yourself?"

"No," he agreed, "maybe not. Not if the plant is sited somewhere equitably instead of stuck in a poor neighborhood with no political clout. Not if the plant is sized correctly, utilizes the appropriate technology, and comes with money earmarked for odor control. What are the odds that as a civil engineer schlepping around for some big-time firm out here on the Island I'd ever have the slightest say in any of that? Slim and none."

"You don't know—"

"Yes I do know," Jon insisted. "I've spent twelve years finding that out. 'Here, this is what we want . . . now go size the pipes and select a pump.' Yes, Elaine, I want to do that until the Social Security check kicks in. Anyway, the job you're talking about is purely theoretical. This whole discussion is theoretical. Maybe there is a job out there that will let me influence policy for hundreds of thousands of people. Maybe in a year or two of intense searching, I'll find that job. Hey, wait a second . . . I just remembered something. That's the job I have right now. And I'm at the climax of over two years' worth of work. Walk out? I can't walk out now. That's probably what Paula wants me to do—walk away. Ride off into the sunset and go draw lines on a desk in a little room somewhere and leave the real decisions to people in the know—people like her. People whose job it is to get fifty-one percent of the vote, even if the other forty-nine percent rot in condemned buildings somewhere."

"Well, I feel guilty, Jon," Elaine said. "I feel guilty for making you move out here. You live like a nomad. Maybe we should never have left the city."

"What's the difference?" Jon asked. "If we had stayed, I'd be coming home *every* night and complaining ad nauseam about Paula. Then you'd probably shoot yourself. Or me."

"I'm just sorry the way everything's worked out."

"Just be happy you're out here smelling the fresh ocean air," he said, "while I'm sucking in asbestos particles from a ruptured steam line. And you know what? Maybe in a year, when this whole thing blows over, I'll leave the Borough President's Office on my own terms and get a job out here. But while Paula Derbin digs in her heels, I'm digging in mine. You know what the odds are of your getting me to leave now?"

"About the odds of my getting you to stop building that batting cage?"

"Less," Jon said.

Chapter 15

It had been twenty-three days since Paula's decree. As five o'clock neared on this Thursday afternoon, Jon saw a growing chance that the day would end without him being called down to Paula's office. Maybe he would even get out of the week unscathed, considering all the preparation that senior staff had to do for the dreaded meeting Friday afternoon. By about three-fifteen or so, fear of the call no longer even occupied his conscious mind. Of course, that was when the call came. It seemed to Jon there was some kind of strange mental cause-effect process at work that would only be revealed to him in the next life.

Melissa did not sound angry over the phone, but it was not her job to sound angry. However, she did sound shaken, like she had just spoken to someone who was angry. Like X rays, Paula's words were supposed to pass right through her, but like a small bullet, they left an entrance wound and an exit wound. "Whatever else you're doing now, could you just drop it?" Melissa asked.

"Well, I *was* in the middle of surgery, but sure, okay." As Jon turned to lock his office door behind him a minute later, he saw Naomi at her desk sifting through documents.

"You're back," Jon said.

"Hi, Jon," Naomi said pleasantly as she wheeled around on the rolling base of her chair. "How are you?"

"I'm about to have my head handed to me," he replied, "though I have no idea why. Other than that, I'm okay. How were your finals?"

"I'm all done," Naomi said, "and I'm ready to plunge back into this."

"You did okay on your finals?"

"I *think* so," she answered. "Does Tuesday sound good for our trip to North River?"

"Tuesday sounds fine," Jon said. "It'll give me something to look forward to while I'm waiting for sentence to be passed."

"Okay, see you later," Naomi said, resuming her involvement with the documents. As Jon passed by Al Gibbs and headed for the door, Old Al stood up and went into a song and dance routine that seemed to come from a 1940s Broadway musical: "It's a date . . . don't be late . . . it's a date, don't be late, it's a date . . ."

As Jon emerged from the main corridor of the nineteenth floor and walked up to Paula's door, Melissa held up her palm like a crossing guard trying to get a bunch of wild fifth graders to stop, although her hand was held closer to her body than a crossing guard's—more like a Miss America pageant contestant waving good-bye. Jon stopped short right before the threshold of Paula's door, acknowledged Melissa's sign language with a quick nod, and saw Laura Ober standing in front of Paula's desk, looking down at the seated Paula but taking a half step back.

"You're just advertising to the world that something's wrong in this office," Laura said sternly to Paula. "I've been there three years. Now I say something a little controversial and I'm gone. Not even when I asked to be. Banished to Board Six. Do you think these people are stupid?"

"You let *me* worry about how this move plays in West Harlem and the Upper West Side," Paula said sternly. "You need to go back to your desk and start familiarizing yourself with East Side issues."

"Oh yeah," Laura quipped, "I'm gonna jump right on that." She turned abruptly and walked out the door, giving Jon a scowl she hoped Paula would somehow catch. As Laura blew by him, he proceeded into Paula's office and stopped four feet from her desk.

"Have a seat," a seated, moderately disturbed Paula said, pointing to the quicksand chair. Jon quickly grabbed a plastic, stiff-backed chair that had found its way into the office, pulled it over to just in front of the quicksand chair and sat. Paula buried her head in her hands for just a moment, pushed her glasses back up the bridge of her nose, then addressed Jon in a controlled tone.

"Now I'm going to ask you something, and I need the truth. Have you been helping a detective from the Tenth Precinct with the sewer murder case?"

"Yes, I have been."

"Well, you are ordered to stop immediately," Paula said.

"What's the big deal? He needs some information about sewer flows at Fourteenth Street—"

"Let me clear up some of the misconceptions you have about your job."

"Isn't my job to help people in the borough of Manhattan with matters relating to the infrastructure?"

"Your job," Paula continued, her short black hair flapping several times, "is what we *tell* you it is. Not what you *feel* like doing when you get up in the morning or what you think will get someone to like you or what you think will make you a hero in someone's eyes."

"What are you talking about?" Jon said. "I've spent a grand total of two hours on this. It hasn't even marginally diminished my ability to execute my other responsibilities. I do it at night, on my own time, between midnight and two in the morning."

"This is *not* an open discussion," Paula said, pounding her fist on not. "We're not talking about how you budget your time, Jon. We're talking about what you do and don't do as a representative of the borough president and this office. We don't *want* you getting involved in this or anything like it. *End* of story."

"This guy puts his life on the line for us every day and no one who works for the city will even help him. What's the worst that could happen—we help him solve a murder case?"

"There are political implications you can't even fathom."

"Try me."

"What if the information you provide leads to an indictment, and that indictment, for whatever reason, is later dropped? Whom do you think the defendant's lawyer is going to turn around and sue? The borough president, that's who. And who do you think the police department is going to blame publicly?"

"Not us . . ."

"Yes, *us*," Paula exclaimed, "'us' being the borough president. *You* may be able to crawl under a rock at that time. Art Shuler won't have that luxury. Art Shuler will have to stand up and defend his office."

"Who *is* Art Shuler?" Jon asked. "And why do I never see him and Clark Kent together?"

"This is not the kind of liability we're looking to accept at this time," Paula continued, oblivious to Jon's wisecrack. "And it certainly isn't in the best interest of this office. This is something we're going to address thoroughly at tomorrow's meeting. We have a bunch of loose cannons running around here. And you're not the only one. Well, all that is going to end. And this debate has now ended. It should never have begun. Cease and desist. That's it." Paula pounded her open right palm on her desktop.

"Okay, can I go?" Jon asked, putting his weight forward onto the balls of his feet.

"No, there's something else we have to discuss."

"More?" Jon said, still leaning forward in the chair.

"I want you to cool it on North River for a while," Paula said.

"Cool it?"

"That's right, cool it," Paula said, pushing her glasses back up the bridge of her nose. "It's soaking up way too much of your time, and we have other priorities for you now."

"I do plenty of other stuff," Jon said.

"Well, you'll have plenty more of it now," Paula responded. "The Buildings Department has a huge backlog of buildings all over Manhattan that are unsafe and need to be inspected. Right now the borough president has half a dozen community boards on his back asking him to do something about it. Some of these buildings may be ready to fall, and the district managers are worried about safety issues. Some of them are abandoned, with homeless people or crack addicts living in them. What if kids wander into them?"

"Where do I fit into all of this?"

"You're going to inspect these buildings," Paula explained, "and issue an engineering report on each one. Once you've done that, the community boards can trigger the Buildings Department to action, and ultimately trigger whoever owns these properties to act as well. In most cases, these buildings have to be repaired immediately by their owners or be demolished. Either way, we're going to jump into this thing aggressively. We can win a huge amount of political goodwill in Manhattan by pursuing this."

"And how long will I be doing these inspections?"

"Until we tell you to stop," Paula replied. "At the moment, we have thirty or so on our list. I expect you to do at least four a week."

"I don't know if you remember," Jon said, "but I have an intern whose sole reason for being here is to study North River. What do I do, send her up Shit Creek without a paddle? We have a site visit scheduled for this coming Tuesday."

"You can keep that," Paula said, "but from then on just answer her questions when they arise."

"What about Clarissa's meetings? I'm a regular speaker there, for over two years. The next meeting is this coming Thursday."

"Go to it," Paula said, "and tell them it's your last one for a while. We're getting a new liaison for Boards Seven and Nine. I'll ask him to cover those meetings."

"That person's not an engineer—"

"This discussion is over," Paula said as she slammed shut a legal tome that had been open on her desk. "Pick up your mail. Get busy. I have a lot of work to do for tomorrow's meeting."

Jon got up abruptly and pushed the plastic chair directly up against the quicksand chair, as if to protect the next victim. He walked briskly down the nineteenth floor corridor, stepped into the tiny mail room, and pulled a sheaf of papers from his slot in robotic fashion. As he waited for the elevator a few seconds later, he felt physically ill from the notion that Big Brother, in the bespectacled form of Paula Derbin, was watching and listening.

He searched his memory for whom he had told about his work for Detective Mercado—Larry, Laura, Jay, Pat . . . Old Al Gibbs had overheard it, but usually either spoke to everyone at once or to no one at all. It wasn't worth tracking it through the others. With the exception of Old Al Gibbs, he considered them all his friends. He had neither thought of his work for Mercado as a closely guarded secret nor presented it that way to any of them. So it wouldn't be fair to badger them regarding whom they spoke to, nor would it necessarily tell him anything valuable regarding how Paula got the information. But he would have to remember to be more careful from now on.

Jon mulled over the fact that not even once during the course of his being raked over the coals by Paula had he mentioned the imminence of the thirty-day mark, which would arrive in seven days, next Thursday. It was a calculated move on his part, and he applauded himself for it. Tossing that issue onto today's bonfire would have been a mistake. It would have burned with everything else. It was better to start fresh on a brand new, friendly Thursday, when things were going his way.

Still, today hadn't been a total loss, reassignment and all. As the elevator doors closed on him alone, he reached deep into his left pocket and pulled out a microcassette recorder. He hit the stop button, then the rewind button, waited about thirty seconds, then clicked it off. When he hit play, he heard Paula's shrill voice with passable clarity: ". . . huge backlog of buildings all over Manhattan that are unsafe and need to be inspected . . ." As the elevator doors to the twentieth floor opened, he hit the stop button and plunged the microcassette recorder back into his left pocket. Larry greeted him as he walked briskly into room 2035 and past Larry's desk.

"King, are you all right?"

"No. I was just demoted to building inspector."

"What?"

"That's right," Jon said. "Paula ripped the stripes right off of my uniform. Starting Monday, I'll be hanging out with the crack addicts in every rat trap in the borough."

"That bitch. This time she's gone too far."

"Yeah, this is definitely why I did four hard years of Columbia engineering," Jon said, "and twelve years of fifty- and sixty-hour weeks—to inspect abandoned tenements."

"I'm surprised you even stay here," Larry said. "Why don't you get some job out by your house?"

"Forget that," Jon replied. "The gauntlet has been dropped. I'm gonna see this North River thing through, and you can thank Paula Derbin for that."

"How the hell did she get to be so goddamned mean?" Larry asked rhetorically.

"I think she was left here by aliens," Jon said.

"I do know one thing," Larry said. "She and her husband have been trying to have a baby for the last two years, and they can't."

"That's because you have to have sex first."

"They're way past that," Larry said.

"I'm sure."

"They've been going to doctors," Larry continued.

"She *needs* a doctor," Jon said.

"It's a tough thing to go through," Larry noted.

"Give me a freakin' break, Larry. She was nuts way before that.

Plenty of people have trouble conceiving. Like me. I can't conceive of her being anything but from outer space. Larry, where do you hear this stuff anyway?"

"I talk to Melissa once in a while. She's really nice, at least when Paula's not up her ass."

"Larry, you can't stand Paula, just like the rest of us. Why do you care so much why she is the way she is?"

"I don't generally go around hating people," Larry replied. "It's uncomfortable."

"Well, get used to it." Jon nodded at Naomi as he walked past her and opened the door to his office. He pulled the microcassette recorder out of his pocket and placed it in his top right-hand desk drawer. He fumbled through the sheaf of mail and pulled out a long sheet of glossy fax paper folded several times, looking less than fresh from the city's war-horse relic fax machine in the mail room. The cover sheet described it as a transmission from Fred Barrow of DEP. Immediately following it was an hour-by-hour listing of the flow through the West Eighteenth Street trunk main— the trunk main fed primarily by the Fourteenth Street sewer, from March 1 to April 20 of the current year.

Jon's eyes homed in on the trunk main readings for the night of April 5 and the early morning of April 6—the hours surrounding the murder. Using this data, he could proceed with the calculations he had begun the previous week and have an answer within a few short minutes. Jon now heard Larry's voice.

"King, could I talk to you a second?"

"Come in, Larry," Jon shouted reluctantly. Larry opened the door, walked in, closed it behind him, and sat down almost in one motion. "Don't tell me someone out there wants a map."

"Well, there was a guy in here before," Larry replied. "An old guy, must be in his eighties, looking for a map of the Seventy-second Street and Columbus Avenue area. You were downstairs. He waited a few minutes and left, 'cause he had another appointment. He filled out a request form and said he'd call you or come back another day."

"And you couldn't have taken him to the map room yourself?"

"I'm sorry, I just can't give in to that bitch."

"You mean that poor woman with fertility problems?" Jon quipped. "Imagine being her kid. You wouldn't even have the *option* of quitting."

"She's a bitch *and* I feel bad for her," Larry said. "Anyway, that's not why I came in here . . . and I'm gonna keep my voice low. Do you know yesterday, while you were out, your intern—"

"Naomi."

"Naomi," Larry continued, "was in your office the whole day?"

"Larry, I gave her the key to my office and permission to use it whenever I'm not using it. Is that what you came in here for? Forget it. Go pick a daily double."

"But King, the reason I'm mentioning it—" The phone rang and Jon lifted the receiver with his left hand while using his right index finger to tell Larry not to go.

"Hello?"

"Jon, this is Fred Barrow. Did you get my fax?"

"Yes, I got the fax," Jon answered flatly. "It just came."

"It just came?" Barrow said. "I sent it Tuesday afternoon." Jon looked at the date and time stamp on the cover sheet: 4-27 14:17. It had come in on Tuesday, a little after 2:00 P.M.

"You're right," Jon said, "you did. Maybe the guy in the mail room took one of those long lunch breaks, know what I mean? And I was off yesterday."

"Just want to let you know I got to it as soon as I could," Barrow said. "Are you still interested?"

"Yeah, I'm still interested," Jon responded without hesitation.

"I got back Monday morning and got your message, but then it got crazy here till Tuesday afternoon."

"Hey, no problem," Jon said. "You got me what I needed. You got me *more* than I needed." As Jon spoke, receiver held in place between his left ear and shoulder, he continued to sort through his mail. There was the list of building inspections from Paula. Right away he spotted several buildings in neighborhoods he could do without—one at 120th Street and Lexington Avenue, another at Ninth Street and Avenue D. The envelope beneath was from the National Weather Service. He tore it open and pulled out the several pages with the data he'd requested the previous week—an hour-by-hour chart of precipitation as measured in the Central Park weather station, covering the first two weeks of April.

"Jon, let me ask you something," Fred continued. "Is this for that murder case from like three weeks ago?"

"Yup," Jon confirmed. "I need to figure out if it's possible for a body to have been dragged by the flow that night. A detective from the Tenth Precinct is working the case, and I'm helping him out."

"Sounds like fun," Barrow said. "You're lucky you have the freedom in that office to do more or less what you want."

"Yeah . . . I know," Jon said without conviction. "Funny you say that, because this detective mentioned to me that he had reached out to your agency for help and got the cold shoulder."

"I'm sure he did," Barrow confirmed. "We were issued an agency-wide memo telling us not to get involved in that case—that the Assistant Commissioner's Office would figure out how to deal with those kinds of requests. Technically, I'm risking my job just by having this conversation. And the fax—"

"Don't worry," Jon said. "I won't tell anyone about this. If someone asks me where I got all this flow information, I'll tell them that I got it as part of my general research on North River."

"Okay, thanks," Barrow said. "As far as that body goes, I'm not a coroner or an expert on ergonomics, but I'd say you need a flow height of at least twenty inches to drag a man even a few yards at typical flow velocities of two to four feet per second."

"That's not far from what I had figured," Jon said.

"By the way, how is that report going?"

"I'll let you know next Thursday," Jon replied. "I finished it months ago, Fred. It's been shelved for a while. Things aren't as great here as they seem."

"They never are," Barrow said. He paused and resumed. "Jon, uh, could you meet me after work at the Pier 17 Pavilion, same place we had drinks last time?"

"Today?"

"Yeah, around five-thirty. The weather's good. I'll be at the same outdoor table as last time."

"Sure," Jon said. "Okay. What's the occasion?"

"I'll tell you about it then."

"Okay, Fred. South Street Seaport. See you there."

Jon put down the receiver. He saw the message light flashing, as he had for the past ten minutes, but still didn't feel like dealing with it. He looked at Larry, who had continued sitting, and who for the past several minutes had been literally, and not just figuratively, twiddling his thumbs.

"King," Larry said, "does Paula know you're working on this?"

"Yes and no. She knows I was, but she thinks I've stopped. Because she's *ordered* me to stop. That's why I've been taken off of North River. You've gotta promise me you won't tell *anyone* about this last conversation I had."

"You have my word on it, King."

"I need more than that, Larry," Jon said. "I need you to be careful—consciously careful. I know that since you abandoned the concept of work in this office, you've had a lot of time on your hands, and the *Racing Form* alone isn't always enough to fill your needs. I know you hang out in different pockets of the office and schmooze. You talk to Melissa, even though you hate Paula. Now you know everything about her—when she ovulates, the name of her fertility clinic . . . How do I know she doesn't know everything about me?"

"King, I would never tell Melissa anything like that, especially concerning you."

"Larry, I'm not saying you *did* say anything to her with even a hair of malice toward me. It's just that I know how these things go. Someone tells you something juicy and you feel you have to match it. I've done it too."

"King," Larry insisted, "I'm absolutely positive I didn't mention that."

"To her or to anyone?"

"To . . . well, definitely not to her," Larry responded. "I might have told Alex from the mail room—"

"Whatever," Jon said. "Look, I don't want to badger you. What's done is done. I didn't even tell you not to tell anybody, so I don't want to turn around and be an asshole about this. This could have leaked through any number of people. My point is that the atmosphere of this office has taken a drastic turn for the worse."

"Tell me about it."

"And I'm talking about just the last few *weeks*," Jon continued. "You've told me how much better it was in general in the old days, but now the downhill run has accelerated. I can't wait to see what kind of shit they're gonna shovel at us tomorrow. I hate to see things get this way, and I'd hate not to be able to tell you what's going on. But this is how it has to be from now on regarding anything sensitive—strictly confidential."

"You have my word, King. That's the reason I'm telling you about your intern. I realize that you gave her permission to use your office and a key and everything, but I wonder how she came here first thing Wednesday morning after being away for a week and planted herself in there all day like she knew you weren't going to be around. You just *got* that day-off deal. Yesterday was your first one. How does *she* know it and feel so comfortable moving right in?"

"I don't know, Larry," Jon said, looking at Naomi's doodle of a cat humping another cat. "I just wouldn't worry about it. My Wednesday deal isn't exactly a secret. I told lotsa people. Maybe one of them told her in the elevator on her way up yesterday morning."

"Okay, King, I'm just letting you know. You're telling me to be careful, and I'm telling you to be careful."

"Point taken," Jon said. "Okay, Larry, there's a lot of stuff I have to get to now, so I really need you to go back out there and continue doing nothing."

"Your wish is my command, King." Larry got up, opened the door, and gingerly closed it behind him.

Now, picking up the telephone receiver, Jon punched in his four-digit voice-mail code. The monotone told him he had three messages. Preoccupied, he listened anyway: "This is a message to all staff from Ned Richter. Everyone is expected to attend tomorrow's staff meeting on the new guidelines. The meeting is at two o'clock sharp, and that's when you're expected to be there. If for any reason whatsoever you cannot attend, you need to come down right now and see either me or Paula. Otherwise, we'll expect to see you all there. Check your mail for more information. . . ." Jon looked at a one-page memo sticking out of his sheaf of mail. He saw something in it regarding "closely managed public speaking." He couldn't bear to read the rest.

The second message played—the voice of an elderly man, speaking articulately but with great effort: ". . . Yes, my name is Wallace, Bernard H. Wallace. I was in to see you earlier today, when I met your assistant, Mr. Golick. He said I might have some luck if I called you. You see, I really do need a topographical map of Columbus Avenue and Seventy-second Street, which has become a dangerous intersection. I was an active member of Community Board Seven until well after my retirement, and I'm still fairly active. I hope you can find the time to get back to me. I left my number for you, Mr. Kessler, but here it is again . . ."

It was a shame, Jon thought. These well-intentioned, hapless people running around gravely concerned with issues that didn't make his or anyone else's top-one-thousand list of priorities. Once in a while, he stepped in gallantly like Prince Charming out of a mixture of guilt, pity, and duty. But that old guy on this miserable day didn't have a prayer.

The third message played. It was the unmistakable, unidentified low voice he'd heard before: "April Fool's, my friend . . . April Fool's . . ."

At 5:34 P.M., Jon was swamped by the smell of fish as he jogged across South Street, beneath the viaduct, and began climbing the metal stairs to the second-level outdoor deck of Pier 17. Though the pier had been converted to a steel and glass mall, the look of eighteenth- and nineteenth-century New York City was all around. The South Street Seaport museum featured a collection of historic sailing ships, which were not locked away in a glass case, but rather, were floating alongside the pier.

Though South Street had been paved over, nearby Fulton Street still had cobblestones, the Belgian blocks originally used as ballast in European sailing ships. And many of the four- and five-story brick buildings that lined the street leaned to one side, most visibly at the windowsills. Jon knew why. Originally underwater, South Street was filled in during the early 1800s. The structures that sat on top were slowly sinking. Jon considered it ironic that the most stable entities were, in effect, collapsing, even if they managed to hold up much longer than he did.

From behind, Jon noticed Fred Barrow's large head of small blond curls first, then upon walking around to face him, Fred's fair, reddish complexion and hearty smile. Barrow looked like he could have been a fisherman in another life, perhaps in this very neighborhood. But the smile came only when he spotted Jon. A moment before he had appeared pensive, even glum, as he looked straight down a half-empty bottle of McSorley's Ale.

"What's up, Fred?" Jon said, taking the seat opposite Barrow.

"Hey, Jon," Barrow said. "Why is it that the greatest things in New York are basically relics?"

"I dunno," Jon said. "Maybe you're just getting nostalgic in your old age."

"It's not only that," Barrow said. "I don't think we're so crazy about the present, and nobody's too secure with the future, whatever that may be. But what we can all agree on is how wonderful the past was, especially if we were never there. That's why we have all this preservation."

"And you don't like it?"

"I like it as much as the next guy," Barrow said, "maybe more. Maybe too much. See, I don't have much of a present right now. Other than my supervisor snooping around my desk and asking me who I'm calling. I'd like to take Carolyn and Amy, get one of those boats, and just get the fuck out of here."

"Is that why you brought me down here? I'm not much of a sailor."

"No, that's not it." Barrow reached into the lining of his jacket and pulled out two eight-and-a-half-by-eleven-inch pages stapled together at the upper-left-hand corner. Each page had a column of dates and a column of three-digit numbers.

"What am I looking at?" Jon asked, perusing the front page.

"Those are the North River daily flow numbers," Barrow said. "Look at the second page, where I highlighted."

"Whooa, what the fuck?" Jon studied the picture the numbers painted. The daily March readings were up in the 180s, 190s, or even higher, as they had been for years. The March 30 reading was 192 million gallons per day. The April 1 reading, however, was down to 175 mgd. April 2 was 169; April 3, 165; and April 4, 162 million gallons per day. The numbers remained in the low 160s after that, right through April 20, the last day listed.

The anxiousness Jon had wrestled with since Barrow had asked him here now resolved itself acutely into two components—one of excitement at having seen this irregularity and the other a jarring feeling—literally one of being struck—as the meaning of the data hit him. Here it was, the arrowhead of all the behind-the-scenes manipulation that seemed to be going on lately, captured in a few simple three-digit numbers.

"I can't believe this," Jon said.

"You shouldn't believe it," Barrow said. "Not unless you can believe a hundred thousand people on the West Side just got up and . . . sailed away one day. Or maybe six major breweries in Manhattan went out of business that week. Not that we had even one." Barrow looked at his McSorley's bottle and took a sip.

"Well, thanks for bringing this to my attention, Fred." Jon shook his head and looked at the numbers again.

"No problem, Jon. I've been working on the Third Water Tunnel the past three years. I don't have a helluva lot to do with the North River plant, but I know how wrapped up in it you are, with your report and everything."

"You were sharp to notice this," Jon said.

"Don't thank me," Barrow said. "This guy who works down in the sewer asks me for these numbers every few weeks. Black guy. I figured you should know too. I guess I would have noticed eventually. Soon it'll be a matter of public record anyway."

"Of course it will be," Jon said. "Do you know what this means? The difference between 192 mgd and 162 mgd is the difference between the plant being way over capacity and being well under capacity. It's the difference between building Hudson City and not building Hudson City, for Chrissakes!"

"There you go," Barrow said. "Big money. This is what passes for sound policy in this city. Real convenient."

"Even more convenient than you think," Jon said. "There's a special committee meeting coming up to determine if Hudson City can get a permit. I found out last week that the committee has already been fixed, four to three, by Art Shuler."

"The writing's on the wall, Jon. They'll say hey, look, the flow is way down. Capacity problem? What capacity problem? Come on down and hook up. Bring on the backhoes."

"You got that right," Jon said. "And they'll attribute it to water conservation. DEP will pat itself on the back and say yeah, the sonar leak detection, the low-flow toilet bowls, the metering—it all suddenly kicked in."

"That shit is just a blip on the screen," Barrow said. "I've looked at all that. Three years from now, all of it could maybe save five mgd. Thirty overnight? Gimme a break—you have to flush those low-flow toilets twice anyway!"

"So where is the thirty million gallons a day going, Fred? Right into the Hudson?"

"Either that or the meters at the plant have been tampered with," Barrow replied. "And to think this is my agency. It's embarrassing. My boss is a jerk."

"Didn't you guys just get big fat merit raises?"

"Yeah," Barrow said. "It felt like a *de*-merit raise. They just want us to shut up and behave. I think I'm gonna do a little more poking around."

"Fred, you've done enough. Let me see what I can do with these numbers. I guess it's going to have to be on my own time, though. My office is like the Kremlin too, these days. They have me inspecting buildings all day as punishment for helping that detective with the Haney case."

"Another DEP sore spot," Barrow said. "Maybe Haney was the guy dumping sewage, and they're protecting themselves by distancing themselves from him."

"From what I've heard about that guy, I wouldn't doubt it," Jon said. "Maybe he worked for Ronald Arlen and was going to rat him out to the press."

"Well," Barrow said, lifting his beer bottle, "here's to one good thing. Here's to the fact that Ronald Arlen doesn't own the South Street Seaport. And here's to spring. To April, May, June."

"Holy shit," Jon said, putting his hand on his forehead.

"What?"

"Someone told me 'April Fool's' today, and I just figured out why."

Chapter 16

It was Friday, April 30, at one-fifty in the afternoon. Twenty-four days had passed since Paula's decree. Jon quickly found a seat as the room filled with what seemed to be every one of the 103 staffers on the payroll. Ned Richter stood at the podium and tapped the microphone three times with a knuckle. Richter was good-looking, mid-fortyish, with dark hair and a neatly trimmed beard, both peppered with gray. Ned always wore suspenders over a white shirt with dark tie. He had a lean but solid build and didn't actually need the suspenders to hold up his pants. As far as people could tell, the suspenders were there to give him a very business-like appearance, more like the people who ran newsrooms and back rooms in the 1940s than the people who ran governments in the 1990s. The suspenders were his trademark.

Ned Richter was also the ultimate apologist for Art Shuler's borough presidency. His official title was Assistant Chief of Staff, but his real function was more specific than that. He was so affable that he could bring any bad tidings and make them sound moderately acceptable. With his smooth and soothing delivery, he could, if he chose, utter the exact same words as Paula and not be loathed. He went a step beyond, though, and chose his own words. Only the ideas were scripted by Paula Derbin. Paula now sat isolated in a metal folding chair in the left-hand corner of the room, distanced, but facing the audience. Having choreographed everything, her job was almost over. She stared straight ahead with icy tunnel vision.

"Okay, why don't we begin?" Ned Richter said. "I know there have been a lot of rumors going around regarding what this meeting is all about. You've probably heard that we're going to be censoring everything you say in public and that we want to know where you are every second of the day, even when you go to the bathroom. But I want to calm those fears right now—this is nothing at all like that."

In reality, it was a lot like that. The monthly progress reports required of everyone now became daily progress reports. A weekly advance schedule would also be required, describing a staffer's planned activities—including location—day by day, hour by hour. Finally, there was a public speaking disclosure form to be filled out after and, if possible, before addressing any members of the public—from a roomful of well-informed community board members to a constituent on the phone with a simple question.

Before Richter was done, Roy Watson, a six-year veteran liaison to Board Three in lower Manhattan, forty-five years old and a former black activist, stood up and headed for the door. His only words were, "I'm gonna go get myself a *job*, man." The whispers elevated to a murmur. A few minutes later Al Gibbs cracked up the room with a tai chi display and a couple of bizarre remarks.

At that moment, Art Shuler walked in from the front door. He seemed pleased with the laughter but oblivious to the cause. Old Al Gibbs had by now made a vaudevillian exit out the back door. Shuler stepped toward the front row, but avoided the podium, relying instead on the confidence and vocal projection that twenty-five years of public service had brought. His huge, jet-black hair-piece was curiously framed by a pair of short gray sideburns. At fifty-eight, he was in reasonably good shape, well-dressed, and possessed the ability to put people at ease. He could have been Ned Richter Senior.

"I'm so glad I could stop by for a minute to see all of you here and see how well this is working out. This is an amazing, unique office, with so many talented people working under the same roof. And there's nothing in the world I like more than doing my job. What is my job? My job is to find ways to get you to be at your best. And this, today, is a perfect example. Now, for the first time, we're really going to communicate. One hand is going to know exactly what the other is doing. As a result, you're going to be easier to manage and freer than ever to live up to your potential and do the best job possible. And that brings me great satisfaction.

"And this is just one more feather in our cap. This is really part of a larger theme. What we're doing here is reinventing govern-ment. The way it worked in the past was, directives came down from the top and the troops carried them out. We're on a whole different plane of existence here. In this office, the ideas work their way up, and after they've circulated for a while, we work as a team and develop a policy. Today is just one example of that. And the thing that makes me proudest of all this is that this expe-rience is working. I get the greatest feedback from our own con-stituents all over the borough, not in spite of our unique approach, but because of it. I'll let you go back to what you were doing now. Ned . . ."

As the meeting broke up fifteen minutes later and staff mem-bers filed out, Pat Truitt crossed paths with Jon at the rear door. "Was that the biggest crock of shit you've ever heard in your life?" Pat asked.

"Ask me if I care," Jon replied without emotion.

"Well maybe you don't mind living in Orwell's *1984*, but I think it sucks. All these forms to fill out."

"I won't be filling out any forms," Jon said, palming Pat's shoulder for an instant. "I don't feel like it. This is all a distraction anyway. C'mere."

Jon turned his back to Pat, who followed him briskly down the main nineteenth floor corridor to the map room. Jon pulled out his fat key chain, inserted the map room key into the lock, and flipped on the inside light switch practically in one sweeping motion. Illuminated were rows of large flat metal files stacked six feet high, containing thousands of hand-drawn maps, telling the story of Manhattan's land development from the 1700s to the present. Other items of incalculable value lay strewn about. Unknowingly, Pat's right hand rested behind him on an open, forty-pound, two-by-three-foot volume from 1801 detailing in original ink and watercolor lot ownership of all property in Manhattan. It was one of a set of fourteen, the only set of its kind. Jon closed the door behind them and turned to Pat.

"What would you do if I told you the new North River flow numbers dropped by thirty million gallons a day around April first and stayed there? Nice timing, huh?"

"You're fucking kidding me."

"I wish I were," Jon said.

"Does anyone else know about it?"

"The anonymous caller who keeps bugging me does. Why don't we tell everyone else? Tell Laura, tell Jay . . . I'm sure they'll be happy to hear it. Tell everyone. It'll be a matter of public record soon anyway."

"Who's this anonymous caller?"

"I don't know," Jon said. "That's why he's anonymous."

"It's like Deep Throat, from Watergate," Pat said. "Hey, maybe you ought to call this guy Deep Bowel."

"Beautiful," Jon said. "Deep Bowel."

"Let me ask you something else," Pat said. "What the hell does DEP do with thirty million gallons of raw sewage?"

"I think they're sending it to Paula's office," Jon replied.

"You wanna hang out on the nineteenth floor for a couple of minutes and call a quick meeting?"

"No, that's okay," Jon said. "*You* tell them. I have something to do right now. I'm gonna go upstairs and reinvent government."

Upstairs in his office minutes later, Jon raced through the Fourteenth Street sewer problem. He saw that the peak hourly flow for the wee hours of April 6 at the Eighteenth Street trunk main was a whopping 6.4 million gallons per hour. He checked the National Weather Service report for that day and saw that it had indeed rained a quarter of an inch during the hour from two to three A.M. alone, so the metered number was consistent with reality. Next, Jon divided the 6.4-million-gallon figure by three to get the assumed peak flow for the Fourteenth Street sewer, which was a fraction of the Eighteenth Street trunk main flow. By then taking from the sewer plans the slope of the sewer, which was one-half of one percent—or 0.005—and the numerical roughness factor for concrete—which was 0.016—he was ready to use the Manning Chart, famous to engineers looking for a short cut to solving complex flow problems. Via trial and error, Jon could determine both the velocity and height of the flow by starting with an assumed flow. After converting the flow into units of cubic feet per second, he tried a few assumed "wetted areas" to see how closely he could come to having the two lines on the Manning chart intersect properly.

Within a few minutes, all was clear. The flow velocity in the Fourteenth Street sewer between two and three A.M. was about 8.5 feet per second, or about six miles per hour. The flow height was approximately half the diameter, or just under three feet along the run east of where Haney was found. Even factoring in all sorts of possible errors, there was easily enough flow height and momentum to whisk away a human body. The only question was why hadn't the body been whisked all the way to the North River plant? Jon lifted the telephone receiver and punched the number for the Tenth Precinct.

"Tenth, O'Connel speaking . . ."

"Detective Mercado, please. This is Jon Kessler."

"Jon . . . thanks for helping us out. I'll get him. Hey, Jimmy, it's Jon Kessler," O'Connel shouted. There was a three-second pause before Jon heard Mercado's voice.

"Hi, Jon."

"I have your answer. Do you still need it?"

"Absolutely," Mercado said. "We have a few leads, but this case is still wide open."

"Okay, then," Jon said, "here it is. It started raining a little after midnight that night."

"Yes it did," Mercado concurred.

"Then it came down real hard," Jon continued. "I got what I needed from DEP, ran the calculations, and I can tell you that the sewer was *easily* flowing full enough to drag that body—or Hulk Hogan's body for that matter."

"Thank you. That will be very helpful."

"And there's lots of room for error," Jon explained. "That sewer might have been as much as half full at the peak of the storm, and that's overkill for what you're interested in. You only need a few minutes or seconds of conditions like that to do what you're asking about and more. My question to you is how did you find this guy's body resting at Hudson and Fourteenth Street? He really should have turned up as a piece of ground beef on the bar screen at the North River plant."

"The bar screen?"

"That's at the entrance of the North River plant. It keeps garbage out of the plant."

"I see," Mercado said. "Haney's arm was hooked into a service ladder, inside the elbow. When we found him, flow was pretty low, but that was some time later. Now we know for sure we can pursue an investigation east of Hudson Street."

"You told me he was killed well before he was dumped into the sewer, right?" Jon asked.

"Yeah," Mercado confirmed. "That's what the coroner said. He didn't reach for the ladder. It's just the way his body was positioned. One of those things."

"Gotcha," Jon said.

"I would appreciate it if you could give me something in writing regarding what you said about the flow," Mercado said. "Something in layman's terms. I'll send over a DD5 form. And would you be willing and able to testify as an expert witness if this goes to court?"

"Willing, yes—able, I don't know," Jon replied. "I'm not even supposed to be doing this to tell you the truth. I was already charged, prosecuted, and convicted in this office for it. If they find out I made this call, *I'll* probably wind up on the bar screen at North River."

"Well, you've been a big help to us, Jon, and I'm sorry we messed things up for you over there. If there's anything I can do . . ."

"Tell you what," Jon said, "don't fax that form here. Could you have someone drop it off? Someone not in uniform?"

"Not a problem."

"Other than that, just keep me posted on this case," Jon said. "That's what you can do for me. Keep me posted within appropriate guidelines and just keep our conversations confidential for now."

"That's fine," Mercado said.

"I'll send you that form," Jon assured the detective. "I'll send you the actual calculations as a backup and a cover letter with a clear explanation. I'm going to send that back to you through the regular mail. The fax machines are all downstairs on the nineteenth floor, and I don't even want to chance being seen standing around faxing that document. And don't rule me out as an expert witness in the long run. We'll see how the timing goes. Right now, things in this office have hit bottom. I don't necessarily see myself here in a year."

"Hey, you're young," Mercado said. "You could still make detective by the time you're forty."

Chapter 17

Twenty-seven days had passed since Paula's clock started ticking. It was Monday morning, May 3, and the stations and towns along the Long Island Railroad's Port Jefferson line passed by Jon Kessler's intermittently open eyes: Stony Brook, Huntington—where he changed from a diesel to an electric train—Syosset, Garden City. He had departed from Port Jeff at seven-twenty after a twenty-five-minute drive to a park-and-lock, and would arrive at Penn Station around nine-fifteen if he were lucky. If he were even luckier, he would arrive at Penn Station at nine-thirty. All he wanted this morning was sleep to make up for the sleep he'd missed over the weekend.

Saturday and Sunday had been cluttered with dread and dispute over his upcoming first week as a building inspector. Elaine had flipped, pleading with him not to enter or even go near any of the buildings without police protection. The Tower card had turned up as a future event in her last tarot reading. This card signified a possible disaster or physical accident. Jon took one quick look at the card, which pictured two medieval people hurtling out of a tower which was on fire from having just been struck by lightning. "So that's how crack addicts looked in those days," he said. Why was his thought process so one-dimensional? Elaine wanted to know. Moreover, why wasn't he actively searching for another job?

Jon didn't necessarily mind Elaine's reactive approach, but wished she would save it for other things. She did not seem to understand that in this case, someone had thrown down the gauntlet. That overrode all other considerations. Why didn't she get it? Rather than run, if he could think through the situation carefully and methodically, the game would eventually swing back in his favor.

That's exactly what had happened over the weekend when the Rocky Point White Sox came back to beat the Wading River Red Sox 10–8. After falling behind 7–0 in the first inning, the White Sox could have thrown in the towel psychologically. Instead, everyone on the team knew the unspoken truth. The game was young. If they could remain calm, loose, and focused, they could chip away—one or two runs an inning—play defense, and find themselves back in the game by the fourth or fifth inning. Moreover, it was possible to out-think the opposition. In the third inning, Charlie Murdock noticed Wading River's pitcher always threw a second consecutive curveball if he got one over for a strike. Jon quietly informed everyone else on the White Sox of this fact.

The White Sox pulled it off. Jon went three for four with a walk in the effort. His final at-bat was an eighth-inning double up the right-center-field gap that scored a man from first and gave the White Sox run number ten—the insurance run. In the simple form of a baseball game, the philosophy was confirmed. Remain determined and observant, and things eventually go your way. But how would Elaine know? She was a no-show. She was at home making panic-stricken long distance calls to relatives.

Now, a few minutes after ten-thirty Monday morning, as he walked eastward on the north side of 110th Street, just south of Morningside Park, it was the long eighth-inning double, barely felt coming off his aluminum bat and disappearing over the flailing arms of a sprinting right fielder, that Jon chose to dwell on, not the numerous signs of urban decay along the street: empty, crushed Olde English 800 cans in the gutter, graffiti along foundation walls showing stick figures raping each other, peeling cornices and window frames, one fifteen-year-old banging chests with another and warning: "You fuckin' with the wrong gangsta, homeboy."

But 352 West 110th Street, the first building on Jon's list, made the rest of the block look palatial. Like the other buildings on the street, 352 West was a six-story brick structure built in the early twentieth century. The foundation was poured concrete and the floors were supported by wooden joists. With unions and the mob well before their peak in New York, and a steady supply of skilled immigrants looking for work, labor was comparatively cheap in those days. Decorative wood cornices and concrete gargoyles were thrown in with hardly a second thought.

Even though the materials were expensive, granite and marble were used liberally as surfaces for floors, walls, and stairs. Fancy, spiked wrought-iron fences surrounded the buildings. Pride and craftsmanship tended to dominate the work. Jon was reminded of a book he'd seen while browsing through the section on New York architecture at the Strand bookstore, and one passage now sprang to mind: "Luxurious living overlooking inviting Morningside Park. The rustic and the urban combined, for the discriminating New Yorker."

Today, the buildings along 110th Street offered the feeling of shelter more than luxury, and the residents likely saw themselves as the victims of discrimination rather than its beneficiaries. But 352 West 110th Street was in a class all by itself. Aside from the obvious—that it was abandoned and sealed with cinder blocks and plywood—it had a major structural problem. Jon's engineering eyes immediately went to the heart of the matter. There were large diagonal settlement cracks running up the building's exterior brick walls. It wasn't a single long vertical crack but a similar one beneath each windowsill, beneath one column of windows in particular. Each crack was slanted in the same direction, down to the east at about forty-five degrees.

The left, or east end, of the building had settled about a half foot lower than the west end. The resulting stress had resolved itself around the window frames since that was the weakest area of the exterior wall. The movement was visible all the way from the cornice down to the foundation and sidewalk, both of which dipped.

But the situation was more complicated than that. The building was attached to another along its east side—350 West 110th Street—which occupied the corner of 110th Street and Manhattan Avenue. The building revealed structural problems that were a mirror image to those of 352 West. Large diagonal cracks ran up the building, corresponding to a particular column of windows. These cracks, however, were slanted down to the west rather than the east. Somewhat less severe but similar sets of cracks formed on both sides, also in mirror image to 352 West.

A sixty-foot-wide chunk of building between the two main sets of cracks was sinking. Whatever was causing it, whatever was devouring this section, was not aware of the party wall between the two structures. Yet the corner building, 350 West 110th Street, for all its similarities to 352 West, was different in one important way—it was occupied.

Jon walked around to the back lots, which faced 109th Street. Rather than construct new buildings on these vacant lots when the original buildings were demolished, the Green Thumb organization purchased the lots for conversion into a small community playground. But this playground, like the buildings that bordered it, had its problems too. A long, four-foot-deep, ten-foot-wide settlement ditch ran north–south through the playground, rendering it virtually useless. A concrete-based, wood-slatted park bench had fallen at one end into the ditch. Pressure-treated lumber, used decoratively to box in the area, had sagged and split. A metal-pipe-constructed set of playground swings tilted forward at more than a thirty-degree angle but somehow remained erect. The lot was overgrown with grass, weeds, and trees that hadn't been pruned in many years. There was not one child in sight.

Jon's eyes followed the ditch all the way back to the rear of the buildings. The rear of both buildings showed the same structural damage—the same cracking patterns, aligned with the cracks at the front. But here in the back lot, the picture was even clearer. The focal point of the cracking was aligned with the center of the playground's ditch. The pattern was familiar. The soil was eroding and taking the building with it slowly. The building settlement was less pronounced than the ditch itself because the surrounding walls were holding up the sinking section. But that wouldn't last long.

As far as Jon was concerned, only moving water could erode the soil that way. In truth, buried garbage disintegrating or an active fault might have produced similar results, but it was a known fact that there were active underground streams all over the borough of Manhattan. In the seventeenth, eighteenth, and first half of the nineteenth century, they were visible aboveground all over the island and were sources of drinking water or of irrigation for farms. They were also, less fortunately, receptacles for refuse and sewage, tossed in by hand, bucket, or shovel. This use of the streams cut down on the viability of the first two uses. After enough time, the streams simply stank.

Eventually, none of that mattered. By 1917 the massive Water Tunnel Number One carried fresh potable water to New York all the way from the Catskill Mountains, along with several other tunnels that carried it from regions just north of the city. There was little farmland left on rapidly developing Manhattan Island, and a growing system of sewers took human waste to the rivers, out of sight. Like a culture subverted, the streams went underground. Smaller ones were filled in and forgotten, buried like corpses, yet with no headstones other than buildings and pavement. Larger ones were often accommodated, like the one beneath the Museum of Natural History. There, the lower portion of the foundation was arched to allow the stream to pass through. This was done less in deference to the stream than for survival of the museum.

Yet, like any subverted culture, the streams lived on. They pushed their way into basements, the owners and managers of which mistakenly complained to the city of a water main leak. When the city investigated and told the manager it wasn't a leaky water main but a stream, there was usually only one feasible solution. Since even highly thorough waterproofing couldn't entirely keep the force of the stream from penetrating the walls and floors, building management typically installed a sump pump, continually moving water from a sump pit in the basement floor to the city sewer system via the house main.

The Transit Authority dealt with the problem in the same way. Streams penetrated its thick subterranean concrete walls all over Manhattan, creating smaller streams that ran between the tracks. A permanent pump drained the F train tunnel at Fifty-third Street and Sixth Avenue. The constant flooding of this area sufficiently complicated matters so that in 1992, a two-block portion of the Sixth Avenue roadway reconstruction was set aside from the ongoing contract so that the city could figure out what to do with this stretch without delaying the rest of the project.

The New York City DEP, meanwhile, was desperately trying to get out of the business of treating millions of gallons per day of underground stream water at its sewage treatment plants. The streams tended to push their way into old, deteriorating sewer walls in greater volume than they did basement walls. To determine exactly where that was occurring, the DEP took water temperature readings in sewers throughout Manhattan. Since groundwater temperature was ten degrees or so lower than that of waste water flushed from buildings, anywhere the temperature turned up low probably pointed to a sewer in need of repair. That sewer was then placed near the top of the DEP's priority sewer repair list.

Occasionally, the unseen streams were considered a resource rather than a problem, not entirely unlike organs of the dead donated to living persons in need. In 1987, when the city was experiencing its worst drought in twenty years, a study was done on whether Manhattan water rather than Catskill or Croton water could be used to fill Manhattan's huge Highbridge swimming pool. Located in Washington Heights and overlooking the Harlem River, the deep pool and the shallow pool combined required almost two million gallons initially and partial replenishment on a daily basis. However, when lab tests revealed the local groundwater contained large doses of oil and lead, this option was thrown out and the kids swam in chlorinated tap water as always.

Only a soil boring near 350 and 352 West 110th Street could confirm whether an underground stream was in fact the cause of the building's settlement, but that was outside the scope of Jon's quick inspection. A look back at the office at engineer Robert Viele's 1874 survey of Manhattan streams was the best bet. Although streams were known to dry up or change their course over a century's time, many did not. Regardless of the cause, one thing was clear to Jon. He would have to recommend that both buildings be inspected and, as necessary, repaired immediately. That meant the occupied one as well as the vacated one. In fact, he would say it was prudent that the occupied building be vacated unless repairs were made quickly.

That was not what the forces that be wanted to hear. Community Board Seven's objective was to trigger the city to demolish the vacant building or to rehabilitate it and use it to provide low-cost housing or various community services. As long as the crack addicts were driven out for good, of course. The cinder blocks and cement in the windows hadn't done the trick. To them, unsealing a building was as easy as doing a rock of "ice." But Jon didn't worry about what people wanted to hear. He had his license to protect. He had taken an oath with the state of New York to call them as he saw them. Regardless of the cause—stream or no stream—these buildings were unstable, and if left unattended, the situation could only get worse.

Now, carrying a clipboard with blank paper, he walked gingerly through the backyard toward 352 West, the abandoned building. A look at the basement floor and walls might give him firsthand knowledge of whether water was really the problem. He spotted a partially open window at the rear basement level. The plywood had been ripped off and tossed aside. As Jon came within twenty-five feet of the rear wall, he felt his throat tighten. It was as if he'd just passed through an invisible security wall surrounding the tower depicted on the tarot card. It was Elaine's force field. But he wasn't going to let that shut him out any more than he was going to confine his report to the vacant building.

As Jon jumped off a shallow retaining wall and got to within eight feet of the rear wall of 352 West, he wondered how so many empty beer bottles, empty crack vials, and used condoms could be concentrated in such a small area. In their midst was the empty cardboard box for a set of Lego. Nice. Apparently, crack addicts were concerned parents as well. Overhead, at the third-floor level, he saw a couple of wires illegally patched into the building—one for electricity and one for cable. To Jon it was both a fascination and a disgrace that addicts had the talent and self-discipline to pirate utilities but not to go cold turkey. Where was the satellite dish?

He stuck his head into the open window and in partial darkness saw a more intense version of the refuse outside. Here, however, there was also an obstacle course of fallen Sheetrock, rotting wood, broken windowpanes, hanging rusted pipes, discarded appliances, and disintegrated mattresses. It was a chicken and egg proposition. Did you wind up living here because you used drugs, or did you need drugs to tolerate living here?

There was very little floor or wall area visible, but if he could get inside, he could clear some trash away and get a better look. He stuck his right foot through where the glass should have been and prepared for his shoe to land on a loose wooden board on the floor inside. As his shoe made contact, there was a sound five times louder than the one he expected. Now he realized the sound had come from another part of the building—an upper floor. The sound of impact was followed quickly by a half dozen more like it—the sound of someone bounding down a staircase.

Jon's left leg and head were back out the window when he heard a high-pitched but rough and furious male voice shout: "Who the fuck there?" Jon was up and over the retaining wall in two seconds and halfway through the back lot in four more. He prayed not to lose his balance as he sprinted back through the ditch. His clipboard fell into a pile of leaves. He avoided the leaning swing set, his heart racing. As he reached the sidewalk like a drowning swimmer lunging for a dock, he heard the same raspy voice cry out: "Come back here, mothafucka!" Jon twisted his right ankle as he made a sharp left-hand turn on the sidewalk. As he dashed across Manhattan Avenue in a frenzy, he heard a pop and a snap.

While running east on 109th Street, toward Central Park West, Jon was almost disappointed to see an entrance for the 110th Street IND subway station, just south of Frederick Douglass Circle. While it made sense to disappear underground quickly, he didn't want to stop running, ever. He wanted to run south through Central Park, down Fifth Avenue, down Broadway, down Lafayette, up the sealed stairs of the Municipal Building to the nineteenth floor, down the hall, and into Paula Derbin's office, where he would choke the life out of her, then go to the men's room, throw up, and leave the city forever.

Instead, he ran down the subway stairs and jumped the turnstile for the first time in his life. He wanted to be caught. When he was, the chief borough engineer had quite a story for the cop, and why the fuck was he so concerned with fare beaters? But instead Jon ran unimpeded into the open doors of a waiting C train, which pulled away in oblivion. The people on the train were oblivious too. This was New York. They weren't at all impressed with the fact that he was soaking wet on a dry day and out of breath. Just so long as you don't take my seat, asshole.

Now standing still for the first time since the terror began, Jon realized the pop and the snap were the sound of a gun being fired and ricocheting off a car body about fifty yards behind him. His mind raced back in time to the first time he solved the engineering problem of a concrete retaining wall holding back ten feet of soil with a building foundation footing on top. Would the wall slide or overturn from the forces or would it be stable? There was a lot to consider—the thickness of the wall, the characteristics of the soil, the pressure from the footing.

His mind rolled forward ten years to the same problem on the professional engineer's licensing exam. In a stuffy room with fifteen hundred other engineers, he had twelve minutes left to solve that problem. Ignoring a raging headache unchecked by four Advil, he drew on all his resources and scribbled out his final answer as the proctor started collecting the exam booklets.

Hallelujah. He was a professional engineer. What on earth had he done wrong? How did that effort bring him here today to crawl through garbage, be cursed at, chased, and shot at?

Chapter 18

Robert Viele's 1874 map showed that there was in fact a stream, albeit a small one, running beneath 110th Street and Manhattan Avenue. Most likely it was still active. By late Tuesday morning Jon had filed his report, which stated: "The potential exists for a more pronounced drop or even a collapse of the exterior wall to occur at any time. This is an unsafe condition. It is recommended here that either a thorough inspection be performed and appropriate structural repairs be made immediately as necessary, or the inhabited portion of the structure be vacated immediately, until such time as such repairs and inspections can be performed."

For Jon, it had been a night of frequently interrupted sleep on Keith's couch. Every hour or so, he found himself awake and staring at a different object in the living room, each time jarred by a dream of the morning before, each time hearing the pop of a gun and the snap of the ricochet. He must have made the run from the crack house to the subway a dozen times in those dreams, each run altered slightly from the previous version. In one version, Paula was yelling from a fourth-floor window of the building as he ran, warning him to "freeze" or she'd shoot. In another version, Paula was a cop who grabbed him as he tried to hop the turnstile. She held him back as his feet moved frantically but could not touch the ground.

In one more version of the run, Jon had made it to the C train, which was now hurtling downtown. Ned Richter walked up to him and told Jon he'd done a good job, but that he had to go back in a couple of days to get a better look at the foundation. Between full-blown dreams, Jon dreamed he saw the reflection of a dark, unfamiliar face in the drip pan of a water fountain from which he was drinking.

In the real world on this late Tuesday morning, May 4, twenty-eight days since Paula's decree, Jon had written a short, sweet memo to Paula matter-of-factly describing Monday's incident and stating that he required police protection henceforth as a precondition to any inspection of a vacant building. He mentioned nothing of the incident to Elaine in his Monday night phone call. He knew the mere suggestion of an I-told-you-so from her would have brought a reaction from him, escalating the dispute into something so much greater that it would have taken on a life of its own.

Now, as Jon and Naomi walked into the Panda Garden on Chambers Street for their pre–North River lunch, the attractive young Oriental waitress who usually served the Stink Tank greeted them.

"Will the others be coming?" she asked.

"No, just us," Jon replied. "Two, nonsmoking." They were led toward the back, to a smaller table near the large circular table, now empty, which the Stink Tank usually took. Naomi's complexion was the best it had been in weeks, as if she was finally getting sleep. She was groomed more carefully today, catching Jon's eye. The new tailored gray gabardine pants, the tight-fitting pink, short-sleeve top with lace trim at the collar, the carefully brushed light brown hair accented by small circular silver earrings, all suggested a young woman who was free for the spring and ready for a change of pace. The faded denim overshirt—a throwback to the semester gone by—had been draped over her arm minutes earlier, and now, along with a brown leather handbag, hung over the back of her chair like a misguided afterthought.

"So this is one of the nights you stay over in the city," Naomi said. "Or do you go back to Long Island tonight?"

"Back to the Island tonight, thank God," Jon replied. "Last night was my Manhattan night. I have Wednesdays at home now anyway. You know that, right?"

"Oh, right," Naomi said. "So you stay over Monday night and go back Tuesday night. Where do you stay, with friends?"

"With one of my best friends," Jon replied, "A guy I went to high school with. He has an apartment on the Upper West Side. He's divorced, so it works out nicely—in a weird, unfortunate kind of way. I'm half crasher, half psychotherapist. Monday night's usually when we're both neediest."

"If you ever find yourself needing a place to stay on an odd night, you can crash at my place," Naomi said.

Jon paused to digest this. "Don't you have a roommate or something?"

"Or something?" Naomi repeated wryly. "I had a boyfriend who was also my roommate. That ended in December. He kept his guitars and music stuff in a spare room, so now I have an extra bedroom."

"Then I assume you're *looking* for a roommate," Jon said.

"Well, I should be, shouldn't I?" she said. "But I'm in no rush to. It's strange, but I'm not as lonely as I thought I'd be. I kind of enjoy the extra space and the peace and quiet. So if you ever need a place to crash, you can use the extra room."

"Uh, well . . . I think my wife would freak out," Jon said. "She's freaked out half the time anyway. But thanks. Who knows, maybe one night my friend will finally go out on a hot date and I won't feel like making the trek home." Jon shifted gears. "But you might have the room filled by then. Doesn't it get expensive?"

"I have a few months to play with," Naomi explained. "It's rent controlled and I'm subletting it from a friend of the family who's working in London for another year and a half. It's a beautiful apartment on West Third Street in the Village, and I'm only paying five seventy-five a month. I've been working my whole time in grad school and I'm actually making a little more now at the borough president's office. So I just don't have the time to get involved right now with putting ads in the paper and screening people."

"Yeah, it's probably better to keep it available for the next boyfriend . . . and his Fender Strat."

"To tell you the truth," Naomi said, "getting a new roommate is more likely than that."

"Really . . ."

"I was with Perry for over three years," Naomi continued, "going back to college. You know the band Purple Crush?"

"I've heard of them," Jon said, "but never heard them. That's your boyfriend?"

"*Ex*-boyfriend," Naomi said. "Yes he was. He started the band when we were juniors at U. Mass. We decided the best thing would be to move to New York after graduation so he could work the club scene, you know, try to get a deal. We agreed to split expenses down the middle."

"He must have gotten a deal," Jon said.

"Yeah, he got his deal all right, a three-album deal from Roadrunner Records—a major independent label. Not enough money to pay me back, but enough attention and gratification to think he was God's gift to women and rock and roll."

"Sounds like a feature article in *Rolling Stone*."

"It's a classic," Naomi agreed. "Two and a half years of supporting him, nursing his fragile ego, telling him he really was good enough and that he was going to make it. Dealing with his fucked-up friends in the band coming back to the apartment to party after a gig, smoke dope, listen to the live tapes over and over . . . screaming, pointing out every mistake and who made it. Then in the morning: 'Nay, babe, you got five bucks for me? I'm runnin' a little low . . .' "

"And then he got signed," Jon said.

"Thanks to *me* they got signed," Naomi said. "I financed all three demos they made, wrote their band bio, took the photos, shopped them to every label, pushed them on every college radio station within fifty miles. Then one day, like a bad dream, Perry is sitting me down, telling me I don't understand the pressure on him and that he has to take every opportunity that can help his career. I'm like . . . 'you piece of shit.' "

"Sorry to hear that," Jon said, "but it sounds like you have more peace of mind these days. I tell you, though, unless you got a percentage of his deal, you should have been paid back for everything the day he got signed—and gotten an agent's fee on top of it."

"Suing Perry for that would mean having some sort of continued relationship with him, even if it's just a legal one, and that's not worth it. What I get out of this, *my* deal, is my time back and half my brain back. I'm good at what I do. You're going to be surprised at what I know. One more year of school. I have a very retentive mind and a high aptitude for public policy, and I'm going to make my mark. When I think of how much time I lost worrying about his problems and who he was sleeping with when they toured, it makes me sick."

"Yeah."

"My grades should have been better," Naomi continued. "Everything should have been better. You know what the ideal relationship is for me for the next couple of years? Find someone who's a mature guy, a professional, not needy, go out once a week and have wild sex, get it out of my system, and work hard on my own stuff for the next six days."

"Sounds like a good plan."

"It probably sounds warped," Naomi said.

"Nah . . ."

"You probably think I'm demented," Naomi said, digging a long hard noodle into the hot mustard and sticking it between her lips. As the hot mustard burned her palate, she extended her leg under the table and for a moment pushed off of Jon's right shin with her low-heeled black shoe. "I'm not even giving you a chance to talk. I'm interested to find out how you wound up way out on Long Island."

"In Rocky Point?" Jon said. "Nothing that exciting. About six years ago Elaine decided she'd had it with the city. She's from the Island originally. You know how overwhelming the city can be, plus she was groped a couple of times on the subway. Not while I was around—I woulda killed the guy. Anyway, her parents owned a little summer house, a shack, on an acre in Rocky Point. So Elaine's idea was this. We already have extra land in the family, I knew how to design and build a house—more or less—so why not build a house out there?"

"Makes sense," Naomi said.

"We figured we could do the whole thing for fifty thousand dollars," Jon said. "It wound up costing more like ninety, even with all the weekends I put in. Two years of weekends, holidays, and vacations. We did a lot of neat things because we had free reign. Environmental things. A roof collection system captures rainwater and sends it to a storage tank underground. To this day that system provides almost half the water we use for bathing and watering the lawn."

"Cool," Naomi said.

"But I ran into a lot of problems. Although I know what I'm doing, I'm not a professional carpenter. I framed the place myself, but I had trouble squaring things off. I once had to tear down half the first floor walls and start over. By the end, when it came to specialties like putting in Sheetrock and roughing in plumbing, I had a lot of subcontractors involved. I'd really had enough."

"But you masterminded it," Naomi said.

"Did I? I guess I did. It's all a blur now. The strange thing is, we had to cut a deal with my mother-in-law in exchange for half the land. We had to agree never to tear down the three-room shack she spent all her childhood summers in. So if you go out there today, you'll see a gorgeous split-level house with a slate-shingled gable roof, next to a shack you'd expect to see Granny from the 'Beverly Hillbillies' come out of."

"That's hysterical!" Naomi said. "But I'm really impressed that you actually framed it all yourself. I love a guy who can work with his hands," she confided. "That was always one of my biggest turn-ons."

"Now if I can only learn to play guitar . . ."

By two-thirty in the afternoon, with an expansive open-air view of the Hudson to the west, Jon and Naomi were staring sixty feet down into the concrete wet well at North River. Directly below, millions of gallons of raw sewage poured in every hour, each gallon of the pounding waterfall passing through a vertical steel-bar screen that extended all the way up to the concrete deck on which they were standing. Steel teeth on a large comblike structure continually raked large objects such as cans and pieces of cardboard up along the bar screen and, once at the top, dropped them onto a conveyor belt.

Though there was plenty of room on all four sides of the railing, Naomi stood right next to Jon and leaned into him a bit as she got into position. In reaching for the top bar of the railing, her hand found Jon's. He made no move to pull away before her hand found some open space a few inches over.

"So this is the wet well I read about," Naomi said. "Half of Manhattan's sewage comes in through this pit."

"Minus thirty million gallons," Jon shouted above the roar of the flow.

"Why minus thirty million gallons?" Naomi asked.

"Because that's how much has been missing since April first,"

Jon replied. "Just in time for the Hudson City sewer hookup committee to declare North River under capacity for the first time in its seven-year existence. Works out nicely, doesn't it? How's that for urban planning?"

"Strange," Naomi said. "I've looked at those numbers right up through the end of last year and they're always very high. You really think it's some kind of a fix?"

"Yeah," Jon said. "And I'll tell you what else I think. I don't know how it was done, but I think that people like Art Shuler, Paula Derbin . . . they know about it. They're part of it on some level. A bunch of us believe that."

"Why?" Naomi asked.

"From day one," Jon responded, "all those people have done is acted in Ronald Arlen's best interest, right down to putting me out to pasture inspecting buildings."

"So where did the thirty million gallons go?" Naomi asked,

"Maybe into the Hudson," Jon replied. "Maybe it's under-metered. I don't know yet. But I know how to find out. That's the main reason I'm still at this job. That and getting my odor report released. I'm not hanging around just to inspect a bunch of dilapidated buildings."

"Oh my God, that is one nasty smell," Naomi said. "I see why there's been so much controversy."

"Actually, it's several nasty smells blended into one. Lucky us—we're up here on a bad day. Not an ideal time to give the uninitiated a tour of one of New York's infrastructure highlights. This is the stink West Harlem has to put up with on that random bad day when no one else is paying attention. Sometimes it's worse. A low dissolved oxygen content in the stagnant water, a little heat and humidity outside, anaerobic microorganisms beating out aerobic microorganisms, and bingo, enough hydrogen sulfide and sulfur dioxide production to make dining al fresco—or, uh, doing anything al fresco—a nightmare. Once it starts, it's hard to stop that chemical reaction."

"Was it always like this?"

"Oh yeah," Jon said. "Years ago, before I had this job or even knew what this place was, I would drive by on the Henry Hudson and catch a whiff. The first thing you think is that someone else in the car passed gas. If it's just you in the car, you begin to suspect yourself."

Jon and Naomi strolled along the concrete deck past the first of eight sets of four tanks, each one measuring 120 by 15 feet. Naomi carried a yellow legal pad and a pen in her left hand, her denim overshirt draped over her left forearm. She nudged Jon's shoulder and pointed down at the open tank.

"Those are the primary tanks, right?" Naomi asked.

"That's right," Jon said.

"They're like swimming pools," Naomi observed, "one lane wide apiece."

"I wouldn't do any laps unless you want a case of hepatitis B. That is, if the rake arm in there doesn't get you first."

"Don't worry about my jumping in and skinny-dipping," Naomi said. "I'm saving myself."

"For what, when you have your bikini with you?"

"For the Jersey Shore," Naomi replied, smiling as she visualized the beach. "Only three weeks to go. I can't wait."

"You have a share house down there?"

"Yeah, in Belmar," Naomi said. "A small Cape Cod with three other couples. I guess I'll be going down alone this summer. Unless I find someone at the last minute."

"You never know," Jon said, looking over at the Hudson for a moment, then back at Naomi. "I'm sure going down alone is fine too."

"It's not the same," Naomi said. "Making love in the bedroom off the deck, with the sliding doors open and salt air blowing in. Hearing the waves break all night long. I might as well give that room to one of my friends."

"No, don't give it up," Jon said, stopping.

"Why not?"

"Well, like I said," Jon replied, "you never know. But aren't you working at the borough president's office throughout the summer anyway?"

"Most of it. I guess I'll still get to go down on the weekends," Naomi said, smiling and brushing her hair away from her face and locking her eyes on Jon's.

"Well, you'll be glad to know," Jon said, turning away after a moment's uncomfortable eye contact, "this plant will be keeping beaches like Belmar clean all summer. The primary tanks will be pulling the grease and scum from the top and the sludge from the bottom. All with that rake arm." Jon pointed to the beltlike mechanism, moving as slowly as the hour hand on a clock, across the top of the open primary tank nearest them. "This place is going day and night, even while we sleep. And beneath the concrete deck just over that way are the aeration tanks. You can't see it, but below, the water is bubbling. Oxygen is being pumped in under high pressure to promote Mother Nature's own purification process."

"Hold it," Naomi said. She had been trying for a few seconds, without much success, to take notes. "I want to get some of this down. Could you turn around?"

"Huh? Oh, sure."

Jon did an about-face. Naomi pressed the pad against his back with her left hand and began scribbling with her right. As Jon bent forward slightly, he felt her fingers gently touching the left side of his rib cage. They seemed to massage him between every syllable she wrote. As occasionally happened at North River, a fresh breeze blew in off the Hudson and drove the rotten egg smell away.

Jon looked toward the river through an open concrete arch and thought of what he would do to Naomi in a room by the sea, far from home. He couldn't remember the last time he had gone away somewhere with the express purpose of satisfying a woman without the possibility of disturbance. Jon was glad he had his back to Naomi, because an erection was making itself conspicuous through his pants.

"I'm almost done," Naomi said, misinterpreting Jon's shifting.

"Take your time." Jon prayed for the smell of hydrogen sulfide to return. Instead, he heard Naomi softly pronounce the last few words.

". . . purification process . . . Okay."

Her fingers were gone from his rib cage and he turned slowly to face her, hands in his pockets. "Got everything you needed?"

"For now," Naomi replied with a wicked grin. "But I might need you to do this again for me."

"No problem."

By three o'clock, Jon and Naomi had reached the south end of the plant, where they walked through a series of doors and entered an area entirely dedicated to sludge treatment. A group of sludge thickeners, each circular tank seventy feet in diameter, gradually dewatered the sludge, stirring the repugnant stew with a sweeping mechanical arm. The water removed was sent back to the head of the plant for full treatment while the thickened sludge was pumped to a series of digesters. In these huge enclosed vats, reminiscent of brewery kettles, the sludge literally cooked itself for days, resulting in large quantities of methane gas. The now further condensed sludge was pumped to a holding tank until a 323 foot long DEP tanker carried it away for further dewatering at a separate treatment facility on Ward's Island. As of only 1991 it was illegal to dump sludge into the ocean. The methane, meanwhile, was piped to a gas holding tank on the North River premises.

"I remember reading that the sludge is still roughly ninety-seven-percent water when it gets to these thickeners," Naomi said as she and Jon looked down into one of the large circular vats. "But it seems so dense already."

"It's all relative," Jon said. "The human body is mostly water. It's that remaining twenty percent or so that gives us structure."

Jon believed deeply in structure—his own and society's. It was the basic essence of his job. And where had it gotten him? He was slinging tiny pebbles at a Goliath of a political system. He was crawling through tenements. He was sleeping on floors. He was getting shot at.

The incident on 110th Street the day before was just beginning to sink in. Every few minutes it seemed to take on a different meaning. At this moment, it reminded him that life was short and uncertain. This was reinforced every time Naomi touched him, smiled at him, or said his name. Given his ongoing struggle with Paula, his insistence on doing what he believed was right, and the absence of any sort of guarantee of success, could a physical relationship with Naomi be held against him?

His parents had raised him to bring honor to his family and profession. Too often, that seemed like a demand for perfection. Why couldn't a few mistakes be painted unobtrusively into a corner of the big picture instead of being splattered all over the canvas? As it was, he and Naomi had already come together in other ways. He had given her his time, his thoughts, his guidance. She had given him interest and attention, and what he took to be affection. Now, with the sound of gunshots still ringing in his head, who could look him in the eye and tell him that one incredible sex-filled weekend with her was any worse than thinking about it a hundred times?

Like everyone else's, Jon's body was mostly water. But his had turned to ice. He was brittle. Only melting could keep him from cracking.

"Jon?"

"Huh? What?"

"What happens next?" Naomi asked.

"What do you mean?"

"With the dewatering process. What do you think I mean?"

"Oh, the dewatering process. Sorry. Well, it goes on and on until it's trucked to a separate plant in South Carolina or somewhere, and you end up with solid fertilizer pellets."

"And thirty percent of the plant's energy is supplied by the methane?" Naomi asked.

"More like thirty-five percent," Jon replied. "That includes most of the pumps."

"By the way, Jon, I read your report thoroughly for the first time a couple of days ago," Naomi said. As she turned toward him, her denim overshirt swung and brushed across his arm, making his skin tingle. "It was well written, but now that I've been here, it's even clearer."

"Thanks," Jon said, more or less recovered. "It's not exactly brain surgery, just methodical, analytical thinking. I measured the surface area for every process area of the plant, took the typical hydrogen sulfide readings corresponding to each of the areas, multiplied one by the other, and got a weighted average model of how much odorous gas each area tends to produce. We now know, for instance, that the sludge digesters produce four percent of the plant's total odor. So when they enclose and filter the air from specific areas of the plant, we'll be able to say: 'Okay, that will knock out four percent of the plant's odor and will cost X dollars. Exactly what do we get for this much money?' That's what we call value engineering."

"But some of the processing areas are *already* air-controlled and filtered, right?"

"Absolutely. Like the area we're in right now. You can see it's enclosed. Remember how hard it was to open the door to get in here, 'cause of the suction?"

"Yeah, it's like a private vault," Naomi said. "Just us. The rest of the world has disappeared."

Jon wiped a bead of sweat from his forehead and continued.

"Well, that's from the massive ventilation duct fans drawing air from the room and sending it through scrubbers and carbon filters. If those fans were to stop right now, you and I would pass out in a few minutes. I already feel faint as it is."

Naomi smiled again. "So that's the air that gets sent out of those huge stacks towering over the park upstairs?"

"Exactly," Jon said. "That's some of the cleanest air in West Harlem. It's the unfiltered air that I'm concerned about. In the report, every area that's already odor controlled is accounted for with either a zero or near-zero odor weighting. That's how the model paints the picture of the situation as it exists today. Then it goes on to look at which areas are going to be enclosed and filtered under the new program and predicts what the benefits will be. Unfortunately, the city's plans don't include the secondary tanks, the largest area of the whole plant."

"You also did some good dispersion modeling," Naomi said. "I like those imaginary cones that start at the arches, then expand to show the effect on the surrounding neighborhood."

"I'm glad *somebody* noticed," Jon said. "The upshot of the whole damn thing is that in three or four years, when the whole program is complete and the entire fifty-five-million-dollar wad is shot, about half the problem that exists today will remain. And half of horrendous is still pretty damn bad."

"Any chance of the report coming out any time soon?" Naomi asked.

"My thirty-day waiting period is up in two days," Jon replied. "I'll be in Paula Derbin's office first thing that morning. I don't care what her agenda is—this thing *better* get released. You've never dealt with Paula, have you?"

"I interviewed with her briefly when I was applying for this position."

"What did you think?" Jon asked.

"She seemed nice enough," Naomi said. "Maybe a little high strung."

"She should be high strung—like from the point of the Chrysler Building. Take it from me," Jon said, "if you're really lucky, that'll be the only encounter you ever have with her."

"Well, good luck with the report, anyway," Naomi said, putting a hand on Jon's shoulder and letting it linger just a couple of seconds longer than necessary. "What are you going to do if you don't get what you want?"

Jon turned to face her. "I haven't decided yet."

Chapter 19

A few minutes before midnight on Sunday, May 2, Detectives Mercado and O'Connel walked east along the north side of Fourteenth Street between Sixth and Seventh Avenues. The air was warm and still with an excess of humidity that threatened to turn into rain. Unlike Fourteenth Street near Eighth Avenue, this area had little nighttime activity. The metal security gates were pulled down on most stores and few lights were on in the windows of the various three-to-five-story apartment buildings above them. Pedestrians walked by at the rate of two or three per minute, each of them seemingly in a rush to get from somewhere to anywhere else.

"Did I ever tell you I hate graveyard?" Mercado said.

"Let's see—you told me last night, the night before, Friday night," O'Connel said. "Oh yeah, and you told me ten minutes ago."

"Just as long as I've made myself clear," Mercado said.

"Crystal," O'Connel said. "But with what we know, a daytime canvass is more or less a waste of time."

"You mean like the nighttime canvass?" Mercado said.

"At least we're getting paid time-and-a-half."

"Waste-of-time-and-a-half," Mercado said. "On a Sunday night, it should be double. Tell you what. Why don't we say right now this store is gonna be our last one?"

"For tonight?"

"For tonight," Mercado said, "forever, whatever. As long as we never make it across the street." Across the street was the fourteen-story brick Salvation Army building. "You think I wanna go in there and interview two hundred bums who don't remember what they saw an hour ago, let alone a month ago?"

"Look at it this way, Jimmy. This is probably only the second night we're canvassing anywhere near the right area."

"Yeah, Kessler opened up a Pandora's box."

"You gave him the key," O'Connel said. "Cheer up, Jimmy. You know who I got a call from Friday?"

"Who?"

"Sarnow," O'Connel said. "He wanted to see if we got the copy of Haney's disciplinary file he sent over. I spoke to him for a couple of minutes. He doesn't have a clue where we are. Last week I told him we questioned one of Haney's prostitutes and she steered us to a pimp Haney owed money to."

"I love it," Mercado said.

"This week I told Sarnow that pimp was a major investor in Haney's porno films and had a big chip on his shoulder. Apparently, Haney was twenty thousand dollars over budget."

"Beautiful," Mercado said. "Sarnow believes his own lies? He ate it up?"

"With a fork," O'Connel said. "Now he wants to give me the name of someone in his agency that knew about Haney's cocaine habit."

"I know about Haney's habit," Mercado said. "He was clean right up until his death. Right after that's when the trouble began."

"I almost feel bad about how we're lying to Gene at the same time," O'Connel said.

"I don't," Mercado said. "He asked for it by sucking up to that wuss. Reinhart thinks we're still going door-to-door at Hudson Street. And we might as well be. Impossible there is impossible here."

Flanked by Libros-Libros, a Spanish bookstore, and Park Luck, a Chinese Restaurant—both of which were closed—Cathy's Gourmet was the only open store for a hundred yards in either direction. The green awning, cluttered front window, and neon Budweiser sign all advertised to night people that they didn't need to walk for blocks to get a pastrami on rye and a cold one.

The inside was long and narrow like a bowling alley. The front end featured the imposing, durable glass and stainless steel deli counter from the old days, complete with tubs of coleslaw, chicken salad, and two dozen other appetizers sky-high in cholesterol. Hanging from above by their delicate feet were four chickens, well done and headless. The middle section of the deli represented a concession to the 1990s, with its long salad bar and clear plastic sneeze guard. Farther back were a few small square tables with chairs, signifying that takeout was not mandatory. The store's interior was lined with white linoleum floor tiles, white acoustic ceiling tiles, and mirrored walls, bouncing the white fluorescent light endlessly throughout the room.

There were a half-dozen people milling about the deli when Mercado and O'Connel walked in. Three men in white kitchen uniforms worked feverishly behind the counter, juggling orders from three customers standing by the counter and another calling one in by phone. The counterman on the phone squeezed the receiver tightly between his neck and his right shoulder, freeing his hands to slice up a pound of roast beef.

"Tuna, whiskey down, grill cheese, Swiss, bacon, tomato, side of fries," the one on the phone shouted. A black man in his mid-twenties, muscular, with a shaved head, let these words sink in for a moment and went to work on the tuna. The other man behind the counter, a Latino man in his thirties with a thin mustache, continued dishing out fruit salad. The man on the phone now placed the receiver back on the wall-mounted hook and looked at O'Connel, who had stepped up to the counter just ahead of Mercado. The deli man was about forty, burly, with jet-black wavy hair, long black sideburns, and eyebrows that arched over his deep brown eyes like curious, furry doorways. He had a slight Greek accent.

"What can I get you?"

"We're detectives from the Tenth Precinct," O'Connel said. "I'm O'Connel and this is Detective Mercado." She pulled out and flashed her badge in one fluid motion. "We're investigating a homicide that took place on the night of April fifth, and we have reason to believe it may have taken place in this neighborhood, along Fourteenth Street."

"I wish I could help you, but I don't see nothing. I'm in here all night working."

"No commotion from outside the window a month ago?" O'Connel asked. "About four weeks ago? It was a rainy night."

"Look," the man said, "I'm telling you. I'm so busy, I don't even know if I see someone killed in *here*. And if I do, I tell the police right away . . . of course."

"All right, thank you, Mister . . ."

"Papadatos. Gus Papadatos. I manage this business."

"All right," O'Connel said, "we're going to talk to your employees and customers, if that's okay."

"Yes, of course."

Mercado had already begun questioning the black counterman, who by now had moved on to slicing provolone cheese.

"I remember that night, man. Rained like hell. I had to make eleven deliveries that night. The last two of them were in the rain. And I didn't have nothin' on but my Knicks jacket."

"Did you see a scuffle or anything unusual?" Mercado asked.

"No, just a couple of people from the Salvation Army hanging out about an hour before it rained. By the time it was raining, they were gone. Everybody on the street was gone, and I was bookin', head down."

"Did you hear any screams or unusual sounds?" Mercado asked.

"No," the counterman said, "just cars rolling by. A couple of buses. There used to be a lot more noise outside when they were diggin' up Fourteenth Street. Now that's over. It's quiet around here at night . . . for New York."

"Did anyone else who works here or anyone who walked in that night mention anything?"

"No, nothin' like that. Not that I remember. Sorry, man."

"I have one more very important question for you," Mercado said.

"Yeah . . ." The counterman eyed Mercado warily.

"Could I get a pastrami on rye?"

"No problem."

Ten minutes later, having questioned all the employees in the restaurant and most of the customers, Mercado and O'Connel stepped back outside and stopped beneath the green awning. Mercado shoved the last bite of his pastrami sandwich into his mouth, chewed, and swallowed hard.

"That's it," Mercado said. "I'm done. Finished. I'm a free man."

"After that sandwich," O'Connel said, "you don't have a little extra energy?"

"After that sandwich, I want a Bromo Seltzer, and I want to go to sleep," Mercado said. "And when I wake up, I wanna know my door-to-door on this case is over."

"You had a lot more energy when you broke me in," O'Connel said.

"Breaking you in was fun," Mercado said. "This is killing me. I'll tell you what. Just for good measure, I'll do one more guy." Mercado looked over and down at a black-haired man of about thirty crouching on the sidewalk, beneath the other end of the awning. He was wearing a white kitchen uniform, which he had partially unbuttoned. He had oval, melancholy eyes, a large black mustache, and a tan complexion that would require little sunlight for maintenance. He puffed on a cigarette and pushed it away for observation, seeming to savor it. Mercado walked up to him and O'Connel followed. The man did not rise from his crouch, but looked up briefly at Mercado with glazed-over eyes and then looked back into the street, eyes still glazed.

"My name is Detective James Mercado, Tenth Precinct. My partner and I are interested in whether you saw a scuffle or anything unusual on the night of April fifth."

"Do you believe in fate?" the man asked in a Greek accent thicker than Papadatos's.

"Only when it works in my favor," Mercado said. "So you didn't see anything, then? I'll take that as a no."

"Take it as a yes," the man replied.

"What did you see?"

"Something that bother me every night since," the man said. "I come out here every night about midnight for my break. To smoke. They don't let me smoke in the back no more. New city law."

"I know all about it," Mercado said. "What did you see?"

"A van come and stops," the man said. "A van from city. White van with letters DEP. No big deal. I see city van all the time. Construction on Fourteenth Street every day, every night for three years. Even after, they come to work on street some more. But I'm looking. I got nothing else to look at. Right through two parked cars I see. The doors open up in back. A man gets out. He takes the lid off sewer, right there.

"Then something come out of van. It is a long roll of plastic, but I see two feet sticking right out. Two boots. The man pulls him. I think someone inside push him. They stick the feet in sewer hole and they drop him, straight down. That's it. They close the hole, the guy gets back in van and drive away. Two minutes, whole thing. I tell myself every night this is none of my business. If someone ask me about it, *then* I say something. Now you ask me, and the moon is almost the same as tonight. I'm sitting here in same position smoking my cigarette. In a few minutes it will start to rain. This is fate."

"Can you describe the man who got out of the van?" O'Connel said.

"Skinny guy," the man said. "Not weak skinny. Strong, mean-looking. Older than you. Fifty years old. Fifty-five years old. Gray hair."

"What's your name?" Mercado said.

"Theo," the man said, now standing up for the first time and making extended eye contact with Mercado. "Theo Pappas."

"Mr. Pappas," Mercado said, "would you be willing to come down to the precinct and give a full description to a police artist?"

"I . . . I'm not sure." Pappas looked down at the sidewalk.

"Mr. Pappas," Mercado said, "you don't have to worry about anything going on in your own life right now. You have my word on that. We just need a positive ID."

"All right, then," Pappas said, looking Mercado in the eye.

"Can you come now?" Mercado asked.

"Yes," Pappas said. "Come in and talk to my boss and I go now."

"You got it," Mercado said, turning toward O'Connel. "Call Sarnow first thing in the morning and tell him we're gonna keep canvassing till we hit the East River."

Chapter 20

"This better be good, for you to get me up at two in the morn-ing," Vicki Moyer said, glaring down at Detectives Mercado and O'Connel. Moyer was an attractive, fortyish police artist who nor-mally worked out of NYPD headquarters at One Police Plaza. At this inhospitable hour her brown shoulder-length hair and bangs hung down flat and straight, not adequately flattering for her high cheekbones and dimpled jaw. Her large blue eyes were squinting, not from an earnest attempt to make a verbal description come to life, but from a grudging attempt to stay awake.

"Don't worry, Vicki," Mercado replied, "soon you'll be glad you came in. When we're all done, this one's gonna hang at the Met."

"Right alongside the last one I did, of that junkie who liked robbing all-night pharmacies," Moyer said.

"Hey, you do a great nose ring," Mercado said.

"Put in for whatever overtime you want, Vicki," O'Connel offered.

"*We* are," Mercado said.

"We'll sign for it," O'Connel said. "We've got a material witness in there, on a homicide case we're working. He saw someone dump the body. You don't wanna know what we went through to find this guy."

"You're right. I don't."

"It was a one in a million shot," O'Connel continued anyway. "We've been down in the sewers and gotten advice from engineers. This witness is ready to go *now*."

"Something about rain and fate," Mercado quipped.

"If we let him go home and come back, he might lose his clarity and willingness. Or we might lose *him*."

"Okay, okay," Moyer said. "I'll see if I can regain *my* clarity and willingness. Where is he—conference room?"

"Yup," Mercado said. "He's in there now looking at mug shots. C'mon, let's take a walk."

Mercado, O'Connel, and Moyer walked down the aisle through the detectives' desk area, toward the metal-framed, translucent-windowed conference room just off the main hallway of the second floor.

"I'll see ya back at the desk, Jimmy," O'Connel said as she continued walking toward the staircase to the first floor. Theo Pappas looked up from the fat portfolio of laminated shots at Mercado and Moyer.

"Any luck?" Mercado asked.

"I don't see him," Pappas responded. "Really, I don't. One guy who reminds me of him, but different nose, different chin."

"Well, we brought someone here to help you," Mercado said. "This is Vicki Moyer, our sketch artist, Mr. Pappas."

"Hello," Moyer said politely. Pappas acknowledged her with a nod.

"Work with her, okay, Theo?" Mercado said. "Describe the guy you saw getting out of the DEP van that night. Tell her every little thing about him you remember, even if you're not a hundred percent sure."

"Okay, good," Pappas said. "But please, how long will this take? I would like to get back to work tonight still."

"I wouldn't count on that," Mercado said, reaching into his pocket for his wallet. "Look, we appreciate what you're doing. It's a big help to us." Mercado pulled three twenties out, folded them once, and tucked the small wad into Pappas's front shirt pocket. "That's to offset your expenses."

"Thank you."

"Hey," Moyer said, "maybe you can commission one of my works."

"I just did," Mercado said.

"Will I have to appear in court?" Pappas asked.

"We're still a long way from that," Mercado said, "but I hope the answer is yes. If we find someone based on your ID, we'll ask you to come in and pick someone out of a lineup. But this is where we start, so take your time and get it right. I'm gonna be back at my desk drafting a written statement for you to sign. Come and get me when you have something."

"That's my last planned stop before I head back home and back to bed," Moyer said.

"Just stay awake until my suspect is staring back at you from the pad. There's coffee in the room next door."

Mercado was back at his desk two minutes later with his own cup of coffee. He looked around at the empty, drab room with the front set of fluorescent lights turned off, and with only a moment's hesitation he pulled out a pack of Camels and lit up. He stared for a moment at the blank witness statement form in the typewriter and began hitting the keys.

He would employ an old trick of the trade in writing the statement—make one or two obvious errors intentionally, in the witness's name or home address, for instance, and have the witness correct and initial them. This lent additional authenticity to the document and prevented witnesses from claiming the statement was coerced or the signature forged. Confession to a capital crime, however, called for a statement written by the suspect in longhand and a videotaping. Now Mercado looked up and saw O'Connel, who had just smacked a manila envelope onto his desktop.

"What do we have here," Mercado asked, "our overtime pay?"

"Another advantage of working graveyard," O'Connel said. "Tomorrow's mail a day early."

"Or Saturday's mail a day late."

"Depending on how you look at it," O'Connel said. "It's our report back from Anticrime. The prints from the videocassette in Haney's apartment matched the prints taken off your notebook that day."

"Sarnow . . ." Mercado looked closely at the two sets of thumbprints—same narrow loop on each, same angular delta in the same position. "This is good news. We should go back and get a written statement from that super. Call Sarnow in the morning and tell him we think a loan shark was into Haney."

"There's more," O'Connel said. "There was another set of prints on the cassette and also on the bag of coke, and a couple spots that were dusted. They ran it through the FBI database and got a match. The prints belong to a Jerome S. Patterson, with a prior. Did seven years in Ossining for manslaughter. There's his photo."

Mercado flipped to the next page of the report, which had pasted to it a black and white shot of a white male in his early thirties with short, dark wavy hair, a narrow nose and angular chin, and icy eyes that stared like the dim lights of a train emerging from a tunnel.

"Hmm," Mercado said, "this guy was released in 'eighty-three, and this photo was taken in 'seventy-six. I wonder what he looks like today."

"At least we know he's got great taste in movies," O'Connel said.

"And drugs," Mercado said, continuing to leaf through the report. "It says here the cocaine was . . . cocaine. And we didn't get to keep any. That's okay—more left over for Sarnow."

"So what've we got here?" O'Connel asked aloud as she logged on to her IBM 486 computer terminal, which was hooked into the police department's central database. "Sarnow is desperate to cover up a murder committed by someone in his department—in DEP. He and some ex-con get into Haney's apartment and leave suggestive items around. Then he comes here and tells us Haney's all wrong. Jimmy, look at what it says for previous occupation. Patterson was an assistant plumber before Sing Sing. Maybe Patterson's the guy who dumped Haney's body."

"And maybe Sarnow is the one in the back of the truck, pushing," Mercado added. "I don't know. Does someone walk out of Sing Sing after a capital offense and get a job with the Department of Environmental Protection? Not so easily. Then again, I had a record before I was on the job. But that was a record for scoring with girls from FIT."

"He doesn't need to be a DEP employee, Jimmy. He just needs to have access to a DEP van. Our friend Sarnow could have given him that."

"You could be right," Mercado said. "But we can't rule out his working for the city. Maybe under a different name."

"I'm running him through now under 'Patterson,'" O'Connel said.

"Look," Mercado said, "I'm all for making life easy. I hope the city has a skel-hiring program funded by Albany and that Patterson is their poster child. I hope he lights up your screen with a couple of employee-of-the-month awards. Then we pull his address, get a warrant, pick him up, get Pappas back in here for a lineup, have him charged, and send him back up the sewer to the pen, maybe with Sarnow paddling a little boat right behind him."

"But," O'Connel said, her shoulders now slumping, her eyes looking down and away from the screen, "it can't be that easy."

"Nothing?"

"Nothing," O'Connel confirmed. "I have fifty-eight other Pattersons, four of them with DEP, but no 'Jerome S.'"

"Tell you what," Mercado said, "let's pick up Sarnow and tune him up anyway. It'll be fun. I promise I won't smoke."

"Sure," O'Connel said, waving away Camel fumes, "starting now."

The room fell silent and continued to fill with smoke for twenty minutes as Mercado typed out the witness statement and O'Connel hacked away at various computer files containing criminal histories or personnel records. Now, once more scrutinizing the printout of Jerome S. Patterson's conviction record, Mercado leaned back and looked toward O'Connel.

"I'll tell you, he could have done it. He could have hit Haney hard enough on the back of the head to kill him. Six-three, 190, tough-looking, but basically a weasel. Killed this guy in 1976 in a barroom brawl. Hit him with a chair. Victim was a union rep— bricklayer's local."

"If it is him, he's learned to have fewer witnesses," O'Connel said.

"Not few enough," Mercado said, looking again at Patterson's photo. "I don't know, maybe I'm pushing it here. I just don't like the look in his eyes. I wish we knew what the hell he looked like today."

"Maybe like this," Vicki Moyer said, dropping her pad with the freshly completed sketch onto Mercado's desktop. Mercado pored over the individual facial features in the sketch, then refocused his eyes to take in the whole entity. He looked back at the file photo of Patterson and back over again at the sketch.

"Same guy," Mercado said.

"Pappas still in there?" O'Connel asked.

"Yeah, and restless," Moyer said. "Can't wait to spend his sixty dollars."

O'Connel got up and leaned over Mercado's shoulder to look at both images. "I think you really got something there, Vicki," she said. "I'll tell you, though, if it's him, this perp aged a lot in seventeen years."

"Haven't we all?" Moyer said.

"Not like this guy," O'Connel said. "Look how buff he was here and how gaunt he is here. I guess the joint wasn't too kind to him. Or the 'eighties weren't. And how 'bout this scar on his left cheek? That wasn't there when he went in."

"Love in the joint can be hell," Mercado said.

"So can trading on Wall Street," Moyer said. "But I still see a strong resemblance. Now I'm gonna go home and study the resemblance between the end cushions on my sofa bed." She slumped in the extra chair near O'Connel's desk.

"Here's where we really need Sarnow," O'Connel said, "to let us have a good look at DEP's personnel folders and see if we can come up with a match. But I'll bet you my pension we're handed a stack of folders minus Jerome S. Patterson—if they have one to begin with."

"Whatsamatter, Janine," Mercado said, "I thought you had access to everything through your computer."

"By the time the whole city goes on-line," O'Connel said, "I'll be collecting my pension. It takes real work to actually scan in all those photos and files."

"If we wanna poke around without tipping off Sarnow," Mercado said, "why don't we start with that guy Sharpe from Haney's old crew? He doesn't strike me as much of a company man. Maybe he'll recognize Patterson, or maybe one of the other guys in the crew will." Mercado paused, looked at the composite, looked over at his city Green Book directory, and continued. "Better yet, let's pay a visit to the New York City Department of Personnel."

"And sift through thousands of personnel folders?" O'Connel said.

"Sure, why not? Work the case the old-fashioned way," Mercado said.

"Hate to admit it, Jimmy, but you're right," O'Connel said. "They have the same information over there that DEP's internal department of personnel has . . . maybe more."

"There are two sides to every coin," Mercado observed. "On the downside, the city has wasted millions upon millions of dollars having agencies duplicate each other's functions. On the upside, folks like Sarnow can't put a stranglehold on the flow of information." O'Connel glanced at the clock on the wall, which read 3:05.

"Well, if we finish these fives by three-thirty," O'Connel said, "we should be able to get some sleep and get down to Personnel by lunchtime."

"Lunchtime?" Mercado said, putting out his butt in an Arlen Armada ashtray. "That's pushing it."

"I'll give you a wake-up call," Moyer said.

Chapter 21

Thursday morning, May 6, ten o'clock, was the time Jon Kessler had focused on during a sleepless Wednesday night, a dream-shrouded train and subway ride in, and thirty-seven aimless minutes of shifting papers upstairs in his office. It was D-Day, thirty days since the decree. By 10:20 A.M., he'd already walked past Paula's office six times. Each time, Paula was on the telephone, her free hand moving from the inside of her hair, down to a fat folder, then back up to the bridge of her glasses. As of sighting number four, the free hand was fully engaged in the task of organizing her desktop. Jon could have walked in anytime. The telephone conversations did not appear to be overly important, so there was little risk of any stray bullets hitting him. But that wasn't enough. The beauty of walking in cold on somebody, he knew, was that you controlled the moment. If that person was on the phone, they controlled the moment. He would have to sit in the quicksand chair while Paula choreographed his waiting with her eyes and her hand signals.

The seventh pass was the lucky one. Paula was off the phone. Jon walked right by Melissa, whose head was buried in something else. Paula looked up from her desk as he strode in.

"Yes . . ."

"We need to talk," Jon said.

"I have three minutes and that's it," Paula said. "If you think it's going to take longer, get my schedule book from Melissa and schedule something. I have a lot going on right now."

"It shouldn't take long—"

Paula's phone rang. Advantage Paula. It was a worst-case scenario. Paula was obsequious on the phone, seeming to yield to every point made or order given by the person on the other end. Including Art Shuler, there were only a few known individuals who could accomplish this.

Jon knew the principle. When it came to tyrants, a perverted kind of equilibrium had to be achieved. When she took it on the chin, she had to deliver a knock-out blow to someone else within a matter of minutes. He glanced at the door and considered making a quick exit, perhaps returning sometime later in the day. No sooner had this option crossed his mind than Paula's eyes caught his. She held up her free index finger, signaling that she would be only a minute. There were no spare chairs in the room—just the quicksand chair. Jon stood alongside it, determined now, his back against Paula's wall.

"Yes, well, let's call this one my oversight," Paula said into the receiver. "I'll pull her files and give you a written summary . . . It is a priority . . . It will happen today . . . Your position is the right one . . . It's the same one I would have to take . . . Okay . . . Okay, that will be fine." Paula placed the receiver down gently in an exaggerated fashion. The same hand that had held the receiver now held her head for a moment in self-consolation and disgust. Recovering quickly, she sat up and looked straight at Jon on a rising angle.

"I got your memo," she said with no emotion. "In light of the circumstances, it's not unreasonable for you to request a police escort to a vacated building."

"I was *shot* at."

"Have you reported it to the police?"

"No," Jon replied.

"You need to do that immediately," Paula replied. "As far as future inspections are concerned, you need to coordinate those through the district manager of each community board a day or two in advance. Ned Richter is putting out a general memo to the D.M.s making them aware of your situation."

"That's fine," Jon said, "but the reason I came in was to talk to you about my report."

"What about your report?"

"Remember you told me the review process would be done in a month?" Jon began. "That was thirty days ago today. I'd like to know the status."

"The status is it is *being reviewed*," Paula responded, with two quick flaps of her short black hair. "Furthermore, the status of our relationship as supervisor and supervisee is that you are not in any way entitled to hold me to some arbitrary number mentioned offhandedly in a conversation a long time ago."

"That's right. It *was* a long time ago."

"In the context of policy that this office carefully developed over the course of years, it's nothing. It's a minute. It's a second," Paula argued, now in more heated fashion. "And the notion that one day you pressure me into saying . . . *something,* and then sit upstairs glibly counting off the days . . . is disturbing, to say the least. It's reprehensible. If I held every one of you to deadlines you mentioned offhandedly, none of you would have jobs left."

"I have nothing else to go by except what you say," Jon replied, combatively now.

"Then go by this," Paula fired back. "Take another month. We're very busy here. Your personal deadlines are not part of the picture. You are overreacting again, Jon. You're overreacting."

"Another month is unacceptable," Jon asserted. "This report has now taken about as much time to review as it did to develop. This is a farce. I could review an equivalent report in two days. Give me the name of the consultant."

"That information is confidential," Paula said.

"That's unacceptable too," Jon said. "Do you realize how much hydrogen sulfide and sulfur dioxide is being released daily, not to mention a host of other noxious gases? We're just letting the months go by, letting it happen. Do you realize what these people are breathing?"

"I don't care what the fuck those people are breathing!" Paula barked, now beet-red. "I've been hearing this shit like a mantra from day one, and I have had it up to here. These people have a hidden agenda to stop all legitimate development below 110th Street out of political spite, expedience, and one-upmanship. They are simply using this issue as a means to that end and blowing it way out of proportion. And *you're* too stupid to see it. Without some guidance, Jon, you're totally lost."

"I'm not going up to that meeting tonight and giving the same old bullshit," Jon said. "These people pay your salary, Paula, and *you're* too stupid to see it."

"Don't you ever speak to me like that!" Paula yelled. "All I have to do is pick up the phone, tell Art Shuler this is not working out, and you are history here. You can tell these people tonight in West Harlem whose *asses* you kiss that this will be your last meeting, period. You have other duties to take care of. In fact, you're done. I don't want you there tonight. I'll have David Saunders cover it."

"It's not so simple," Jon said with self-restraint. He turned and walked out the door, but jerked his head around for a moment as Paula shouted one last time.

"Kiss those Wednesdays off good-bye right now! I want you here nine A.M. sharp every Wednesday! And I expect to see three inspection reports on my desk by Monday!"

Jon turned his head and continued walking, past Melissa and down the hall. He bypassed the mail room, walked straight to the elevator, and returned the hello of no one who crossed his path. On the twentieth floor he walked right past a map seeker, past Al, past Larry, and past Naomi. As he put his key in the lock, Larry spoke.

"King—"

"No disturbances," Jon shot back. "I mean it this time." Jon closed and locked the door behind him. He pulled the micro-cassette recorder out from his left pants pocket and tucked it inside his right-hand top desk drawer. He ignored the flashing message light on his phone and turned the ringer off. He didn't care about visiting the dilapidated building on the Lower East Side, which was next on his schedule. What he cared about was closing his sleep deficit from the night before. He threw a spare jacket on the floor in the corner, on the carpet, and began to stretch out. For the next couple of hours, no one could touch him in his little box, tucked away in partial darkness two hundred feet above Manhattan's hot, thankless pavement. He would now hide in a box within a box, disappearing within the confines of his own brain. Even here was less safe than it used to be. But sleep was still the thing. Maybe he would wake up with some answers.

At 6:48 that same Thursday evening, Jon bumped into David Saunders at the entrance to the community room of 626 Riverside Drive. Jon saw the awkwardness of the situation spelled out all over David's face. At twenty-five, Saunders—a petite version of Cary Grant—did his job and wore few battle scars. His work doing economic analysis on city budgetary issues and occasionally filling in for the liaisons had brought him three modest pay raises and praise from above in the space of eighteen months at the borough president's office. In this short period, he hadn't gone looking for conflict, and it hadn't come looking for him. But those days were over.

"Hi, David," Jon said flatly.

"Jon, I know this is an uncomfortable situation," David began. "I know you have a long history up here and a role you've established, and I'm not trying to usurp that."

"Good," Jon said.

"Since you decided to show," David continued, "I'll defer to you this time and not even get up there and say anything, so you can just go up and say whatever you had planned to say, and I'll just tell Paula that Clarissa Marbles insisted that you say something since it was your last . . . official visit, and that I felt I had nothing to add to that."

"Deal," Jon said.

Inside, Jon took his usual seat in a folding chair in the ninth row. David took a seat five rows farther back. Various regulars, most of them West Harlem residents, waved or nodded a greeting to Jon as they milled about and looked for a seat themselves. Though Jon acknowledged them in return, his uncharacteristic blank expression told them not to bother starting a conversation. Only Clarissa Marbles herself had the guts to invade his space. On her way up to the dais, she stepped into the ninth row and leaned in to talk to him. "Did you get a chance to thank Laura for me?" she asked.

"Yeah."

"What she did took courage," Clarissa said.

"Yeah."

"And I know she and I have had our differences, but I respect what she did," Clarissa added.

"Uh-huh."

"She made us proud." Clarissa stepped away and continued her trek to the front.

It was one of the worst-smelling days of the year. The rotten egg hydrogen sulfide stench, along with other chemically related stenches, came wafting in the windows not unlike tear gas that preceded a raid, though these gases were invisible. There was no hiding from or ignoring the gas today. On less intense days, the nose eventually became numb. Today, the intensity was enough to affect the eyes, and eyes never went numb. It was not even a particularly hot spring day for New York, but the building custodian turned on the three air conditioners serving the room and began shutting the windows. The smell and the tears were evident in Clarissa Marbles's voice and her scowl as she called the meeting to order.

"I am Clarissa Marbles for those of you who don't know me. I am the chairperson of the West Harlem Environmental Review Board. Welcome, all of you, to our monthly meeting. We've got a full agenda tonight, and I want to get right to it. Unless y'all came in here in a bubble, you know this is a particularly horrendous day among many horrendous days. That our government would allow us to live this way is an affront to me, as I'm certain it is to you.

There is no choice for us but to fight. We've lived here for years, most of us before there ever was a plant. We've invested in this community, and are in no position to run away somewhere. And even for the few of us who could run away, that just don't sit right. And it solves absolutely nothin'.

"But they've got some other ideas downtown. They're gonna let Mr. Ronald Arlen build a huge development on prime real estate, pocket the profits, and send the sewage uptown to you and me, where this stinkin' plant has proved, day in, day out, it simply cannot take it. But they figure *us* folk are gonna sit here and take it . . . sit here and smell it. But *are* we?"

A thunderous, spontaneous "No!" burst from the audience of over two hundred, with an angry "Hell no!" a defiant "No way!" and an outraged "Unite!" cutting through the storm of sound. Clarissa's scowl let up for only a second before she concluded.

"Then let us start, as we always do, with Mr. Edward H. Connor, area engineer for DEP. Mr. Connor will be reporting to us on the odor monitoring devices they have installed in our neighborhood." Sitting at the dais, Connor looked pale, tentative, and even more reluctant than usual to address the anxious faces.

"Thank you, Ms. Marbles."

"*Chairperson* Marbles."

"Chairperson Marbles," he proceeded. "As you know, we've installed seven air pollutant monitors at different locations in the neighborhood. I'm sure you've seen them by now. They're approximately four feet by four feet, and seven feet high, with a steel casing housing the actual unit inside. These units will be giving hourly readings of several pollutants, including hydrogen sulfide, sulfur dioxide, carbon monoxide. This past month, our engineers identified and corrected a number of problems with these units—"

"When?" a tall Latino man with angular features, glasses, in his early thirties shouted from the back of the room. "*When* do we find out what we're breathing?"

"We were supposed to find out six months ago," a heavyset forty-year-old white woman with bouffant hair added aloud from the fourteenth row. A wave of muttering passed from the rear to the front of the room and back again. Connor tried to hold back the flood.

"Believe me, we are closer than ever to being where we want to be—"

"This is a farce," a tall, bespectacled black man in his late forties said as he stood for a moment by his seat in the tenth row for all to see. "This is like that math problem when you move half the remaining distance to the goal line each time, but you never *get* to the goal line. Mr. Connor, we want to get to the damn goal line."

The room exploded with a powerful mixture of approval and indignation, temporarily dwarfing other sounds, thoughts, and smells. Connor lifted his right hand meekly, slowly, with resignation, and tried to continue.

"I know this is not what you want to hear or deserve to hear, but these are very sensitive, complex, instrumentation systems, and they need to be constantly calibrated and recalibrated. It would be irresponsible for our agency to issue numerical readings of any sort until we were confident of those numbers." Groans pervaded the room, reaching where even hydrogen sulfide could not.

"Mr. Connor," Clarissa Marbles said, "are you prepared to explain to us what each component of the system does, and precisely what is wrong with it?"

"I could begin to tell you some of it," Connor responded, "but I couldn't go on in depth and do it justice at this time."

"Fine," Clarissa concluded, "no use in embarrassing yourself anymore. You come back next month with a full report on those components, unless of course you give us all a heart attack and actually tell us what we wanted in the first place."

"Yes, that would be fine," Connor said.

"Thank you very much then, Mr. Connor. Next on our agenda, we have Mr. Jon Kessler, chief engineer from the borough president's office."

Jon approached the dais more relaxed than he had felt in a year, as if a weight had suddenly come right off his shoulders. He sat on the main table, instead of behind it, his arms bracing him, his feet just reaching the floor as he faced the audience. The words rolled off with little effort.

"First, I'd like to apologize to all of you. I had a whole speech worth of bullshit worked out in my head, but I forgot all of it on my way up here. So instead, I'll have to improvise by telling you the deep dark secrets of North River."

Scattered hushed conversations throughout the audience evaporated into silence.

"Hydrogen sulfide is a noxious gas given off during biological decomposition. You breathe it every day. You're breathing it right now. So am I. When that gas exceeds ten parts per billion in the air you breathe, the human nose can smell it. At twenty, thirty, or forty parts per billion, the symptoms get worse . . . eye irritation, throat irritation, respiratory difficulty, fatigue. I'm sure you're familiar with these too. The hydrogen sulfide level of the air here is almost always over ten ppb. It's often over forty. Sometimes it's over a hundred. And that's after it's been dispersed over several hundred feet between here and the plant. As you get closer to the plant, that concentration intensifies, of course. These are not *my* numbers, by the way. These are numbers the Department of Environmental Protection has on file. I was allowed to see them because I work for the borough president. And only after I badgered everybody and promised I wouldn't do something irresponsible . . . like this."

The room was quiet enough not only to hear the hum of the air conditioners, but to hear when their compressors kicked in. All eyes were intensely focused on Jon, including the few people sitting to his sides and behind him on the dais. It felt like theater in the round.

"Those are the raw numbers. What analysis have I done? Well, I'll tell you. You've been told again and again for months that whatever the air pollution problem here may be, it doesn't matter, because it'll all be gone. The foulest areas of the plant are being methodically enclosed and air-filtered, so within three years there won't *be* any odors, with a hydrogen sulfide level of roughly zero, or maybe one or two due to naturally occurring levels. Is that claim true or false? Answer—it's false." There was now a buzz in the room, with isolated hushed conversations breaking out again, but squelched by Jon's raised eyebrows and raised voice. "I studied the plant area by area and created a model using actual hydrogen sulfide levels as they exist today, measured right at those areas. So . . . cover and air-filter this area or that, and we can determine exactly what the effect is.

"You see, while we have fifty-five million dollars to enclose and air-filter certain areas, remember that we have a twenty-eight-acre plant here. Huge areas of the plant won't be enclosed, because that's seen as just too expensive. For instance, the secondary treatment tanks, which cover four times the area of the primary tanks, are going to be left open. Several other important areas will be left open as well. So what's the bottom line? When all is said and done, about half the existing odor problem will be eliminated and half will remain. So is this glass half empty or half full? In my opinion, it's half empty.

"On marginally bad days, at let's say the corner of Riverside Drive and 142nd Street, fourteen ppb becomes seven ppb. So your nose gets a break in that particular situation. But how about at forty, fifty, or one hundred ppb? Well, twenty, twenty-five, and fifty ppb is still enough to make you feel sick. I mean, it's great that something is being done about this problem. Fifty-five million dollars is no drop in the bucket. But don't let anyone tell you it's all going to go away. They need to enclose the rest of the facility, no doubt about it. But there are no plans to do that right now. And unless there are, you can look forward to experiencing days like this one through the year 2000 and beyond."

The silence in the room had now given way to the sounds of restlessness and curiosity—muttering, grumbling, chair legs rubbing against the floor tiles. The Latino man who had spoken earlier now asked a question, the words spilling out even before his hand went up.

"What about all the other gases being released?"

"Sulfur dioxide, scatole, ammonia, methyl mercaptan . . . there isn't any information available on those gases," Jon responded. "We know from other sewage treatment plants that they're being released, but we don't have any numbers. Maybe we will when DEP gets its act together with those new stationary air monitors. You know, they're in shakedown mode—perpetually. All I was able to do is model the one gas we have a wealth of data on. We also know that these gases tend to be released together. But that's not good enough."

Jon now pointed to a strikingly beautiful black woman of not more than twenty, who had her hand raised for almost a minute. Her long hair pulled straight back, near perfect posture, and keenly focused dark brown eyes gave her the aura of an African princess. Though the fumes were a great equalizer, she seemed to float above them.

"Yes, Mr. Kessler," she began, "what is known about the long-term health effects of hydrogen sulfide and the other gases?"

"Key question," Jon responded. "A lot is known, but there's not much of it that I can tell you. We need health experts to attack that problem—epidemiologists, occupational health physicians. I've advocated this within my office from day one. One study that should be performed is a health survey of this neighborhood that considers the incidence of respiratory illness of residents versus the distance of their homes from the North River plant. Several studies need to be done, and once they're funded, we'll need more data to proceed—a lot more. Very good question."

"What about capacity?" an elderly white man in a New York Jets cap inquired. "We hear a lot about the plant being over capacity. What has this got to do with the odor problem?"

"It has something to do with it," Jon replied. "When the pumps are overburdened, they're more likely to break down, and we get stagnant sewage. When you run raw sewage through the plant too quickly, you tend to get anaerobic respiration—basically, what you've been smelling. Of course, if we have a completely enclosed plant, they can run four hundred million gallons through it every day and we won't smell it. Okay, I'm gonna take just one more question right now, but maybe I'll take some more later. My mouth is getting kind of dry, so I'm going to take a break and get a drink of water. Miss . . . ?" A stout black woman of about sixty spoke.

"Is this report available in print?"

"No, it's not," Jon replied. "Art Shuler wants to sit on it until the problem goes away by itself. He wants me to go away too, apparently, since I'm not even supposed to be here tonight. So if you want more answers, call me or write to me at my office. Or better yet, call Art Shuler and tell him to get off his ass."

Jon stood and walked down the aisle toward the rear door. As he walked, he heard Clarissa Marbles's booming voice behind him. "I think we owe Jon Kessler a show of appreciation for the research he's done and the courage it took to stand up here and deliver." With these galvanizing words, a single clap swiftly turned into a booming ovation as Jon disappeared out the door and walked down the corridor toward the water fountain. Fatigue had caught up with him now, and the closer he got to the fountain, the more he needed the drink. He pressed the stainless steel button and lowered his face to the cool arcing stream.

He swallowed again and again and tensed up as he saw a distorted colorful reflection in the stainless steel drip pan six inches below, distorted even more by the running water. As a hand touched his left shoulder, he whipped around like a prizefighter, hands out front, water dripping from his mouth.

"Mr. Kessler," the woman said, startled. It was the beautiful dark princess who had addressed him in the room minutes earlier.

"Jeez, I'm sorry," Jon said. "You surprised me."

"I'm sorry," the princess said. "I just wanted to thank you for what you did. I'm studying environmental science at City College."

"That's great . . ."

"And when you were speaking," she continued, "I was thinking how the next time I'm burned out on studying, I'll think about everything you said and just keep going. That's the whole point—to make an impact. I mean, I think you made an impact. Do you think you made an impact?"

"Oh yeah," Jon said, rolling his eyes, "I made an impact."

Chapter 22

At two-thirty in the afternoon of Thursday, May 6, Detectives Mercado and O'Connel sat in a file room on the fifth floor of the New York City Department of Personnel at 2 Washington Street. Hundreds of folders were spread throughout the square white room, the stacks near the wall of windows waiting to be scoured and the stacks near the opposite wall having already proved to be fruitless. In between, the few dozen folders spread out on the table represented the hope of quick relief. Mercado tossed another folder onto the dud pile as if tossing a log on a roaring fire.

"At this point," Mercado said, "I'm playing a game with myself. Every ten folders represents another thousand dollars I'm going to win in a lottery."

"Whatever it takes to keep you from lighting up," O'Connel said.

"That's not going to be easy," Mercado said, throwing on another log. "When that game gets boring, which isn't long from now, I'm going to have to think up a new one—rating the female folders on a scale of ten."

"What about Linda?"

"She doesn't work for DEP," Mercado said of his wife. "At least not that I know of. She's not the sewer type. Not unless they have a Bloomingdale's down there." Mercado opened a new folder and did a double take. "Here's a nine."

"Must be assigned to the Park Avenue Sewers," O'Connel said.

"Maybe we can get her involved in this case," Mercado suggested, "you know, as an expert witness."

"Or maybe you can just call her up and ask her to the movies," O'Connel said. "There's her phone number."

Mercado threw down the folder, rubbed his eyes, and heard the blaring horns of the cars backed up at the mouth of the Battery Tunnel just outside.

"Four days of this shit," he said.

"Two and a half," O'Connel said. "Monday was a half day, and Tuesday we caught up on the Chemical Bank robbery."

"Feels like four, though."

"Hey," O'Connel said, "at least we're not doing night canvassing anymore."

"What I wanna know," Mercado said, "is if we hit the end of the DEP pile, do we go on and start with another agency? I mean, at that point, I think we're grasping at straws. And that's when I start grasping at Camels."

"No need to light up, Jimmy . . . look at this." Mercado leaned toward O'Connel as she slid over an open folder roughly to the halfway line of the desk surface between them. To the detectives' two sets of weary eyes, and with the composite drawing etched firmly in their brains overnight, the photo was an easy match.

"He fits," Mercado said. "Let's go snatch this son of a bitch. Those eyes, like out of a fifties sci-fi flick. The facial lines . . . even that nasty scar is there."

"You were right, Jimmy. He probably did pick up that scar in the joint."

"That, and he may be on horse too," Mercado said, using cop slang for heroin.

"Max McCord, huh?" O'Connel said, pulling the Jerome S. Patterson file alongside the McCord folder. "Look at that—now I can make detective first grade. Same prints here, here, and here.

Patterson, McCord, the guy planting videos in Haney's apartment, the one dumping Haney's body—they're all the same person."

"They're all the same flunky, running around doing Sarnow's dirty work for some reason we haven't figured out," Mercado observed. "Somebody took Patterson out of the joint and gave him a city job for a reason. But it wasn't Sarnow. He was over at Parks at the time, or maybe kissing ass somewhere else."

"There are college kids who can't get that job," O'Connel said, nodding in agreement. "He gets it fresh out of Sing Sing in 1984, and a new name to go with it."

"He'll wish he got a new face too."

"Look at this, Jimmy," O'Connel said, flicking at page three of the McCord folder with her index finger, "a suspension in 1985, disciplinary action in 'eighty-seven, another disciplinary action in 'ninety."

"Like I said, someone with some juice is behind him. Someone who keeps stepping in on his behalf."

"No doubt," O'Connel said. "I mean, even with all those black marks, he's still held down the same job for nine years. How many people can say that?"

"You, me, and him," Mercado said. "Here's his last listed address—146-06 Parsons Boulevard in Flushing. Why don't we get a warrant, pick him up tomorrow, hold him, and get Pappas in here for a lineup?"

"Sounds like a plan," O'Connel said. "I'm just glad I don't have to look through any more of these folders. DEP is hiring some ugly dudes lately."

"Yeah, I spotted a couple of those myself," Mercado said. "Must be to scare away the alligators."

"Hey, what about Sarnow?" O'Connel asked. "I was looking forward to telling him Haney's death may be ruled a suicide. Now that we're picking up McCord, he's gonna know we're getting close. What do I tell him?"

"Tell him he's next."

It was a well-known fact that Art Shuler was afraid of heights. Though his own staffers often did advance work, making sure the borough president never had to give a speech from a balcony and always got an aisle seat on a plane, Ronald Arlen was trying a different approach this morning.

At 11:15 A.M., Friday, May 7, when Arlen's helicopter took off from the heliport on the roof of the Arlen Palace Hotel at Sixty-third Street and Third Avenue, Art Shuler was nearly incapacitated. Sitting in the second row, next to Arlen, Shuler saw the roof of the hotel suddenly drop out from under him. He felt virtually weightless for an instant when the copter swerved quickly and plunged fifty feet in a sudden strong breeze. The pilot seemed to find it almost amusing, and Art Shuler would mention it to him as soon as he stopped digging his nails into the armrests.

As Shuler got up the courage to look around, the Dodger was quick to point out the sights on this clear day. To the left were relatively flat Queens and Brooklyn, converging in the distance with the blue mass of the Atlantic. To the right were hundreds of buildings of granite and concrete and steel and glass, with towers such as the Citicorp Building, the Empire State Building, and the Chrysler Building rising above the gray, brown, and red cluster. As the copter turned west, the Hudson approached and the Atlantic partially receded behind the skyline.

"Every one of these buildings represented a dream to someone at some time," Arlen said, appearing to enjoy the fact that he had to shout to be heard above the whop of the rotor blade. "Even the little ones. Someone had to dream it, to pay for it, to fight with the imbeciles who got in the way, and ultimately to put the damn thing up. That's what I see when I look down there. You ever build anything, Art?"

"Uh . . . no. Well, a constituency." Shuler loosened his tie and collar with his right hand, looking up for a moment, then looking back down.

"A constituency?" Arlen sneered. "Give me a fucking break. I don't mean a weak alliance of fickle people who say they stand for something then disappear. I mean something solid and real that lasts forever. Not even a house, Art?"

"Uh . . . no."

"You see, that's the problem," Arlen said. "I got a lot of people criticizing me who don't know the first fucking thing about what I do. If you've never built anything, you can't know. It's a fight, from start to finish. Most people couldn't stand up to it. But they have no problem standing around when it's all done and critiquing the thing. And they have no problem paying me rent either, do you understand me?"

"Yeah," Shuler answered, trying to lift his head once more. "Where are we going?"

"Going? You wanna land already? We're just starting to have some fun, Art. No one should get in the way of anyone else's fun. I firmly believe that. I came this close to putting up a 150-story building right down there. For the fun of it? You're damn right for the fun of it! And the sheer sense of accomplishment. All right, and to stick it to Trump. But a bunch of morons with nothing better to do got in my way. *You* got in my way. Do you remember that, Art?"

"Uh . . . yeah."

"It's funny how what goes around comes around. Now you're helping me."

"Yeah, that's right," Shuler agreed.

"Sometimes I wonder if it is," Arlen said. "You're *supposed* to be helping me. I'm paying you to help me. But—and help me here, Art—why doesn't it seem like you are?"

"What do you mean by that?" Art Shuler now held up his head for a full five seconds—a record.

"Let me tell you a little story," Arlen said. "When the Arlen Palace was being put up in 1983, I was walking along Sixty-third Street, right off of Lexington Avenue, and I noticed something. I was almost two blocks away, but I could tell a terrace slab on the twenty-eighth floor was out of place by about a half inch. I walked in, found the foreman, and told him somebody fucked up. I told him I wanted whoever it was fired, and I wanted that slab ripped out and repoured. And that's exactly what happened. Do you know why I'm telling you this?"

"No," Shuler said. "No."

"Because I'm a builder," Arlen said. "That's what I do. I had a lot of money then and a lot of success. I had a lot of offers from a lot of women. Beautiful women. I could have dated Princess Caroline of Monaco. But I was too busy putting up buildings. And I didn't mind it. I could have left all the details to someone else, crooked terraces and all. Who would have known? But you see, I needed to be where the building was going on. But when it comes to politics, I don't want to be worrying about the nuts and bolts. That stuff is beneath me. That's why I have people like you, Art. You're supposed to be taking care of that stuff. But you're letting me down."

The pilot swerved and plunged the helicopter just as it passed directly over the north end of the old Penn yards, around Seventy-second Street. Art Shuler stuck his head between his knees and gripped his seat tightly. Arlen paused to look down at the future site of Hudson City. From three thousand feet up, the imperfections of the seventy-acre site largely disappeared. The weeds, most of which had turned green in the spring, now appeared closely cropped and gave the impression of a lawn, as if the park Arlen had promised was already realized. Even the elevated Henry Hudson Highway, which cut through the property, seemed to complement the strips of land on either side.

"You're letting me down, Art."

"How am I letting you down?"

"I'm supposed to be building something great down there. This could be better than Rockefeller Center and Battery Park City combined. But I can't so much as start until you get your house in order. Is that too much to ask? For what I'm paying you? My friend at the *Times* tells me your engineer is playing hero to West Harlem. I'm told he gave quite a speech up there last night. Thinks he's Mr. Smith Goes to Fucking Washington."

"We're taking care of that," Shuler said, and struggled again to lift his head.

"Taking care of it?" Arlen said, pounding his fist into the back of the seat in front of him. "He already let the cat out of the bag!"

"Not about the drop in flow, from what I understand." Art then pointed toward the pilot, his eyebrows raised.

"What? You're worried about Bill? He's been with me for eleven years. I own him. But I don't own Kessler. That drop in flow cannot be made public now. It is not for public consumption, and it is not for public debate. They can't find out until after the committee hands me that permit. Based on what I've seen, Kessler might make that public the next time he wanders up to West Harlem."

"I don't think that's likely," Shuler said. "I doubt he even knows about it. There are no leaks at DEP. We're taking care of that."

"Sure you are," Arlen said, "just like you took care of that odor report. Well, I'm calling the shots now. You have a terrace that's out of place. You don't even know your own people. This is the kind of guy who's not only going to find out about it, not only going to tell everyone about it, but he's going to figure out how we're doing it. I can't have that."

"What do we do with him?" Shuler asked.

"We can't make a martyr out of him," Arlen said. "That's the last thing we need right now. It has to be discreet and unrelated." Arlen pulled a business card out of his wallet and handed it to the borough president. "Give this guy a call. Today. He'll set everything up. Just follow his leads. And no more fuck-ups, please."

"Okay, okay," Shuler said. "But you don't have to speak to me like that. Joel Haney wasn't my fuck-up. If I recall correctly, it's my people who have been running around covering your man's ass on that one."

"But Art, if there's ever an arrest made, who do you think will get the legal bill?"

"You don't even have to worry about that," Shuler said. "From what I hear, the detectives working that case are way off and getting further off track every day."

"Good," Arlen said. "At least we don't have to worry about some engineer fucking up that one too."

"Nope," Shuler said, swallowing hard. He placed his head once again between his knees as the copter swung east.

At 6:00 P.M. on Friday, May 7, Detectives Mercado and O'Connel walked up the three wooden stairs to the front porch of 146-06 Parsons Boulevard. The neighborhood, like so many others in the borough of Queens, was somewhere in the middle of an unseemly transition from suburban to urban. Virtually half of the Colonial, Victorian, and Tudor-style single-family homes on the many sixty-by-hundred-foot lots in the surrounding blocks had been torn down and replaced by three-story concrete and brick box-houses, typically with six or seven one- and two-bedroom apartments. A zoning of R-3 and the utter absence of landmark status had made this windfall a possibility for any developer with access to a few hundred thousand dollars and the desire to make a killing on the latest wave of immigration.

Scattered throughout the neighborhood, in numerous one- and two-story garagelike, stucco-walled, roll-down, metal-gated commercial properties were sweatshops, 1990s style. A side door left open for ventilation revealed twenty to thirty Asian women and men hunched over sewing machines, crammed together like Diet Coke cans in a case, churning out shirts and pants that would bear labels like "New Era" and "Good Life" and sell for $9.95 at the stores along Fourteenth Street in Manhattan. With a wage of typically a dollar an hour, six to eight of these workers could pool their money to afford one of the box-house apartments that surrounded them.

The two-story Victorian house with gambrel roof, hand-carved awnings, and white wooden siding on whose porch the detectives stood seemed to be on its last breath. Asphalt roof shingles curled up, cracked and distorted from decades of alternating heat and rain. Paint on the wooden window frames was little more than a smattering of chips. The next contractor to take care of the house would likely be driving a bulldozer.

The front door opened on O'Connel's fourth ring. The woman in the doorway was five-foot-six, about 110 pounds, with grayish-blond hair hanging straight down and breaking in random directions over a threadbare blue sweatshirt. Her narrow nose and dainty cleft chin contrasted with the dull yellowish pallor of her skin. Though she had walked the earth about forty years, it had walked on her another twenty.

"Who are you?" she said abruptly.

"Detectives from the Tenth Precinct in Manhattan," O'Connel replied. "I'm O'Connel, and this is Detective Mercado. We need to talk to Max McCord. Is he home?"

"That son of a bitch?" the woman said. "You're about four months too late. He moved out right after New Year's. The last time I saw that asshole was like two months ago when he came by to pick up some mail."

"Can you tell us where he is now?" Mercado asked.

"I'd tell you in two seconds if I knew," the woman said. "He's probably in his other house, sticking it to a girl half my age."

"His *other* house?" O'Connel asked.

"He don't own this one," the woman explained. "We rented it. I didn't even know he had another place until he let it slip in December. It's out in Suffolk County, some rich neighborhood, that's all I know. Tell you what, if you find that asshole, you let *me* know."

"Are you his wife?" Mercado asked.

"No," the woman said, "common law, maybe. Although Max don't do much according to any law. Whattaya looking for him for?"

"We just wanna question him in connection with an old disciplinary matter on his record," O'Connel said. "Nothing earth-shaking. We just need some information on somebody else we're investigating. Maybe if you could tell us where he works."

"In the sewer," the woman said, glancing back into the house for an instant. "You wanna come in?"

"Thank you," Mercado said. He and O'Connel followed the woman into the first-floor hallway, past the living room, and into the dining room, where the three stood around the table with newspapers and magazines spread out on it. In the living room and dining room were about two dozen cardboard boxes in various states of fullness.

"I got everything in boxes," the woman said. "I have to be out of here by the end of the month. That asshole tossed me three thousand bucks on his way out of here. This was as far as I could stretch it. What am I gonna do, go back to dancing? It don't matter. They're gonna knock this place down anyway."

"So he works in the sewer?" O'Connel said.

"Depends what you mean by work," the woman said. "What do they do down there anyway—make sure the shit's going in the right direction? Tell you the truth, I don't know how much he was really there. A couple of days a week maybe? I went down to visit him a few times on Eighty-fourth Street. He wasn't around, then he wasn't around again. Then when I found him one time and said, 'Hey, Max,' he screamed and yelled at me and told me never to see him down at the job again. Then at home that night we got into it and he beat the shit out of me. That's how I got this." She pointed to a scar on her left cheek.

"His and hers," Mercado said.

"I was halfway out the door with my bags the next day, and he comes in with diamond earrings."

"Is he still over at Eighty-fourth Street?" O'Connel asked.

"No, I doubt it. That was years and years ago. They moved him around. That schmuck. No, I'm the schmuck. Takes me all those years to figure out he's holding out on me. I mean, what son of a bitch who works down in the sewer is friends with Ronald Arlen?"

"Ronald Arlen?" O'Connel said. "The developer?"

"Can you believe it?" the woman said. "First time it happened was like six years ago. Max disappears for a few days, and this guy keeps calling the house, like he's annoyed, but he don't say who he is, just that he'll call back. Finally, he calls back like the fourth time and says, all pissed off, 'You tell him Ronald Arlen called.' I'm thinking Ronald *fucking* Arlen? How 'bout we forget Max and you build me a casino on the boardwalk?'"

"You gave Max the message then?" Mercado asked as the woman nodded. "You ask him what that was all about?"

"Yeah, sure. He tells me thanks for the message and it's none of your fucking business, Jeanie. He called the house every once in a while after that and never identified himself, but I'm like, 'Hi, Ron.' Tell you what, I'll save youse some trouble." She walked over to a corner of the living room, lifted a medium-size box off the couch, and placed it on the dining room table. "This is all Max's stuff that's left. I was close to throwing it out. Maybe you can get some use out of it. I sure as hell don't want to see it."

"You sure it's all right with him?" Mercado asked.

"Yeah, whatever," the woman said. "He wants you to have it."

"Thanks a lot," Mercado said, picking up the box. "If we find something of interest, we may give you a call."

"Just do it before the thirty-first," the woman said. "And don't expect to find the diamond earrings in there. I'm selling those. I'm looking to get myself a one-bedroom in Bayside and have enough left over to keep up my methadone program."

"Good luck with that," O'Connel said as she and Mercado took several steps toward the front hallway. "Could we get your full name?"

"Jeanie Griffin."

"Thanks for talking to us," Mercado said.

"Yeah, my pleasure," Jeanie said, following them out and opening the door for them. "You let me know what happens. Call me if you need a witness against that prick." The door closed behind the detectives, who walked back down the wooden stairs.

"Piece of work," O'Connel said.

"Yeah," Mercado said, stopping for a moment to rummage through the box and coming up with a notepad with scribbled notations and a Ronald B. Arlen Corporation letterhead. "But a helpful piece of work."

Chapter 23

Strangely, Friday, May 7, had passed without incident. Several times Jon had picked up his phone, braced for a left hook, and gotten only a breeze. Someone wanted a map. Someone wanted to know about the new curbs on Sixth Avenue. Several times he'd picked up the phone with the cranky, defensive "Yeah," instead of with the more formal "borough president's office," or even "Jon Kessler." The knocks on the door were all blanks too—Naomi asking about the North River air compressors, Larry announcing he hit the trifecta.

Then, over the weekend, Jon had resisted the temptation to phone in and retrieve his voice mail messages. On Sunday, he went two for four. These hits were sandwiched by two strikeouts, one of which came with him looking at a fastball for strike three. His head was not on the game.

Now, at nine-forty on Monday morning, May 10, four full days since D-Day had come and gone, Jon opened the door to his office, and the message light flashed at him through the stale air. Rather than play it cool, he rushed over and dialed in for the messages. There were eleven, and the dreamlike silence was over. The *Amsterdam News*, the *Westsider*, the *Daily News*, the *New York Post*, and the *Sun* all wanted to speak with him. Jay Gonzalez seemed both troubled and pleased in the message he had left: "We gotta talk, man, as soon as possible. They're talkin' about you down here like you're some kind of comic book superhero. Call me." Pat's message said: "Well, you gave these SOBs what they deserve. I'm having fun down here watching them cover their asses."

The message from Dennis Roseberry, the borough president's office press secretary, was not unexpected: "You are to direct any and all calls from members of the media directly to me, and abstain from making your own statements." Do not pass Go. Close the barn door after the horse escapes. Laura, in her message, revealed feeling shortchanged: "Jon, you should have told me what you were going to do. I thought the meeting was going to be the same old crap. I would have *been* there." Jon had surprised himself as well.

The message from Ned Richter was the most jarring of the eleven. It was called the Zebra Pattern, a phenomenon not limited to the borough president's office. It went something like this. The person at the top had unfriendly designs but a pleasant demeanor. That person hired a hatchet, who executed most of those designs and appeared openly belligerent. The hatchet, in turn, required the services of a gofer, a lackey, who was particularly cheerful, especially while carrying out a select few assignments—usually the most unsavory ones. Here, Art Shuler sat at the top, Paula Derbin was the hatchet, and Ned Richter was the lackey.

"Jon, this is Ned," Richter's message said. "Call me back as soon as you get in. We need you to inspect Four-forty-eight East Tenth Street, *this morning*. I'm in my office. Call me. Thanks."

Now the phone in Jon's office rang. He picked it up on the second ring. "Hello. Jon Kessler."

"This is Mark Rosario of the *Westsider*. I'm doing a story on the North River sewage treatment plant. Would you be willing to confirm some of the statements attributed to you this past Thursday evening at the West Harlem Environmental Review Board?"

"Well . . ." Jon hesitated, scanned his baseball wall of fame, and replied, "What did you hear?"

"Is it true you said that in spite of fifty-five million dollars' worth of updating to the plant, roughly half of the odor content will remain into the next century."

"That's correct," Jon replied. "That's what the numbers from my study revealed."

"Is this study available to the public?" Rosario asked.

"No, it's not," Jon replied. "This office has had it in review for months."

"Why do you think that is?" Rosario inquired.

"Well, I can only speculate," Jon answered. "The borough president has a lot at stake regarding the Hudson City approval. Maybe he feels the report jeopardizes it."

"I wouldn't doubt it," Rosario agreed. Jon saw the light for his alternate phone line flashing and interrupted the reporter.

"I'm sorry, I have another call. Let me clear it. Don't go away."

"Okay."

"Jon Kessler."

"Jon, this is Ned. We need you to get to Four-forty-eight West Tenth Street by ten-thirty *this* morning."

"The Glass House?" Jon responded. "What's the rush? Anyway, I'm not going into the Glass House or any other building like it without police protection."

"I know all about that," Ned Richter said, "and that's all taken care of. You'll have police protection, but only if you get over there now. Didn't you see what happened there last night on the news?"

"No, I was way out on Long Island."

"To make a long story short," Ned said, "the squatters living there were kicked out by the police. The city had looked the other way for a long time, but yesterday evening the fire department responded to an alarm for the building. Some of the squatters threw bricks and wood at the fire trucks, and there didn't seem to be any fire. So the firemen left, and an hour later the police came and cleared the place out. Threw the squatters out into the street."

"Where do I fit into all this?" Jon asked.

"Community Board Three wants the building assessed pronto for structural safety. They want it refurbished or torn down immediately, and we're in a position . . . where we have to take a position. The police are guarding the place, and there's a guy from the Department of General Services waiting for you right now. His name is Bruce Gregory. DGS controls the building for the city. He knows the place, and he's expecting you. If you leave right now, you can catch him. Otherwise, he'll leave and everything gets messy."

"I got it," Jon said.

"So can you drop everything right now and get over there, Jon?"

"Okay, let me just clear this other call and I'm out of here."

"Thanks, Jon."

Jon got back on the other line with Mark Rosario of the *Westsider.* "Hello, Mark?"

"I'm still here."

"Listen, I've been called to a semi-emergency. Can I call you back later in the day so we can do justice to this story? It can't be covered in five minutes."

"Definitely," Rosario replied. "I'll be back in my office after four today. Call me." He gave Jon his phone number.

Jon repeated it, scrawling the numbers down alongside a Naomi doodle of two large lips and a four-digit number. "Speak to you then." Jon put down the receiver, grabbed a clipboard with blank paper, and stepped quickly out the door. A small lump formed in his stomach as he looked out at the front desk of room 2035. He had never seen this elderly man before, but was certain who it was.

"Wallace. Bernard H. Wallace," the gentleman said.

"I'm sorry, King," Larry began.

"You never returned my call, and I do need that map of Columbus Avenue and Seventy-second Street."

"You lucked out," Jon said as he made sure his office door was locked. "Wait right here. I'll be back with your map in five minutes." Jon dashed out the door of room 2035 and caught an elevator right away for a change. As he ran down the hall on the nineteenth floor toward the map room, he minimized eye contact with various staff members who would have him answer numerous questions. He was now glad to be on his way to inspect a site, performing a normal function, being part of the team again somehow for a few minutes, cheating his inevitable fate for a moment and seeing how long it could possibly last. He whipped out his fat key chain, inserted the map room key into the lock, and flipped on the inside light switch in one almost fluid motion. He opened flat file number 51, pulled out the correct mylar, and put it through the long roller on the printer that kicked you in the head with the smell of ammonia. Jon felt bad for Bernard H. Wallace and believed that if he didn't get his map today, Wallace might disappear off the face of the earth, brokenhearted and lonely.

"Thank you, sir," Wallace said upon grasping the rolled-up blueprint four minutes later. "This is much appreciated."

"No problem," Jon said as he darted back out the door. But it was a problem.

In the Brooklyn Bridge subway station beneath the Municipal Building a few minutes later, the 4 train, an express, rolled away as Jon stood cursing on the platform. While rushing around for Wallace, he'd used up all his slack time. The train had known it. The platform had known it. Now Jon knew it. Because the next express was maybe ten minutes away and it was already ten-fifteen, he would have to consider taking the next local to Union Square, where he could change for the L train to First Avenue and run the rest of the way to Alphabet City. He had forgotten to stop at a cash machine on the way in that morning, so he didn't have the money for a cab. Jon did not know exactly what he was running from or what he was running to, but somehow he felt safer, more consumed and protected, while running. He looked ahead and knew his heart would be pounding and his clothes sticking to him as he stomped the Lower East Side pavement.

The 6 train, a local, pulled in on the tracks along the wall. Jon got on but did not sit as the train pulled away, northbound. No reason to get too comfortable. The seats were filthy anyway. He considered the four minutes he'd already lost. He didn't quite understand the urgency Ned Richter was talking about. If the police were there to keep the squatters from returning, they would be there for him as well, indefinitely. Who cared if Bruce Gregory left?

As the 6 train rolled into the Canal Street station, Jon thought about the Glass House and how it symbolized the decline of New York. Built in the 1840s, this five-story brick and wood joist structure was used as a glassblowing factory until about the turn of the century, when it was divided into residential apartments. The building at the corner of Tenth Street and Avenue D thrived during the first half of the twentieth century in the working-class Lower East Side. Though never made lavish, the building had been well-maintained.

Shortly after World War II, industry started moving out of Manhattan to the outer boroughs and to New Jersey. The middle-class suburban exodus took hundreds of thousands of prosperous people out to Nassau and Suffolk counties on Long Island, and up north to Westchester. In addition, rent control laws in New York City kept landlords from converting buildings into luxury apartments. Without access to well-paying jobs, the new immigrants and transients replacing the departing members of the middle class needed the artificially low rents, but the low rents weren't enough to keep the buildings profitable. The demographics of the new, non-European immigrants scared off what remained of the middle class, accelerating their departure and further destabilizing certain neighborhoods.

By the 1960s many landlords had begun getting out themselves, the only profitable way they knew how—by burning their own buildings and collecting insurance. Other landlords, less dramatically but perhaps even more insidiously, stopped maintaining the buildings while collecting rents for as long as they could. Eventually, many of them even stopped paying city property taxes, effectively abandoning the buildings as the city took over. Together, the two approaches—arson and abandonment—represented a kind of scorched-earth policy in the war zone known as New York.

Ironically, in the late sixties, the city started granting landmark status to many of these older buildings, either for their architecture, their unique place in local history, or both. The Glass House was one such building. But with a budget dwarfed by the size of this socially, economically, and legally driven problem, there was typically little the Landmarks Commission could do to preserve such buildings. It was one thing to threaten the owner of a profitable landmarked building with fines for making unapproved alterations. It was quite another thing to find an investor masochistic enough to take on an unprofitable building once it had been left for dead—landmarked or not.

As rent-paying customers emptied out of these buildings, the homeless moved in. In an unseemly way, one problem appeared to solve another. But like a pothole and drainage problem, they grew together. The squatters' sub-ghetto grew, with the city as its absentee landlord and curator. On one hand, the city could not come up with the $100,000-plus for the complex demolition, which involved pulling one building down painstakingly by hand while those attached were carefully shored up. On the other hand, no private entity wanted to risk the half million dollars or more necessary to make the building usable again. Buildings like the Glass House existed in a sort of economic limbo, the birthplace of residential hell. Progress was dead.

Progress had stopped on the 6 train as well. After stopping at Astor Place, the doors had closed and then abruptly opened again, the train remaining motionless for the next few minutes. Now the conductor made an announcement: "Attention, ladies and gentlemen. We're being held here due to a police action at Union Square. We should be moving momentarily. We're being held here . . ." People on the train grunted as they got off the car and kicked a seat or slapped a metal strap. The word "shit" came involuntarily out of Jon's mouth, pure and direct. He ran up the stairs, out of the ornate, replica turn-of-the-century kiosk onto the triangle at Astor Place, where he fought off physical and mental duress to make logistical calculations.

He decided to run up to Union Square and catch the M-14 bus going east. As he approached Union Square, he saw huge crowds of people swarming, with the trees and subway kiosks sticking motionless out of the chaos. Sirens from the fire engines, police cars, and ambulances were coming from every direction and ringing in his bones, but he didn't recall exactly when he noticed the sounds beginning. It was as if the usual sirenlike white noise in the city had steadily risen to become overwhelming.

Now Jon was amidst the confusion as it nearly swallowed him at the corner of Fourteenth Street and Fourth Avenue, where he stopped to catch his breath. He asked the person nearest him what had happened.

With a joint brazenly hanging from his mouth and wearing a Nirvana T-shirt, a longhaired man his own age replied, "Someone blew a bomb off down there, dude. On the uptown express. At least three people are dead. A lot of injuries too, man. I saw some people coming out of there covered with soot, on stretchers."

"Oh my God." Apparently, it was the train Jon had just missed.

Jon's impulse was to hang around Union Square and interject himself into the bedlam. But borough engineer or not, the Transit Authority, the police, and Emergency Medical Services would quickly have every base covered if they didn't already. The Transit Police would have all tunnels and stairwells sealed to trap the culprit, if there was one. Transit engineers would quickly be on the scene to assess any potential structural damage to the steel columns or any other component of the subway. EMS would navigate the shortest route to the city hospitals with burn units. As chaos went, it was well under control. Still, even through the strain of long distance running with a knapsack and an ankle still sore from the shooting incident near 110th Street, he wanted to be part of it, and already planned to come right back after this inspection. And if he could remember, he'd thank Bernard H. Wallace sometime for saving his life.

All traffic had stopped, so he had to run east along Fourteenth Street. As he ran toward Irving Place, then Third Avenue, then Second Avenue, the noises and sirens receded. Soon, the catastrophic events would have no more immediate effect on him than they had on someone living in Paris, or Tel Aviv, or in the Northwest wilderness. He was relieved to be running, even though the heat and his shortness of breath were becoming oppressive. The people he whipped past on Fourteenth Street had less and less to do with the bomb at Union Square.

Then he was beyond First Avenue, between Avenues A and B. To his left was Stuyvesant Town, a massive residential development built by Metropolitan Life shortly after World War II. To build it, Met Life first had to get the city to condemn blocks and blocks of tenements known collectively as the Gashouse District. These poor buildings were among the last in Manhattan not to have electricity and therefore used gas for lighting, even as the United States had successfully developed and dropped the atomic bomb. As a result, buildings in the Gashouse District burned like London under attack from the Luftwaffe, whether it was wartime or not. Meanwhile, the nearby gas tanks along the East River tended to leak and give the entire neighborhood a foul odor.

Ironically, a huge Con Edison plant, one of the biggest electricity generating plants in the world, stood right across the street on Avenue C. Con Ed didn't see hooking up these economically marginal homes as profitable. In the late 1940s, when Metropolitan Life opened the doors of Stuyvesant Town, fully equipped with electricity from across the street, it was strictly white people only, as that arrangement was also seen as the most profitable. Met Life subsequently won a landmark legal case in which it was decided for the time being that separate but equal housing was acceptable. One condition was that Met Life develop a similar site uptown where "Negroes" were preferred.

Jon ran from disaster to disaster, more comfortable between the two, more secure in his knowledge of the past than in the unpleasantness of the present. Gashouse, Glass House—it was all running together in his brain now.

Police surrounded the Glass House. There must have been a score of officers. Several dozen homeless people camped out nearby with their possessions in bags and shouted sporadically at the cops: "Squatters rights . . . fuck the pigs!" Even drained of most of his energy, Jon quickly spotted numerous structural problems. The parapet walls revealed missing and loose bricks all around the roof perimeter. There was extensive cracking and spalling along the concrete foundation. There was somewhat less extensive cracking visible along the brick exterior walls. The bricks, originally yellow, were bleached from a century and a half of New York weather, yet at the same time blackened from a century and a half of New York grime.

"Is Bruce Gregory in there?" a panting Jon asked the beefy cop at the front entrance.

"Are you from the borough president's office?"

"Yeah."

"Go ahead in," the cop said. "He's in there. He's waiting for you. He's in there with a Chinese woman. I don't know what floor they're on right now."

"Okay, thanks," Jon said. He looked back at some of the protesting squatters for a moment and confirmed what he'd observed a moment earlier. These people were a cut above the usual homeless people in their appearance. While their clothes were the same random, tattered threads on the backs of most of the homeless, the look in their eyes was distinctly more focused.

Now Jon turned and proceeded into their world. The first floor interior was a shambles. Shoddy possessions left behind, useful to someone at some time, were all over the place in small piles. Though no partition walls remained between them, each pile represented an apartment of sorts. All apartments were equipped with blankets, tattered pillows, an old lamp hooked up to the illegal wiring, a hot plate, assorted books, a makeshift table fashioned from scrap wood. Over on the south end was a luxury apartment, equipped with black-and-white TV, stereo with 8-track, and a Budweiser cooler. With a little more work, the apartment could have been a duplex. There was a hole in the floorboards directly above. Expand the hole, install a circular staircase, and you were done.

However, there were small holes in the floorboards everywhere, above and below. There was a rotting smell permeating the building. Most likely, the roof had gone bad some time ago, allowing rain to progressively destroy everything under it. The wood joists supporting the floorboards were water damaged as well, but in much better shape overall. Unlike the floorboards, the joists were not ready to give. Nor were the deep wood girders and the columns supporting those girders. Though weathered, they had been built to last. So long as he looked carefully at the floorboards ahead and made an effort to walk along the joists, Jon thought, he would probably be all right.

The other smell permeating the air was that of feces. There were human feces in isolated locations throughout the first floor, amidst the broken glass and rubble. It was not, however, enough to explain the intensity of the smell, which in certain spots was overwhelming. Jon wondered why these squatters, so resourceful in other ways, hadn't developed a more hygienic method of relieving themselves.

There were four yellow traffic cones situated in a square about five feet per side in front of a glassless window opening along the east end. Jon assumed that since the brick-throwing incident over the weekend, the building had probably been inspected and reinspected by several engineers representing various city agencies. That added to his confidence as he walked, knowing that the most dangerous spots had most likely already been located and cordoned off. Now he stuck his right foot just inside the square of cones and pushed it completely through the tender floorboards. As he did, he heard footsteps coming down the stairs. He turned and saw a man and a woman approach.

"How long have you been here?" the man asked gruffly.

"Just a few minutes," Jon replied. "Are you Bruce Gregory?"

"Yeah."

"I'm Jon Kessler."

"I know who you are." Gregory was a tall, wiry man about fifteen years Jon's senior. His thinning hair was gray, right down to the ponytail. At six-foot-three with a worn denim work shirt, large work boots, and an earring, he was an imposing figure. His tanned skin was as weathered as the bricks in the Glass House. "You're late, and I have to get to my next site."

"Janet Wong," the woman said, extending her hand to Jon. "Community Board Three." She was attractive, about Naomi's age, and, like Jon, way overdressed for the Glass House. She seemed relieved to see him, as if a half hour or so alone with Bruce Gregory was not what she had in mind when she took the job.

"I think we met once before," Jon said, shaking her hand.

"You spoke about the third water tunnel to my board last year," Janet Wong replied.

"Folks, I don't have the time right now," Bruce Gregory insisted. "I need you to look at something upstairs. If you want to stay and look at the rest of the building after I leave, that's up to you."

"By the way," Jon said, "the reason I'm late is there was some kind of explosion on the train ahead of me, going to Union Square."

"You're kidding me," Janet said.

"I wouldn't kid about that," Jon replied. "I'm going back after this to find out more. I wound up running here, and I feel light-headed from the whole thing."

"That is so sick," Janet said. "Are you okay?"

"Let's go," Bruce Gregory said, leading the two up the rickety staircase to the second floor. "You'll have plenty of time to talk about it later."

"Jeez, all right," Jon said, following the two toward the second floor, which looked very similar to the first floor. There were even four cones in the same pattern, situated along the east-facing window opening directly above the cones on the first floor.

"Look, you can poke around here all you want after I go," Gregory barked. "I need you to look at one thing on the fifth floor and then I'm outta here."

"Okay, okay," Jon said, falling back into line and proceeding up the next set of stairs. "I just don't feel well. The smell is getting to me."

"I don't blame you," Janet said, the rear of her skirt bouncing just in front of Jon's face. "This place is filled with the signs of human suffering. A lot of PWAs lived here."

"What's a PWA?" Jon asked.

"Person with AIDS," Janet replied. "This particular group of squatters has a lot of them. They're actually part of a national group of squatters that preaches self-reliance. They're very organized. I'll show you something upstairs. There's the leader's room in the back of the third floor. It's all finished on the inside. There's a nice bunk bed, carpet, and a huge Led Zeppelin banner hanging from the wall for some reason. They've got a small library of radical books: *The Autobiography of Malcolm X, The Communist Manifesto, The Anarchist Cookbook* . . ."

Jon's body was giving out now. He doubled over with stomach cramps and felt the involuntary rush of a cold sweat. The events of the past few days—the shots fired at 110th Street, the speech in West Harlem, the bomb in the subway—were choosing this instant to hit him, landing their long-overdue blows in his intestines. He could not run anymore. He could barely walk. He stumbled out onto the fourth floor, which, unlike the floors below, was almost completely saturated with human feces. "I'm sorry," he said. "I think I'm gonna throw up."

"Isn't it terrible?" Janet Wong remarked, not entirely in tune with Jon. "This is the bathroom. This is the floor they chose as the bathroom."

"I need you to look at the stress cracks below a window on the fifth floor," Gregory said.

"I heard you the first time," Jon said.

"Don't fuck with me today," Gregory said.

"Who's fucking with you?" Jon said. "Now I'm not going to the fifth floor—how's that?"

"Okay, okay, I'm sorry," Gregory said, quickly assuming a conciliatory tone. "I got people riding my ass back at the office. Why don't you take a look at the outside of the wall beneath that window right there. It's got the exact same type of stress cracking anyway."

"I'll take a look," Jon responded, "right after I use it to throw up." He walked toward the window, sincere as well as sarcastic about vomiting. As his weight came down on his left foot, there was a snap and the floor gave way. He experienced his falling as the building rising quickly around him while he was weightless. A floorboard rushed toward his head like a baseball bat being swung and broke across his right shoulder. He landed on his left ankle in a far from ideal position. The rest of his body followed like a rag doll.

The spot where he landed on the third floor had begun to give way also, but it barely held, somehow, as he rolled away, dreading when the physical pain would kick in. The soundtrack to this event was Janet Wong's lone, shrieking voice from one flight up, not subsiding even after he knew he would live, scaring him into thinking maybe he wouldn't.

Under his right palm, human feces, probably viral, was crushed like paste. Looking up, he expected to see the face connected to the screams. Instead he saw a joist, hanging, not in particularly bad condition, sawed off cleanly at one end and notched at the end from which it still hung. Then he knew. He was not supposed to stop falling at the third floor. He looked back at where he'd landed and saw four cones.

Chapter 24

Jon's heart was beating its way out of his chest as he stood up on two bad ankles. The relief from realizing the left ankle was not broken was tempered by the sharp pain he felt in that same ankle, in his right shoulder, and in a half dozen other points of impact. A moment of light-headedness passed and was replaced by unfettered rage toward Bruce Gregory and anyone else who had the sick nerve to try to take away his life.

"C'mere, asshole, I have something for you," Jon yelled as he staggered toward the staircase. Loud footsteps were coming toward him from the vicinity of the stairway, apparently from both above and below. With Janet Wong following right behind, Bruce Gregory appeared at the foot of the third-story stairs.

"Are you okay?" Gregory said.

Jon ran and lunged toward Gregory, knocking him backward onto the bottom few steps and stuffing into Gregory's open mouth the human feces that still stuck to Jon's right palm.

"Aaaaargghhh!" Gregory's scream was bloodcurdling, then he spit desperately and flailed his arms madly, managing to strike Jon with a blow across the right temple.

"Yeah, I'm okay now," Jon said amidst the blows. "How are you doing?" Jon felt himself pulled backward by the huge force of two broad, iron arms. They belonged to the beefy cop who had been guarding the front entrance. There were others behind him as well.

"You fucking son of a bitch, I'll kill you!" Gregory shouted, still spitting and now managing to land a right-hand blow against Jon's leg, which was furiously pumping for a last kick at Gregory. "I'll fucking kill you!"

"You had your shot!" Jon said. "You blew it!" The officer's arms continued to pull him back, and now Jon was surrounded by blue, involuntarily hobbling down the stairs toward the second floor. Two more cops restrained Gregory as he disappeared from Jon's view.

"That asshole set me up," Jon said. "That beam was ready to go."

"The whole building is ready to go," the beefy cop replied.

"Look, I know what I'm talking about," Jon protested. "That beam was notched. That doesn't happen from rot. That asshole had it planned out. I wanna go back up to the fifth floor. I'll bet you a month's salary those beams were notched too." The beefy cop shoved Jon out the ground floor front exit, onto the pavement, and released him somewhat tentatively, his blue chest puffed out. Another cop blocked the front doorway.

"Do you want me to call an ambulance?" the beefy cop asked.

"No . . . no, not right now," Jon said, rubbing his right shoulder with his left hand, feeling for stress cracks. "Maybe later. I need to go back up there."

"I can't let you do that," the beefy cop replied. "They're in there asking your buddy if he wants to press charges."

"Against *me*?" Jon said. "Give me a fucking break. *He tried to kill me.*"

"That's what you say. All I know is I hear a thud, a girl screaming, I come up, and I see you on top of this guy." The other cop stiffened in the doorway while the beefy one continued. "Do *you* want to press charges against *him*?"

"Yeah . . . no, not right now." Amidst the sharp physical pains, Jon tried to sort out what the rest of his day should be like, the rest of the week, the rest of his life. "I want to talk to my lawyer first." A cop with a thick mustache stepped out from behind a third cop who blocked the front door and addressed the beefy cop.

"No, he says he doesn't want to press charges. He just wants to kick his ass."

"Okay, then," the beefy cop said to Jon, "I'll ask you again. If you want to press charges, we can all go back to the precinct. But I'm not letting you back in there unless he leaves first."

"What's your name . . . Simpkins?" Jon said, looking at the cop's nameplate. "That piece of shit is lucky if all I do is press charges. I'll be calling you."

"Whatever you say, chief." Simpkins scowled. Jon began limping away, down Avenue D.

"You tell him that for me," Jon said, over his shoulder.

He turned westward at Ninth Street and limped toward Avenue
C. His various wounds seemed too tame, as if they were not ham-
pering him as they should have and as if they would reveal their
true colors the moment he stopped moving. So, he kept moving,
toward Avenue B, then through the Ninth Street footpath in Tompkins Square Park, asking himself the obvious questions but not
fully accepting the obvious answers.

Was it that simple? Did Paula set him up by turning him into a
building inspector and arranging for him to fall through the
cracks? Did she, Ned Richter, and Bruce Gregory sit down and
map out his demise over lunch? Jon wondered how the incident at
110th Street and the subway explosion fit into this puzzle. And
then there was Wallace. Bernard H. Wallace. If not for the man's
annoying, trivial map request, he would have been on the subway
that blew up.

Furthermore, had he not been ejected from the subway system
and forced to run, he would not have been out of breath and would
likely have made it to the fifth floor of the Glass House. Then he
probably would have fallen through the fourth floor, third floor,
second floor, and first, down into a basement full of rats, rusty
nails, and shards of glass. Wallace had saved his life not once but
twice. Next time, on the spot, he'd get him a map of Jupiter if he
asked for it.

But the life that Wallace had saved was one of extremes. Jon
felt at once liberated and shackled, more so both ways than ever
before. Having lived through this day, no one could tell him anything anymore. He was free to do whatever he damn well pleased
for the rest of his life, for the simple reason that he had stared
death in the face. Yet from now on, every piece of ground was no
more stable than the fourth floor of the Glass House. Having to
tiptoe forever was in some ways worse than falling through to the
basement.

Now, kicking a half-crushed empty can of Colt 45 Malt
Liquor, he resolved that no one would ever force him into that
subterranean existence. He'd confront everyone he had to, finish
his project, and go down with dignity if anyone had the guts to
take him on. And there, whipping him around 180 degrees yet
again, was the answer. *Nothing* was that simple. He had Elaine
and the kids.

Jon lifted the receiver of the pay phone on the northeast corner of Ninth Street and First Avenue. There was no dial tone. He dropped the receiver and trotted with visible difficulty to the pay phone on the southeast corner. On this one, a private pay phone bolted to the side of a bodega, the mouthpiece for the receiver was missing, leaving an assortment of red and green wires staring him in the face, mocking him. Jon slammed the phone down onto the metal hook.

"Damn it," he shouted, "is there a single fucking pay phone that works in New York?"

"That one works," a black man in his seventies clutching a cane said, leaning into the half booth and pointing to the AT&T pay phone directly across First Avenue. A few moments later, at the southwest corner of First Avenue and Ninth Street, Jon punched in Elaine's work number, then punched in his calling card number. Elaine picked up on the second ring.

"LILCO computer help desk. How may I assist you?"

"You can assist me by going home, packing, and getting Stacy and Steven out of the house."

"What happened, Jon? Are you all right?" Elaine fought with each syllable to steady her voice. Jon's speech was sharp and direct, as if some drastic resolve had already taken hold.

"I'm okay, but I'll be a lot better as soon as you're in hiding. I took a fall through the floor of a building a few minutes ago, okay? I'm pretty sure it was a setup, and I'm pretty sure I know who's behind it. Unfortunately for them, I lived, and now I'm gonna be their worst nightmare."

"Jon, you've got to get out of there," Elaine pleaded.

"That's exactly what I'm doing," Jon said. "I'm heading back down to the office to get what I need, and then I'm disappearing."

"And *then* what?" Elaine asked.

"On the way downtown, I'm making a list of everything I need," Jon said, "and of everyone I might be able to contact who can help me get to the bottom of this. That may or may not include the police. I'll live at Keith's apartment . . . or somewhere." There was a short beep on the line.

"I have another call," Elaine said.

"From who—*another* husband who almost just got killed by a bunch of money-hungry developers and has to go into hiding?"

"Hang on five seconds, damn it." Elaine's voice was now replaced by the tail end of a Barry White song and then an announcer's voice boasting: "Love songs—nothing but love songs." Jon tried to envision his brief trip back to the office. He would try to slip in and out unnoticed, like a ghost. Elaine's voice was quickly back on the line.

"Jon, I knew something bad was going to happen."

"You don't know the half of it."

"Look, I don't want to sound selfish, but there's nothing more you can do now. There's nothing more you *should* do. Just resign, get a job out here, tell them you're not interested in this issue, and let them keep that stupid report."

"And send them what message?" Jon said. "That all you have to do is take a couple of potshots at someone and you can have what you want?"

"Why do you have to take on everyone else's problem? You can't even keep your wife happy, and now you're going to save Manhattan."

"Saving Manhattan's a lot easier," Jon said. "Anyway, even if I was the wimp who you so desperately want me to be, your plan wouldn't work. It's too late. Obviously, they already believe I know too much. And no matter what I say on the way out, no matter how many olive branches I throw on their desks, they're never going to trust me. We'd have to live our lives in fear anyway. That option is closed. We might as well make the best of it by nailing their asses to the wall. And the idea of sucking up to Paula makes me sick. 'Oh please, Paula, will you let me ride off into the sunset without shooting me in the back?' Gimme a break."

"Well, I don't want any part of this," Elaine said. "I'm taking the rest of the day off and bringing Steven and Stacy to my mother's."

"Great. That's what I wanted to hear. When you get back to the house, take a look at the wooden box on the floor of our bedroom closet, on the left side. There's almost two thousand dollars in cash in there. Take it. You might need it."

"You never told me about that," Elaine said.

"I was saving it for a rainy day. And now it's raining bullets."

"I'm in shock, Jon, but I really can't say I'm surprised. I saw this coming."

"Whad'ya do, pull the sewage card from your tarot deck?"

"I pulled a migraine, okay?" Elaine said. "Jon, what are we going to do? Is this ever going to go away? I mean, can I even come back to work tomorrow?"

"I'm not sure," Jon said. "You're probably relatively safe at work. You've got a lot of people around."

"Jon, I'm worried about you."

"Just worry about yourself and the kids. I have part of a plan. I'll work the rest out on the subway."

"Call me later."

"I'll track you down," Jon said. "Don't forget that I love you."

Jon put down the receiver and continued walking west. The list of things to do would have to be compiled in his head for now. His engineering notepad and the knapsack it was in were lying somewhere in the rubble and feces of the Glass House. So was a page on which he had scribbled some conjecture regarding the whereabouts of the missing thirty million gallons a day of raw sewage. Like the sewage itself, it was gone for good.

For the first time since the collapse, Jon took a look at himself. His pants were torn in three places, his shirt in two, and both were soiled extensively. In the reflection of a store window he noticed the open cut on the left side of his chin and made a conscious effort not to touch it at least until he could clean his hands first.

A half hour later he limped along Chambers Street toward the massive arches of the Municipal Building. Since the IRT and BMT lines at Union Square were still closed in both directions due to police investigation of the explosion, he had walked to Sixth Avenue to catch the downtown F train and changed for the A train at West Fourth Street. Now, fifty feet from the revolving door entrance of the Municipal Building, he stood face-to-face with a smiling Jay Gonzalez.

"What happened to you?" Jay asked. "Were you mugged?"

"I wish," Jon said.

"Well," Jay said, still smiling, "I heard about the building."

"You know about it already?"

"Sure," Jay said. "Everybody knows. It was all over the nineteenth floor."

"And you find this amusing?"

"Hey, it makes you look good," Jay said. "I'm happy for you. It's not like anyone got killed or even hurt."

"Wait a second," Jon said, "*I* got hurt. And I almost got killed."

"I don't understand," Jay said. "You were *in* the building when it happened? What were you doing, waiting around for it to collapse, so you could be there to take credit?"

"Credit for what?" Jon said, annoyed. "I was led to a weak spot and fell through the floor. It's a miracle I lived. And then I had to walk a mile through Alphabet City covered in shit."

"Hold on, hold on," Jay said, losing his smile. "I'm talking about 110th Street. What's this about Alphabet City?"

"What's this about *110th Street*?" Jon pressed.

"Then you don't know about it? That building on 110th Street you inspected last week and predicted was in danger of collapsing—well, it collapsed. What do you carry—an engineer's crystal ball next to your slide rule?"

"And you say no one was hurt?" Jon asked. "Was it the abandoned building?"

"No, the occupied building next to it, on the corner," Jay said. "It was only a partial collapse. The foundation and front bearing wall dropped about three feet. Everyone got out of there. I heard it was a scene. A 20-inch water main was crushed and went off like a geyser."

"Unbelievable," Jon said. "Now I've got a story for *you*. Ned Richter sent me to inspect a building on Tenth and Avenue D, and it was a setup. Some piece of shit by the name of Bruce Gregory from DGS did everything he could do to get me to walk over a weak spot, and it finally worked."

"Oh my God," Jay said. "And you're sure you were set up?"

"Yeah, I'm sure," Jon said. "Pretty sure. I looked at the beam that gave way. It was notched, not rotted. Someone sawed just enough out of it so it would stay up on its own but give if somebody walked on it. And they made sure I was that somebody. The police dragged me out of there, so I didn't get a chance to check out the other floors, but I'll bet you anything they were all like that. I was supposed to drop all the way through, like Yosemite Sam in a Bugs Bunny cartoon."

"Holy shit," Jay said, "I'm glad you're still alive. You really think Paula and Ned are behind it? It's hard to believe this has really gone far enough that they would resort to something like that."

"Put it this way," Jon said, "I'm not going to hang around here long enough to find out. They're not going to get another clean shot at me. I'm going upstairs, pack a few essentials, and disappear."

"I heard Art's going to announce his candidacy any day now," Jay said. "You might want to give it a week."

"No way."

"I understand," Jay said. "I hope I'm not next. Could you do me a favor and stay in touch?"

"Sure, Jay. I'll keep you posted and let you know where you can reach me."

"The only thing is," Jay mused, "I still don't know if you're going to want to leave. You're going to get a hero's welcome up there. I don't know if it's sunk in yet, what you look like to the outside world. One day you expose the situation at North River. A few days later you predict a building's gonna collapse and it does. You're a rare commodity. They can't afford to let you go."

"But they *can* afford to kill me."

"They might be glad they failed."

In the elevator on the way up, Jon prayed the doors wouldn't open onto the nineteenth floor. None of the other three strangers in the elevator car had pressed 19, so there was a good chance he could proceed straight to the twentieth floor without having some potentially awkward interaction with someone else from the borough president's office. Get in and get out—that was his goal. But the moment Jon felt a few pounds lighter from the deceleration of the car, he knew his prayer hadn't been answered.

As one of the building custodians pushed his cart onto the elevator car, Jon locked eyes with Ned Richter, standing in the marble-floored hallway, flicking his suspender straps, confused for a moment, lost somewhere between point A and point B. As Jon stared, Ned stopped flicking his suspender straps, stared back blankly, and searched for some words as if he was tenderly chewing gum. Ned lifted his right hand and said "Hi" as the elevator doors closed. Jon knew he had to get out of there. Even the bathroom could wait.

A half minute later, as he walked urgently through the front portion of room 2035, it was a stereo snore-a-thon, with Larry in the right speaker channel and Old Al Gibbs in the left. Naomi was not at her desk. No sooner had Jon unlocked and opened his door than he found himself almost mechanically going through his folders for information he might need to take with him into hiding. While flipping through the main North River folder, he hurriedly considered which problem at the plant would be more significant—odor or flow—and decided it wasn't worth sorting through right now. He'd just take the whole fat folder.

He ripped two sheets of paper off the wall that had two dozen or so important phone numbers scribbled on them. As he pawed more folders, he realized he would have to grab most of his computer diskettes and toss them into a bag rather than go through them now. Then he would make a new backup of his hard drive and delete everything on it. Now, as he held in his hand the folder that contained the calculations on floating bodies he had developed for Detective Mercado, there was a double knock on the door. Quickly, even before the sound of the second knock could fade completely, the door opened. It was Paula.

"Hi, Jon," Paula said, somehow both resonantly and furtively. Sitting, folders in hand, Jon froze for a second before replying in the steadiest voice he could muster.

"What brings you up here? You're like a fish out of water."

"We got a call saying you took a fall this morning," Paula said with an air of concern. "We were worried."

"I'm sure you were," he said.

"Well, a few things have come up that I know you'll be interested to hear about. But first, are you okay?"

"I think I'll be fine in a few minutes."

"Okay, then," Paula said, racing on, "because it's been an incredibly hectic day. We got your odor report back from our consultant."

"And who was the mysterious consultant?"

"Herb Jacobs of Greely and Davis," Paula said, "and the news is good. He thinks the bulk of your work is valid. A couple of revisions and we can release it in a week or two."

"You're kidding me . . ." Jon put down the Mercado folder.

"No, this is certainly no joke," Paula said.

"You could have just told me Greely and Davis," Jon said.

"It worked out better this way," Paula said. "I told you to bear with us. Art has always had a soft spot for West Harlem, but we had a responsibility to make sure all the i's were dotted and the t's were crossed. And there is one small stipulation."

"What's that?" Jon asked.

"We'd like to release it in two parts," Paula explained. "Most of the report deals with the odor issue, which is fine. Let's focus on putting that out. You deal more briefly with the issue of flow to the plant. The consultant felt that portion was basically inconclusive and detracted from the report as a whole."

"Uh-huh . . ."

"Which is fine," Paula continued. "We can put out part one while you take a couple of months to refine part two."

"So I'm allowed to work on North River again? I'm allowed to *think* about North River again?"

"Look," Paula said, "what we had was a timing problem. We want what you want. But we were out of step with each other. Now it's time to get back in step. Yes, I've lost my cool. I've been upset with the situation at times, that's true. But I know we're most effective when we cooperate."

"I'm no angel myself," Jon said without affect. "Sometimes all I want to do is make other people eat shit."

Paula hesitated, gulped, and continued. "Well, just sit tight, and you'll get what you want. If anyone else from the media calls, tell them the report will be out in a matter of days, and you'll be able to discuss it with them at that time."

"Does it matter?" Jon asked. "The cat's pretty much out of the bag already."

"True, but you'll accomplish more if you save your fire for the release date. Same thing with your observations on flow. Hold off on *that* topic till *that* report comes out. I don't think that's asking too much of you, given that we're sticking our necks out for you. Art's willing to risk Hudson City, even though he advocated the project publicly."

"And why the one-eighty on *that*?" Jon asked calmly.

"There's really no one-eighty," Paula replied. "Art just wanted to make sure your report was solid. As far as Hudson City is concerned, it will have to live or die on its own merits. Art thinks it will live. And if the city has to come up with some additional money to further improve the odor condition at North River, so be it. Fair is fair. Jon, I was trying to explain this to you all along."

Jon said nothing.

"Well, I'll let you clean yourself up now," Paula said. "You still have a long day in front of you. Did you know that there was a partial collapse at 350 West 110th Street?"

"Yes, I just heard about it on the way up," Jon said.

"Well, congratulations," Paula said, with a bubbly air. "You've graduated from engineer to soothsayer. If you want to be a celebrity for a few days, go with that story. I imagine some reporters will be calling you. Go full blast on this one—you have our blessing. Tell them the mayor should be doing something about these deteriorating buildings. Let 'em have it."

"I will," Jon said.

"Good," Paula said, gently tapping the top of Jon's computer monitor and reaching for the doorknob with her other hand.

"Hey, what do you know about the subway explosion on Fourteenth Street?" Jon said. "Was it a bomb?"

"We were told it was a transformer that blew," Paula replied, "just one of those things."

"I just missed being on that train," Jon said.

"Really? This must be your lucky day. If you want to get involved in that too, go ahead. Just keep a low profile on the North River flow issue until we're in step on that one. You understand where I'm coming from."

"Sure, I understand where you're coming from." Paula stepped out and closed the door behind her. "I just want you to go *back* there," Jon said under his breath.

He got up, peered out of his doorway, and watched Paula walk past the stereo snoring and out the front door of room 2035. He pulled his head back into his office, then closed and locked the door. He considered the fact that he hadn't taped this last conversation with Paula—that from the moment she pounced, he hadn't been able to find a good opportunity to casually reach into his desk drawer, locate the microcassette player, and press record. No great loss, he thought.

Now he looked at the flashing red message light, which he hadn't dealt with consciously since first entering his office. The bathroom could wait another couple of minutes. It wasn't as if he had to impress anybody. He picked up the receiver, punched in his code, and learned that he had four new messages. He let the first one play: "Jon, Mark Rosario, *Westsider*. Couldn't wait to hear back from you. I heard you predicted that building on 110th Street was going to come down. Now I have *two* things I want to talk to you about . . ."

Jon put down the receiver for a moment and decided his first order of business was to call Elaine. He tried her office number first, but was told she'd left for the day. As he dialed their home number, he started taping one of the lists of important phone numbers back onto the wall. He then heard Elaine's exasperated voice on the phone.

"Hello . . ."

"I'm staying."

"You're staying?" Elaine said. "Where, at your job? Are you crazy?"

"The picture here changed just a few minutes ago," Jon said. "Not completely, but enough so that it's worth it for me to hang around at least a little longer. And maybe longer than that. My report came back from the consultant. They're going to release most of it in two weeks."

"Congratulations," Elaine said with festering sarcasm. "For that you're willing to get yourself killed. Well, I'm not. I'm not staying."

"That's fine—"

"By suppertime the kids and I will be gone. I'm taking them to my friend Judy's house. I already spoke to her. She has a finished basement that's not being used. I don't want to get my mother involved. That's the first place they'll look. I'm not even telling Mom and Dad about this whole thing. It'll just scare the you-know-what out of them."

"Elaine, you're overreacting—"

"Someone tried to kill you, you said, and—"

"Maybe someone did try, and maybe not. Maybe the squatters notched that beam for the police. So whether someone tried to kill me or not, I'm still here. And I'm going to see this thing through. I will not be stopped. Anyway, Paula was just in here a few seconds ago. If she absolutely needed me dead, don't you think she could have walked in here and shot me?"

"Would *that* convince you?"

"Things have changed, Elaine. I'm not sure exactly why. But when they release my report, that gives me stature—stature I didn't have before. I no longer become someone they can dispose of so easily. How's that? You don't know every little last thing about me, okay? I went in and inspected a building last week and predicted it would collapse. Well, today it did. And I did it without tarot cards."

"So they call off the dogs for a few days and you think you're out of danger."

"That's not the point at all," Jon protested. "The point is I'm finally in a position to do some good. I'm worth more standing up here for environmental justice than I am hiding in someone's finished basement in Long Island."

"Worth more to whom?" Elaine said.

"To everybody. What do you think, I'm suddenly going to stop being vigilant? I'm going to be more vigilant than ever. It's not like I trust these assholes. I caught a couple of breaks, and I'm gonna ride them a little while, okay?"

"You're showing me a lot about your priorities today," Elaine said.

"That's a low blow, Elaine. I didn't ask to be in this situation. It landed on me, and I'm trying to deal with it the best I can. Don't worry about it. I have a plan."

"I have a plan too," Elaine said dryly.

Chapter 25

A few minutes past ten on the overcast morning of May 11, Detectives Mercado and O'Connel emerged from their unmarked blue '87 Plymouth Fury and walked west along the north curb of Fourteenth Street. Forty yards ahead, Charlie Sharpe was using a metal rake with a long wooden handle to clean out a catch basin. Even before Mercado could speak, Sharpe stopped and looked the detectives up and down once quickly.

"Yeah," Sharpe said, breathing out forcefully.

"Mr. Sharpe," Mercado said, "Detectives Mercado and O'Connel. Need to ask you a couple of questions."

"You got anyone yet?" Sharpe asked.

"Maybe," Mercado said. "You can help us. Ever see this guy before?" Mercado opened a folder and pulled out the personnel file photo and the composite sketch of McCord, holding one in each hand and putting them forth for Sharpe to see. Sharpe looked at each hand for a second and looked up at the detectives again.

"Max McCord," Sharpe said. "He works over at Eighteenth

Street, all the way over on the West Side . . . that area. My old job. That's who killed Joel?"

"Eighteenth Street again," Mercado said, shaking his head.

"We have some evidence that indicates McCord was involved to some extent," O'Connel said. "Can you tell us anything else about him?"

"McCord?" Sharpe said. "What do you want me to tell you? We got hundreds of folks working for the department. You think I hang out with all of them and shoot pool? What do you want to hear—that he beats his wife? What the hell do I know?"

"We don't know *what* you know," Mercado said. "That's why we're asking. Anything you can tell us might help—who his friends are in your department, anything about his past . . ."

"Nope, I don't know nothin' about his past," Sharpe insisted. "The only thing I know about is *my* future. I got eight more catch basins to clean out today and eleven months to go before I go on an all-expense-paid trip outta here for good."

"Remember you said something last time about permit trouble the city was having with the sewers?" O'Connel said. "Any developments with that lately?"

"I don't know and I don't care," Sharpe said vehemently, placing his right hand firmly on his hip. "I stay out of their business and they stay out of mine. The day they come down here and check for missing bricks is the day I go up there and tell them what to do with North River. If you wanna know how they run this system, read that guy from the *Westsider* who's always bitchin' about it. Or go ask them yourselves."

"Them?" O'Connel asked. "Them who?"

"I don't know," Sharpe said, "whoever signs my paycheck. Hey, I don't have any problem with them. They just gave us all big, fat merit raises—ten percent, retroactive to last June. You guys are only getting four percent this year, and no fat payday like us. So how could I possibly have a problem?"

"When did you get this increase?" Mercado asked.

"I don't know—a few weeks ago, something like that."

"Like right after your partner was killed?" Mercado pressed.

"Look, I don't know," Sharpe said. "Yeah, that same day, whatever. They passed out checks at his funeral, is that what you're lookin' for? All I know is it fattened my pension ten percent."

"Everybody get these merit increases?" O'Connel asked.

"Everyone I know," Sharpe said. "We got a thank-you note— 'Thanks for shoveling shit.' You know what a gift horse is, Detective?"

"Mr. Sharpe," O'Connel asked, "can you ever recall hearing the name Ronald Arlen in connection with McCord or anyone else in DEP? Even something minor?"

"Yeah, sure," Sharpe replied, "Ronald Arlen's down here all the time, showing us how he cleaned the sewers when he was working his way up. Sometimes we all get on his helicopter and fly down to one of his casinos in Atlantic City. We drop a few thousand at the tables and Arlen takes us up to his penthouse and lays some champagne and caviar on us."

"All right, that's enough," O'Connel said, snarling. "We're trying to figure out who killed your friend and why, and all you can do is stand there and make smart-ass remarks. We know Joel Haney is innocent."

"I told you where to find McCord," Sharpe said. "Go ahead . . . pick him up. Ask him what you asked me."

"We'll do that," O'Connel said brusquely. "Thanks for the information."

"Yeah, sure," Sharpe said, starting to push the rake around the edge of the open catch basin again. The detectives had turned and walked ten feet back toward the unmarked Fury when Mercado stopped and turned back toward Sharpe, and spoke.

"You might want to stick around for a few more months after you become eligible for your pension. Who knows—maybe you'll get Lee Sarnow's job after he gets the boot."

Sharpe stopped for a moment, fought off a smile, and resumed cleaning. When the detectives had walked another twenty feet toward the car, it was Sharpe's turn. "Hey."

Mercado and O'Connel turned around to face Sharpe again, who had one last utterance.

"If you want to pick up McCord, try the graveyard shift."

Twenty minutes before midnight, May 11, Detectives Mercado and O'Connel sat without interior lights in the unmarked Fury parked along the shoulder of the southbound side of Eleventh Avenue, fifty yards north of the Eighteenth Street underground regulator chamber. They craned their necks periodically, looking north, south, east, west. The night was cool, damp, and overcast, but the fog had not settled as low as the pavement along the Hudson River. With the help of a streetlight, the detectives hoped to spot McCord from whichever hole or patch of darkness he emerged.

"I don't know," O'Connel said, slapping the locked steering wheel with two open palms, "should we have filled Gene in like we did about this arrest?"

"Look, we've been over this half a dozen times," Mercado said, "and we're damned if we do and damned if we don't. If we blindside Gene with this, then we look bad in front of the D.A. or Gene pressures us to turn McCord loose."

"But we have a witness," O'Connel said, "and some good circumstantial evidence."

"Exactly," Mercado said. "That's why we go with it straight up and take our chances. I feel better with the bench warrant. Sarnow is going to have to know about this sometime anyway—like the day we pick him up. I wish we had enough on Sarnow to make him right now too, but we don't. Our best bet is to lean on McCord and make him sing. Hopefully, everything sticks."

"Yeah," O'Connel said, "and hope that in between now and then, that little twerp doesn't have enough time to cover his ass."

"McCord will be feeding him information," Mercado said, "but we can make that work in our favor."

"And what about Gene's little thing with Sarnow?" O'Connel asked. "Starting a few hours ago, Sarnow may have already begun coming up with alibis."

"Let him," Mercado said. "He's still in for a surprise soon. As far as Gene goes, we've kept him pretty much in the dark. He doesn't know about Sarnow's fingerprints in Haney's apartment, or about Kessler and exactly how we came up with Pappas, or about that Arlen memo, or everything we know about McCord and Sarnow. All he knows is that we came up with a witness in a deli on Fourteenth Street."

"Bottom line, Jimmy—do you think Gene has already picked up the phone and called Sarnow?"

"Fifty-fifty," Mercado said, "but as self-serving as he is, I don't think Gene is gonna throw it all away that easy. He plays us, we play him, he plays Sarnow. At a certain point the evidence becomes overwhelming and takes on a life of its own."

"Okay, I'll go along with that," O'Connel said, sighing. "We'll be showing some of our cards to McCord soon, like you said. I'm just tired of walking this tightrope."

"You're almost at the other end," Mercado said.

"Jesus, it stinks down here," O'Connel said, shrugging and rolling up her window. "It's like a thousand dead fish."

"You got that right," Mercado said. "I read that the Hudson River water quality was getting better over the past few years, ever since that treatment plant opened up."

"Apparently not," O'Connel said.

"How 'bout if I light up?" Mercado said. "That'll make the dead fish smell go away."

O'Connel thought for a moment. "Tell you what," she said, "I'll take the fish."

"Sorry you feel that way," Mercado said. "Looks like Sharpe wasn't kidding when he said the city was having problems with the state and the feds over environmental matters. Maybe this is what he means."

"I'm sure it's a lot more complex than that, Jimmy. Anyway, what's up with Sharpe? Why is he holding out on us like this? He should realize we're on his side."

"He has a pension to protect," Mercado said. "Tell you the truth, I feel for the guy. The last thing he needs is for someone like Sarnow to mess things up for him just for cooperating with us. How would *you* like to be mugged in the final 365 yards of the New York City Marathon?"

"It's not like I don't give a shit," O'Connel said. "You know that. But I feel like this guy's a potential wellspring of information, and it bothers me."

"Just be glad you're sitting here."

"Oh, I'm real glad," O'Connel said.

"We owe half this arrest to Sharpe."

"Let's see what pops up first," O'Connel said. "We could be here all night and get nothing. But you know no matter what happens, we're missing something big here, and you know damn well Sharpe knows what it is. Doesn't that bother you?"

"Everything bothers me, Janine," Mercado said, now reaching into his pocket for a pack of Camels.

"Like that comment about McCord beating his wife," O'Connel said. "Right there, you know he knows something about McCord.

The merit raises he talked about, the sarcasm about Ronald Arlen, his whole attitude . . ."

"Sure. And he's holding something on Sarnow too," Mercado said. "Don't worry. He's aching to let it out. We'll try him again. At the moment, we just have too much time on our hands sitting here spinning our wheels."

"Yeah, that's how the trouble started in the first place," O'Connel said, rolling her eyes and fighting off a smile.

"Wait a second, someone's coming out of that manhole," Mercado blurted out, pointing straight ahead, due south toward the Eighteenth Street regulator chamber. The detectives were stone silent for a moment as they watched a heavyset, broad-shouldered man with a goatee emerge.

"That looks like one of the rough-looking dudes DEP hired," O'Connel said. Emerging right behind him was McCord, wearing gray pants and carrying a walkie-talkie.

"That's a hit," Mercado said, "let's go." Mercado and O'Connel popped out of opposite sides of the unmarked Fury and took their first few deliberate steps toward the two, who now squinted in the headlights O'Connel had turned on.

"Freeze and put your hands up," Mercado shouted, now along with O'Connel flashing his shield and revolver. "Detectives Mercado and O'Connel from the Tenth Precinct." Both McCord and his partner complied immediately, raising their hands, McCord still clutching in his right the walkie-talkie, rolling his eyes back in his head and lifting his arms halfheartedly, as if this had already become a tedious exercise.

"Max McCord, you're under arrest in connection with the murder of Joel Haney on the night of April fifth," Mercado said, removing the walkie-talkie from McCord's extended hand and giving it over to O'Connel, who pocketed it. As O'Connel stood five feet away, with both McCord and his partner in easy range of her revolver, Mercado turned the grinning McCord around and cuffed him from behind. Mercado began to pat down McCord and pulled from his rear pants pocket a .22-caliber Smith & Wesson snubnose.

"Shoot a lot of alligators down there?" Mercado said, nodding toward the steel regulator cover and handing the piece to O'Connel.

"That's a licensed gun," McCord said.

"Yeah, licensed to someone else," Mercado said.

"All right, do whatever you have to," McCord said glibly. "You're wasting your time. I'll be out in a couple of hours. I wasn't even around when Haney was killed."

"Where were you," O'Connel said, "taking a sauna with Ronald Arlen in your pad out in Suffolk?"

"I'm a working man," McCord said. "I take home eleven hundred and ninety-eight dollars every two weeks."

"What do you do with the rest?" Mercado said. "You have the right to remain silent. Anything you say can and will be used against you in a court of law. You have the right to an attorney. If you cannot afford one . . . but, hey, we all know you can."

"Are you arresting me too?" McCord's partner asked.

"Not unless you want us to," O'Connel replied.

"You want me to call Fuckface?" McCord's partner asked.

"What I want you to do is shut the fuck up," McCord answered.

"Fuckface, huh? Is that your name for Lee Sarnow?" Mercado laughed and grinned at O'Connel, who smiled back wryly.

O'Connel now patted down McCord's partner as Mercado covered her. O'Connel came up with an assortment of wrenches but no weapons. With O'Connel leading the way, Mercado pushed McCord toward the unmarked Fury.

"What could I possibly have against someone like Joel Haney?" McCord said.

"I dunno," Mercado said. "Maybe that he was good-looking."

"What do you two do for a living anyway?" McCord asked.

"Shut up and get in the car, Jerome," Mercado said.

In the interview room on the second floor of the Tenth Precinct, O'Connel sat across a worn oak table from McCord, who was now uncuffed and looking at the acoustic tile ceiling to avoid eye contact. Mercado paced around the perimeter of the room, occasionally stopping to tap the green metallic walls and gather his thoughts. McCord thumbed a mug of black coffee, took a sip, and placed it back down.

"I'm *glad* you're not cooperating," Mercado said. "We have enough to put you away for life."

"Then *do* it," McCord said.

"I *will*," Mercado said. "If you're so stupid that you're willing to be a patsy for someone like Lee Sarnow, you deserve to rot in a cell somewhere." ·

"Hey, my lawyer's on his way," McCord said. "You can tell this shit to him."

"Who's paying for that lawyer, Jerome," Mercado said, "Lee Sarnow?"

"I don't know what you're talking about," McCord said, fixing the collar of his work shirt.

"You know—Fuckface. Who's Fuckface's lawyer gonna be looking out for," Mercado said, "you? I seriously doubt it. I've seen this a hundred times before, Jerome. This guy will want you to shut up and take the rap for everyone. He'll tell you to believe in him like he's your savior. Meanwhile, Lee Sarnow is saving his own ass, putting everything on you. Is that who you really are, Jerome? The kind of guy who lets these upper-echelon bureaucrats walk all over you?"

"Look, I swear I didn't kill Joel Haney."

"Okay," O'Connel said in a soothing, conciliatory voice that contrasted with Mercado's, "then tell us the truth about the whole thing, and you're really not looking at much time. We want to help you."

"Speak for yourself," Mercado said.

"Max," O'Connel said, "we have bigger fish to fry."

"No, no, let those fish fry *him*," Mercado said. "He's a sucker anyway."

"Why would I want to kill Joel Haney?" McCord said. "I worked with the guy. We never even had words."

"Then the question is why would you want to tamper with evidence, Jerome," Mercado said.

"Stop calling me Jerome."

"We have your prints all over Joel Haney's apartment, Jerome," Mercado continued. "Remember the videotapes you planted? Remember the blow? Those are all separate charges, and this stuff is just mounting up against you, Jerome. I guess you miss your old friends at Sing Sing. I guess you miss getting slashed and getting it up the butt."

"Shut the fuck up," McCord shouted, swiping the cup off the

table and sending four ounces of hot coffee streaming across the oak tabletop.

"Go ahead, Jerome, provoke me," Mercado yelled, grabbing McCord's collar and delivering his message point-blank. "I *wanna* see you go away, you know why? Not because you conspired to kill an innocent man, Jerome. But because you're so spineless you don't deserve to walk around free in New York. If you want to live the rest of your life watching people take advantage of you, we'll put you somewhere where that can happen."

"Leave me alone," McCord said, breaking Mercado's grasp and burying his face in his hands momentarily.

"We have a witness who puts you on Fourteenth Street between Sixth and Seventh Avenue dumping Haney's body," O'Connel said calmly. "He got everything right. But maybe that's *all* you did . . . dump a load in the sewer. Maybe you didn't even know what it was you were dumping. The time to get out in front of this is now, when you can still help yourself. You can probably plea way down on this. You can be back out in a year or two and still have a life."

McCord stared straight up at the ceiling.

"Right," Mercado barked, "then you can go back to whatever it is that gives you kicks. Like dumping toxic sludge from the sewers illegally in the Fresh Kills landfill."

"Who told you that?" McCord snapped, for the first time in a long time looking directly at Mercado.

"Who the hell do you *think* told me that?" Mercado said. "Your friend Lee Sarnow. You think we haven't interviewed him yet? We had him up here a little while ago. He was picking that big schnozz of his, telling us all about you, putting everything on you. Telling us how you hit Haney over the back of the head and drove him out to Fourteenth Street, where you dumped him and about how he's tired of covering for a chump like you."

McCord's face turned progressively redder, while his fists were firmly clenched and pressed into the oak tabletop. Mercado continued.

"You know something? I don't even believe half the shit Sarnow's telling us, but I could care less. I just wanna close the book on this case and get back to my *boat* on the *South Shore*, know what I mean? So I'm cool. The more you shut up and take it in the rear, the faster I can do that."

"I didn't kill Haney!" McCord blurted out. "Paul killed him by accident. I helped him get rid of the body and that's it, I swear! I'll take a lie detector test—"

"You won't take anything," a portly, fiftyish, bespectacled man in a three-piece suit said, opening the door to the interview room and slamming it behind him, "except the Fifth and two Prozacs. You just shut up and say nothing to these people." McCord literally bit his own tongue. The portly man looked straight at Mercado.

"I'm Reggie Lang, Mr. McCord's attorney. You two oughta know better than to badger my client without his attorney present."

"Your client just admitted to dumping Joel Haney's body in the Fourteenth Street sewer," Mercado said.

"That means less than nothing," Lang said. "It's under duress, you didn't get it on tape, and he won't be signing anything. I'm taking Mr. McCord out of here and finding out every last way in which you violated his rights." Lang now looked at McCord, who was staring down at his own hands. "From now on, you talk to me."

"He can talk to whomever he wants," O'Connel said. "He just offered to take a lie detector test."

"Forget it, honey," Lang said. "Take the test yourself and let me know if you pass."

"You might want a deal for Jerome here after you hear what we already have," Mercado said.

"Not interested," Lang said. "Is my client even being charged? If not, I want him cut loose this second."

"He's as good as charged," O'Connel said. "The D.A. will be here in the morning and so will our witness. We're pulling together a lineup, and right after your client is ID'ed, he's charged. We're holding him overnight downstairs."

"I'll be waiting in the building the whole night," Lang said, "within earshot."

"Your time must be cheap," Mercado said.

"It'll be costly to you," Lang said. "Go ahead, make the mistakes you cops always make. I'm gonna be all over them, and Max is going to be a free man by lunchtime."

"Can we arrest *you* then, for being an asshole?" Mercado said.

"We're done," Lang said.

"Jerome," O'Connel half pleaded, "once you go along with him, that's it—you've cut your lifeline, your one chance to walk away from this thing in a few months."

"I got nothing to say," McCord replied.

Chapter 26

At 9:35 on the morning of May 12, Detectives Mercado and O'Connel stood inside the viewing room, separated from the lineup room by a wall and a large pane of one-way glass. As O'Connel looked on, Mercado read from page two of that morning's *Times*, which featured an article by Leonard Kretchner.

After a lengthy internal investigation, the New York City Department of Environmental Protection has conceded that the city's sewer system has most likely been used for the trafficking of large amounts of illegal narcotics, including crack cocaine and heroin. A report released by Deputy Commissioner Lee Sarnow states that apparently, small, tightly sealed bags of narcotics were flushed down toilets and received by human couriers waiting in nearby large sewers in an effort to bypass police surveillance of those buildings . . .

"Who has time to think this stuff up?" O'Connel asked.
"Wait, listen to this," Mercado said.

According to the report, the couriers then proceeded on foot through the sewers to manhole locations beyond the purview of police surveillance and eventually to their final destination. The report states that there is evidence pointing to the involvement of DEP personnel in this trafficking scheme . . .

"That must be why everyone got a raise," O'Connel said.
"Here we go," Mercado said.

The report concludes that the apparent ring leader of this operation was Joel Haney, a DEP maintenance worker who was found dead last month in the sewer beneath Fourteenth Street.

"Beautiful . . ."

Haney has already been implicated earlier as a producer and distributor of underground pornographic movies. Deputy Commissioner Sarnow states the entire matter is being turned over to the New York City Police Department and that the DEP will offer full cooperation throughout the entire investigation.

"Poor son of a bitch," O'Connel said. "The longer he stays dead, the worse his reputation gets."

"And the sicker Sarnow's imagination gets," Mercado said. "As ludicrous as the whole story is, you know what really bothers me about it?"

"What?"

"The timing," Mercado said. "We haven't seen anything from the Haney smear campaign in a while. Now, right on the heels of the arrest, here it is, at our doorstep."

"You think Sarnow knew exactly when this arrest was coming?" O'Connel asked.

"That's what it feels like," Mercado said. "Who knows? My inspired guesses have been pretty good lately. I guessed right about McCord having a pool and a boat. I guessed right about his dumping toxic sludge in the Fresh Kills landfill. All I had was that memo with the words 'Fresh Kills' and a bunch of dates and times. You see McCord's face? Too bad he lawyered up."

"If you're right, Jimmy, we have a serious leak in here. Or maybe Jeanie Griffin is still talking to McCord."

"I doubt it," Mercado said.

"Me too. Or maybe someone at Two Washington Street tipped off Sarnow, but that's a long shot. Then there's Gene."

"It doesn't matter," Mercado said. "We have Pappas. And a pile of other evidence. The *Times* can print that Joel Haney was the Antichrist—in this state, it's still a capital offense to kill the devil if he has a Social Security number, a beating heart, and is a registered voter."

"Let's not kid ourselves, Jimmy. This is getting out of hand. I mean, we book a sewer rat and who's his attorney? Reggie Lang. This guy represents big politicians caught in bed with prostitutes and major developers—like Ronald Arlen. His firm did Arlen's last bankruptcy. And he's getting out of bed in the middle of the night for a guy making eleven eighty every two weeks? Let's get real."

"I know, I know," Mercado said, pressing his face up against the one-way glass and watching it fog up. "We don't know exactly why all this juice is behind the murder of a guy shooting dirty home videos, but we know this is an iceberg, and we know some of the players above the surface. Once we nail Jerome with Pappas, we'll be in position to go after the rest of the iceberg."

"Reinterview McCord after we charge him?"

"You got it," Mercado said. "I want his butt back in interrogation. It'll be hard as hell with Lang around, but Jerome just may break with the pack. Did you take a look at him? He does not wanna go back to the joint. It's right there in his beady little eyes."

The door to the viewing room opened and in walked Assistant District Attorney Rose Caffey, a fortyish, trim, and well-groomed brunette whose businesslike extra-short haircut and gray suit were offset by pumps and nicely put together calves.

"What's up in there, Rose?" O'Connel asked.

"We have Pappas," Caffey said. "They're still trying to get one more guy for the lineup."

"What's the problem?" Mercado complained. "I gave them a list of fills, phone numbers and all."

Mercado continued to look through the glass, where he saw a uniformed officer position McCord second from the right. McCord, still in his gray pants and denim work shirt from the night before, looked haggard. He came in at just under six-foot-three. Mercado studied the gray hair, the gray eyes, and the scar on the left cheek and put himself at ease. McCord was a dead ringer for himself.

The center position in the lineup was still vacant. But the other three, though all white males in their forties or fifties, shared perhaps only one or two physical features each with McCord—one was about the same height, another had similarly sallow, weathered skin, another gray hair. But none of them other than McCord himself had the combination of hardened and time-worn features identified by Pappas the night he described McCord to Vicki Moyer.

By comparison to the obstacle course of finding Pappas in the first place and his superb effort in describing the suspect, this morning's exercise was a cakewalk. Pappas was their insurance policy against all other things that might go wrong in a case—illegal searches, failure to Mirandize, inadmissible testimony, or even public innuendo by a deputy commissioner. If McCord was the tip of the iceberg, Pappas was a piece of the rock.

Still, Mercado now felt unexplained pangs of upset in his digestive tract and reached for a Camel. After lighting up, he clicked the fingernails of his left hand against the viewing glass and turned to Assistant District Attorney Caffey.

"What's taking so long?"

"Nothing's taking so long," Caffey said. "This thing is coming together pretty fast considering you just picked up the suspect last night and it's barely ten A.M. They're rounding up one more fill. As a matter of fact, Reinhart just found somebody they're sending in."

"Reinhart? Well, let's get this show on the road," Mercado said.

"Relax, Jimmy," O'Connel said. The door to the viewing room opened and in walked Reggie Lang, his three-piece suit now a bit crumpled.

"You get a good night's sleep?" O'Connel asked.

"I don't sleep on the job," Lang said. "I'm not in a union."

"Then you probably heard McCord singing all night from his cell in the basement," Mercado said. "Amazing. All it took was one good, hard bitch-slap and he told us everything we wanted to know about ditching Haney's body, blowing Lee Sarnow, making money on the side with Ronald Arlen. By the way, how is Arlen doing? Still seeing that waitress over at Goldfingers?"

"You're pathetic, Detective," Lang said without affect.

"That's what happens when you work for a living," Mercado replied. The door to the viewing room opened again.

"We're just about ready to go, Detectives," a uniformed officer said, leading Pappas into the room and leaving him there like a frightened kid dropped off at sleep-away for the first time.

"Thanks for coming down, Mr. Pappas," O'Connel said.

"No problem," Pappas said. "I told you I do it. As long as I get back soon. I'm on the early shift now."

"It shouldn't take more than a minute," O'Connel said.

Mercado had dropped his cigarette and was now transfixed

against the viewing glass. The uneasiness in his stomach had become a piece of hot lead. The first thing he noticed was the scar on the left cheek. Then the leathery skin. Then the icy gray eyes, both in a skull that topped out at six-foot-three. All would have been okay if it was McCord, but it wasn't.

It was the last man in the lineup, inserted into the vacant center position a moment earlier by one of the uniformed officers. Even the work clothes were similar. In a sense, as he and McCord stood side by side, flanked by nonentities, they were more alike than identical twins. Identical twins, though having the same genetic makeup, eventually had different life experiences. These two had the same life experience, and it showed. It was as if one was named Max McCord and the other Jerome Patterson.

"Wait a second," Mercado said, smashing his open right palm against the glass, "What the hell is going on? Janine, take a look at this."

"Oh my God," O'Connel said. "Can we hold it a second?"

"What's the matter," Lang said, "your perp's not in there?"

"He's in there," O'Connel said.

"Then put your witness's face in the glass," Lang said.

"How 'bout if I put your face in the glass?" Mercado said.

"Why don't you do that, Detective?" Lang said.

"Can we break for five minutes?" O'Connel asked.

"Forget it," Lang said. "Waste any more of my time and I'm pressing my own charges."

"I have another case to get to, Janine," Caffey said, looking at her watch. Lang had already shoved the pliable Pappas up to the glass, as if he had the authority to do so. O'Connel leaned over to Pappas and tried to speak with a steady voice.

"Take your time. Make sure you get it right. Remember, they can't see you." Mercado slumped with his back to the front wall of the viewing room and cradled his face in his right hand. Maybe Pappas would pull it off. Maybe he was a witness for the ages. Maybe he had an epiphany that rainy night, seeing clearly not only a few outward physical characteristics, but right through to the man's soul. Pick number four, Pappas. Pick number four.

"I don't know for sure," Pappas said. "I think it's one of those two. Number three or number four."

"Which one, Mr. Pappas?" O'Connel said. "Which one?"

"Three or four," Pappas repeated.

"Sir, that's not of any use to us," Caffey said. "We need a definite response. If you're not sure, you shouldn't be up there guessing." There were five seconds of dead silence. Inside the lineup room, the suspects twitched and turned slightly, impatient, as if freedom or imprisonment were both preferable to this state.

"Three or four," Pappas said.

"Pappas," Mercado said, lifting his head but looking at no one, "try to remember what you're here *for*. *For* what did you come to this country?"

"Number four?" Pappas said.

"That's it," Lang barked, "this lineup is invalid. He was coached. Release my client this second."

"I'm sorry, Janine," Caffey said, "we can't hold him."

"Number three?" Pappas said.

"Rose, we have a lot of other evidence," O'Connel said, pleading, panic-stricken. "We have fingerprints—"

"We can talk about it later," Caffey said. "From what I was told this morning, we just don't have enough to charge him. Not after this."

"Rose, we have probable cause."

"What you have is circumstantial," Caffey said. "We will talk about it later this afternoon in my office."

Mercado shoved Lang out of the way and bolted out the door. Blue uniforms and plainclothes alike whipped around as Mercado stomped and breezed past them in the first-floor hallway like a half bull, half matador. The creaks of the old wooden steps to the second floor could not catch Mercado's angry black heels. The yellowed walls of the second-floor hallway collapsed like an accordion around Mercado, who swung open the door to Captain Reinhart's office. Reinhart, still in his wake-up ritual, looked up from his desk and put down his *New York Times*.

"Jimmy—"

"You fat piece of shit."

"What the hell is wrong with you?"

"This," Mercado said, slapping the newspaper toward Reinhart's face. "You and Sarnow and the borough president and Ronald Arlen and whoever the fuck else is lining your pocket."

"You're crazy," Reinhart shouted. "What the hell is wrong with you, Jimmy?"

"You fixed that lineup," Mercado said. "Admit it. That was a righteous bust. You fixed that lineup. You killed all our work. Now stand up and say it, you piece of shit."

"Are you on drugs, Mercado?" Reinhart said sternly. "The lineup? The lineup? We were lucky to get anybody for your fuck-ing lineup. They had to call some guy down from DGS at the last minute who helps us out once in a while. Bruce Gregory. And we were lucky to get *him*—he isn't feeling so well. So what hap-pened? Did your witness pick out McCord or not?" The rear of Reinhart's office was now jammed with O'Connel and five uni-formed officers, with more in the hallway trying to catch a glimpse.

"You made it impossible for him," Mercado said. "*You* belong in a lineup."

"Jimmy, you're looking at this whole thing from only one angle. If we go charging city employees, don't you think it ought to be airtight? Wouldn't you want the same scrupulous treatment if you were named?"

"Come off it, Gene. You crossed the line here."

"*You're* the one crossing the line," Reinhart said. " And I got news for you. The whole lineup turned out to be a waste of time anyway. McCord has an alibi for that night. He was with Lee Sarnow the entire time. A waiter at the Judson Grill on Fifty-second Street backs them both up. Sarnow was giving McCord a promotion, personally. Gotta turn him loose, Jimmy. Sorry. I'm taking you and O'Connel off the chart anyway. Nothing else is getting done. It's sucking your time. You're chasing asinine leads up and down Fourteenth Street. I can't have this."

"Then you can have *this*," Mercado said, tossing his shield onto page two of the *New York Times*."

"Jimmy, take a few days to reconsider—" Mercado turned and pushed his way past O'Connel and through the cluster of officers. "I'm gonna hold this for you, till you cool off." As Reinhart shouted, Mercado was already out of view. At the end of the hall-way, with all eyes upon him, Mercado put his foot through the decorative glass of the Coke machine. A moment later he was down the stairs and out the front door.

Chapter 27

Jon Kessler awoke at 7:50 A.M. on the morning of Wednesday, May 19, in the master bedroom of the house in Rocky Point. Evidently, he had shut off the clock radio instead of hitting the snooze button. Now he rolled over to Elaine's side of the bed, which was unoccupied except for a ten-day-old sweet, faded scent of her perfumed soap and overnight perspiration ground into the sheets.

Jon recalled bits and pieces of the dream he was having just before waking up. In it, a steel pipe was suspended in midair, surrounded by trees, as if in a forest. The pipe had sprung a leak, and water was dripping down, forming a hole in the soil below. Earlier in the dream, the hole in the ground looked to be maybe a few inches deep. Now it was bottomless. Jon offered to fix it, but Elaine stood off in the distance, arms folded, shaking her head and warning him that it was too dangerous.

Naomi, however, had placed a workman's ladder before him, extending up to the leak, and was encouraging him to fix it. "Go ahead, give it a shot," she said repeatedly. As Jon took careful, methodical steps up the ladder, he felt something strange in his mouth. Reaching in with the fingers of his right hand, he removed his two upper front teeth.

Now, fully awake in Rocky Point, Jon watched the digital readout hit 8:00 on the clock radio and considered which train into New York he might still catch. Then he recalled that there really was a leak. He had noticed it several times over the past month and again the night before, during a heavy rain. The aluminum gutter along the west side of the house had pulled apart at a joint between two sections. About half of the storm water was not making it to the downspout at the front of the house, instead running straight down, eighteen feet to the flower garden below, where a hole three inches deep had already formed.

Twenty minutes later, in sneakers and sweatpants, Jon stood beneath the separated joint in the gutter. The sun had come out, and it was now easy to see what had happened. Two nails connecting the gutter to the eave of the second-floor roof were missing. Jon looked around the yard, at the empty batting cage, at the swings—now still except for a faint breeze nudging at them, at his gray Chrysler minivan with a registration sticker already three weeks past the expiration date. The minivan looked almost abandoned without being flanked by the red '89 Honda Civic as it usually was.

Jon looked back up at the missing nails and considered what kind of time would be involved in getting the ladder out of the garage, looking for the right nails in the basement, and actually doing the work. He would lose an hour when it was all said and done. He looked down at the hole that had formed from the erosion. Then it dawned on him. He had no reason to be here.

Jon sat at his desk at eleven-forty that Wednesday morning sifting through precipitation charts from the National Weather Service when the phone rang. He grabbed the receiver in the middle of the second ring.

"Jon Kessler . . ."

"Hey, buddy." Jon recognized the voice instantly.

"Keith, what's up?"

"What's up with you, buddy?" Keith asked. "I haven't seen you in a week, but I can't get away from you, you freaking celebrity. Everywhere I turn you're in my face—the *Daily News*, the *Post*, the *Westsider*, the *Voice*, Channel One."

"What can I say?" Jon replied. "I got lucky."

"Just don't tell me *my* building's gonna fall down," Keith said.

"Well, if I do," Jon said, "you'd better get the hell out of there and find someplace else to sleep."

"I will," Keith said. "Which brings me to why I called."

"You mean you didn't call just to congratulate me?"

"Not just," Keith said. "You know the reason you haven't seen me the last couple of times you slept over?"

"A girl?"

"That's right," Keith said. "A woman named Diane from my office. Works in my unit."

"Hooo yeah . . . Is that in your unit or on your unit?"

"We wound up at her place the last few times," Keith said.

"She's the first woman I've ever cared about since Allison. She's great."

"But you need your apartment tonight," Jon said.

"Just in case you were thinking of using it. I hate to ask . . ."

"You didn't have to," Jon said. "Hey, no problem. I'll sleep on a park bench somewhere. A safe bench, in a safe park—like maybe in Crown Heights. Don't worry about me."

"Her roommate's having her old boyfriend over tonight," Keith explained, "so I told Diane I didn't think you were coming over tonight."

"Kind of like a domino effect," Jon observed. "Now I'll have to tell that guy on the Bowery I lent my cardboard box to that I need it back."

"No, seriously. Will you be okay?"

"Don't worry about it," Jon said. "I can stay with my aunt and uncle in Queens, remember? I'm a celebrity now. They'll be glad to roll out the old cot for me."

"I was thinking maybe you could go home."

"Where's home, Keith?"

"You know, Rocky Point," Keith said. "Maybe you could surprise Elaine."

"The only way I could surprise Elaine would be to quit my job and give up my mission," Jon said. "She's not even there."

"You're kidding me. What happened?"

"Long story. Basically, she's afraid of the boogie man. She's over at her friend's house. She's freaked out ever since I fell through the floor of that building on the Lower East Side. She's got the kids."

"I'm sorry to hear about this," Keith said. "Is there anything I can do?"

"Yeah. Get laid and don't worry about it," Jon said. "I've got my hands full with stuff I'm working on here, and I don't have time to worry about it either. Did you know I have a major report coming out in a few days? If you think I'm a celebrity now, wait till this thing comes out. And I'm working on more stuff right now as a follow-up. You think she cares about any of this, Keith? Not at all. She's paranoid, okay? And superstitious. And at this point, I really don't give a shit anymore."

"But you have kids to think about."

"And I think about them constantly," Jon said, trying to avoid the subject. "Hey, listen to this. Remember the missing thirty million gallons of sewage I told you about? Disappeared overnight, April first, and hasn't been back since? Well DEP just put out an official explanation. They claimed that there was a huge snow cover from this winter that melted all throughout March, making flows to the North River plant seem high. Then, they say, around March thirtieth, there was no more snow cover left. So the melting stopped and the flow to the plant dropped significantly."

"So . . . ?"

"Total bullshit," Jon said. "I have the National Weather Service report from March right in front of me. From the Central Park Station. It includes how many inches of snow cover there were each day. Turns out that by March twenty-first, it was all gone. Zero point zero inches. The thirty million gallon drop came well after that and had nothing to do with it."

"Something doesn't smell right," Keith said.

"Couldn't have said it better myself," Jon said. "But I'm on top of it. Now that I'm free to do what I want, things are really happening. Just by methodical research and process of elimination I'm getting closer to the answer every day. It's exciting. I'm having a great time."

"Good," Keith said. "Just don't forget what's most important."

"I won't. You either," Jon said, "you stud."

A few minutes past four in the afternoon, Jon walked into room 2035 with a markup of his odor report in his right hand. Naomi was hunched over a set of North River plans, her light brown hair spreading estrogen all over the sterile, oversized blue-line prints which still reeked of ammonia. Larry was leaning back in his chair and listening to the final innings of an afternoon Mets game on the radio. Old Al Gibbs was standing, singing "Take Me Out to the Ball Game," acting out each line, knocking over a penholder by accident on strike two.

"Whatcha got there, King?" Larry said.

"My odor report," Jon said. "Revision number five. This one's from Dennis Roseberry. Just punctuation and getting the executive summary to be politically correct. No big deal. Nothing I can't live with."

"This is taking forever," Larry said. "Five drafts!"

"I turned each one around in a day or two, Larry," Jon said.

"Whatever it takes. This ought to be the last one. I'm just riding with it now, not getting into any petty arguments, because I'm getting what I want. A couple more days and over a year's worth of work will have paid off. They want me to jump through a couple of extra hoops? Hey, no problem."

"Good for you, King," Larry said. "To tell you the truth, I never thought I'd see it happen. You hang in there, King. Next thing you know, the Mets'll win the pennant."

"Uh, let's not get carried away, Larry." Jon walked briskly into his office, closed the door, sat down, and dialed Elaine's number at LILCO. Elaine picked up on the third ring.

"LILCO computer help desk. How may I assist you?"

"You can assist me by coming home," Jon said.

"Jon, is this something important? I have two people on hold. It's been a crazy day." Elaine's vocal cords sounded as if they were muffled by a hard shell case.

"I wanted to see how you were doing."

"Well now you know," Elaine said.

"How's Steven's cold?" Jon asked.

"Still there," Elaine said coldly. "Sleeping in a basement doesn't help."

"Well, I'm making a lot of progress over here," Jon said. "My odor report should be out any day now, and I'm narrowing down where that thirty million gallons went to."

"That's great, Jon," Elaine said flatly.

"What do I have to do to make you come home, Elaine? Do I have to solve this entire North River problem?"

"You know what you have to do. Oh yeah, I remember what I was going to ask you." Elaine's voice had now shifted gears, into placating mode. "Did you get a chance to fix the gutter?"

"Why do I need to go back to the house, Elaine?" Jon snapped. "Why are you even asking me this? Did you pull the Gutter card last night?"

"I have to go now, Jon. I can't make these people wait any longer."

"No, you can't," Jon said. "Those poor, poor people."

"Goodbye, Jon."

Jon heard himself disconnected. He put back his own receiver as if to ready for a slam dunk but then restrained the impulse and lowered the phone so it made only a gentle tap upon returning to the hook. He forced his eyes to look down at his marked-up report, with its bright red comments in the margins. As soon as he focused in on sentence one of paragraph one of the executive summary, the phone rang again. Elaine had reconsidered, Jon thought. Even if she wouldn't come back to the house, maybe she'd at least let him take her out to dinner and maybe go to a motel for a few hours. At least she'd make an attempt to see things his way.

"Yes," Jon said into the receiver.

"Check out Eighteenth Street, my friend. Check it out."

"You know something?" Jon said. "You are a coward. A fucking coward, okay? You evidently know I'm trying to solve a problem here, you give me diddly-squat to work with, and I'm getting sick of it. I'm not even asking you to tell me who you are. You could be one of those guys that lives in a tent at the base of the Municipal Building for all I care. But you apparently know something I don't, and it's apparently got something to do with North River, so could you do me a favor and either explain to me in plain English what the hell it's all about or never call me again?"

"Eighteenth Street, my friend. That's all for now. Check it out."

"You wanna make me beg, you asshole? You know, we have a name for you around here—Deep Bowel." Jon heard a click and a dial tone on the other end. This time, he slammed the receiver like Charles Barkley. The phone survived the blow. Again Jon forced his head down toward the executive summary of the report.

At five-forty in the afternoon Jon emerged from his office and stretched his arms toward the ceiling. Larry and Old Al Gibbs were long gone, but Naomi was still at her desk, making notes on a yellow legal pad on top of the engineering drawings she had spread out. She wheeled around to face him, looking up. "Still going at it, huh?"

"I was going to say the same thing to you," Jon said.

Naomi used three fingers of her right hand to gently move her hair away from her right cheek. "Have you eaten?" she asked.

"Dinner?" Jon said. "No. And lunch was a pretzel and a little thing of orange drink."

"Wanna grab something?"

"Um, well . . ." Jon hesitated.

"C'mon, Jon, you need a break. You can always come back afterward if you want and work some more."

"Okay," he agreed. "Let me just go gather up my stuff. I don't feel like coming back here. I'll take my work home."

"Where *is* home tonight?" Naomi asked.

"Damn good question," Jon replied.

By six-thirty, Jon and Naomi had a table by the window of the Village Corner, a bar and restaurant at the southwest corner of Bleecker and La Guardia. Jon sat on the long, worn wooden bench along the La Guardia side of the room and looked across a small freestanding table at Naomi, who sat in a regular chair and fondled her skull-and-crossbones earring with her right hand.

The waitress had just brought two Heinekens. Any minute, Lance Hayward, a blind black gentleman in his seventies with a shaved head, would take his usual seat at the piano to Jon's left and begin tickling the ivories, coaxing out one jazz standard after another. Jon, as always, had an extra pair of Jockey shorts and a clean shirt in his knapsack.

"To celebrity," Naomi said, raising her bottle, motioning for Jon to do the same.

"Whose?" Jon replied, feeling his bottle clink with hers.

"Yours," Naomi said. "How does it feel to see your name in the paper so many times in one week?"

"As long as it's not in connection with the World Trade Center bombing . . . pretty good, I guess."

"You ought to be proud," Naomi said.

"Well, it's really all a complete absurdity," he replied. "You plug along for fifteen years, drawing lines, doing calculations, analyzing structures . . . in total obscurity. And then one day six newspapers want to quote you."

"But for good reason."

"Nah, I don't take it too seriously," Jon said. "This will come and go in a Warholian fifteen minutes. Anyway, for real fame these days, you have to go on television and admit to the world you're sleeping with a goat."

"A transvestite goat."

"Exactly," Jon agreed. "One that's in recovery."

"But at least *you* know that what you're doing is important," she said.

"*I* know it," Jon said, taking a big swig from the bottle, "but you'd be surprised how many people just don't care."

"*I* care," Naomi said.

"Well, that's one of the things that's great about you," he said. "You see the big picture. You see that whatever we do to the environment, it will sooner or later do to us. You wouldn't believe how many people out there gear their whole lives to getting home in time to tear open a bag of Cheez Doodles and watch *Hard Copy*."

"Come up with anything on that snowmelt theory?" Naomi asked.

Jon paused for a moment to think. "Did I mention that to you already?"

"Yeah, you mentioned it," Naomi said.

"Oh, 'cause I thought I just came up with it last night," Jon said. "Hey, what do I know—I don't even know where I'm sleeping tonight. Yeah, the DEP snowmelt theory—not worth the paper it's printed on. The snow was all melted in Manhattan way before the thirty million gallons disappeared. But why should I believe the National Weather Service, right?"

"So what do you think is happening with all that sewage?"

"I wish I knew," Jon said. "I can tell you what *may* have happened. Maybe it's all there, but someone tampered with the meters at the plant. Or maybe someone's bypassing the sewage right into the Hudson, before it even gets to the interceptor. But knowing exactly where, when, and how that's being done is another story entirely. I'm still a ways from that, but I'm gathering a whole bunch of data right now that's going to allow me to narrow it down."

"That's fascinating," Naomi said. "Where'd you get this data?"

"I have a friend at DEP," Jon said. "A guy named Fred Barrow. It's a sick sign of the times that I need a friend on the inside to get trunk main flow data, or any other data for that matter. As borough engineer, I should be able to get whatever I want with one phone call to whomever. But unfortunately, that's not the way it works, especially these days."

"Well, once you have all this data," Naomi asked, "what do you do with it?"

"Are you gonna be in tomorrow?" Jon asked.

"Yes . . ."

"Okay," Jon said, "I'll go over this with you tomorrow, when we have a desk and a pen and some paper and I can really explain it, with a schematic drawing. When you see how the system is put together, and the data we have, you'll see how we can locate the problem spot."

"That'll be great," Naomi said, wide-eyed. "It's kind of like fixing a big leaky pipe."

"Something like that," he said, pausing. "The whole thing is just an elaborate application of a single rule—conservation of matter. Other than in a nuclear reaction, matter can be neither created nor destroyed."

"This is pretty exciting, Jon," Naomi said. "Could I tag along? I mean, even if you're not going out into the field, just show me the nuts and bolts of what you're doing?"

"Sure, that's what you're here for," he said. The waitress stopped at their table and looked down.

"How are you two doing?" she asked.

"Two more Heinekens?" Naomi said.

"Coming right up," the waitress said, just before an about-face.

"This round's on me," Naomi said. "I just got my final grade report."

"How'd you do?"

"Three A's and a B," she said. "I knew what three of them were going to be, but the last A was a surprise. I was braced for a B-minus."

"That's what they all say." Jon looked down at his belt and pressed the time function on his beeper. "Excuse me, I'd better call my uncle and let him know I'm coming into Queens."

"What about your friend Keith?" Naomi asked.

"He's got a hot date tonight."

"Well, he's doing better than me," Naomi said. "My apartment is very underutilized. So . . . you're staying in my extra bedroom."

"You sure it's okay?" Jon said.

"Please, Jon, don't even mention it. It's a few blocks away. You'll get a lot more done this way instead of taking a long, slow subway ride into Queens."

"Okay," Jon said. "Thanks a lot."

A few minutes before 10:00 P.M., Jon followed Naomi through the front door to her apartment on the third floor of an old brick walk-up on West Third Street, just east of Sullivan Street. Naomi pushed a dimmer switch, and track lighting revealed a neatly furnished room with lightly stained wood floors, eggshell-white walls, and a deep Oriental rug. A framed color reprint of Van Gogh's *The Night Café* hung near a love seat. Except for the billiard table in the middle, the painting, with its oppressive, distorted yellow leaking everywhere, reminded Jon of the Village Corner and the six beers he had just drank.

Six beers was nothing for him in college, where even one or two at breakfast was a possibility. Now, however, they gave him a strong buzz that blurred the distinction between what had already happened and what he anticipated. He needed a sturdy chair somewhere to ground him. Naomi tossed her thin leather jacket onto a one-piece, clear Plexiglas coffee table.

"First door on your right," Naomi said, pointing to the hallway on the left.

"Thanks." Jon walked with his knapsack carefully down the hall to the spare room. When he flicked on the light switch, he saw a queen-size brass bed, piles of women's clothing on two oak dressers, a cluttered bulletin board, and a large poster of Iggy Pop. He felt apologetic, panicky, and excited all at the same time. This wasn't the spare room. This was Naomi's room.

"Is there something here you wanted me to see?" Jon shouted.

"Yeah," Naomi said, "this."

When Jon turned around, he saw that Naomi had unzipped her yellow zip-front shirt to her navel, exposing her two firm white breasts, which now had only a distinct tan line for a bra. He had already dropped his knapsack and was ready when she stepped forward forcefully to kiss him open-mouthed. After a second of being passive, as if to hang on a little while longer to the innocent role of merely viewing the act, he kissed Naomi just as hard and slipped his hands into her open shirt, wrapping them around to the muscular small of her back and then to the top of her tight buttocks beneath her jeans.

After reconciling himself seven years earlier to the tasting of one set of lips and smelling one scent of skin for the rest of his life, it dawned on Jon now that *his* life had something else in store for him after all. Though the realization seemed powerful for an instant, it had nothing to bounce off of and simply disappeared into the night. What he was left with was a beautiful, aggressive, half-naked woman devouring him in complete privacy. Suddenly, he did not need a greater context. This was his entire world, and that world felt good.

Naomi backed her way onto the queen-size brass bed and Jon pushed her as much as followed. Now on top of her, his tongue penetrated deeper than before into her mouth and his erection fought its way through his cotton slacks to a tight place between the thighs of her jeans. Naomi's short nails dug into Jon's back through his pin-striped shirt, which he now sat up to unbutton and remove.

Naomi took this opportunity to sit up as well and remove her skull-and-crossbones earrings. With her back to Jon, and facing a night table cluttered with clothes, books, and magazines, she labored over the removal of these earrings and then seemingly agonized over where to put them amidst the clutter. As she did this, Jon reached around from behind her, unzipped the rest of her shirt, and pulled it off her, now once more with her help.

Jon cupped her breasts with her hands and licked the nape of her neck. Naomi put her hands over his and helped them along before thrusting backward. Jon let her fall, so that she was now on her naked back staring up at him. He leaned over and traced her tan line with his tongue. As he worked his way down to her navel, she unzipped his fly and gripped his erection. Jon felt just a scrape of her tooth and tongue when Naomi paused, her body now noticeably stiffer.

"Don't worry," she said. "This is just a short commercial break." She slid out from under him, sat up, kissed him succinctly on the lips and put her feet on the floor.

"When I come out, I want you to fuck me till I scream."

She walked a few steps to the adjacent bathroom and closed the door behind her. Jon now lay facedown on the thin white quilt and breathed in the remains of her scent. He heard a zipper open behind the door, then a snap, then the water go on in the sink. Here was his window of opportunity. For all he had misbehaved so far, once that bathroom door opened again, another door would shut forever. It was easier to ignore this a minute earlier, when the sex had a life of its own. Now he was almost responsible again, and he didn't like it. He could get dressed now and salvage something, however small. But why be left with the worst of both worlds?

He looked up at the digital clock radio. It was ten-fourteen. The water still ran in the bathroom. He reached forward and put the radio on and recognized the song instantly. It was "Don't Let Me Down," by the Beatles, a rare play even for a classic rock station.

The chorus delivered repeated blows to Jon's head. "Don't let me down. Don't let me down."

He flicked the radio off, but he still heard the lyric "Don't let me down," and Elaine was saying it now instead of Lennon and Mc-Cartney. There were so many broken promises wreaking havoc on the Earth, and now his was one of them. There was so much mediocrity on display, and now he was part of the window dressing. There was alcohol in his head, but not enough to mask what he was. These reflections combined with the alcohol made him feel sick. He reached over and fished his shirt off the floor.

He could button the shirt halfway in twenty seconds, grab his bag and be out the door in a few more, he calculated, leaving Naomi to figure out the obvious. The awkwardness at work he could live with. That was the least of his problems. But now Naomi's phone rang, causing him to rush the buttoning and therefore get nothing done. He was frozen now. The water still ran loudly in the bathroom. Instead of a fifth ring, an answering machine clicked on. In recorded voice only, Naomi was in the room again.

"Hi, this is Naomi. Tell me who you are, what it's about, and where I can reach you." Frozen as he had been, Jon entered his own private ice age right after the beep. It was Paula's voice, shrill and demanding.

"Naomi . . . , Paula. When you get in, call me and let me know what you got out of Jon. Whatever he knows about the missing sewage, *we* have to know, before he gets too close. You figure it out. Talk to him, sleep with him, drug him . . . get everything you can. I don't know . . . I still wanna try to off him again, but we have a stop order on that since that idiot at DGS fucked up. Call me when you get in."

The water was still running in the bathroom. With his shirt half buttoned, Jon stepped up to the machine. He looked down, listened and waited for the tape to stop. It was an old machine, with separate tapes for the outgoing message and the incoming messages. Jon saw that there was a spare cassette tape, nearly identical to the ones in the machine, sitting on the dresser.

He lifted the lid, removed the cassette for incoming messages, placed it in his front right pants pocket, and substituted the spare tape. He lifted his knapsack, walked out of the bedroom, stepped out into the third-floor hallway, and ran toward the staircase. The last thing he remembered was the sound of the water still running.

Chapter 28

Jon ran north on Sullivan Street on this cold spring night which had seen the temperature drop ten degrees since he and Naomi drank their first round. He didn't bother pulling the wool sweater out from his knapsack or closing the top three buttons of his shirt. The alcohol had made him numb enough to ignore the chill. The realities now slowly setting in were numbing him to the same chill. If only, he thought, the alcohol could numb him to the realities themselves.

The pretty Village women passing Jon on the sidewalk were all conspirators to him. The ones with a serious look painted on their faces were in deep thought figuring out how to further screw up his life. The ones with happy faces had just done it. As a rational thinking engineer, he had always advised others to avoid paranoia at all costs. But what was paranoia when all suspicions were confirmed? Simple—it was his life.

Now, as he cut north through Washington Square Park, one hip-looking couple made out on a bench. Two middle-aged men played chess. Two terriers went berserk under the arch. A dealer in a Yankees cap, perched on a steel pipe railing, offered Jon some weed. It was worth considering. He didn't have that much to lose anymore, except the memory of what he was doing in bed a few minutes earlier. He knew the only reasons he was wandering in the park instead of committing marital treason were an uncooperative diaphragm and the phone call from hell, and he desperately sought to expunge that realization. They said drugs worked wonders for that sort of thing.

Aside from the fact that he was somewhere in New York, he was more lost than he'd ever been or had ever imagined he could be. The net result of fifteen years of hard work and dedication to principle, mixed with a few minutes of indiscretion, was complete chaos, despair, and hopelessness. A fair deal. He wrote off the notion of catching the 11:19 train out to Port Jefferson, or the 11:49, or any other one for that matter. Based on what he'd done, that was not home anymore. Nor was the office. And what would be the appropriate segue to barging in on Keith and his date—an urgent inquiry regarding Keith's advice on divorce?

Jon took a quick inventory as he left the park and walked west along Waverly Place. The most valuable thing he owned was the tape in his left pants pocket. He had a couple of other tapes of lesser value in the office, along with reams of important files. He also had a reputation as a structural forecaster and as an odor engineer. Throw in the knapsack, and that was about it. A voice told him he could build his inventory up once more by going back and reviewing things he remembered telling Naomi over the past few weeks and even the past few hours. The task, though, seemed far too daunting. Better to get drunker and empty an inventory of urine on a tree.

He walked into the White Horse Tavern at 11:35. He had tied one on many times during high school and college at this 1880 bar on the corner of Hudson and West Eleventh Street. It had been a speakeasy during prohibition and a favorite watering hole for Welsh poet Dylan Thomas shortly after World War II. Jon recalled that it was one of the last remaining buildings in Manhattan framed completely of wood. There was always the chance that it would go up like a tinderbox. Now, he walked past the outdoor picnic table seating—vacant due to the cold—and took a seat at a small table near the window facing Hudson Street. He glanced toward the bar, behind which was a huge antique mirror lined by a half-dozen rows of liquor bottles. Within a few minutes a five-foot-eleven waitress with hair down to her ass brought him a pitcher of Bass Ale. Jon noticed her youth and estimated she had been about seven the first time he got blitzed at this very table.

He poured himself a full pint and emptied half of it quickly into his esophagus. A jolt of light-headedness hit him. It had been many years since he'd come even near that threshold. He put the glass down heavily on the table and dropped his head into his hands just as heavily. He was approaching another threshold now, not just one of alcohol poisoning. He was boxed in, chased, cornered, bruised, trapped.

There was nowhere to go, but he had to go somewhere. He

knew this was the easy way out—to drink to oblivion and let the rest take care of itself. But what if it didn't? Was being scraped off the floor at 2:00 A.M. and tossed into the street a solution or just procrastination? Then again, was procrastination even possible when you had no idea what to do next?

The only thing he knew for sure was that he wasn't lifting his head again until he had a real next step. He was not going to look at this room full of glib, carefree people and pretend to be one of them. A sound started in Jon's head. It got louder and louder, until it was mildly, then acutely, painful. He was going to have to lift his head and break his vow, just to shake the sting. But when he did, he saw that all the carefree people were in pain too. This was due to a real, live police siren, coming from a vehicle right outside the window. Even after it pulled away moments later, the other customers still appeared annoyed. Jon's pain, however, had subsided. For the first time, he knew what to do.

At the pay phone near the front entrance of the White Horse Tavern, he fingered the folded-up piece of paper from his wallet on which he kept about four dozen phone numbers. Detective James Mercado's number had somehow wound up in the lower right-hand corner, next to Naomi's. Jon put a quarter in the phone and took extra care to dial the right number. He didn't expect to get the detective at this hour, but perhaps even a message would jump-start the process. Surprisingly, on the second ring, a human voice responded. A female voice.

"Tenth. O'Connel speaking."

"Uh, hello. I was calling for Detective James Mercado."

"He's . . . not here. Can I help you with something?"

"This is Jon Kessler."

"Kessler?"

"Yeah, I helped him out with some sewer calculations."

"I remember," O'Connel said. "Are you okay? You sound rattled."

"Oh, I'm rattled, all right. The people who run my office are trying to kill me. This is the borough president we're talking about. So could you leave him a message?"

"I'm going to do better than that," O'Connel said. "Where are you now?"

"The White Horse Tavern, at the corner of Hudson and West Eleventh."

"Are you in any danger at the moment?"

"No," Jon said looking back at his table. "Not due to anyone but me, that is."

"Okay, what's your number there?"

"Uh . . ." John gave him the pay phone number.

"Listen to me," O'Connel said. "Wait by the phone. Someone will call you back within five minutes. If the phone doesn't ring by that time, I want you to call me back. Okay, Jon?"

"Okay," he replied. "I'll wait."

"Five minutes," O'Connel repeated. "No longer. Keep the line clear. 'Bye."

Jon heard a click and placed his own receiver back on the hook. The tall waitress with the long hair was checking his table for an instant, looking at his pitcher. Still three-quarters full. She and Jon happened to make eye contact for a moment. She got the message. Leave it there. He wasn't quite done with it yet. Meanwhile, a fiftyish man in a cashmere sweater stood impatiently waiting for the phone, eyeing Jon and snapping his fingers rhythmically. Too damn bad, Jon thought.

He picked up the phone on the first ring. "Jon Kessler."

"This is Jimmy Mercado, Jon."

"Thanks for calling," Jon said. "Did I disturb you at home? Sorry."

"That's okay. I need a break in the monotony. Can you sit tight where you are?"

"I got a guy waiting by the phone," Jon said.

"Not by the phone," Mercado said. "Just take a seat. I'll be down there in fifteen minutes."

"Sure. I'm not going anywhere. I don't even have a place to sleep tonight."

"Just wait there."

Back at his table, Jon tried to sip his beer instead of swigging it. It wasn't easy. This seemed like the longest fifteen minutes of his life. His mind could perhaps begin to stop racing if he knew where he was going to sleep. Not Rocky Point. Not Keith's. Not Naomi's. Somewhere, there was a bed with his name on it.

Jon saw Mercado walk hurriedly through the front door about half past midnight. The detective was less dapper than the first time Jon had seen him. Mercado wore a gray trench coat over slacks and a blue-collared work shirt. No tie. There was about two days' worth of beard on his face. He spotted Jon, walked over, and took the chair opposite without bothering to remove his coat.

"So Art Shuler's trying to kill you."

"Paula Derbin, really," Jon said. "She's the attorney who runs the office."

"Paula Derbin?" Mercado said. "She's married to this asshole I was trying to take down. Lee Sarnow."

"Over at DEP, right?" Jon said. "I met him once. You're trying to nail him?"

"At the very moment, I'm not trying to nail anybody. That's my problem. We'll get to that later. Tell me the rest of your story."

"Yeah, sure," Jon said, trying to keep his enthusiasm in check. "Paula Derbin has made life hell for me ever since I handed in this report on North River. You know, that defective sewage treatment plant up there in West Harlem?"

"I've read about it. I've read about you."

"From the day I handed in that report," Jon said, "she's been on me. She badgered me—more than usual. She shelved the report indefinitely. Hassled my friends too. You see, the most important thing in the world to her and Art Shuler is to pave the road for Hudson City, that massive project on the West Side."

"I live up around there," Mercado said. "I've signed a couple of petitions against it."

"She took me off my regular job and sent me in to inspect a bunch of dilapidated, abandoned buildings," Jon said. "At first I thought it was just to get me out of her hair."

"But then she tried to kill you," Mercado said in a deliberate, steady voice.

"She set me up," Jon said. "First I get shot at from a building on 110th Street. Then I fall through the floor at a building in Alphabet City. The beams were notched. I'm an engineer. Believe me, it was no accident."

"And you're a hundred percent sure Paula Derbin was behind it."

"Got the evidence right here in my pocket," Jon said. "On tape. I didn't even want to believe it at first. But the writing was on the wall. I'm looking back on some things now. Even the guy they sent down there to guide me to that weak spot, he looked like he could be a hit man. A guy from the Department of General Services named Bruce Gregory."

"Bruce Gregory?!" Mercado said, his palm slapping the table-top and his eyes stretching to touch his brows.

"Yeah . . ."

"That's the guy who fucked up my lineup," Mercado said. "I had Joel Haney's killer in custody with an eyewitness ready to make an ID, and Bruce Gregory got sent in as a ringer. My witness got confused, and the D.A. let the perp walk."

"Bruce Gregory?" Jon said. "Guy with gray hair and a sick-looking bony face, tall . . ."

"Same guy," Mercado said, shaking his head.

"I was wondering whatever happened with that case," Jon said. "I never heard back from you, and I never read anything else about it. Only about what a psycho Joel Haney was. I'm not trying to pat myself on the back or anything, but I stuck my neck way out to do those calculations. In fact, that's what got me transferred to those crack houses in the first place."

"Jon, it did help us, and I'm going to make it up to you if I can. You helped us make that arrest."

"Are you still working on the case?"

"As of a few seconds ago I am," Mercado said with a smile. "I haven't told you something. I'm on a leave of absence. Unpaid. The captain at the Tenth is on the take. I lost it for a couple of min-utes when that lineup incident went down. Kicked the shit out of a Coke machine. My partner cooled me off afterward. Now I'm supposed to take some time to think about my future. The Detec-tive Benevolent Association took care of the rest."

"Then you *are* going back," Jon said.

"Not till we clear this case," Mercado replied.

"Which case is that," Jon asked, "the attempt on my life or the Joel Haney case?"

"Jon, they're the same case," Mercado said flatly.

A chill went through Jon's body.

"Remember what I said about Lee Sarnow?" Mercado said. "He's the son of a bitch who got my perp off the hook. Max Mc-Cord. McCord works for Sarnow at DEP. McCord dumped Haney's body into a manhole on Fourteenth Street between Sixth and Seventh. Lee Sarnow and the captain at the Tenth put Bruce Gregory into that lineup as a fill. Sarnow and McCord tampered with evidence in Haney's apartment. We have their prints. And you know something—that asshole McCord still walked. I think

McCord or one of his men killed Haney all the way over at Eighteenth Street and Eleventh Avenue and dragged him over to that manhole just to make it look like Haney screwed up on the job. And Sarnow's been covering up ever since."

"Wait a second," Jon said. "Did you say Eighteenth Street?"

"Yeah."

"You're right," Jon said, "this *is* all tied together somehow. What you should know is that thirty million gallons a day of raw sewage has disappeared at the North River plant. It happened around April first."

"Right before Haney bought it," Mercado said.

"And that thirty-million-gallon disappearance clears the way for Hudson City to hook up. The committee vote's coming up, and that's all fixed too. Paula Derbin set me up with an intern who I just found out was a spy. Caught the whole thing on her answering machine tonight. Paula knows I'm on to the thirty million gallons. She even admitted to trying to have me killed before, can you fucking believe it?"

"And what about Eighteenth Street?" Mercado said.

"I have this anonymous caller I call Deep Bowel who keeps bugging me," Jon said. "Keeps leaving me clues."

"Any idea who it might be?"

"Nope," Jon said. "But I get the feeling he's very powerful. Way up there, that's why he can't reveal himself. One of the clues Deep Bowel gave me—this was just today—was 'Check out Eighteenth Street.' Very cryptic. But while I was sitting here waiting for you, it dawns on me. That's where one of the regulators is located. I'd been playing with numbers, trying to figure out where all the sewage is being dumped, and I think, 'Shit—Eighteenth Street!' And now you tell me this!"

"One big mess," Mercado said, slapping the table again. "Amazing."

"Personally, I think they may be bypassing sewage at a few of these regulators."

"Well, Eighteenth Street smells, I'll tell you that," Mercado said. "I *knew* this thing was huge. Sarnow's married to Paula Derbin. Derbin tried to have you whacked. She hires Bruce Gregory. Paula Derbin works for Art Shuler, who's looking to make a mayoral run. Meanwhile, Shuler's doing Ronald Arlen's laundry. This thing goes all over the place. I'm doing some routine homework on my perp, some skel who used to be a plumber, and I find out he's on *Ronald Arlen's payroll*! When we book him, Ronald Arlen's attorney comes down, and this guy lawyers right up."

"And what about Joel Haney?" Jon asked. "How did he wind up dead? Was he mixed up in this somehow?"

"The more I think about it," Mercado said, "the more I'm convinced that poor schmuck was just in the wrong place at the wrong time."

"But I read he was a porn filmmaker," Jon said, pausing to drain his beer mug. "And I read something else recently. I heard he was using the sewer to smuggle drugs."

"At least three-quarters bullshit," Mercado said. "Your boss's husband had those stories fabricated to make Haney look bad."

"Wow. You sure?"

"Yup. No respect for the dead . . . or the living. My partner and I turned over some rocks. Haney had problems in the past, but by the time he was killed, he was a legitimate documentary maker."

"Then what was he doing at Eighteenth Street?" Jon said. "You say he was killed there."

"I think he was there as a filmmaker, because he knew the territory, knew that's where he could find the hookers he needed to interview. I'll show you some films. And yeah, okay, there was some sex included in some of the early ones. In all the early ones."

"Yeah, that's just what I need to see now." Jon poured another glass of beer. "Remember I told you I found out what was going on from my intern's answering machine?"

"Yeah."

"What I left out," Jon said, "was I was over there with her tonight, at her apartment, doing something I shouldn't have been doing."

"Don't tell your wife, Jon. Then you might wish it was only Ronald Arlen who wanted you dead. Believe me. Even if . . . you were separated at the time. It won't solve anything. Chalk it up to experience. We all make mistakes. You made half a mistake. The most important thing right now is your answer to the following question: Do you want to nail these bastards?"

"More than anything." Jon put his mug down hard on the table.

"Good."

"It's not just what they're doing to the environment," Jon said, "or what they've done to me—believe me, that would be enough.

But I loathe to the core the way they look at the world. If something stands between them and the money, get rid of it. It's that simple. Get rid of you, get rid of me, get rid of West Harlem, get rid of thirty million gallons of raw sewage. There's nothing I'd like more than to fuck up them and fuck up their plan."

"For that," Mercado said, "we'll have to come up with a plan of our own."

"Well, I have that tape," Jon said, "and some others. I'll have to get my files from the office. I'm working on a mathematical proof of where the sewage is being diverted."

"No matter what we can prove," Mercado said, "we're going to need someone behind us—someone to turn this evidence over to when we're done. And it's gotta be someone we can trust."

"There's only a handful of people on the planet I trust," Jon said, "and I doubt any of them are in a position to do anything. You know someone?"

"I'm going to reach out to an old friend at Internal Affairs," Mercado said. "I should have done this a week ago, when I walked out, but instead I sat around angry, trying to figure if it was really time to get out. Now it's time to get back in. Another factor for me was that I knew I was lacking in some of the technical aspects of this case. That's not a feeling I get too often, and it's not one that I enjoy. But you know the sewer system cold, right?"

"Not cold," Jon said. "Not like I wish I did. I had to split my time fifteen ways in this job. But maybe I can use some of my contacts too."

"Like we said, though, be careful. Leaks happen all the time. Did you ever consider the possibility that you were bugged?"

"Yes," Jon said. "I wondered why my intern seemed to be two steps ahead of me sometimes."

"There you go," Mercado said. "I may be able to help you out with that one. Another thing we need is someone in the media to counter the stories they're going to be writing about you."

"About me?"

"Yeah, you," Mercado said. "You've got yourself a nice little image right now, Jon. But let me tell you, the second these assholes catch wind of what you're doing and find they can't get to you physically, they will trash you in the media like there's no tomorrow."

"Like Haney."

"Like Haney," Mercado said, "only worse. Get ready for that."

"I might have a contact in the press," Jon said.

"And we have to think about getting your family some security."

"I think about that every minute," Jon said. "Almost every minute. I probably spent too much time thinking about my odor report. For some reason, they were ready to release it. That's why I stayed as long as I did. Pathetic."

"That's not pathetic."

"Okay, you want to hear pathetic?" Jon said. "I don't even have a place to stay tonight."

"I've already thought of that," Mercado said.

"You're kidding me."

"No I'm not," Mercado said with a broad smile. "And you're gonna love the location."

At 1:25 A.M., Jon staggered along Nineteenth Street, a step behind surefooted Jimmy Mercado.

"You gonna be okay, kid?"

"Eventually."

"Well, here we are," Mercado said, "so pull yourself together."

"I'm okay," Jon said. "I'm just not that crazy about living in a dead guy's apartment."

"It's not like he died in the apartment or like his body's in there now," Mercado said.

"Still . . ."

"Still what? Every apartment in Manhattan was once inhabited by someone who's dead. Except the ones Ronald Arlen is building." Mercado stepped up to the single metal-framed glass door and hit the intercom button that read SUP. He waited five seconds and hit it again.

"Who the hell is it?" said a gruff, perturbed male voice.

"Detective James Mercado. It's very important."

"Aw, shit." The buzzer sounded and Mercado pushed open the door, Kessler right behind him, using the hallway wall to steady himself. As they proceeded, they heard three separate locks click open. George Fazekas met them just beyond his doorway.

"I thought you was done with this case," Fazekas said.

"I have a tenant for the Haney apartment," Mercado said.

"Four A?"

"Yeah."

"Building's full. I already got someone moving in two weeks," Fazekas said. "The family didn't want it, so I was gonna start gettin' rid of Haney's furniture tomorrow."

"Save yourself the trouble," Mercado said. "This guy likes the old furniture just the way it is." Fazekas looked warily at Jon, who was slumped headfirst against the adjacent wall.

"He's not . . . gay, is he?"

"Not yet," Mercado said. "Look, I can pay cash."

"I don't know," Fazekas said. "What am I gonna tell this other guy movin' in?"

"Tell him if he sits tight, he'll eventually get the place."

"I don't know."

"Look," Mercado said, "this building is leaning. I noticed a couple of bricks loose along the front. Ever heard of Local Law Ten? They're cracking down on this stuff over at the Buildings Department. Huge fines. And there's this other guy at the borough president's office. He'll make a federal case out of it. Let's see . . . no ventilation—"

"Okay, okay, I'll get you the fucking keys." Fazekas disappeared for twenty seconds, returned to the doorway, and slapped a set of keys into Mercado's open palm. "That's eleven hundred a month."

"No problem," Mercado replied, now pulling crisp hundred-dollar bills out of his wallet and counting to twelve. He handed over the small wad to Fazekas, who quickly counted it out.

"There's an extra hundred in there for you," Mercado said, "for being such a stud." Mercado stared longingly at the wad of hundreds.

"Hey, what's the guy's name?" Fazekas said.

"Ben," Mercado said, "Ben Franklin." Mercado began pushing a sluggish Jon along the hall, toward the steps.

"Hey," Fazekas said, "what about security?"

"You'll have lots of it," Mercado said.

When Mercado had Jon halfway up the first flight of stairs, Fazekas called out one last thing.

"And keep the music down!"

Jon came to in what he thought was the late morning, based on the high angle of the sun in the sky. The rays came blasting through the window but did not hit him directly. Instead, they splattered and bounced off of a dozen surfaces—the floor, walls, a metallic lamp, a framed movie poster of Peter Fonda in *Easy Rider*—and reached Jon's eyes in diluted form. Still, this was enough to wake him once he had unconsciously pushed his head out from under the blanket.

Jon did not remember exactly where Haney's apartment was, nor exactly how he had found his way into the bedroom. He did have disjointed recollections of being moved around like a sack of potatoes and of being on his knees at one point. The sleep that followed was filled with bizarre dreamlike images that followed one another mercilessly, each without resolution: falling out of his office window, completing the sex act with Naomi, watching Elaine drown, seeing his house in Rocky Point blown to smithereens.

But none of it was as unpleasant as the profound nausea he felt now as he began to adjust his position on the bed. The agony had two distinct centers—one in his stomach and one in his temple—but the pain radiated toward any limb that dared make a move. Mercado sat near the west-facing window, reading the *New York Times*, relaxing in a swivel chair.

"Oh my God," Jon said, "why did I drink like that?"

"To get out of a situation," Mercado said. "But that's going to take more than a couple of beers."

"How many should I have had?"

"How'd you sleep?" Mercado asked.

"Terrible. What time is it?"

"Almost three in the afternoon," Mercado said.

"Holy shit!" Jon said, sitting up and opening the floodgates of the pain he had earned. He realized now that the window behind Mercado faced west. "Three o'clock!"

"What's the problem?" Mercado asked with a grin. "You have to be someplace?"

"Um . . . no," Jon replied, thinking it over. "Well, yeah. I should get to my office one last time and get my stuff."

"That's a good idea," Mercado said. "You should be careful, but I think you'll be okay going in for a few minutes."

"Did I explain the sequence of events in my intern's apartment?"

"Right after we got upstairs," Mercado said.

"I don't even remember telling you," Jon said, rubbing his eyes.

"You'll be okay in a little while," Mercado said. "Just get in and get out. I'd go with you, but I don't think it's necessary, and I have some things to take care of. The phone will be turned back on tomorrow, maybe even later today. For now, we can use my cell phone. But use it sparingly," Mercado said, handing it to Jon. "It can be intercepted. I had the locks changed, and I had a set of keys made for you. They're over there on the dresser. I'm going to be meeting with my friend from Internal Affairs in a few minutes."

"Okay," Jon said, hanging an arm over the side of the bed, his bare knuckles grazing the cool wood floor.

"Now that you've . . . slept on it," Mercado said, "you're still in, right?"

"I'm in," Jon said. "I have to be in. Mostly, I'm in pain."

"Okay," Mercado said, "just making sure it wasn't only the booze talking."

"The booze *is* doing some talking," Jon said, "telling me 'I'm coming right back up.'"

"There can't be much left over after last night," Mercado said. "All over Joel Haney's nice towels. Really enjoyed cleaning it up."

"Jeez, sorry," Jon said. "So this is the bed where Haney shot his porn flicks, huh? If I wasn't so sick . . . I'd feel sick."

"You'll have to change the sheets yourself," Mercado said.

"I do have one real misgiving," Jon said. "After all the months I spent on that report, I was dying for it to finally come out. Now it won't. But I'm confused. With what I know now, why was Art Shuler ever going to release it—late or at all?"

"Here's why," Mercado said, getting up, walking over to the bed and dropping the paper next to Jon's head. Jon picked it up and struggled to focus his eyes on the banner headline of the Metro section: ARLEN GETS FOUR BILLION FOR HUDSON CITY. Now Jon read.

Macrotel International Ltd., a group of Hong Kong–based investors, agreed yesterday to buy a seventy-percent interest in Hudson City for the reported sum of four billion dollars. Developer Ronald Arlen, president of the entity now known as the Hudson City Corporation, stated yesterday that city officials had assured him that a sewer hookup permit, the last link in a long chain of required permits, was virtually assured.

"Get the picture?" Mercado said.

"Wow. That's a lot of money I was blocking," Jon mused. "Almost too much to comprehend."

"See what happened?" Mercado said. "This was going on behind the scene while they tortured you and your friends. Arlen could never build this project himself. At this point, his total assets are a couple of casinos and a lot of hot air. He planned to sell off most of this project from day one. That's how you make a ton of cash quick. And who has more available cash than filthy rich Hong Kong investors looking to unload it before the Chinese get hold of their island? They're anything but stupid, though. They don't simply throw around their billions.

"Arlen wasn't going to get a cent before he could prove to them this was truly a done deal. And that couldn't happen until the sewage situation was fixed. I guarantee you McCord and company took care of those thirty million gallons and are still taking care of them as we speak."

"I didn't tell you this yet," Jon said, "but the sewer hookup committee has already been fixed, four to three. They got Ted 'Kill the Trees' Santorini for that one."

"Sure," Mercado said. "This was all planned a while ago. And once this was all a done deal, why would they care if your little odor report came out? As long as the project was permitted and financed, somebody else would have to worry about North River and West Harlem stinking. You know what they'll do—hire a consultant for two million dollars to do essentially what you did, only not as well.

"Hell, releasing your report was going to be *good* for Art Shuler. It would have made him look like there's no way in the world he was in bed with Ronald Arlen. It fooled *you*. How well do you think it would have worked on people who know *nothing* about all this? But then you started tampering with their bread and butter—the thirty million gallons. Just like when my partner and I snatched up McCord. They made me flip him, and I flew off the handle. You had it worse, Jon. They were biding their time before they tried to kill you again. And until then, they were going to pick your brain clean."

Jon let the *Times* drop to the floor and put his head in his hands.

"We're not done," Mercado said. "Look at page one of the A section. Right column." Jon reached back down and did so. The headline jumped off the page at his aching cerebral cortex: SHULER ANNOUNCES MAYORAL RUN.

"Unbelievable," Jon said.

"All planned," Mercado said, "all timed. We were just obstacles. I'll bet you right now Art Shuler's got a war chest somewhere with a few million bucks for buying TV spots and major endorsements."

"You know the strange thing?" Jon said. "Art Shuler's announcement and the four-billion-dollar figure were supposed to make me understand the full impact of what I've been dealing with. But you know when it hit me? Last night, right after the incident with my intern. She's beautiful, likable, and smart, and should have had a great life. But for some undisclosed sum of money, she became a cunning animal. The level to which she fooled me scares the crap out of me. That's what it comes down to, Detective. If she can be turned into that, how about some high-level operator with no redeeming qualities to *start* with?"

"They'll take you down in two seconds if they feel they need to," Mercado said.

"One good thing," Jon said. "Elaine's already in hiding. But I'm not sure it's enough."

"I'll see if I can help you on that one," Mercado said. "Right now, you need to reorient yourself. Hate to be a pain in the ass, but you need to think differently from before. Starting now, we gather and catalogue evidence every waking hour. The sooner we put this together, the better. So get up, take a shower, and retrieve those files from your office. They probably don't know anything's up yet. But they will soon, especially once you take the stuff. Like we said, just get it over with today."

"Do you want to listen to the answering machine tape?"

"I already did," Mercado said. "Nice work, Jon. I'll be playing it for my friend at Internal Affairs." Jon reached into his left front pants pocket, which was now empty.

"I have other tapes," Jon said, "and other weird little things I've noticed."

"Good," Mercado said. "Get them to me and make notes of every observation you've made. The same way Ronald Arlen collects properties, we're going to collect evidence. This is *our* greed.

Make sure you get it all on paper. And don't assume they played fair. Like I said, don't rule out the possibility that your phone and office were bugged and that your voice mail was listened to. Write down everything you may have inadvertently given them while schmoozing in your office, including anything you might have told your intern."

"For starters," Jon said, "Naomi knew about my theories even though I had never told anybody, other than my friend Keith over the phone. And she seemed to know I had nowhere else to go last night because my friend had a date staying over. You know, she had the keys to my office, and my boss gave me a couple of Wednesdays off."

"Jesus, Jon. When you fall, you fall hard. Now get up, throw up again if you have to, this time *in* the bowl, and get over to your office. I may be back from my meeting by then. Just let yourself in. By the way, the super might call you Ben Franklin."

"One more question," Jon said. "Where exactly are we?"

"Chelsea. Nineteenth Street, near Eleventh Avenue," Mercado said. "Nice quiet neighborhood."

Jon stood up and felt the blood flee from his head. He walked over to the window near the swivel chair, looked out, and took in the view of the Chelsea piers.

Chapter 29

At 4:15 P.M., as Jon walked briskly eastward toward the Municipal Building along the north side of Chambers Street, a brown '88 Lincoln Continental veered to the curb as the side window opened. Without thinking, Jon ducked behind a mailbox. As he peered around its bolted, blue edge he saw a woman with gray hair and horn-rimmed glasses leaning out of the open window, dumbfounded. Now Jon stood up and approached the car.

"I'm so sorry, I didn't mean to scare you," the woman said. "Did we pull too close?"

"No, no," Jon said, "I'm just jumpy today."

"Can you tell us how to get to the World Financial Center?"

"Just keep going until you hit West Street and make a left. Then it'll be about a quarter mile down on your right."

"Thank you so much."

"No problem."

Four minutes later, as he was riding the elevator up in the Municipal Building, Jon caught his breath, wiped the sweat from his brow, and considered whether he was prepared to live the rest of his life braced for a drive-by shooting. The answer was a resounding no. A few minutes in and he was already cracking. His best bet now was to get in and out of the office as quietly as possible, minimizing his time in harm's way.

Having run through a dress rehearsal for this only days earlier, he anticipated no problem deciding which files to pull and which papers to yank. He knew what to do with the computer. The whole thing should be five minutes, tops. As long as he didn't pass out first. Here was his first lucky break—the elevator car passed the nineteenth floor without stopping.

As he walked into room 2035, he saw that Naomi was not in, but that Al and Larry were. As Jon grunted, Al looked up from his newspaper and followed Jon with his eyes. Larry emerged mentally from a Garth Brooks song and spoke.

"King, you look like shit."

"Exactly," Jon said.

"You better take a few days off," Larry said. "This job is killing you."

"Bingo." Moments later Jon was in his office with the door locked behind him and two important folders already snatched up. A wave of nausea came and went as he briefly tasted his own bile at the top of his throat. The more he rushed, the more something inside told him there was another way to go about this. In a radical departure from his original game plan, he decided to check his messages while present, even while knowing he could check them at any time from outside the office using his remote code. But the reward for following instinct came quickly. The first message was from Naomi.

"Jon, it's ten-thirty, and you're not here. I'm sitting here in my apartment thinking I blew it. I don't know whether I was too fast or too slow, but I just want to apologize for whatever it was I did wrong. So when you get in in the morning, I'd really appreciate it if you'd give this some thought. I really like working with you, and I don't want that to change. I just want to let you know that you're in the driver's seat. If you want to forget everything that happened and never mention it again, that will work. But if you ever decide you want something more from this relationship, that will be here waiting for you. Okay . . . that's really all."

The remaining three messages were all map inquiries. Jon sat as still as possible in his chair. Larry had unwittingly triggered the thought, and Naomi perhaps unwittingly completed it. It was to his advantage to string this out as much as possible. Calling in sick was probably the best bet. While he needed to be out of sight for safety reasons, it was to his advantage not to tip anybody off that he knew their intentions. It was entirely possible that switching the answering machine tape had worked. It was entirely possible that Paula and Naomi never mutually understood that Paula's message was intercepted.

Therefore, calling in sick for at least a few days might not raise any suspicions. He could check in with various people and even pretend to be doing work while actually using that time to continue gathering evidence, unhampered by physical danger, throwing Paula and friends off track, and taking no unnecessary chances all the while. Even the mentally thorough James Mercado hadn't suggested this approach. Larry Golick was a genius.

The logical extension of this train of thought was to cover his tracks and make it appear that he hadn't gone into hiding, even to anyone who might be snooping in his office later. That would mean leaving the files on his hard drive intact, even after taking backups out of the office for his own use. It would mean making photocopies of all the important files and returning the originals to the file cabinets. These measures were useful only under the assumption that Naomi and the others were already very familiar with what was and wasn't there. As Jon now thumbed through the main North River folder and noticed several items not in the order he had last left them, he knew that was a reasonably safe assumption.

The trade-off, however, was that leaving the computer and paper files meant giving Naomi and company ample, even unlimited time to go through everything carefully. This was too complicated to analyze further. He simply needed to create breathing room for himself, and that breathing room could only be spent away from the office, out of Paula's sights. Jon's head was throbbing as hard as ever now from the hangover and from the problem at hand. The pain was compounded by the thought that maybe he should look for an electronic bug.

An ancient part of his brain, largely unhampered by the alcohol, made the snap decisions for him, one after the other. Leave the computer files on the hard drive. Forget about the possibility of a bug for now. Take the papers and folders out of the office, photocopy them in safety, and have a friend inside the office return them in a day or two. Let Naomi, Paula, Ned, and even the Dodger spend twenty-four hours a day studying his files if they wanted to. They were a thousand times more useful to him than they would be to anyone else. And unlike them, he had no deep, dark secrets to hide. None that were in the files, in any event. The important thing was to buy time. By doing so, he'd be buying time for Elaine as well.

As Jon walked out briskly through room 2035, he threw a quick verbal pitch to Larry. "I'll be out for a few days. I think it's the flu. Taking some work home."

"Feel better, King." Meanwhile, Old Al Gibbs looked up at him again and rose as Jon reached for the door.

"Could I talk to you for a minute?"

"I don't think so," Jon said, walking out. Jon was now near the elevators and reaching for the heat-sensitive down button. He saw with his peripheral vision that Al had slipped out behind him before the door from room 2035 had automatically closed.

"I really do need to talk to you," Al said, walking right up to Jon and attempting to speak softly to him. Seeing Old Al Gibbs acting discreet was like seeing Muammar Qaddafi acting contrite.

"What is it you want to tell me?" Jon asked. "How you stormed the beaches at Normandy or how you instigated the Bay of Pigs incident?"

"Look, I don't blame you for being pissed off," Al said.

"Pissed off?" Jon said. "About what, something *you* did? You flatter yourself by assuming I even give a shit. You're a slug, Al. If I sat around expecting any production out of a slug, *I'd* be the crazy one, wouldn't I? What does amaze me, however, is why the slug standing in front of me has picked this late date to address me directly. That makes me a very special person, doesn't it? Why can't I grasp just how lucky I am?"

The look on Old Al Gibbs's face was expressive, not in a maniacal or obsessed way but in a concerned, almost compassionate manner. Disgusted and uncomfortable, Jon looked away, up at the illuminated elevator floor indicator, ever so slowly working its way up to 20. Because of a city contract to replace the elevators, two of the six elevators on the north side were always out of commission. By the time the contract was complete, it would be time to start all over again.

"You're not coming back, are you?" Al asked rhetorically.

"No, I'm not coming back," Jon said, visibly annoyed. "And I'm leaving you in charge. Congratulations—this is that promotion you were counting on. Don't be modest. You've earned it."

"See, I knew you weren't coming back," Al said. "I know that look anywhere. I knew it the second you walked in the door. I've been there, man."

"Where, Iwo Jima?"

"Look, Jon, I know you're in trouble."

"Woooa, he knows my name. They must be doing something right down at the clinic."

"You think I don't know what they're doing to you with this Hudson City thing?"

The elevator door opened. No one else was in the car. Jon stepped in. "Have a nice life, Al." But Gibbs had stepped into the car right behind him.

"Jesus Christ." Jon pressed 1, stuck his head into the left rear corner of the car, and looked point-blank at the black printed lines on the fake wood paneling. The doors closed and the elevator began falling.

"You probably don't even realize what kind of danger you're in," Old Al Gibbs said. "Once this kind of money is involved, people are just obstacles . . . ants."

"But not if you know tai chi, right, Al?"

"I was in your shoes once, Jon. You probably think I was born a slug, but until I was just a little younger than you are now, I was one of the best engineers to come up in a decade. And black too."

"No kidding?" Jon looked up and saw that the elevator had gone below the fifteenth floor. That meant it would plunge uninterrupted to the lobby. On the negative side, he would have no other passenger to hide behind. On the positive side, it would all be over soon.

"You know how hard you've had it?" Al said. "Well if you were black, double it. Minimum."

"That's a shame," Jon said. The elevator door opened and Jon stepped out quickly, past Old Al Gibbs and through an elderly couple trying to get in. Gibbs followed Jon closely and continued speaking.

"There's a lot you don't know about me."

"And boy am I dying to learn," Jon said.

"I was second in command when we built the interceptor in 1970," Gibbs said. "The deep part, north, near the plant. That's what made your whole North River plant possible in the first place." Gibbs's last few words were muffled as Jon jump-started the north set of revolving doors and Gibbs entered the compartment behind him. Jon consciously avoided Chambers Street, where he would almost undoubtedly be held up by a traffic light, and instead made a U-turn onto the brick pavement of St. Andrew's Plaza, then walked toward Police Plaza. Gibbs was again a step behind him, breathing desperation.

"I was the link between the Bureau of Sewers and the sandhogs. We tunneled through bedrock a hundred feet below street level. Every damn day, drill a few holes, put in a few charges, set 'em off, and send up the debris. Then we put up another section of a steel shield to hold it in place. Thick, curved steel plates bolted and welded together. Always problems. We had water down there, trickling in from little streams and pockets. We tried grouting. Then we boosted the air pressure up to triple normal atmospheric to hold it back while we worked. I got the bends a couple of times coming up in the elevator. So did most of the men. Ever feel a little nitrogen bubble move its way around through your veins? That's something you'll never forget."

Jon continued walking, the click of his heels reverberating throughout the plaza but now slowing a bit in their rhythm. The main ramp to the Brooklyn Bridge loomed large before Jon as Gibbs continued.

"I knew something was wrong, you see. The bedrock was getting looser and looser, with more silt and sand between the schist. More water was starting to turn up, even under the air pressure. I wanted to stop the whole thing and take some precautions. Put the shields in earlier. Double the thickness. Put a refrigeration system down there—pipes with refrigerant—to freeze the water.

"But my boss turned me down flat. He had a commitment to finish the thing by a certain date, and that would set us back too much. The general contractor was mob controlled and was making a killing the way the bid process was already set up. I think they were into my boss too. Officially made only five thousand more than me but had a three-car-garage place in Short Hills. You tell me how. Had dinner with the foreman two times a week."

For the first time, Jon, weary and ill, stopped to look at Gibbs directly. The late afternoon spring wind whistled through the plaza and made its way toward the East River.

"You see," Gibbs went on, "I had a real bad feeling, and I was in my boss's face every day with that refrigeration system. He wouldn't listen. I knew the deal. That system had to be provided at cost under the contract, if the Bureau of Sewers asked for it. That meant no big fat expensive change order for DeChiara and Sons, and holding the job up too. So one day I'm pushing my boss for this system, and he turns to me and says: 'Boy, you're damn lucky you're watching these sandhogs instead of digging it yourself. If you know what's good for you, you'll shut up, or you won't even be able to get a job cleaning catch basins. Quit while you're ahead.' "

"What did you do?" Jon asked.

"I put my head down and went back to work," Gibbs said. "I had two little kids at home. Four days later, there was a collapse. Three people died. One of them was my best friend. Jessie Curtis. Grew up with the dude in Jamaica, Queens. He never had a chance—crushed almost instantly. I had another friend down there at the same time—Charlie Sharpe. The three of us were like this." Gibbs held up three fingers on his right hand and squeezed them together. "We all worked for Sewers. Charlie got away with a broken leg."

"And what happened to you?" Jon asked.

"I got away with a nervous breakdown. I let those guys down, man. I was the only one set up like that to get my degree. My pop put in some crazy hours. I was there to stand up for my boys, and I fucked up."

"Sounds like you were damned if you did and damned if you

didn't," Jon said, finding it hard to believe he was actually having a conversation with Al Gibbs.

"No, hearing that from people doesn't do shit for you when you come face-to-face with it," Gibbs said. "You probably know that yourself by now. They covered that shit up before you could blink. Changed the log books to show no warning signs of the collapse. Boss tells me if I ever said anything, they could easily make it look like me who blew it. Show my sign-off on all sorts of forms over the preceding days."

"Holy shit."

"I lost it after that," Gibbs said. "Those days were like a blank. I didn't sleep for weeks. Every time I dozed off I'd see Jessie under those rocks, screaming for his life, calling my name. I was in Bellevue for a while. After about a year, I was together enough to walk around and maybe not cry in public. That's when they gave me this job at the borough president's office. They told me if I wanna get paid, just sit down and shut up."

"Well, at least you broke rank on *that* one," Jon said.

"That Vietnam shit?" Gibbs said. "That's been an act for some time now. But for a long time after Jesse died, it wasn't no act."

"Look," Jon said, now with a hardened look on his face, "that was a fascinating story, you are the most bizarre person I've ever met, and I'm very sorry your life turned out to be a train wreck. But I have my own train wreck to deal with. There is nothing I can do for you, and there is nothing you can do for me."

Jon turned and walked back toward the arch at the base of the Municipal Building, the sound of cars from the Brooklyn Bridge now bouncing off the towering walls that shadowed them. When he was about ten yards away, Gibbs shouted out two words.

"First Fidelity."

Jon turned, looked at Gibbs, and dropped his heavy knapsack to the pavement.

Gibbs called out again: "First Fidelity."

Chapter 30

Jon felt numb for a moment, and then it hit him. He ran twenty yards to the nearest planter and threw up into it. He let out a big groan in anticipation of the second wave, which, unlike most other things in his life, came on schedule. Gibbs was behind him now, holding Jon's knapsack in one hand and gripping Jon's shoulder with the other.

"You're gonna be all right, man," Gibbs said. "Let it out."

"If you knew something that could help me, why the fuck didn't you just tell me?" Jon griped into the planter. "You're . . . Deep Bowel? Why didn't you just walk across the room and tell me?"

"That's my own damn problem," Gibbs said. "No matter now. I'm gonna tell you everything I know."

"Like about April Fool's," Jon said, wiping his mouth, "and Eighteenth Street."

"That's right," Gibbs said. "You see, Charlie Sharpe and me stayed friends. He could have told me to go to hell after what happened, but Charlie's not like that. He understands. After the collapse, he gets a lower risk job with Sewers and says he's going to suck the city for the biggest pension they've ever seen. He tells me I oughta do the same. This isn't even right away. This is maybe three or four years later, when I'll agree to talk to certain people. Charlie says, 'You have a desk job, motherfucker. You can sit there and do whatever you want.'

"Funny thing is, Charlie was never like that himself and never could be if he tried. He was full of angry ideas on the outside, but you better believe he went right back to work his butt off. You can't change your basic nature. And as for me, for about eight years I couldn't have worked if I wanted to. Couldn't concentrate."

"Then what happened?" Jon asked.

"I started to come out of it," Gibbs said. "Very slowly. Like waking up very gradually from a bad dream, but taking months instead of hours."

"Really?" Jon said. "You seemed certifiably insane to me until a few minutes ago."

"Sadly, I got to be pretty good at it," Gibbs said. "You have to understand what it was I woke up to. I was divorced. My professional engineer's license had been revoked. I had maybe three friends instead of three dozen. I was living in a hovel, like an unwashed orphan. And I heard myself talking nonsense."

"At least you had this wonderful job." Jon nodded up toward the top of the Municipal Building.

"That's about all I had," Gibbs said. "I used it as my foundation. I told myself no one was ever gonna fuck with me again. So I just kept right on doing these little routines. They kept people off my back. And they were pretty damn funny too."

"So you sat there and read the same issue of *Playboy* for another fifteen years?"

"That's what I wanted you folks to think," Gibbs said. "Actually, I was reading, studying, and planning almost all the time. I ran a few little businesses on the side. I played the stock market. I turned about twenty thousand dollars into about half a million."

"You and Hillary Clinton," Jon said.

"Hey, this was accrued methodically over a period of many years," Gibbs said. "I studied my butt off like I did in Columbia and made diversified moves very carefully. I got into silicone before the big boom. I did a little real estate in the Reagan years and got out before the bottom dropped out."

"Sounds like you did better than Ronald Arlen."

"Not really," Gibbs said. "He'll do whatever it takes to get what he wants. I never learned that."

"Good," Jon said. "But why didn't you take that money and just get the hell out of this place?"

"Hey, eighteen more months and I hit thirty years. I can leave and collect about seventy percent of my salary right away. They owe me. I'm not letting those little fucks off the hook."

"I know exactly what you mean," Jon said. He did his best to straighten up, feeling his stomach finally begin to settle down. "Tell me how you know all this stuff about my situation. And what's this about . . . First Fidelity?"

"Let's get out of here first, so no one spots us," Gibbs said. He pulled a handkerchief from his pocket and slapped it into Jon's right hand. "Here, clean yourself up. Start walking that way. And whatever you do, don't give that thing back to me."

Two minutes later Jon and Gibbs were walking west along Chambers Street, not far from where Jon had ducked behind a mailbox earlier. They milled through the rush hour crowd that was beginning to form. Gibbs gesticulated with his hands, as if to clear a little space around himself and Jon.

"Charlie started telling me a few months ago about some of the strange things going on at DEP," Gibbs said. "It started when they moved his crew off the Eighteenth Street regulator and that general area over to Fourteenth Street. They brought in a bunch of goons to replace them, and a shroud of secrecy surrounded what they were doing from day one."

"Yeah, I just figured out last night why you wanted me to check out Eighteenth Street," Jon said. "That's probably one of the places they're tripping the regulator and dumping raw sewage out of the tide gate. Makes perfect sense."

"You got that right," Gibbs said. "They work at night. No one's seen most of these guys ever before. You tell *me* what they were doing. In fact, Charlie told me a lot of dirty people were put in place at DEP over the last year or two, right after the Hudson City deal became imminent. Not just at the bottom level of the department—way up too. Lee Sarnow is one of them."

"Uh-huh," Jon said. "That's Paula's husband."

"If you want to call it that," Gibbs said. "Art Shuler and Sarnow go way back, to when Art was a council member. Sarnow was his page. You ever hear about when Nixon fired just about everybody from his staff in 1972, but wrote a memo to keep George Bush because, and I quote, 'He'll do anything for the cause'?"

"Rings a bell," Jon said.

"Lee Sarnow is Art's George Bush, except much worse. No spine, will do whatever he's told, eager to please in the worst possible way. Art put him in DEP for a specific purpose—to ram that permit through at all costs. Get the flow down. Hire more assholes like himself—more plants. And when do they finally pull the whole thing off? April Fool's! Sons of bitches, as if nobody's watching. Charlie was onto this thing practically from the day they pulled him off Eighteenth Street. He checked the daily flow readings to the plant with a friend of his upstairs at DEP. Checked it out every few days. He knew a big drop was coming, and one day, bang, there it is."

"What about First Fidelity?" Jon asked vigorously.

"Oh yeah," Gibbs said. "My daughter works at the one on two-seventeen Broadway. She's an account manager. One day, she sees Lee Sarnow walk in. See, once in a while, Althea takes me to lunch across the street at Foley's. One time, I spotted Sarnow eating alone at the counter and pointed him out. She never forgot the face."

"How could you?" Jon said.

"So now he goes up to the window to make a deposit," Gibbs said, "and it turns out to be fifty thousand dollars in cash. So Althea checks his account and there's over two million in there. Huge deposits and withdrawals every week. That's his slush fund. He's the point man for this whole operation at DEP."

"And he's married to Paula," Jon said. "How perfect is that? She's the point . . . woman, here. Is that just another bizarre coincidence, like your daughter working for First Fidelity?"

"Nope," Gibbs said. "That's what I started to tell you before. That was practically an arranged marriage. Paula used to work for Ronald Arlen. She was one of his young attorneys working a hundred hours a week closing less-than-kosher real estate deals. From what I hear, she was sleeping with him too."

"Okay, this is too fucking much." Jon stopped cold for a minute on the sidewalk in front of the Panda Garden and smelled the fried rice.

"Wait, I'm not done yet," Gibbs said. "I don't really know the whole deal, but from what I heard, Art Shuler and Ronald Arlen more or less brokered that marriage. They haven't been married that long. When the plans for Hudson City started taking shape, I guess these folks were spending a lot of time together, maybe wining and dining in one of Arlen's hotels. So they made a trade. Art sent his top player over to DEP, where Arlen has always had a few plants. And Arlen sent Paula over to Art's team."

"Jesus, I got my job by answering an ad."

"So to spell it out for you," Gibbs said, "Art and Arlen knew that most of the coordination for this whole thing was going to be between their two point . . . people. What does that mean? That means a huge log of phone calls between the two of them was going to pile up over the next couple of years, maybe attracting undue attention and one day perhaps forming a massive body of evidence in court. So what better way to cover the whole thing than marry off the two of them? Who's going to question a husband and wife calling each other on the phone constantly?"

"You know, I owe *my* wife a call," Jon said.

"And who's going to question a husband and wife being seen together frequently?" Gibbs said. "I heard they were even pressured to have a kid, but Sarnow was sterile."

"Wait a second," Jon said, "you may think this is a stupid question, but was there any attraction there at all?"

"Maybe," Gibbs said. "Maybe not. But I do know this—a couple of million is a hell of a lubricant. Not a bad dowry either. All *I* got was two thousand in savings bonds."

"As an engineer, I have to ask this question too," Jon said. "You know how engineers love symmetry?"

"Yeah . . . ?"

"Well," Jon said, "the only thing keeping this whole story from being perfectly symmetrical is . . . um, were Art Shuler and Lee Sarnow ever . . . lovers?"

"As an engineer, I couldn't tell you for sure," Gibbs said. "But I do know there wasn't much between Art and his wife. I heard they had separate apartments for the last ten years of their marriage. Art got married to please his father. That was another arranged marriage. She was the daughter of one of his father's business partners. When Art's father disowned him, he had no reason left to put on a charade and got a divorce. I don't know—you figure it out. The main thing is, without his father, Art needed someone else to back him for his mayoral run. Art never saved much. He lived high on the hog. From what I heard, he practically sought out Ronald Arlen in the beginning, and was greeted with open arms."

Jon stood and looked up for a moment into the unforgiving sun baking the sticky Chambers Street pavement and him along with it.

"I feel like a schmuck," he said. "I considered you a village idiot, and you not only see the big picture, you know every little detail of it. And I knew practically none of it."

"That's because you spend all your time working," Gibbs said. "Nothing to be ashamed of. So tell me, how do you know that Eighteenth Street is just one of the places they're dumping sewage?"

"That trunk main only handles about five million gallons a day. We need to account for thirty million. You said there's a lot of plants in DEP. They probably have a few other regulators tripped too."

"Good man!" Gibbs exclaimed. "See, I knew I wasn't wasting my time with you. And how 'bout the girl, Jon? Did you watch the girl?"

"What girl?" Jon asked.

"Naomi," Gibbs said.

"Oh, her," Jon sighed. "Yeah, I watched her. From three inches away with her top off."

"Oh shit, see?" Gibbs said, sucking his teeth. "I knew she was bad news from the beginning."

"Hey, I didn't go all the way or anything."

"I should have stepped in earlier," Gibbs said.

"Why would you want to step in at all for me?"

"Charlie and I knew it was time," Gibbs said.

"Look, I don't even know this Charlie guy."

"He feels he knows *you*," Gibbs said. "He's the one who gave your name to that detective working on the murder of his foreman."

"The Joel Haney case?" Jon said. "That was his foreman? Small world. And getting smaller."

"You remind me of myself in 1970," Gibbs said. "You're arrogant, but your heart's in the right place. And that means you get screwed. I'm sick of watching it happen. And there's something else. Charlie and I developed our little me-first philosophy because we were burned. But it gets to the point where you're pushing retirement, you see the same shit over and over again, and you ask yourself if you ever tried to make a difference, or were you just another passive critic?"

"And that's what this is to you," Jon asked, "philosophical redemption?"

"We're doing it for Jessie," Gibbs said.

"Then how would Jessie feel about this?" Jon said. "I'm being warehoused by a detective from the Tenth Precinct who wants Lee Sarnow's head on a silver platter. We're trying to put together a plan right now."

"Mercado?"

"Yeah, how'd you know?"

"I'm in," Gibbs said without hesitation. "I was in a while ago."

"Then why don't we head up to my new cell right now?" Jon said. "You're gonna love the view."

At 5:35, the buzzer at 434 West Nineteenth Street sounded, somewhat muffled and distorted. With Gibbs behind him, Jon pushed his way into the old brick building and walked up the rickety stairs inside. A minute and a half later they arrived at the fourth floor, Gibbs following Jon with a cautious light foot down the hallway to apartment 4A.

"Just don't say anything for a minute," Jon said several steps before his new key worked its way into the lower lock. Ten seconds later, Jon and Al saw Mercado sitting impassively on the couch, slumped forward, his head in his hands, the right one rubbing his brow. Jon stopped for a moment as Mercado looked up wearily, then took three more steps into the apartment, with Gibbs still behind him. Gibbs closed the door.

"Wait a second," Mercado said, "that's that nut from your office."

"It turns out he's not so crazy," Jon replied.

"Right," Mercado said with a smirk. "He's the grim reaper. He is Death."

"He's Deep Bowel," Jon said.

"What?" Mercado said, his Spanish eyes bulging.

"He's the guy," Jon said. "Admitted it to me on my way out. His whole act was just that. You wouldn't believe what he knows. Where Sarnow keeps a two-million-dollar slush fund to pay the people dumping raw sewage into the Hudson. Turns out we were right about Eighteenth Street."

"Keep talking," Mercado said.

"We said we wanted someone who knew the sewers inside out," Jon continued. "Well, this guy helped *build* the interceptor, how's that? Over twenty years ago. He knows how the whole system is put together, how sewage can be diverted from the interceptor into the river."

"That ought to be useful," Mercado said.

"And if that's not enough of a jackpot," Jon said, "listen to this. He's been a fly on the wall for a long time. He knows how this conspiracy is put together—how Paula Derbin wound up marrying Lee Sarnow, why Art Shuler approached Ronald Arlen, how Arlen has plants all over the city. A friend of his even knew there was going to be some kind of huge, sudden drop in the flow to the plant."

"Hang on a second," Mercado said, "your friend knew that? What are you, in on this conspiracy or something?"

"My friend," Gibbs said, "is Charlie Sharpe."

"Charlie Sharpe?!" Mercado stood up, took one long stride toward Gibbs and Jon, and stopped. "Why the hell did he hold out on me and my partner like that?"

"Don't take it personally," Gibbs said. "A few months to go before retirement. Him *and* me."

"I understand, but—"

"Plus," Gibbs said, "where we come from, we don't go trustin' no cop too fast. It didn't look like this was gonna be an exception. Police draggin' their feet."

"I wasn't dragging *my* feet," Mercado said.

"We figured that out," Gibbs said, "but it took a while. We knew Sarnow had his hooks into somebody down at the Tenth. For all we knew, it was you."

"Not in this lifetime," Mercado said, shaking his head once quickly.

"Well, we had to make sure," Gibbs said. "Charlie heard evidence was planted, in this apartment, right here. I knew you were working with Jon, but I didn't know if it was just bullshit, going through the motions."

"So what changed your mind?" Mercado asked.

"Not any one thing," Gibbs said. "The way you kept working with Jon helped. When you stopped Charlie in the street last Tuesday, he wanted to help you but we still had some doubts. His youngest son just got sick, and all he thinks about is gettin' out clean. He was this close to giving it all up that day, especially when you asked him about McCord and then made some crack about putting Sarnow in jail."

"Okay," Mercado said, "I guess he did the best he could."

"We're gonna do better," Gibbs said. "I seen what they did to Jon. And I understand Sarnow fucked up your investigation."

"Just a small speed bump," Mercado said. "Not even the most recent one. My friend at Internal Affairs, Ray Florentino, told me he couldn't make a commitment on this thing. Known this guy fifteen years, and he said I'd have to wait for an answer. I've got to sit tight, keep him posted."

"All dressed up, no place to go," Jon said.

Jon took a swan dive onto the couch from which Mercado had just stepped away. He turned over, stretched out, and cradled the back of his head in his hands. He felt somewhat relaxed for the first time in many days, but could not entirely comprehend why. It was as if he'd known somehow he would eventually have to walk through the desert to get where he was going, and now that he'd done it, he was relieved.

He had crossed over. No job, no hours, no real home, and no responsibilities—other than to nail Paula and her partners in crime. This was his oasis—a dead man's one-bedroom flat in Chelsea. It was the first time since the day he graduated Columbia that he didn't have some kind of clock to punch, and it was almost a guilty pleasure. And the price seemed reasonable—the simple cutting of all worldly ties. Why hadn't he discovered running for his life sooner? But almost as quickly, the euphoria was gone. He remembered he still had to call Elaine.

Mercado and Gibbs were now gazing out the west bedroom window, like a couple of real estate moguls, down past several rooftops and rooftop cooling units, toward the tiny steel valve chamber cover in the extreme southbound lane of Eleventh Avenue. Several construction workers, packing it in after a day of laboring on the Chelsea piers, and several pedestrians walked by the rectangular plate, oblivious to its significance.

"This is great, right?" Mercado said. "We'll set up a video camera on a tripod right here, with a telescopic lens, and we're set."

"Of course," Gibbs said, "we're going to need a unit with night vision capabilities. These guys work mostly in the night. I know where we can get a phosphorus unit that multiplies the available light by a thousand."

"But can you pay for it?" Mercado asked. "I already shelled out a small bundle for this apartment."

"Not a problem," Gibbs said, "but think about this. What are we going to film through that lens? A bunch of guys entering and leaving the valve chamber at various times. There's nothing illegal about that—they're just doing their jobs. That's what they're going to say. We may be able to get a fair look at their faces, but we could do that by walking over there tonight and taking a good look up close."

"But it's a start," Mercado said. "At least we can establish a pattern—something we can corroborate with other evidence."

Jon had walked into the bedroom. "I overheard what you were talking about," he said. "About corroborating evidence. I may have an idea on that."

"Let's hear it," Mercado said.

"We're assuming every time those guys go down there they're tripping the regulator or making sure it stays tripped. That means sewage goes right out the outfall instead of down into the interceptor and to the plant."

"What exactly is this outfall thing?" Mercado asked.

"It's just an opening in the seawall," Gibbs explained. "Nothing that spectacular. I don't know the exact size of the one down there at Eighteenth Street. Could be a tide gate in there to prevent river water from washing back into the system. Kind of like a big check valve."

"So we can film sewage coming out of this outfall?" Mercado said.

"Maybe," Jon said. "I'm not sure. We'd need a boat for a good angle. But I think most outfalls are located below high tide, sometimes even below low tide, so there's a question of visibility."

"So we find out when low tide is," Mercado said.

"When *night*time low tide is," Gibbs added.

"Like I said," Jon asserted, "we'll have to check it out. Each outfall is a little different in size and elevation. If it's completely below sea level a hundred percent of the time, we may be fucked. I mean, do you own scuba-diving equipment?"

"There might be other alternatives," Gibbs said. "Once we're in a rowboat, in position, we could stick a probe down and take a differential pressure reading. It wouldn't be exact, but it would indicate unusual flow."

"That sounds like it might be worthwhile," Mercado said. Jon, meanwhile, sat on the couch, sucking his lips and shaking his head back and forth with slight movements.

"Another way we can go," Gibbs said, "is to take water samples near the outfall and have them analyzed for fecal coliform."

"You mean," Mercado said, "like shit?"

"No, not *like* shit," Gibbs said. "*Shit*. What we do is take a couple of background samples upstream and compare them to the fecal coliform levels taken near the outfall. If, say, the lab tells us the background levels were 150 coliforms per hundred milliliters and the outfall samples are 1,100 per hundred milliliters, then we can show there's dumping going on."

"Look," Jon said, "I don't want to sit here and second-guess everything you're saying, Al. I mean, this stuff sounds just great for an environmental assessment. The problem we're going to run into, though—even assuming we get past all the logistical problems—is that we're not showing cause and effect. Something's *probably* happening over here. Something *may* be causing it over there—"

"We use time-coding on the videotapes," Mercado said.

"No, my man has a point," Gibbs said. "Combined sewer overflow happens fairly often as it is. Sometimes it's because a storm trips the regulator. Sometimes the regulator malfunctions and trips on its own. These are problems DEP contends with legitimately. If we can show the system malfunctioning, that's great. But that's not the same as showing that it's deliberate."

"Exactly," Jon said. "But it's still a hell of a lot better than nothing. You're right, Detective, we should time-code everything. Showing that the overflow is occurring at roughly the same time as these guys going down into the regulator does establish the probability of cause and effect."

"Of course, DEP will tell the judge it was the other way around," Gibbs said. "They'll say there was a chronically tripped regulator that they sent a crew to respond to."

"You really *were* paying attention during your coma," Jon said. "That is exactly what they'll do. But if we can do this kind of surveillance repeatedly, we'll be able to show a pattern, a very suspicious pattern, that shows no evidence whatsoever of anything being repaired. In fact, the more of this type of evidence we gather, the greater the chance of catching DEP in a lie when they try to defend themselves. For instance, showing that there *was* no overflow occurring during the daytime will blow apart their claim that they were repairing anything. Of course, there's no reason to show our whole hand until we have to. Let them make a few mistakes first."

"Remember," Mercado said, "we have to find someone to go to bat for us, or all this is a waste. I'm still hoping Ray comes through."

"I'm optimistic," Jon said. "We have some circumstantial and supporting evidence as well. We have that tape from Naomi's machine."

"Yes we do," Mercado said. "We have your own testimony, Jon—how you were harassed and almost killed. I want you to write all that down for me."

"I have a few more tapes for you," Jon said.

"Good . . ."

"Nothing as incriminating as the first tape," Jon said. "Maybe nothing that could stand alone. But they do support the answering machine tape. Same person—Paula Derbin, badgering me."

"Okay, good, good," Mercado said, "let me have all of it. I'll make copies of everything and label it. And what about Lee Sarnow's bank account?"

"My daughter works at that bank," Gibbs said. "I'll have her give me a balance sheet showing all activity."

"Great," Mercado said. He paused and looked up for a moment, as if to count the booty in his head.

"I have a friend at work who has extensive tapes of Paula Derbin," Jon said. "Probably better stuff than most of mine. I can give her a call."

"Okay, okay," Mercado said. "Give them a call. The phone's already in. But like I was telling you, Jon—assume the worst when you're making a call. Assume it's being recorded."

"And traced?" Jon asked.

"We don't have to worry about that aspect right now," Mercado said. "Last night and today I've been going over this whole thing again and again in my mind, trying to cover everything—the small details and the big picture."

"I have my hands full just trying not to throw up," Jon said.

"Just listen closely," Mercado said. "It all comes back to protocol—what we can and cannot do. For instance, we can use the regular phone to call potentially hostile people."

"We can?" Gibbs said.

"Yes, we can," Mercado said. He sat in the swivel chair in the bedroom and pulled a yellow legal-size pad from the desk nearby. He snatched a half-chewed Bic pen from his shirt pocket and began making notes sporadically as he continued talking.

"I called NYNEX this morning," Mercado said, "and had them block the caller ID coming from the line. I already tried it out on a friend at the Tenth. It worked. The message he got on his caller ID box was 'Out of town.' "

"So I can call my wife?" Jon asked.

"Maybe, but I don't know what her situation is," Mercado said. "Do they know where she is?"

"Yes and no," Jon said. "I doubt they know where her friend's house is. She didn't want to go to her parents' house because that was too obvious. But she's still going into work every day."

"That's gotta stop," Mercado said.

"I know," Jon said, "that's one of the reasons I've got to call her."

"Let's hope she hasn't been followed back to her friend's house," Mercado said.

"Well, even though technically I should be panicked," Jon said, "I'm really not. The way I figure it, there's still probably a little slack time, and we may be able to stretch it out a little further still."

"Great minds think alike," Mercado said. "I know exactly what you're thinking, and we're on the same wavelength. From what you've told me so far, Paula Derbin and her friends may not know that you're on to them or that you've bolted. You grabbed that answering machine tape and replaced it. Paula may just assume your intern got the message and not mention it. Your intern may just assume you walked out because you felt guilty."

"Assume away, Naomi," Jon said.

"They may never put two and two together," Mercado continued, "unless you give them a reason to. Right now, your job is to give them a reason *not* to."

"Sure, I've already thought this through," Jon said. "When I went back to the office, I realized I could buy some time by calling in sick for a few days. I acted very casual."

"You sure fooled me," Gibbs said with a smirk.

"Gimme a break," Jon said, "I had to think on my feet when it was hard enough just *standing* on them. I didn't remove much from my office, and I'm going to have to put it back as soon as I can have it photocopied. I even told Larry I was going to be out sick for a while. And he's someone I *trust*."

"That's a start," Mercado said. "Now what you need to do is call that intern of yours. I don't want to cause any more trouble, but tell her you're sick, and as soon as you're up and around, you want to finish what you started. You have that report you're finishing up, right? Well, you still wanna do that. That's it—you wanna get that report out and you wanna see her. You're still in the ball game, Jon—*their* ball game. That's what these assholes need to think so we can slither around in peace for a few more days."

"But you said I should assume everything's being recorded," Jon said.

"Well, there's a definite trade-off involved," Mercado said. "What's a little harmless phone sex compared to buying us days or even weeks unhampered? But don't tell your wife!"

"Definitely not," Gibbs said.

"Right," Jon said.

"Tell you what," Mercado said. "Write your wife a letter explaining the whole thing, sex included, and send it to yourself in the mail."

"Where?" Jon asked.

"Here," Mercado said with a wink, "to Ben Franklin. One day, if you're ever in a tight spot, hand your wife the sealed, postmarked letter. Hopefully, it'll never come to that."

"It's a gamble," Gibbs said.

"This whole thing's a gamble, gentlemen," Mercado said. "We're free agents. I don't know, Jon, who do you normally call when you call in sick?"

"I haven't been sick enough to establish a regular thing," Jon said. "I guess I call Larry, and he calls Paula's assistant. And I've already done that."

"Great," Mercado said, "then you're halfway there. As for you, I want you back in the office bright and early tomorrow."

"No problem," Gibbs said.

"And work on that story where you almost rescued the American hostages from Iran," Jon said.

"You got it."

"You're our eyes and ears in that office," Mercado said to Gibbs.

"We have other eyes and ears," Jon said.

"But here's what you've got to remember," Mercado said. "These are your friends. Paula Derbin, Art Shuler—they know these are your friends. Just like your phone may be tapped, their phones may be tapped. Hey, you already said they've been harassed. Now all they need is a call from you explaining what you're up to. Then they're screwed and we're screwed. But they're really screwed. We're sitting here more or less out of harm's way. They're dead meat."

"Point taken," Jon said. "But what if I really need to talk to them? Can I call them at home?"

"Maybe," Mercado said. "Let's think about getting someone to act as an intermediary. Let's hold off for a day and work something out."

"Maybe I can let them know," Gibbs said.

"Fine," Jon said, "but make sure you act a little paranoid-delusional. You don't want to put them into *total* shock."

"Don't worry," Gibbs said, "I'm a pro."

"And how are you at making copies?" Mercado asked.

"Hey, that was the one official duty I *didn't* shirk the last twenty years," Gibbs said.

"You *sure* you're not mentally ill?" Mercado said with a smile.

"Anyone who works for the city has to be a bit mentally ill," Jon said.

"Okay, great, then," Mercado said. "There's a copy place over on Eighth Avenue. Copy all Jon's files and put the originals back when you get in in the morning. And I have an assignment for you too, Jon."

"What?" Jon asked. "I already have my hands full. As soon as he gets back, I'm going to start going through all the data from top to bottom, to see what kind of inconsistencies I can find. I've never really done that with the kind of thoroughness it calls for."

"I know you won't have much free time, but don't forget to write down every possible leak," Mercado said.

"Do you know what you're asking?" Jon said. "Can you recall everything you've said today since Al and I walked in the door?"

"Yes I can," Mercado said. "Make notes. Make more notes. I want to know what they know and what they may know. We've got to stay one step ahead of them."

Chapter 31

Twenty minutes later, with Gibbs out running errands, Jon tested the dial tone, then made his inaugural phone call to Elaine.

"Hello?" The voice was soft but harried. The background was filled with the sounds of young children screaming, cackling, breaking plastic objects.

"Hello, Judy, it's Jon. Is Elaine there?"

"Yeah, she just got in. How are you doing?"

"I'm . . . okay. Surprisingly."

"Good. Your son gave my kids a cold. I'll get Elaine."

"Thank you."

Jon listened as Judy called at the top of her lungs to Elaine. "It's him!" Jon heard one of the kids sneezing.

"Hi, Jon." Elaine's voice was more open and lenient than he'd expected. He was happy to hear a voice at all. "Are you okay?"

"Yeah. Feeling a little sick. But I'm okay. I'm glad you seem to care."

"I do care, Jon." Elaine's voice rose and fell with the passion she had withheld for many days. "I'm so glad you called. It was—"

"Psychic?"

"It was," Elaine said. "Jon, I was thinking about you nonstop all day, and I was going to call you. I miss you, and I feel like I've been . . . selfish."

"No you haven't," Jon said. "You have the kids to protect."

"But I should have been more supportive," Elaine said. "I know you're trying to do the right thing in this situation and how hard that is. I know—"

"Look—"

"Let me finish," Elaine insisted. "I know you're defending people who aren't in a position to defend themselves against things they aren't even aware are happening and against a bunch of terrible people they don't even know. If it's your destiny to do this, it's wrong for me to stand in the way. My problem is, I've seen what happens to so many people who fight the good fight, Jon. They're devastated, their family is devastated, and in the long run nothing really changes."

"Well, that psyches *me* up," Jon said.

"I don't want to lose you, Jon."

"You're not going to lose me. When I'm a hundred, you'll lose me. And by then you'll be ecstatic about it."

"The point is," Elaine said, "I'm your wife and I should be standing by you, even if you've done something wrong. And the thing is, you haven't. You're out there taking the high road."

"Come on, I'm no hero, Elaine. Part of this is personal."

"Whatever the details," Elaine said, "if I hold back, I'm just holding everything back—you, me, and the people you're trying to help."

"I appreciate that," Jon said. "When did you have this . . . revelation?"

"Last night, around ten o'clock," Elaine said. "It was the strangest thing. I was sitting in bed reading, and I began to feel sick—physically ill."

"Well, Judy told me the kids have colds."

"No, it was way beyond that," Elaine said. "I felt sick, like having a big lump in my stomach . . . and a knife through my heart."

"What the hell were you reading?"

"I don't even remember. But I felt as if after keeping you at arm's distance, you were suddenly a million miles away. Not like you were dead. Like the bond between us had snapped."

"That will never happen," Jon said.

"For a moment it did," Elaine said. "I mean, I didn't even know where you were or how to reach you."

"You should have beeped me."

"I was going to," Elaine said, "but then something even stranger happened. The whole feeling of dread just . . . lifted. Just like that—poof."

"And in its place love, acceptance, and a willingness to risk your life?" Jon asked. "Is there a missing link here?"

"You're gonna laugh at me."

"No I won't," he said. "Go ahead—give me the whole tarot card reading. Make my day."

"All right," Elaine said cautiously, "here's what I remember. I did a Celtic Cross spread."

"Did you have all your clothes off?" Jon tried to stifle a chuckle.

"See, that's what I mean."

"Continue. I'm done."

"You got the Devil card in the present obstacles position."

"That would be Paula and company," Jon said.

"Yes, it would be," Elaine said. "You got the Strength card in the upright position. That was in the present position. That's a good card, Jon. It balances off the present obstacles. It shows you have the ability to cope in adversity by drawing on your vast reserve of inner strength and self-control."

"That's me," he said with an ironic sigh.

"And Jon, here are the most encouraging cards of all. In the future influences position, you got the Justice card, and in the outcome, you got the Judgment card, both upright."

"Is that like hitting the daily double?"

"It is," Elaine said. "It's telling you the forces of justice are at work and the result will be fitting."

"Great," he said. "Now I'm *really* glad I called."

"I don't want to mislead you, Jon. There were a couple of cards that gave some cause for concern."

"Oh?"

"In the future events spot, you got the Ten of Swords, in the reverse position."

"That doesn't sound good." Like a tea bag that got fat through osmosis, Jon seemed to recall the image shown on this particular card. A man lay prone, lifeless, with ten long metal swords sticking from his back.

"And in the personality spot," Elaine said, "you pulled the Five of Coins. That's generally associated with financial worries or poverty. Don't get overwhelmed by those two cards. No reading can be completely rosy and perfect."

"Thanks. I'm not that worried," Jon said. "I get the general idea—good results, but trouble along the way. Just like when I took my engineer's licensing exam. Now let me tell you the main reason I called."

"Wait a second," Elaine said. "There was one more card that really bothered me." Between them, they listened only to each other's breathing. Then Elaine continued. "You got the Fool card in the home life position, reversed."

"That's probably because I haven't fixed the gutter," Jon said.

"I doubt it's that trivial," Elaine said. "It typically means someone is prone to act foolishly, without regard for consequences. It's associated with impulsive behavior. It's funny—when I pulled that card, I got a little bit of that feeling that I'd had earlier. Sick to my stomach."

"Hey, you're the psychic," Jon said. "You shouldn't need a deck of cards to tell you I'm a fool. I hope I'm not getting psychic too. Yesterday, I had a dream where I lost my two front teeth. Really bothered me."

"Jon, that's a universal dream symbol for betrayal."

"Actually," Jon said, "that makes perfect sense."

"I know things haven't been great between us, Jon. I want to straighten them out. I want to come home."

"That's the one thing you can't do," he said. "That's what I've been trying to tell you. They *have* been trying to kill me. It's real. You were right on the money, and now there isn't even a shadow of doubt."

"Oh my God. How did you find out?"

"Almost by accident," Jon said. "My intern stupidly left things lying around my desk. Like her voice mail access code. So I did a little detective work. I checked her voice mail and I heard Paula's voice talking about how they tried to put me away. I'm pretty sure it was in reference to the day I fell through the floor of that building on Avenue D."

"So I was right to move out."

"Absolutely right," Jon said. "I've moved out too. I have no immediate plans to go back. I don't want you within a five-mile radius of that place. In fact, you shouldn't even be going back to work. It's too risky."

"What do I tell them?"

"Tell them there's a hit out on your husband and there may be one out on you too."

"Jon, I can't live like this—" Her voice cracked.

"Elaine, it's bad, but it's not as bad as that. At least not right now. I may have overstated my case. They're not trying to kill me at the moment, and as far as I know, they don't know that I'm aware that they ever were. They know that I know there's some kind of conspiracy with the thirty million missing gallons, and they know I'm trying to find out where it went. And I'm closer than they think. But they're letting me live for the time being because I'm too high-profile. Essentially, they're trying to spy on me to see how I'm unraveling their mystery, probably so they can ravel it back up again."

"You let me go through a whole reading before telling me this?" Elaine's voice was now stern and reprimanding.

"We had a good couple of moments going there," Jon said. "I didn't want to ruin it right away."

"What's your plan?" Elaine's alarm would not be so easily dampened.

"Right now, I'm buying time by calling in sick and making them continue to think I'm not quite on to them. As far as they'll know, I'm still anxious for my report to come out. But I'm staying out of their reach just in case that changes. Do you have a pen handy?"

"Yes."

"Take the number down where I'm staying, okay?" He gave it to her.

"Where's that?"

"With Detective Mercado," Jon said. "Remember the guy I told you about who was working the sewer case?"

"Yes," Elaine said. "Really? He took you into his apartment?"

"Not exactly," Jon said. "He set me up in Joel Haney's old apartment. That's the dead sewer worker."

"Oh God, you're kidding me."

"It's not easy to find an apartment in New York," Jon said. "And this one overlooks the scene of the crime. Before you know it, we'll have enough evidence to prosecute."

"And what if you prosecute and win?" Elaine said. "Do they stop trying to kill you? Does this all go away?"

"Your tarot card reading says it does."

"In the meantime, what are you going to do for money?" Elaine asked. "Looks like I'm out of a job too."

"Just call in sick for a while," Jon said, now audibly frustrated. "Stop with the money already. We'll figure it out. If we're lucky, we'll barely even feel it."

"I don't have that many sick days left. Our checking account is low. What are we going to be living off of?"

"They're still paying me, remember?" Jon said. "I'll have a friend pick up my paycheck. Right now all I need is some clean underwear and a good meal. And you have the two thousand bucks from the closet."

"I never took it."

"What?!"

"I was in a rush."

"How can you be in too much of a rush to take two thousand dollars?!" Jon demanded. "Great. Just fucking great. Now I know why you pulled the Five of Coins."

"Should I drive over and get it?"

"No," Jon said adamantly, "don't even think about it. I'll do it when I get the chance."

"Take money out of your Municipal Bank checking account," Elaine said.

"I will, but I may need that two thousand at some point."

"Be careful, Jon."

"Don't worry, I won't trample the azaleas. Look, I'll call you back later. It's going to be crazy here for a couple of days. We'll talk some more and you'll feel better."

"Jon . . . ?" Elaine's voice trailed off before she forcibly got it back under control. "Even though I'm upset, I'm serious about what I said. I want to help you. How can I do that?"

"By doing what you're doing now," he replied. "And since you're so computer literate, why don't you dig up some information for me on Paula Derbin and Lee Sarnow. That's S-A-R-N-O-W."

"I can do that, Jon. There's a company on the Web called Do-cusearch. They'll sell you salary information, telephone records, medical histories—"

"Go for it, Elaine. And, oh yeah—one more thing. Don't leave any messages on my voice mail at work. As far as they know, I'm sick at home with you. You'd have no reason to be leaving me messages."

"Got you," Elaine said. "Jon . . . ?"

"Yeah?"

"Next time I want a bigger assignment than that."

"You got it, babe."

A few minutes before 11:00 P.M. that Thursday, Jon fixated upon the calendar on the side of Joel Haney's refrigerator. Though it was May, Haney's calendar was opened to April, as it would be for eternity. Jon's focus on the calendar grew so intense he eventually saw past the numbers and the lines, but unfortunately, whatever was behind them was not yet clear. It was now May 20, and he was looking more backward than forward. He could recall a few of the things he had said either directly to or in the presence of Naomi but not precisely when he'd said all of them.

He recalled telling her, during their North River site visit, that he was absolutely committed to solving the mystery of the missing thirty million gallons. He remembered bragging to Larry about how he was helping Detective Mercado of the Tenth Precinct, and that Naomi had been within earshot. Yet both of those oversights had already come back to haunt him, and he had trouble seeing where the rest of the mines were hidden. He knew they were there, and that they were potentially deadly. However, his brain was already saturated from hours of going through data, an exercise that was also proving futile. It was one thing not to be able to handle Mercado's assignment. It was another thing entirely not to be able to handle his own.

Jon stepped into the living room, where Gibbs was seated at a large table and poring over hundreds of sheets' worth of data he had photocopied for Jon that same evening.

"Well, this sucks," Jon said. "I have a mental block going on this whole surveillance thing, and we're both striking out with this North River data analysis."

"Speak for yourself," Gibbs said. "I just struck gold."

"Gold?"

"Okay, silver," Gibbs said. "You know, finding coins in the sewer is commonplace. They stick to the bottom."

"What do you have, Al?"

"Take a look at this," Gibbs said. Jon sat in the nearest chair and leaned in toward Gibbs's small stack of papers. "You know how DEP converts wet weather flow into dry weather flow?"

"Sure," Jon said. "On a rainy day, there might be a hundred million extra gallons coming into the plant, sometimes even more. The meters at the plant only know how much sewage is coming into the plant, total. They don't know if a hundred million is rain water and another 180 million is regular sewage. Those meters read 280 million gallons and that's it. But since DEP's permit is based on dry weather flow, they have to come up with dry weather numbers even on a rainy day. So they apply a bizarre statistical analysis to the data. Something like . . . if the flow for the hour is at least two standard deviations above the mean for that hour, they substitute the dry weather average for that hour taken over the past month. I always thought the formula was bullshit anyway."

"Okay. What would you do if I told you DEP used that conversion on days when there was no rain whatsoever?"

"You're kidding me," Jon said, pulling closer to Gibbs's papers.

"Not at all," Gibbs said. "Look at this. April eight, 1993—National Weather Service reports zero precipitation for Central Park. But DEP gives a total flow of 181 million gallons and a converted dry weather flow of 169 million gallons. That's twelve million gallons of raw sewage gone, vanished with the stroke of a pen."

"So DEP reports 169 million gallons for that day," Jon said, "but in reality, there were 181 million gallons, all of them regular, undiluted raw sewage."

"That's right," Gibbs said. "And the city slips in under its 170-million-gallon permit limit, at least for that day. What I showed you was just one sample day. They've done this sixty-five times over the past year alone. Sometimes they get rid of two million gallons, sometimes twenty. Whatever they're in the mood for."

"Al, you're a genius. Especially for someone who's been brain dead since 1970."

"Well, you know," Gibbs said, "this is nice, but it's a far cry from accounting for thirty million gallons every day."

"But it's a nice piece of the puzzle, Al. And it's interesting that they were doing this even before April Fool's Day. This is turning out to be more complex than we thought. It's falsification on multiple levels. They have this thing fixed all sorts of ways. Who knows how much sewage is really being produced all told and where it's going?"

"Hey," Gibbs said with a shrug, "at least it's a piece of the puzzle, like you said."

"An important piece," Jon said. "We can hand that right over to Mercado's file. Good job, man. And look at me. I'm sitting here for hours and I haven't come up with jack shit."

"Take it easy," Gibbs said, "it'll come. You're burned-out. You were throwing up a few hours ago. You need a break. You're in luck. I think Mercado is off the phone." Gibbs nodded toward the bedroom.

"I think it's too late to call Elaine," Jon said. "Her friend'll bite my head off."

"No. I mean call Naomi."

"What the hell," Jon said, pulling out a list of phone numbers from his wallet. There in the lower right-hand corner was Naomi's home number, penciled in on the day she first offered to let him sleep over if Keith ever put him out. Now Gibbs took the base of the living room extension and handed Jon the receiver. Jon took it in his right hand, and with his left punched the seven digits.

As he listened to the phone ring on the other end, he stood up, took the base from Gibbs, and carried both pieces of the phone toward the couch, where he could get a little more comfortable. No sooner had the base of the phone landed on the coffee table and his body sank into the sofa than Gibbs's index finger hit the button for the speaker phone. Jon saw a smirk on the side of Gibbs's face as he scooted over to the straight-back leather chair. Jon heard Naomi's voice in his ear and throughout the living room.

"Hello?"

"Naomi, it's Jon."

"Hi, Jon." The businesslike tone of her voice barely suppressed its breathlessness, which in turn barely masked confusion. "Did you get my message?"

"Yes I did, and I'm letting you know I want to go for the package deal."

"Good. I'm glad." Now that she knew precisely which role to play, a studied casualness returned to her speech.

"I shouldn't have walked out like that," Jon said. "Part of it was that I wanted you so bad I was uncomfortable with myself. I'm not used to feeling like that. But I'm past that now."

"Good. Where are you?"

"I'm at home, in Long Island," Jon said. "It's too late now to catch a train. I can't stay on long."

"Are we on for tomorrow?" Naomi asked.

"Well, I'm going to be out sick for a few more days," Jon said. "It's embarrassing to admit, but the drinking put me out of commission for a while. I can barely move. I might have been coming down with something to begin with, and everything kicked in all at once."

"Well, get better soon," Naomi said. "I want you inside me, Jon."

"Hang in there," Jon said. "It'll only be a few more days. I want to finish what I started."

Gibbs sprang up from the couch and paraded softly around the room holding his arms upright in a touchdown position. Mercado had entered the living room grinning and was looking straight down at Jon, who was still on the couch. Jon tried to wave them both off with his left hand and continued the conversation.

"What about your report?" Naomi asked. "Isn't being sick going to push it back some more?"

"Well, you know how badly I want it to come out," Jon said, "but a few more days isn't going to kill me. I'm set for a while. I had the latest draft of my report in my knapsack last night. I had a feeling we wouldn't be coming back to the office."

"Any new ideas on the missing thirty million gallons?" Naomi asked.

"A couple," Jon said, "but nothing airtight yet. I'll tell you about it when we're together . . . when we take a breather."

"I'm saving it up for you."

"One more thing," Jon said. "Try not to call me at home. I don't want a certain someone to pick up the phone."

"Understood. Call me tomorrow?"

"You got it."

"'Bye." Jon put down the receiver. Gibbs and Mercado burst into loud, spontaneous yelps and chants of "Whooop, there it is."

"Please," Jon said. "You want me to start throwing up again?"

"What I want," Mercado said, "is her phone number."

"You can have it," Jon said, "but she only goes after married engineers holding up multibillion-dollar developments."

"Two out of three ain't bad," Mercado said.

"Forget about it," Jon said. "I'm gonna nail her with the rest of them. She's probably plotting to have me killed right now."

"Excuses, excuses," Mercado said.

"Haven't had this kind of action in twenty-three years," Gibbs said. "It's late. Time for me to get a cab back to Queens. I'll have a smile on my face the whole way."

Jon lay on the couch and slept in half-hour spurts. He mulled over various hypotheses but seemed to be going around in circles. At one point he sat up and turned on the TV to soothe himself into oblivion. Almost every channel, it seemed, had an infomercial going, selling nonsurgical cures for baldness, real estate programs closely resembling pyramid schemes, and thirty-day diets promising to turn Roseanne into Kate Moss. The host of one such infomercial bragged: "Eat as much as you want, as often as you want, and still lose weight so fast you can practically *see* it come off before your very eyes."

Throughout the rest of the night and the morning, this vacant promise echoed in his head. A few minutes after noon, he got up for good. He considered heading into the bathroom to shave, but then figured he might as well grow a beard.

Instead, he trudged over to the dining room table, still cluttered with remnants of work from the night before, and sat down. From the flow reports, to a legal-size pad, to a calculator, and back again, Jon went in circles that were getting him somewhere for a change, like the wheels of a Ferrari. Within forty-five minutes he had what he was looking for.

The euphoria was tempered by embarrassment over how elegantly simple it all was, and his belief that he probably should have figured it out a lot earlier. Fourteen of the nineteen trunk mains feeding the interceptor were metered. The plant and the interceptor were metered as well. Those meters were supposed to be telling roughly the same story. But they weren't. Jon added the daily flow total of the fourteen trunk meters. This total, throughout the months of March and April, remained at around 140 million gallons a day, give or take a couple of million gallons.

The total of the plant remained around 192 million gallons a day, also give or take a couple million gallons. Jon plotted the two curves on the same piece of graph paper, and they tended to rise and fall with each other. Except during March 30 to April 3. During that brief period, the reported flow to the plant plummeted from 192 mgd to 162 mgd. The trunk main total, meanwhile, remained flat at 140. From then on the two curves were synched up again, one at 162 mgd, the other at 140 mgd, gently following each other's leads once more like a veteran Olympic figure-skating team after a leap and triple turn.

Jon looked at the neat graph before him. Millions of dollars and dozens of experts had gone to war to prove the city's water conservation efforts explained the drop, but this lone graph proved otherwise, definitively. Of course there were a few trunk mains not yet metered, but there was barely enough flow in them to account for the thirty-million-gallon disappearance, even if every one of the residents in the corresponding neighborhoods had dropped dead on March 30.

Something in the system had gone haywire, and here was mathematical proof good enough for a judge. The sewage was being sent down the line but wasn't reaching its destination. Surely the goings on just a couple hundred yards outside Haney's living room window provided at least part of the explanation.

It was now early in the afternoon, Friday, May 21. The phone rang, but Jon remembered that Mercado was in the bedroom and yielded to the detective out of courtesy. The phone was picked up in the other room on the second ring. Jon spent the next twenty seconds reveling in his accomplishment until Mercado walked into the living room.

"Pick up, kid," Mercado said, "it's for you. Tell you something—all your women have amazing voices."

Jon smirked and reached for the phone as Mercado walked back to the bedroom. Jon did not hear the other receiver being hung up. "Hello?"

"Jon, it's Laura."

"Laura," Jon said urgently, "first thing—where are you calling from?"

"From a pay phone on the ground floor of the Woolworth Building," she replied.

"Okay, good," Jon said. "So you know the situation."

"Yes, I know the situation all right," Laura said. "Al Gibbs pulled me aside this morning and told me everything. What a shocker."

"They actually tried to kill me."

"I already knew that," Laura said. "The shocker is that Al's not crazy."

"Tell me about it." Jon said.

"I want to help you, Jon. From what Al said, though, it sounds like you still have some breathing room."

"Just a centimeter's worth, and that could change any second. That's why I was so concerned over where you were calling from."

"Don't worry, " Laura said, "I've got that covered. I was being careful about phone calls long before you. I probably should have told you this a couple of days ago."

"What?"

"Well," Laura began, "something that Paula said stuck in my brain. The time she called me in to reassign me to Board Six. You were waiting outside."

"I remember."

"This happened just before you showed up. I was reacting to what Paula was saying. I told her I was considering quitting, right there and then. And she said: 'Why don't you go ask Clarissa Marbles for a job, now that she thinks you're a hero?' "

"So?"

"I listened to my tape of that conversation over and over again," Laura said, "until it hit me. Paula had a spy in that community board meeting, right?"

"Of course."

"Everyone knows Clarissa and I don't get along. But Clarissa never said a thing at that meeting," Laura said. "And Clarissa and Paula aren't even on speaking terms. But we do know Clarissa called you a couple days before to tell you she thought I was a hero, and you then related that to me a few minutes later."

"So what are you saying?"

"I'm saying, Jon, that you're probably being bugged. Your office, your phone, or both."

"Don't forget about retrieving messages off my voice mail," Jon said. "That's the easiest thing for them to do. They have access to the control panel. How hard could it be to access someone's password?"

"Easy," Laura said.

"I've been confronting this whole surveillance issue myself recently," Jon said. "Naomi slipped up at least once or twice and asked me about something there's no way she could have known about any other way."

"Al told me you went halfway with that little viper."

"Great."

"I would have expected better from you, of all people, Jon."

"Hey, no harm, no foul," Jon said. "Give me credit for walking out of that trap. And until you spend a lifetime wearing male body armor, please don't bring it up again."

"Okay, fine," Laura said. "My point is simply that, knowing

this, my head is spinning trying to recall what I've said and when."

"I hear that. Detective Mercado wants me to write all of it down. I don't even know where to begin."

"Remember that day I came into your office half in tears?" Laura asked. "Well, Paula must have heard every word I said to you, including the fact that I tape her. How's that?"

"Not good," Jon said. "I'll bet it freaked her out."

"So it's a safe bet she knows about all of us." Laura spoke with both a heightened awareness and a sigh of resignation.

"Yes," Jon said emphatically, "and don't assume that just because I was the biggest thorn in Paula's side I'm the only one under surveillance. If my phone is tapped, why not yours, Jay's, Pat's? And how about Al? He left cryptic messages on my machine. They probably didn't recognize his voice, though. I know I didn't. I feel like we're all hanging on by a thread. As soon as they figure out what I'm up to, the thread is going to be cut. I mean, Laura, are you still going to show up at work? Is Jay or Pat?"

"For now we are," she replied. "We talked about it and decided that if we all stay away, they're much more likely to know something's up. You might even want to drop by for a day yourself."

"No way," Jon said. "And don't you guys come in to work on my behalf or on behalf of some general plan of action. Don't underestimate the risk you're taking by giving them a live target. They're willing to kill."

"That's why I have a proposal for you, Jon. I went to Yale with a guy named George Nagle. He's now an attorney with the U.S. Justice Department specializing in environmental law."

"Uh-huh."

"Al Gibbs told me your detective friend is getting a lukewarm reception from Internal Affairs at the police department."

"That's right," Jon said.

"Okay, I'm going to talk to George about getting involved. The city is violating the Federal Clean Water Act by deliberately dumping into an open waterway. This is definitely under the attorney general's jurisdiction. I'll call him today."

"Sounds good," Jon said warily, "but can we trust him?"

"Absolutely," Laura said. "He'd love to have someone like Ronald Arlen for lunch. And Art Shuler for dessert. George wants to be attorney general one day. The guy's a straight arrow, almost to an annoying degree. He was valedictorian."

"Well, hallelujah."

"I know no one else cares," Laura said, "but he still does. I think he wanted to go out with me, but I wasn't interested."

"Okay, Laura. As long as he doesn't turn out to be another Naomi."

"Uh, not likely," Laura said. "I have to go with my instinct right now, just like you're going with yours. Believe me, I'm aware of the danger. I was in denial at one point, not wanting to believe that everything is tied together . . . the sewer murder—"

"Believe it," Jon said.

"I do, especially after what happened this morning."

"What happened this morning?" Jon asked, a hint of alarm in his voice.

"You don't know?" Laura asked. "I thought you were in touch."

"No, I'm out of touch. *Way* out of touch."

"A guy from DEP fell down the valve shaft at the Seventy-ninth Street access to the third water tunnel. During an inspection. A scaffold gave way."

"Who?" Jon asked urgently.

"An engineer," Laura said, "Fred . . . Barrow." Jon had heard the full name even before it was uttered.

"Oh my God." His head slumped down onto the arm of the couch, cradled inside his left arm. His right hand, still holding the receiver, flailed like a dying fish against the coffee table. A foot and a half from the receiver, his right ear picked up the dampened, filtered pulse of Laura's voice repeating his name.

"This is on my head," Jon said, propping himself up and again bringing the receiver to his ear. His voice was angry, shaky, disturbed, fluttering, "I knew him. He gave me information. I . . . mentioned his name to that bitch Naomi the night I almost slept with her."

"Jon, this is not on your head."

"Yes it is," he insisted. "You say this happened this morning? I was with Naomi Wednesday night. Now you're back to the old theme of calling everything a coincidence. I told her he was helping me out. Do you understand?"

"You are not the only source of information."

"He had a young daughter," Jon half sobbed. "I was just sitting here going over photocopies of the data sheets he gave me."

"Jon," Laura pleaded, "we just went through how it's possible or even probable that all sorts of people are under surveillance. This guy worked at DEP. How do you know his office wasn't bugged? How do you know they didn't pick up a conversation between you and him off of your phone?"

"I don't know." Jon's array of emotions now funneled their way into his throat and congealed as rage. "But I do know this, Laura. Now we're gonna stick it to those assholes. That's it. No holds barred."

They quickly arranged to leave a series of messages on each other's answering machines misleading Paula about Jon's progress on the missing 30 mgd and about the Stink Tank's commitment to assisting Jon. After agreeing to turn over her microcassette tapes to the Mercado file, Laura informed Jon that the committee hearing on the Hudson City sewer hookup had been moved up to the first Wednesday in June, making the situation that much more urgent.

After putting down the receiver and slumping back on the couch, something dawned on Jon. It was the kind of recollection you got only after excessive sleep, and it penetrated even his grief over Fred Barrow's death. Mark Rosario of the *Westsider* was not only the reporter he saw questioning Ronald Arlen that day at the construction site, he was also a classmate of Jon's at Columbia. Jon had never put this together before, and apparently Rosario hadn't either. It was a big school. They had one political science class together. Rosario was writing school editorials advocating bottle and can recycling years before it was law.

Today, as a professional, Rosario wrote editorials vilifying people like Ronald Arlen who used the resources of the city strictly for their own ends. It made sense to approach Rosario, albeit very discreetly. As a reporter for a relatively small paper, he had a lot to gain. And, as Mercado had explained to Jon, his adversaries had little compunction when it came to assassinations—of either people or their characters.

Chapter 32

That Friday night, May 21, Jon was alone in the apartment except for the remains of two six-packs. Through a self-imposed haze of alcohol and anguish, Jon watched Chuck Scarborough report the local eleven o'clock news. Fred Barrow's death was the second lead story on Channel 4. Jon listened as a police detective was quoted as saying the death was "most likely accidental." About as accidental, Jon thought, as what happened to him in the Glass House.

Two stories later, Donald Trump was interviewed as part of a segment on the possibility of legalized gambling just off the shores of New York City. This was an idea whose time had come, Trump said, and he was getting in on the ground floor—even if it was floating.

At eleven-eighteen, the front door to the apartment opened and Detective Mercado walked in, with Al Gibbs and Charlie Sharpe immediately behind him. The click of so many heels at once on the wooden hall floor unnerved Jon, who sat on the couch. Mercado walked over to the couch and with a broad smile looked down at him.

"Jon, listen to me. This was not your fault."

"That's easy for you to say," Jon replied.

"I've lost people I worked with," Mercado said, "but I didn't blame myself. No, actually I did blame myself, but I realized later I was just being self-indulgent."

"You see, this is different," Jon said. "This really *was* my fault."

"You need to distract yourself from this," Mercado said.

"Mercado's right," Sharpe said.

"How do you know?" Jon asked, eyeing Al Gibbs's friend quizzically.

"Fred Barrow was a friend of mine too," Sharpe said. "He got me some of the information I gave to Al. Did I get him killed? Maybe. Did you? Maybe. But I know who pulled the trigger."

"Who?" Jon asked.

"His boss," Sharpe replied. "Lee Sarnow."

Jon said nothing and slumped backward on the couch. From the right pocket of his navy-blue windbreaker, Mercado pulled out a VHS cassette tape. He tossed it gently onto the couch cushion alongside Jon.

"What's that," Jon asked, "a tape of the Rodney King beating?"

"Nope," Mercado said, "a tape made by a deceased filmmaker by the name of Joel Haney."

"A porno tape?" Jon said. "I've seen them all already."

"Sorry to disappoint you," Mercado said. "It's mostly outdoor shots . . . scenery. It's the tape we found on Haney's body when he was killed. It was partially waterlogged. Even after I let the sucker dry, it killed my VCR. And part of the tape. It's a loaner, so be careful with it. I had a guy down at the Anticrime Unit clean it up and put it back together for me."

"So . . ."

"So it was worth it," Mercado said. "Most of the footage is intact except for being lightened, and the lines running through it. The audio is almost all there. Pop it in and take a look when you can see straight. I have it set to the important part. I think one look at it, and you'll completely understand the connection between Haney's murder, Eighteenth Street, and the sewage issue. Like I said—wrong place, wrong time."

"You were right," Jon said.

"Huh?"

"You did disappoint me."

"Jon, lighten up," Gibbs said. "We're going places. The detective told me Laura's friend already agreed to help us out. That's great news."

"Yeah," Jon said, "that's what Laura said. I'll believe it when I see it. He'll only address us in person, and we don't have a firm commitment on when he's coming in. Maybe next week."

"Still, good news, and more of it on the way," Gibbs said. "Charlie here is in. On Wednesday the detective and his partner are coming up to the office to do some countersurveillance work. I'm letting them in and giving them access. The pretense? I'm getting them a map."

"That'll be a first," Jon snapped.

"Don't worry about it, Jon," Sharpe said. "Whatever you're worried about. You just keep doing what you're doing."

"I'd like to," Jon said, "but I'm almost out of beer. I may have to switch over to vodka."

"He means with the research," Gibbs said. "I told you you'd come up with something once you gave yourself a chance."

"How do you know what I came up with?" Jon asked.

"Are you too drunk to remember our phone conversation?"

"Yes," Jon said. "And I don't think I'll be coming up with anything else. Every time I try to cull through that stack of papers, I think of Fred Barrow. Maybe I ought to just leave it there as a memorial."

"I know what it's like to lose a friend," Gibbs said, "but you'll get over it because you have to."

"Exactly," Jon said. "I'm going to grieve and act like a lunatic for, say, twenty years, and then I'm going right back to work." Jon took a huge swig and looked right at Mercado. "So you're going to do a sweep of my office?"

"Looking forward to it," Mercado said. "I get to pretend I'm Gene Hackman in *The Conversation*. I may even find my way into your friend Paula Derbin's office."

"Aren't there certain legalities you have to worry about?" Jon asked. "Certain regulations and guidelines?"

"Only if you're an officer of the law," Mercado said.

"And you're not . . ."

"Not officially," Mercado said. "Not at this very moment. Not unless I need to be. Now I get to beat these people at their own game. Like I said, I'm looking forward to it."

Jon took another swig and studied Charlie Sharpe's face for the first time. "Where do I know you from?" he asked.

"Fourteenth Street," Sharpe said. "When you did an investigation on the sidewalks."

"And, you're Al's friend from way back," Jon said.

"That's right," Sharpe said. "Way back."

"Jeez, it *is* a small world," Jon said. "If I'd have known it was that small, I would never have fooled around with my intern."

"Life is full of symmetry," Mercado said. "Take you and me. They think you work for the city, but you don't. They think I don't work for the city, but I do."

"Yeah," Jon said, "something like that."

Chapter 33

Sunday afternoon, May 23, at 4:45, Jon had the apartment to himself. The bright spring sun was well into its descent over the Hudson now and momentarily burned a hole into his hair like a crop circle. Bathed in solar heat, his head felt oven-baked regardless of which way he turned it. Even the open casement window and the relatively fresh air it allowed in could not compensate for his overwhelming sense of being penned. But in another few hours, he reminded himself, much of that feeling would finally be released.

Mercado's involvement and supervision had quickly proved both exciting and onerous. With the presence of a law enforcement agent, though temporarily minus his shield, Jon, Al Gibbs, and even Charlie Sharpe felt more empowered than they had only two days earlier. Though George Nagle lurked somewhere in the shadows of the distant background, Mercado's strong persona pervaded everything they did, whether he was standing in the room or not.

The carrot of justice now dangled inches from their noses rather than feet or yards, motivating everyone to work even harder than they had planned. Jon, in particular, took it up a notch, both to stay even with Mercado's pace and to atone for his behavior Friday night. His mind was playing a cruel hoax on him. The more he searched his memory for things he might have said while under surveillance, the more he recalled the stupid things he had said while drunk. So far, a steady diet of number-crunching had been his only way of neutralizing this condition, a kind of self-medication.

The last two days had been filled with a barrage of new technical terms only vaguely understood by Jon: first and second generation night-viewing devices, phosphor screens, harmonic radiation, frequency deviation. Mercado tossed them off as if they were part of Jon's lexicon just because he was an engineer. But there were many subcategories of engineering, and many, many subsubcategories. Jon knew structures, drainage, sewage treatment, and environmental assessment. He didn't know the first thing about bugging a room.

Even now it seemed that Mercado was bugging him. A Panasonic AG-456 S-VHS camcorder sat on a sturdy tripod near the window. Its built-in 12:1 power zoom was enhanced by a Century tele-extender, making the total zoom capacity 24:1. Fitted between the camcorder and a 2/3-inch bayonet lens was an Astroscope—a night-vision module with a series of photocathode intensifiers capable of amplifying the available light thirty thousand times. Al Gibbs was footing most of the bill. This piece of equipment alone cost him seven thousand dollars. The unit was aimed out the window and down toward the Eighteenth Street regulator chamber. But when Jon considered what he was about to do, he felt sure the unit had eyes in the back of its head.

It was five o'clock. Jon picked up the telephone receiver and punched in Naomi's home number. Her expectant voice was heard after only two rings.

"Hello?"

"It's me."

"Jon. I'm glad you called."

"I got your message yesterday on my voice mail," Jon said. "Pretty hot."

"It won't compare to the real thing," Naomi said. "Trust me."

"As it is, I can barely get any work done. I've been thinking about it all day. That whole idea of walking into a hotel room, seeing the woman of your dreams from behind, naked on the bed, not saying a single word, walking over and gently slipping it in . . . my concentration is shot. How do you think of these things?"

"Maybe I've had too much time on my hands lately," Naomi said. "But just remember this—what some people call a fantasy, I call a reality. Pretty soon it will be your reality too."

"I'm counting the minutes."

"I am too," Naomi said, "and I can barely wait any longer. When I get you alone in that room, Jon, I'm going to bring you right to the brink and back again. We'll need the room for a full week just to scrape ourselves off the ceiling. I'm losing my mind thinking about it."

"We are going to do this, Naomi."

"I know . . ."

"Just hang in there a little while longer," Jon said. "I have a few more things to take care of, and then the coast is clear."

"I know, Jon," Naomi said, almost breathless. "The more I want something, the more I become afraid it may not happen."

"You don't have to think like that, Naomi. We're not talking about that much more time, are we?"

"No . . ."

"Then we're as good as there."

"Okay," Naomi said, "you're right. I'll be seeing you very soon." Jon heard the soft sound of a kiss, hardened slightly by transmission across telephone lines, followed by a click.

Jon was still alone at eight o'clock. Mercado and Gibbs were somewhere plotting their coup. No one knew where Sharpe was, but he wasn't due back till tomorrow. Jon now took the VHS tape Mercado had given him and popped it into the VCR for what would be his third look.

The time code on the tape, in small, boxlike white letters, read Friday, April 2, 1993, 9:52 P.M. Thin, white, horizontal lines ran periodically across the screen, moving deliberately from top to bottom. The entire screen lightened for a second here, three seconds there—apparently the effect of the tape's overnight visit to the sewer. Jon adjusted his eyes just as the camera had adjusted its diaphragm to the darkness, which on screen was penetrated by the streetlights along the roadway.

Along the black, narrow asphalt pavement that served as a sidewalk, a slim, almost malnourished female with long brown hair, sad sunken eyes, spandex, and a bomber jacket emerged from the darkness, into the artificial light from a street lamp. Her brisk, burdened stride transformed itself into a slower, more seductive walk as soon as the woman appeared to recognize the camera. Now she spoke directly to it.

"Joel. Like to hook up right now?"

"Sorry, Tiffany," the baritone voice from behind the camera replied. "We already got everything we needed."

"I didn't mean another interview, Joel," the woman said. "I mean do you want to take me upstairs and fuck me? Maybe even kiss me."

"We're out of *that* business, Tiffany," the voice said. "I was dead serious about that. You should be getting out too."

"And do what?" the woman asked rhetorically. "Act in documentaries? That's nice work—when you can get it."

"Okay, here you go," the voice said. A hand reached forward into the lower left-hand corner of the screen. The woman met the hand with her own right and snatched from the blurry mass what seemed to be several bills.

"Thanks, Joel," the woman's voice said, now coming from off-camera. The man's voice responded.

"Take care of yourself, Tiffany."

"Let me know if you change your mind," the woman's voice said, now from a greater distance. "You know where to find me." The camera panned north and zoomed in on a few yellow cones and on two large men in grayish uniforms and high boots, one of whom used a long tool to pry open a large utility cover from its position in the westernmost lane of traffic. The voice from behind the camera spoke again.

"Sometimes an offer like that is hard to turn down. But I don't let the demon in me do the talking anymore. Tiffany had a mother and a father once. She had a tricycle. She had a Barbie doll. She had a boyfriend. But something threw her for a terrible loop. Anyone who formed even one tiny segment of that loop bears some responsibility. I'm one of these people. I bear responsibility. At least today I'm trying, desperately trying, to get Tiffany, twenty of her friends, and, yes, even myself, out of that loop."

There was a pause in the voice-over as the camera continued to study the area inside the cones. The second of the two men had now disappeared into the earth. The voice from behind the camera resumed.

"Of course, if there were any justice in the world, Tiffany or one of her friends would get my old job. God knows any of them could do a better job than those idiots they gave it to. See, here's where this camera falls short as a tool of communication. It can't smell, and I envy it for that. Right now, this place smells like a Penn Station toilet because these goons can't get the regulator out of the bypass position. Or maybe they want it that way. So out everything goes, right into the river. This is how the city protects its environment. Pathetic. Some lonely voice in my head, maybe my dad's voice, is telling me to go over there and . . . help them out. Well, forget it. When it comes to the city, no good deed has ever gone unpunished."

Jon hit stop on the remote. There was nothing more to be gleaned. What Sharpe had suspected and what Mercado had come to know he now understood as well. Joel Haney had stumbled into the situation, perhaps even more innocently than Jon himself had. Haney died not understanding the big picture, of which he so quickly and violently became an important part.

Eventually, Haney had given in to that voice in his head, which told him to look into something if it didn't seem right. But had he heard the *whole* voice, he would have been duly warned that any-one who came within thirty feet of that utility cover risked elimi-nation by men who, in varying degrees, did not understand the big picture either. And for the first time, Jon himself did.

Now, with the transient nature of life painted so vividly before him by a camcorder, he was more compelled than ever to go ahead with his plan. Along with the tape he had just seen, Jon had spent parts of the past two days watching an earlier, unredeemed Joel Haney having sex in umpteen positions with a variety of women he barely knew and for whose services he had paid. By compari-son, what Jon was about to do was hardly a sin at all.

He hadn't told Mercado, Gibbs, or anyone else of his inten-tions, not because they wouldn't understand his urges, but because they would be inclined to overstate the risks. But Jon knew he could leave now and return sometime after midnight without ever mentioning where he had gone or what he'd done. He had already set the camcorder for the evening's surveillance, and it would run eight hours before a fresh tape had to be inserted. He would be back, no problem. Just as long as he could scrape himself off the floor.

At 9:36 P.M., with a buzzing Times Square heard faintly two blocks away, Jon darted across Forty-fourth Street and into the bright white lobby of the Algonquin Hotel's next-door neighbor, the Iroquois. He stroked the stiff beginnings of his new beard and adjusted his dark sunglasses as he approached the desk behind the large cut-out area of the rear lobby wall. From behind it the cheru-bic, fortyish desk clerk, a woman with a bouffant of red hair, looked up at him.

"Can I help you?"

"Yes," Jon replied, catching his breath, ". . . Jon Kessler."

"Oh, yes," the clerk said with a smile. "Room 414." She

reached for a hook and handed him a set of keys. She looked down at her reservation book and looked back up at him. "Naomi Pierce is waiting for you." Jon smiled, let out some air through his nose, and looked up for an instant at the ceiling.

As he stepped off the elevator, walked to his left, and began to focus in on the number 414, he realized this was going to come off without a hitch—with impunity. To dwell on this sequence of events day in and day out and not to finally live it was no life at all. Some would have him believe that the arrival could never measure up to the journey, but as he fitted the longer key into the lower keyhole and pushed open the door, he knew those people were clueless.

She lay completely naked facedown on the bed, just as they had discussed. Upon hearing the door open and now gently close, she did not look back for even an instant, but simply raised her tight buttocks in readiness off the mattress, her arms stretched out before her gracefully like a dancer's, her head partially buried in the pillow almost as if for prayer, her knees braced for reception. He stepped up to the rear of the bed, flinging his sunglasses to the carpeted floor, dropping his pants and Jockey shorts to his ankles, and jockeyed neatly for position on the bed seemingly in one smooth motion.

Erect, it seemed for days, he entered her forcefully, but without resistance. Though joined together only this much, her entire body felt as if it had enclosed and consumed his, the two supple entities now beginning to wrap themselves around each other and move as one. The difference between them was vanishing as quickly as the sun had disappeared beyond the Hudson—a bright glow and then a magnificent shadow more radiant and mysterious than the sun itself. For every sunset that Jon had pondered this eventuality, it had now made itself that much more blissful for the wait.

Jon gripped her with a steering, desperate life force over the top of each athletic shoulder, her head still hiding in the pillow from the brightness and ecstasy, calling his name sporadically, muffled and crazed. They rocked apart, then together for a minute, five minutes, a lifetime, as everything but their consumption of one another and the rocking itself dropped away. He put his lips together and kissed the spot along her spine, precisely where the center of her female energy lay, and fell inside her in ways that defied and mocked any mode of description.

At this precise moment her rocking was no longer hers, no longer even theirs, but that of the Earth's. Her few words became a long, timeless, sensual cry from deep in her belly and his. The cry seemed to have started eons before and gave the impression that nothing could ever silence it. He was crying now too, or was part of the cry—which, he could not tell. It became louder and more synchronized and soon went beyond their threshold to hear it, to sense it.

She came—strenuously, helplessly, menacingly, and now, with what little composure she had, pushed out every ounce of love and chaos she could through wherever it would leave her body. He came as well, distinctly, with a soaring, masculine submission to what was complete and finally a deed. His final drops spilled, he lay atop her, both of them facedown, twitching occasionally, mixing perspiration, and remembering how to breathe.

"Oh my God," she said, "that was a thousand times better than I expected. And I expected perfection."

"Me too. And now we may never get over it." When she rolled over, he saw Elaine's handsomely chiseled face and searing green eyes fully for the first time in two weeks. Except for a couple of worry lines that had thickened, everything was the same as the last time he'd seen her.

"My idea of perfection," Elaine confided, "is to have this whole thing go away."

"It will," Jon said, "it will. Hey, you are one sick puppy giving your name as Naomi Pierce."

"I knew you'd get a kick out of that," Elaine said.

"Are you kidding me? I didn't know whether to burst out laughing or run out the door."

"Well, this is my way of getting even with that little bitch," Elaine said. "I'm glad you decided to check her voice mail. And she was going to try to get you into bed? She's got some nerve."

"You got that right," Jon said.

"Jon," Elaine said, "was this a good idea?"

"You tell *me*."

"No," Elaine said, "I mean was it wrong to leave the kids with Judy? Do you think anyone might have followed us here?"

"Elaine, this is a big city. It's easy to get lost in it."

"I guess you're right," she said.

"I explained this to you already," Jon said. "We have no hard and fast reason to think I'm even being followed at this point. I told you—I've called in sick for a few days, I'm still working on the revisions of my odor report, my friends are leaving messages throwing Paula off, Al returned my original files to the office—"

"Okay, Jon."

"What we're doing is being perhaps a hair less than perfectly prudent," Jon said. "But I'm not going to let anyone tell me I can't have sex with my own wife. I'm entitled to my own money too. One day this week I'm going back to the house to get that two thousand dollars."

"I don't think you should," Elaine said.

"Please, Elaine," Jon said, smacking the mattress with an open palm, "I have this covered from every angle, and I don't want to discuss it. This surveillance equipment is costing us a small fortune, and I don't want to make Al Gibbs pay for all of it. We're not even half done collecting the stuff. Detective Mercado is broke. Paid my rent and he's not collecting a paycheck. I'm getting the money, Elaine. When they really come after me, you'll know it."

"Okay, okay," Elaine said. "Oh, I have some telephone logs for you in my bag. Some stuff you wanted on Lee Sarnow."

"Thanks. You're an angel." Now Elaine sighed and lay her head across Jon's chest. "By the way, how did you come up with this whole devious idea of having me wait for you here with my ass in the air?"

Jon eyed her for a moment and replied, "I guess I've had too much time on my hands lately."

Chapter 34

Jon's gray Dodge Caravan was right where he'd left it a week earlier, professional engineer's plates and all. Now, a few minutes past three in the afternoon of Wednesday, May 26, as he walked through the park-and-lock at the Port Jefferson train station, he was grateful for that much. He'd had his fill of surprises lately and then some. Although the car theft problem on the North Shore was not particularly severe, a decent-looking vehicle sitting idle for seven days was usually an open invitation to grand larceny. Today, however, the only inconvenience he had to deal with was tree sap and some soot on the windshield. Just to be on the safe side, he checked for signs of a bomb under the hood and under the chassis before opening the driver-side door. Once the Sears DieHard battery kicked in, he was on his way.

As he began driving the seven miles east on Route 25A toward Rocky Point, he shook his head and his shoulders in an effort to wake himself fully. He had fallen asleep on the train while trying to do some sewage flow analysis. This had become a pattern over the last few days. The more he tried to focus, the more his mind drifted. Like bubbles, important thoughts and recollections were floating up through the water but bursting at the surface, evading his grasp.

The obsession with a single goal had taken only a few days to wear him down. The strange truth was that no matter how overriding that goal's importance, the human brain had to seek shelter to survive, and if it wasn't getting any cooperation, it would find that shelter on its own.

Jon's brain gravitated toward sex or sleep at times as a reaction to his relentless push. The rendezvous with Elaine was supposed to have quelled the sexual longings, but seemed only to have intensified them. Even the nightly calls to Naomi had become a guilty pleasure. Though their purpose was to enhance his chances of survival, his desire to break up the awful monotony of fear and dread was so great, so desperate, that he needed to play the game for a few minutes each night just for the illicit distraction. This was unacceptable to Jon, who now decided that after retrieving his money, he would go visit Elaine at Judy's house in Miller Place.

Still, the past few days had been productive. He and Gibbs had streamlined much of their independent research and consolidated it into a single, succinctly worded report. Mercado's evidence basket was filling up with all sorts of goodies, including the memo from Ronald Arlen to Max McCord and the videotape found on Joel Haney's body.

The surveillance camera in Haney's apartment had already yielded extensive footage of two, sometimes three, men going in and out of the regulator chamber repeatedly throughout the night. Even at this moment, Gibbs, Mercado, and Janine O'Connel were about ready to get their countersurveillance sweep under way. For his part, Jon had remembered to pack a change of clothes in his knapsack, so he would have something to wear after he spent the night with Elaine. Only now he remembered he'd be visiting his own closet anyway.

Just before the left-hand turnoff at Odin Road, Jon—wearing shades and a Yankee cap—pulled into the parking lot for McCarrick's, the small convenience store on the corner. The work, worry, sleep, and lust had made him thirsty again. Inside, Shari, the busty eighteen-year-old counter clerk, saw him and shouted, "Nice beard," blowing his cover right off the bat.

"Nice breasts," Jon said, getting an immediate giggle and reminding himself that their ten-month repartee probably exempted him from a sexual harassment suit.

Now as Jon looked through the refrigerator glass and tried to choose between Gatorade, Tropicana, and Mott's apple juice, he was annoyed to no end by the repetitive sound of fake explosions coming from a video game in the corner being played by a possessed eleven-year-old with a Baltimore Orioles cap. Jon reminded himself how edgy and reactive he had been lately and shook it off. But as he turned around with a quart of Tropicana grapefruit juice in his hand, he was startled just the same. It was Charlie Murdock from the Rocky Point White Sox, wearing Bermuda shorts instead of baseball pants.

"Jon, what happened?"

"You mean the beard?" Jon asked, now extending his right hand to meet Murdock's. "It's a long story."

"No, I mean the game," Murdock said. "You never missed a game before. Not even a practice. How come you didn't call?"

"That's part of the same long story," Jon said.

"Well, tell me about it," Murdock said. "I have the time. I'm taking this week off. Just hanging out. Is Elaine okay?"

"Yeah, thanks for asking," Jon said. "It's . . . the job."

"I told you working for the city'll kill you," Murdock said, now reaching for a bottle of Miller Lite and letting the glass door slam shut on its own.

"It's not what you think," Jon said. "It's a lot worse. You wanna take a ride for a couple of minutes?"

"Yeah, sure," Murdock said. "I walked here anyway. Trying to work off this." Murdock grabbed a handle of flesh just to the right side of his navel.

"Start by putting back *this*," Jon said, nodding toward the bottle of Miller Lite.

Five minutes later they pulled into the driveway on Jon's property and Jon turned off the engine of his minivan. Murdock looked straight ahead, mesmerized, and nursed his beer.

"Holy shit," Murdock said. "This is like something out of a movie! But it's actually happening to you. Jeez, I don't know if I could handle being in your shoes."

"Don't worry," Jon said, "you don't have to. And don't feel sorry for me. I've found ways to distract myself. Sometimes the research I'm doing is even a helpful distraction. On the train ride over here, I couldn't get something out of my mind. The city has a meter on almost every one of those trunk mains. But there are no meters on the tidal gates themselves."

"Of course not," Murdock said. "That would make life too easy for you. Then you could simply read off a chart what was going into the Hudson. Forget that. You have to work for it. The meters that *are* installed were put there grudgingly anyway. The state made them do it. I know all about it. We bid on that job. We were underbid by about a million dollars by Brown and Smalls. We knew for a fact that they could not possibly make money at that price."

"But there's always a way around it, isn't there?" Jon asked rhetorically.

"Of course," Murdock said. "They put in for a couple of bullshit change orders and wound up billing the city even more than we bid. The whole thing was fixed. And Lawrence Brown was a DEP commissioner before he started Brown and Smalls."

"Don't get yourself too worked up," Jon said. "It happens all the time."

"I know it does," Murdock said. "That's why we steer clear of the city. This goes on and on and nobody ever does anything about it."

"I'm trying to do something about it."

"And look where it's gotten you," Murdock said. "I don't want to sound like a broken record, but this is why you should be working with us."

"Don't think I can accept any job offers right now," Jon said. "Got some stuff to take care of first."

"Well, let me help you," Murdock said. "I'll go inside and get your money. Where is it again?"

"In the closet of the master bedroom, in a box. Look, forget it. You don't have to get involved in this mess."

"It's no problem, Jon," Murdock said. "Hey, you pinch-hit for *me* last year against the Mariners."

"Yeah, that worked out great," Jon said. "I got hit in the knee with a fastball."

"That's what I mean," Murdock said. "I owe you one."

Murdock got out of his side of the minivan and Jon followed from the driver's side, with his knapsack slung over his shoulder.

"C'mon, Jon. Give me the keys."

"Tell you what," Jon said. "How 'bout neither of us bothers with this. I'll just wait for my next paycheck. They may have video cameras set up inside."

"That's exactly what I'm talking about," Murdock said. "You don't need them knowing your whereabouts. If I go in, what are they going to think? They don't know me from Adam. They might think I'm robbing the place."

"Feel free to," Jon said.

"The keys?"

"Suit yourself." Jon pulled the key chain from his pocket and tossed it overhand to Murdock, who, like the utility infielder that he was on weekends, used both hands gingerly to bring the keys to his body.

"And get me some underwear from my top drawer," Jon said. Murdock nodded.

As Murdock walked toward the front door, Jon took a good look at the main house, with its wood siding manufactured from recycled sawdust and its triple-pane windows installed for maximum insulation. Years of his life were sunk in that structure, and now he considered going in and having a beer himself, in pure defiance. Instead, he looked at his mailbox, which was overflowing with a week's worth of *Long Island Newsday* and other items. He walked over to the box, tossed the newspapers onto the ground, and pulled out a dozen other pieces of mail. There were utility bills, credit card bills, a smiling Ed McMahon telling him he may have already won ten million dollars, and a thin nine-by-twelve-inch yellow envelope sealed with Scotch tape. He inserted all these pieces of mail into his knapsack and zippered it shut.

When Murdock turned the lock and pushed the door, suddenly all was light, heat, and sound. The explosion shook Jon like an earthquake and had its way with him like a hurricane. As in lightning, the sound followed the light, only much more closely because of the short distance. Jon felt the impact on his chest as if it was a punch from a heavyweight prizefighter. Though he stumbled backward, he felt stiff as a pillar of salt, somehow frozen in heat by what he saw.

The flames and pure force that had come through every window and created some of its own pathways through the roof had taken Murdock. He seemed gone—vaporized. Though not completely. Still inside the first two seconds of the experience, Jon hadn't the time to make moral judgments or to block out unseemly details. The simple truth was that the impact on his chest was from Murdock's charred hand, which now lay on the ground beside him, still clutching the keys.

What replaced the horror, out of pure necessity, was a clear sequence of actions to take, as logical as those for determining the stresses in a truss bridge, only much more rapid. Jon sensed that he needed to build a bridge to the afterlife, even if it lasted only a short while. The first component in that bridge was the set of keys. They were clearly his, since the initials J.K. were on the key chain. There was no reason to pry the keys loose from Murdock's detached right hand. When the keys and the hand were found together, it would be assumed that the hand was Jon's as well.

It would be days before the hand's true owner was positively determined, and by then Jon would have firmly established his own death and bought himself more time. Even after the hand and Charlie Murdock were linked in a laboratory, few would be quick to resurrect him, thinking he had probably perished simultaneously.

Now, Jon provided such people additional reasons to believe as much. From his knapsack he pulled out a double-knit cotton shirt and a pair of Jockey shorts and draped them both on a burning cinder near his feet. Both items caught fire. Then he pulled from the same knapsack a sheaf of papers and let the wind scatter them. They were only a series of daily climatological reports, probably none of which he needed anymore, and all of which he could have access to again if necessary.

Jon looked at the open wound on his right forearm, which, like a big toe stubbed on the leg of the coffee table, hadn't yet been given sufficient time to ring in the pain. He picked up a rock, a twenty-pound piece of schist, and smeared it with blood from the wound. Dropping the rock, he looked back at the hand and considered the keys once more. He had no use for them. The house, the minivan, the borough president's office—they were all history. Now that a few more seconds had passed, the smoke was beginning to clear, and neighbors were just beginning to make it to their doors and windows, Jon knew he had to vanish as fast as possible.

He knew the woods, or what was left of them. He ran toward the back of his own lot and into the brush. The threat of poison ivy meant nothing compared to the promise of bursting out onto Shamrock Road and into the hereafter. Pummeling tall grass and avoiding both maple trees and sticker bushes, Jon took a catty-corner path and emerged. Here, rather than turning right and being spotted running from the scene by his neighbors on Shamrock, Jon made a left. The fence along Shamrock opposite the wooded area gave him another hundred feet or so of cover.

Now, his sunglasses and Yankee cap planted once again on his head, he ran momentarily back along his own property. Making a right onto Tarpon, where his few years in the neighborhood had led him neither to friendship nor even to acquaintances, he streaked his way through another street, a dead end, and then a right back to Odin. He seemed to be of little consequence to the people who stood on their lawns peering through smoke, wondering whether the Fourth of July had come early.

Jon now emerged on Route 25A and began walking westward along the shoulder. He would have to make it to Judy's house on foot and not draw any more attention to himself. At the moment he was thankful that Rocky Point had become a sprawling, overdeveloped suburban town for the anonymity it provided him. The first and second of what would be many fire engines screamed and barreled past him. The trucks were filled with the sort of young men who played for the Rocky Point White Sox and would soon be discovering one of their own dead at the scene. If Jon was lucky, they would think it was him.

Now, when he least expected it, like snow in a desert, overdue drops of memory hit him. So did the bigger picture. The shock had provided a moment of clarity. Paula needed to give Naomi weekday access to his office. On weekends and weeknights, a guard was on duty downstairs and sign-ins were required. Jon recalled that Wednesday, April 28, was the first of the two Wednesdays he took off. On that day, or possibly on a prior day, Naomi had installed some kind of surveillance equipment in his office. He could almost see her moving a cabinet and adjusting a button, as if it were happening in front of him at that moment. Now the vision faded and the clarity of his recollection took its place, focusing on anything important he might have said in his office after April 28.

He recalled that on the very next day, Larry had expressed his suspicions about Naomi. That meant Larry could be targeted any minute. The same was true for Gibbs, Laura, Jay, and Pat. On the other hand, how well did he really know any of them? Any of them could have leaked his course of action. But since Jon hadn't even bothered to call Larry since disappearing, Larry was the least likely leak. He would have to call Larry as soon as possible to warn him. While having Larry act, of course, as if he had perished in the explosion.

As for the others, it had gotten so complicated now that even in his state of clarity, he was overwhelmed, gagging on his own suppositions in the hot Long Island sun. The plan he'd agreed upon with Laura was to leave messages on everyone's voice mail deriding each one for dropping out in the event that Paula and company found out what he was up to. Apparently, Paula and her minions had found out. And even though Jon suspected the leak to be one of his friends, he didn't know that for sure, and therefore owed them the benefit of the doubt. That meant a fake scathing message on everyone's machine, as planned.

But if he left such a message, Jon realized, Paula and company would discover he was not dead. He would then be surrendering his own margin of safety for the benefit of people he was no longer sure he could trust. Damned if he did and damned if he didn't. As a man with no home, he felt strangely more comfortable than ever with this impossible situation. Like an ear pierced many days ago, the hole was there, but the pain had almost completely faded. He was an animal.

Having run about a mile and watched and listened as three more fire engines blew by, Jon turned into the parking area of an Exxon station along Route 25A and headed for the men's room in the back. The room was vacant, almost spotless. He locked the gray metal door behind him and looked at himself in the mirror. There was black soot on his face and on his arms, along with several small open wounds. His shirt and pants were dirty as well. He removed his baseball cap and shades to begin washing when he remembered the reason he'd come in here in the first place.

The nine-by-twelve-inch yellow envelope sealed with Scotch tape had bothered him since he touched it. Perhaps it was the absence of a return address or the way it was addressed in type to ELAINE KESSLER. Jon now unzipped his knapsack, inserted a fingernail beneath the Scotch tape, and began to tear the envelope along the top.

There had been a delayed reaction after he'd heard that Fred Barrow had been killed. He hadn't yet felt the shock of seeing his house and teammate blown up from a distance of eighty feet. Now, as Jon removed the contents of the envelope, the full force of those events finally hit him, as if to protect him from what was in his hand.

There were two color eight-by-ten photos. The first revealed Naomi, kneeling upright, naked above the waist, her eyes rolled back and her mouth open. Cupping her breasts with his hands from behind was Jon, whose unfocused gaze was half hidden by Naomi's brown hair. The next photo showed Naomi on her back with Jon, bare-chested, hovering over her in reverse position, his mouth near her waistline, the tip of his erect penis clearly in her mouth.

Now Jon hovered over the bowl, but nothing would come out. He was in the perfect place to vomit and felt entitled to the sweet relief this action promised, but his combination of rage and sickness was so profound it would be years before it could work its way up even to his small intestines. With his ability to feel once again muffled, his brain nonetheless continued to hum along, mechanically completing the connections it was supposed to make. Looking again at the photos, he saw their graininess and the white horizontal line running across each and understood that they were stills from a videotape. Naomi had probably activated the camera when she stopped to remove her earrings and placed them on her night table. That theory was consistent with the camera angle.

Jon rinsed his hands and face and continued to think it through. The camera continued to run while Naomi was in the bathroom and he lay on the bed contemplating. The audio portion continued to run as well. The camera had caught him lying there, turning on the clock radio, then listening to the Beatles song. The camera had caught the phone ringing, Paula's voice coming over the answering machine, and his reaction to it. This included his sitting up, buttoning his shirt, and walking over to the answering machine to switch the tapes. At least he thought so. Now Jon looked again at the photos. They both included the telephone and the answering machine in the lower right-hand corner.

But most likely Naomi hadn't bothered to view the tape all the way to its end. She'd probably been so excited to get what incriminating footage she had that she stopped and rewound the tape once she got to all the dead time. That foul-up had allowed him to exist for a few more days without his life on the line and for Naomi to buy into the telephone sex. But once the tape was handed over to Paula and company for photographic reproduction, someone had noticed the remainder of the tape's content. Perhaps Paula herself. Whatever the case, once that had occurred, Paula and Naomi pieced together the rest and understood his full awareness of his plight.

Exactly when Paula and Naomi's recognition had occurred was not clear. It was possible that Naomi had already known when he'd spoken to her on Sunday. Jon now looked at the yellow envelope. It was postmarked 10:28 A.M., May 24, which was Monday morning. Chances were they had known what he'd known by that time and already decided to send the photos to Elaine simply to disrupt his life. Though they knew Elaine was no longer staying at the house, they'd assumed she retrieved the mail, or perhaps that he delivered it to her as a matter of course.

But a follow-up decision had been made. The photos weren't good enough. They needed to set up a trap, and they knew most likely no one was staying at the house in Rocky Point. So they sent out a bomb squad to rig the place. The bomb squad may even have beaten the yellow envelope to the house.

It could have worked out differently. Elaine could have picked up the photos and gotten the shock of her life a few minutes later in her friend's basement. She could have removed the envelope from the mailbox and been vaporized moments later at her own front door, dying not knowing how frail and vulnerable her husband was. Or he could have removed the envelope from the mailbox and been vaporized himself moments later, knowing just how frail and vulnerable he was but not knowing how well it had been documented.

But this was the way it *had* worked out—with him standing soiled, battered, and bleeding in an Exxon station bathroom. With him knowing how well his foolishness had been documented, but with Elaine's feelings spared, his life spared, and an innocent bystander's life lost. *This* was the situation he had to deal with. And deal with it is precisely what he would do.

He considered his friends—Laura, Jay, Pat, even Al. He was neither ashamed that for a moment he'd doubted them, nor particularly proud. The morality of survival allowed for reasonable suspicion. He owed them each a phone call now. Rather, two phone calls each. Not to reveal his innermost thoughts and feelings. The first set of calls would serve to inform them that despite what they may have heard, he was alive, if not well. Those calls would go directly to their homes.

The second would go to their voice mails at work, where most likely the calls were being monitored, and would not come from the late Jon Kessler but from a caller he would have to choose. The caller would inform them that (a) we were dismayed at the lack of cooperation you provided, and (b) none of it mattered anyway now that Jon Kessler was dead and the operation was called off. Have a nice life.

Now one more wave of realization swept over Jon's ravaged body. It was the phone conversation he'd had with Elaine from his office shortly after the Glass House incident. The date was Monday, May 10, well after April 28, the first Wednesday he took off, and a prime candidate for surveillance. Jon had already recalled the general content of their conversation—how Elaine was moving out. But now he concentrated, squeezing every last calorie out of the synapses in his cerebral cortex, looking for the exact wording Elaine had used.

He heard it in his mind once: "By suppertime, the kids and I will be gone. I'm taking them to my friend Judy's house." *To her friend Judy's house.* No last name, no address, no other description. That was probably what had kept Elaine safe over the past couple of days, the difference of a word or two. But then he recalled: there was no guarantee someone hadn't followed her home any of those days. Perhaps that fortunate omission provided the borrowed time she was living on at this very moment. He had no time to waste.

Jon ran the remaining three miles to Judy's house, making a right onto Miller Place and a left onto Hallock Avenue before spotting the two-level Victorian structure redone with white vinyl siding. No one was out front. Jon kneeled up against a small illuminated basement window and spotted Elaine's blond head of hair moving by below. He tapped the window hard three times and made eye contact with Elaine, who looked up through the glass in both excitement and horror.

Using his index finger, Jon motioned for her to come out. As soon as she seemed to understand, he pulled a blank lined sheet of paper and a pen out from his knapsack. Still kneeling on the ground, using the yellow envelope with the photographs inside as a backing, he began writing frantically.

Elaine emerged from the side door with Steven in her arms and Stacy trailing from behind. Jon picked up the paper and yellow envelope and opened his arms for Stacy, who had run to him with urgent glee. The yellow envelope now smacked gently against Stacy's warm white cotton T-shirt as they embraced.

"Daddy, are you gonna stay?" Stacy asked, her vulnerability burning a hole through Jon's heart.

"Not today, Stacy," he said. "Maybe next week."

"But you said you would play baseball with me." Stacy began crying. Jon stood and rubbed the top of her head.

"Very soon," he said. "Mommy will teach you for now." Elaine let Steven put his feet on the ground. Now Stacy hugged one of Jon's legs and cried while Steven, not knowing enough to cry, hugged the other.

"I wanna go home," Stacy cried.

"I do too, Stacy," Elaine said. "But we have to wait until it's safe."

"Don't hold your breath, Elaine."

"Why," Elaine said, preparing for the hit. "What happened?"

"You didn't have the television on?"

"No, we just got home a little while ago," Elaine said.

"They blew the house up."

"Oh my God, no!" Elaine said, covering her mouth with her hand.

"Yup," Jon said. "The strange part is, your mother's old shack is still standing. Funny how things work out, huh?" Elaine dropped to her knees, but Jon hoisted her back up almost immediately, held her up for a moment, then stood her apart as she struggled to regain her composure. "It's gone, Elaine. Gone. But we're not. And we're going to keep it that way."

"How?" Elaine's survival instinct now shone from behind her tears.

"Pack up the car, take the kids, and drive south, to Marilyn and Steve's house. She was your maid of honor, and she lives in the boonies. Just go and stay there till this is all taken care of."

"But when will that be?"

"Pretty damn soon."

"Okay," Elaine said. "We should be able to leave in the morning."

"No good," Jon said. "Now. In thirty minutes, you should be on 25A."

"You went back to get the money," Elaine said, kicking some dirt and staring intensely at him.

"What can I say," Jon said. "You were right and I was wrong. That's the way it goes. Hopefully it'll be the last mistake I make, but I doubt it."

"You don't listen."

"You think I feel good?" Jon said. "If I had the time, I'd feel like killing myself. Charlie Murdock is dead. Blown to bits, right at our door."

"Oh my God, no!"

"Yes, yes, absolutely," Jon said. "There goes that job offer. Now here's a kiss, and you get the hell out of here." Jon leaned over and gave Elaine a peck on the cheek. "Call me at Haney's when you get in."

"Jon?" Elaine had an afterthought, and with it came another few seconds of composure. "I'm still part of this. Remember you told me you'd give me a real assignment. Not just running away. Something to help you."

"Okay," he said. He handed Elaine the piece of paper on which he'd just scrawled the names of his friends and their office phone numbers, each beginning with a 212 area code and a 669 exchange. Elaine looked at the paper carefully.

"When you get part of the way to South Carolina, when you've made a little headway," Jon said, "say somewhere in Jersey in some beat-up gas station, call each of those people at my office and leave a message. Let them know it's you, Elaine Kessler. Cry. Be angry. Tell them your husband died today in an explosion and the whole operation is over. Tell them thanks for nothing. They could have saved your husband's life, but you're sure they leaked information to Paula Derbin instead. Tell them you're going to be out west and they should all go rot in hell."

"But—"

"I don't have time for this now," Jon said. "Just do it."

"I will," Elaine said.

"Good." Jon shook his legs free of his children and took his first few steps away from them all. "Elaine?"

"Yes?"

"In the next few days, you may be hearing reports of my death."

"Uh-huh . . ."

"They'll all be greatly exaggerated."

Chapter 35

At five-fifteen late Wednesday afternoon, Jimmy Mercado stood at the northeast corner of City Hall Park, only a few yards from where a young female German tourist was waiting to use New York City's French pay toilet. The toilet had been brought back by popular demand. There was no such clamor on behalf of Mercado, who got perhaps one or two calls a day from fellow officers wanting to know when he was going to give up the ghost and come back to work. His answer was the same every time. He had some personal business to take care of first.

A low-level noise emerged from his open leather briefcase. Mercado had gone undercover many times before, but never on his own time. Wearing black wraparound shades, a long black leather jacket, a fat silver cross on a neck chain, and a "Vote No on Statehood" button on his lapel, he looked far more like a Puerto Rican militant than an officer of the law. Naomi had seen him only once before, very briefly, and would no more be able to connect him to the dapper detective who had entered room 2035 that day than she would to any of the various New Yorkers who each day walked in pleading and walked out cursing.

That was fortunate, since Mercado would have to get past Naomi to get to Jon's office. Since Monday, Old Al Gibbs had noticed that Naomi, Paula, Ned, and even Art Shuler were staying late, as if in a state of alarm. They came and went somewhat unpredictably throughout the night. Gibbs had to observe this from just outside the base of the Municipal Building, since as a well-known basket case civil service employee, he had no reason to be putting in serious overtime.

But Pat Truitt, who had long ago made a habit of staying late, confirmed from the inside what Gibbs had noticed from the outside. People would meet in Paula's office, close the door, mutter, argue, scream, then retreat to their own spaces. Then they would do it all over again and maybe leave the building alone or in pairs to grab dinner before returning once more.

Now that five-thirty was approaching, Mercado was anxious to get into the building. Security had tightened up significantly since the World Trade Center bombing a few months earlier. After five-thirty, the guard in the lobby would let you upstairs only if you had a city ID or if he knew your face. It was true that even without his badge, Mercado could show the guard any number of other credentials to gain access, but he would still have to sign in, and he wanted no record whatsoever of his having visited the building. But he could not proceed until he heard from Gibbs.

At 5:17 P.M., carrying a rolled-up *Daily News*, Gibbs stood at his desk on the twentieth floor and craned his neck to see Naomi, who continued to sit like an owl at her own desk and scribble notes onto a lined legal pad. Gibbs broadcasted an angry message for the world, which at the moment was Naomi and himself.

"A few more minutes and I'm outta here. Shit, twenty-nine years and I still follow the man's rules. Come in a half hour late, leave a half hour late. Army's got no place for a man who can't follow rules."

Naomi did not flinch. Gibbs tugged at his belt and spoke again. "Uh-oh, here comes that five-o'clock piss. Ain't no one gonna hold that back."

He headed for the door, opened it, and proceeded to the twentieth floor men's bathroom, where he pressed 2 and 4 simultaneously on the combination lock and turned the doorknob. Once inside, he was alone with ten thousand tiny ceramic floor tiles and a half-dozen marble urinals, one of which had a big chunk missing from the day in June 1975 when layoffs were announced. Gibbs pulled a 5-watt, 40-channel citizen's band walkie-talkie out from his rolled-up newspaper. He whipped open the antenna, flicked on the power, and tuned to channel 27 as planned. He pushed the talk button and spoke.

"Jimmy, you there?" On the northeast corner of City Hall Park, Mercado noticed the white noise disappear for a moment and heard his first name in its place. He reached into his leather briefcase for his own walkie-talkie.

"Yeah, I'm here. What's holding you?"

"She's not leaving," Gibbs said. "You better just come up now while you can. She won't figure it out. And we may get a little something out of her."

"I hear you," Mercado said. "I'm gonna have to get started if I'm gonna hook up with Janine a little later. Have you heard from her?"

"Yeah," Gibbs said. "I saw Pat Truitt on the nineteenth floor about a half hour ago. As far as I know, she's just sitting in the ladies' room up there, waiting."

"Okay," Mercado said.

"Hey," Gibbs said, "maybe we'll get the bonus."

"Hope so," Mercado said. "I'm coming up now."

Since things on the nineteenth floor had reached a level of absolute paranoia, using a walkie-talkie there was taking a suicidal liberty. So when Pat Truitt had noticed at 4:56 that Ned, Art, and Paula were all holed up in Paula's office, and that the hallway was therefore clear, he used the telephone in Roy Watson's old cubicle to contact Detective Janine O'Connel. Since the day Roy Watson quit, staffers had used this abandoned phone for personal and long distance calls. It was unlikely that this phone was bugged. Still, when the middle pay phone near the Municipal Building outdoor food court rang and O'Connel picked it up, all she heard was: "Send up a knish." Her only response was: "Plain or with mustard?"

The militant Mercado, briefcase in hand, walked into room 2035, leaned over the counter, and stated his request.

"I need my plans of City Hall Park. You got 'em?" Mercado spoke with a thick Puerto Rican accent.

Gibbs looked up from his desk with a single wary eye.

Mercado continued to state his case. "Hey, I don't got no time to waste, man. You Jon Kessler?"

"Do I look like my name is Kessler?" Gibbs asked.

"Hey," Mercado said, "I spoke to the dude last Monday. He told me he was gettin' that topo map hisself and putting it aside for me when I come in. I just came all the way down from Washington Heights, man. That map's supposed to have everything, man— Park Row, Chambers, Broadway. We're holding a rally at City Hall next week. I gotta get going on this shit."

"You holdin' a rally?" Gibbs asked. "I might be there."

"Good."

"Bustin' heads," Gibbs said. "I won't take no hippies burning the flag, you got that? I'm a loyal soldier of the U.S. Army. Uncle Sam signs my paycheck. I see one butane lighter come within ten feet of Old Glory and death will rain. Haaaayaaa . . ." Gibbs struck a fierce tai chi pose.

"Yeah, I'm shakin', man," Mercado said. "Trembling. Now get me my map."

"Hey, I ain't no damn map fetcher."

"Kessler said he left it in his office in the back there," Mercado said, now more forcefully. "Just let me in there, man, and I'll look for it myself."

"I don't carry that motherfucker's key," Gibbs said. "I ain't no key holder."

"Then I'm coming back there myself," Mercado said, abruptly rounding the counter.

Gibbs stood with his chest stuck out to block his path.

"You wanna go, motherfucker?" Mercado said. "We'll go right now." Just as Gibbs put his hands up, Naomi bounced out of her seat dangling a peace offering from her right hand.

"Here," she pleaded to Mercado, "I have the key. This is the one right here. Let yourself in."

"Thanks," Mercado said, closing his right thumb and index finger around the key from which the rest of the chain hung.

"Just make sure you give them back," Naomi said, "as soon as you're done."

"I'm hoping it doesn't take too long," Mercado said. "You wanna come inside with me?" Mercado puckered his lips and made a grotesque kissing sound.

"Uh, that's okay," Naomi said. "I'll just wait."

"Bitch," Mercado muttered under his breath as he let himself into Jon's office and slammed the door behind him. Naomi stood in place, visibly frazzled. Gibbs marched back to his desk and began assembling his take-home kit: his reading glasses and their case, some loose change on his desk, and the *Daily News*—still hiding the walkie-talkie.

"That's it," Gibbs lamented, "I'm outta here. Unbelievable, I have to deal with this shit. Oh how the mighty have fallen! Do you know that in May 1963, I was approached by a CIA operative to kill goddamn Kennedy? JFK, baby! Don't look surprised, honey. They had a hit out on him, and I was their best bet. I had a reputation for killing. I worked clean, baby—not a trace. But above all, I'm a patriot. I told that son of a bitch: 'Ain't no way I'm takin' out the commander in chief. Off-limits, baby.'

"Then I did what I had to do. Took *him* out. Broke his neck right there and then. Had to. Survival. Once you know about a conspiracy like that, you're next to get hit, whether you do their bidding or not. 'Course what they did in Dealy Plaza was treason. Folks sayin' that second gunman was behind the grassy knoll over there . . . bullshit. Know where he was? In a catch basin. In a sewer, baby, lookin' straight up and over at the President. That's why his head jerked up like that. That's where they wanted me that day. I said: 'I ain't goin' down in no sewer even if I was gonna help y'all.' Then I broke the dude's neck."

Naomi continued to stand in place, making a false start or two toward her desk, but frozen by Gibbs's outlandish, relentless verbal assault on American history.

Meanwhile, inside Jon's office, Mercado was quite busy. He'd locked the door behind him and tuned Jon's radio to a salsa station, which was now blasting.

Like Mercado, Gibbs actually did have the key to Jon's office. But they needed to hide that fact to get the rest of the keys, like the one to Paula's office. Beneath the thumping bass and trebly horn section of the salsa, Mercado went to work switching four keys—two Sargents and two Medecos. He had already checked the room for hidden video monitors and found none. He now pulled dummy keys out of his pocket and slipped them one by one onto the chain from which he'd just slipped the originals off. He hoped Naomi used these particular keys on rare occasion, minimizing her chance of realizing she'd been taken. She would probably never know they were keys to the old locks from Joel Haney's apartment. Since O'Connel carried with her a Lockaid pick gun capable of handling most tumble locks, it was possible that these new keys were unnecessary. But as he and Gibbs had agreed, this was just a bonus. An appetizer.

It was now time for the main course. From his briefcase Mercado removed a five-by-five-inch bug detector. Powered by a nine-volt battery, the device looked like a miniature CB radio and could pinpoint the exact location of transmitters operating anywhere between 5 MHz and 2gHz. Though the salsa still masked even the loudest noises, Mercado switched off the alarm function and depended solely on the LED bar display. The display quickly lead him to the right rear corner of the room. There, between the short file cabinet and the wall, stuck to the back of the cabinet, was a self-contained FM transmitter the size of a stamp.

In appearance it actually was nothing like a "bug," but looked more like a miniature version of the first radio high school kids put together in electronics shop. It featured a condenser microphone and was powered by a 1.5 volt battery, which explained why they needed Naomi to visit the room at least once a day. Those batteries didn't last long. He and O'Connel would be able to avoid that problem. Taped to the side of the cabinet was a five-inch-long, plastic-coated antenna. The unit had a typical range of three hundred feet and was receivable on a standard FM radio within that range. If anyone was listening at the moment to Kessler Radio 104.1 they were getting a healthy dose of Tito Puente.

Mercado's bug detector now led him to the telephone wire behind the short cabinet. This minitransmitter was similar in size, but twice as long and featured more visible capacitors and inductors. It was powered directly by the phone line and therefore did not require Naomi's nurturing. The device also transmitted on the standard FM band within a range of a quarter mile, and picked up both sides of a telephone conversation. This device had allowed local listeners to pick up Jon and his wife arguing on Mellow 106.3 FM.

Phase one was over for Mercado. He left the bugs in place, put away his bug detector, and grabbed a single rolled-up map left atop the tall file cabinet for him by Gibbs. He turned off Tito Puente and opened the door to the large room, where Naomi was now sitting and Gibbs was still lecturing.

"I had something they didn't, honey. I knew where to draw the line. Never bite the hand that feeds you."

"Here you go, sister," Mercado said, tossing the original set of keys onto Naomi's desk. "You should have come inside with me. You missed a lot." Naomi was speechless.

"Whaddya do in there," Gibbs asked, "have some kind of Puerto Rican Day festival?"

"You shut the fuck up," Mercado said. "You could have saved me a lot of time."

"Hey, I told you—I ain't no map fetcher. I'm a CIA operative."

"You're an asshole," Mercado said as he paused by Gibbs's desk for a moment to fumble through his briefcase, then stormed out and let the door close itself behind him.

"What time is it?" Gibbs said, looking at his watch. "Five-forty! This is bullshit. I just logged overtime because of that bastard. I'm calling it in. Time and a half, baby. And it's going on my pension too."

Gibbs went to his phone and punched in Roy Watson's old four-digit extension. Downstairs, on the nineteenth floor, it was Laura Ober's turn to monitor Watson's line, and when it rang, she was ready. She rose from her seat, walked over two cubicles, and picked up the receiver.

"Roy Watson's office," she said.

"Yeah, this is Al Gibbs from upstairs. I just want to let you know that it's five-forty, and I worked ten minutes of overtime, and I expect to be paid for it." She knew exactly what he meant. A little over a minute later, Laura stood in the south elevator lobby on the nineteenth floor, directly in front of the leftmost elevator. The door opened and the militant Mercado slapped a set of four keys into her hand. The door closed, and the elevator continued its descent.

Mercado got out on the eighteenth floor and rang the buzzer by the large swinging iron gate, which now sealed off the main offices of the Department of General Services. While he waited, he considered how little time he'd had to check for a bug on Gibbs's telephone line. Yet he was reasonably satisfied that no transmitter was present. The same could probably even be said for Larry Golick's line nearby.

A man in his middle forties with a big, squarish jaw, squarish glasses to match, and thinning gray hair combed straight back appeared on the other side of the gate.

"Hey, Stan," Mercado said.

"Jimmy, is that you?" Stan replied. He pushed the button to unlock the gate and forced the door open halfway once he heard the lock uncouple. Mercado stepped through the opening and shook his hand. "Jeez," the man said, "you look like you kick ass for a living."

"I do," Mercado said. He felt relaxed for the first time in almost an hour as he followed Stan Beaumont down the main corridor of the DGS offices. This was relatively safe territory. Compared to phase one, phase two would be a snap, at least for him. O'Connel would have to watch her back, upstairs on the nineteenth floor. Mercado, however, was in the company of an old friend and was in neutral rather than hostile territory. Almost. He did a double take as he walked by a cubicle with a nameplate that read BRUCE GREGORY.

Mercado followed Beaumont into his office, which, according to the floor plan Gibbs had provided, was almost directly beneath Paula Derbin's office. Beaumont pulled off the blanket from a flat worktable in the corner and revealed more than a dozen pieces of electronic equipment that Mercado had given him the day before: six FM broadcast band receivers, each one with one-microvolt sensitivity and a frequency range of 70 to 110 MHz, actually extending slightly both above and below the range of standard FM tuning; six scanner recorders to automatically activate a tape recorder when the receiver registered a message above one microvolt, thereby eliminating "dead time" on the tape; and six long-playing cassette recorders, designed to provide twelve hours of recording time on a standard ninety-minute cassette.

"There you go," Beaumont said. "Get to work. You know, you're a fucking lunatic."

"I know. Can I make a phone call first?"

"Be my guest," Beaumont said.

Two minutes later, in the stall near the window of the nine-teenth floor women's bathroom, Janine O'Connel's alphanumeric beeper vibrated against her hip. She adjusted her position in the seat, as much to avoid cramping as to remove the beeper from her belt. She began reading the words on the screen and scrolled down using the green arrow key:

"NO VIDEO. KESSLER DOUBLE
BUGGED. GIBBS CLEAR. GOLICK
CLEAR. KEYS ARRIVING SHORTLY.
GOOD LUCK, CUTIE. AVOID
USING 104.1 AND 106.3."

O'Connel breathed a little easier but shifted in her seat again. The keys couldn't get there soon enough.

Back down in Beaumont's office, Mercado was busy patching together all six sets of surveillance systems with the wires and power strip Beaumont had brought in a shopping bag. Beaumont looked discerningly at each step Mercado took and soon was un-knowingly breathing down his neck. Mercado made a few inches of additional room for his friend and looked at him for an instant.

"So how's engineering, Stan?"

"Okay, I suppose," Beaumont replied. "Believe it or not, I've been working on rehabbing a police station."

"No kidding! Which one?"

"The Sixty-first, in Brooklyn," Beaumont said. "Going there every week got me thinking—I kinda miss the job. It's been ten years. It would be nice to go back for a few years, I guess."

"Guess again," Mercado said, now fiddling with the frequency control on the first unit, which was up and running. "Hey, Stan, let me ask you something. Guy named Bruce Gregory work here?"

"Yeah, sits right down the hall," Beaumont said. "He does property inspections."

"He a stand-up guy?"

"He's an asshole," Beaumont said.

"That figures," Mercado said. "He's in on this whole thing. He was the ringer in my lineup the other week."

"No shit," Beaumont said. "Hey, you're welcome to poke around his desk."

"Sounds like an idea. You sure he's not going to walk in on me?"

"No, no," Beaumont said. "He's been out sick for over a week. Bad case of hepatitis. Apparently he got into a fight and somebody made him eat a little shit."

At seven-fifteen, Laura Ober, who was sitting patiently at her desk, felt someone lean over her shoulder. It was Pat Truitt.

"Okay," Pat whispered, "they're all out of here. All three of them."

Laura abruptly got up, walked down the main corridor and into the nineteenth floor women's bathroom. She knelt down in front of the stall at the end and let them go. On the other side of the door, O'Connel watched the metallic object skid across the tiles and hit her left shoe. The keys had arrived.

Seconds later, with Laura already gone, O'Connel emerged from the end stall wearing a gray smock, loose fitting gray work pants, an old pair of white Keds, and a light brown kerchief, which hid and matted down most of her radiant red hair. She slung her worn canvas zipper bag over her shoulder and emerged from the bathroom. There, only twenty feet or so down the hallway, at the edge of the north lobby, was a large, mostly empty canvas cart used to collect the recycled paper set aside in each office and each cubicle.

She began pushing it. In less than a minute and a half, she was at Paula's locked door at the other end of the floor. The second and third keys she tried worked on the lower and upper locks respectively. Two locks on an office door. This was promising, O'Connel thought. It was fortunate that the bonus had come through. The upper one was a bolt lock with extra pins that would have been difficult if not impossible for the pick gun to open.

Once inside, with the door slightly ajar, O'Connel went to work fast. A look inside the central cabinet of Paula's center mahogany bookcase revealed a mission control not entirely unlike the one Mercado was setting up at this moment on the floor below. However, instead of compact broadcast band receivers, Paula had a stack of six receivers normally purchased as part of a home entertainment center.

There were six corresponding long-play recorders, but no scanner recorders, so it occurred to O'Connel that Paula Derbin must have gone through quite a few tapes. O'Connel counted the number of receivers again—six. She considered where they might lead. Two were accounted for by Jon's office. Perhaps Pat Truitt, Laura Ober, and Jay Gonzalez each had their phones or cubicles bugged. Since they sat in open cubicles, checking this would be easy. But that theory only accounted for five of the six receivers.

There was little time for such contemplation. O'Connel closed the cabinet doors and hooked up a minitransmitter to Paula's phone wire, along the baseboard behind a file cabinet, safely out of sight. Next she found the six-socket electrical adapter into which a lamp, a clock, a television, and a VCR were plugged, and replaced it with an almost identical adapter. The only difference was, this one doubled as a transmitter with a frequency range of 104 to 109 MHz. And its power source was the wall circuit itself, so there would be no battery to replace. O'Connel set the unit to 108.6 MHz by adjusting the tuning coil.

O'Connel now looked at the table near Paula's desk, upon which sat a phone/fax machine hooked up to a separate line. It was an AT&T model 7820, like the one she herself had at the precinct. She recalled that if she pressed Function, then 5, then Function, Start/Copy, the machine would spew out a reception log of the last thirty faxes received, including the subscriber's fax number for each. She now did this, and out came the printed log. A similar programming sequence produced a transmission log. Within a half minute she had this too. Upon tearing the second sheet from the machine, she remembered that she'd promised to send a test message as soon as she had the room transmitter set up.

Downstairs on the eighteenth floor, Mercado was excited. He had already gotten a phone call from Pat Truitt on the Roy Watson line informing him in code language that O'Connel was heading toward the offices of the top brass. Now, on receiver number one, with a speaker attached, Mercado was getting a clear, strong signal on 108.6 MHz. However, the only audible sounds were that of feet on a carpet and small objects being moved. But then came the sound of a fax machine printing out. Better still, he now heard the sultry voice of Detective Janine O'Connel. "Jimmy, if you could see me now, you might lose that crush once and for all."

By seven-thirty, O'Connel was finishing up the third of three offices. There had been no key for the single lock on Ned Richter's door, but the pick gun had taken only seconds on that one. Getting into Art Shuler's office had been a double-lock affair, but the remaining two keys made that easy. Evidently, Naomi Pierce had close friends in high places, and full access to them as well. As O'Connel set the socket transmitter to 108.2, she felt the beeper vibrate against her hip once more. She removed it from her belt and read the message: *Not a chance.* She thought for a moment, then smiled. In case Jimmy was tuned to 108.2, she responded: "You're hopeless."

As she packed her bag and started back toward Art Shuler's door, mission almost accomplished, she had a thought. She removed her own bug detector from her bag and turned it on. The LED bar display naturally led her to the two transmitters she'd just planted, but now it was directing her somewhere else entirely. There, stuck to the underside of Art Shuler's mahogany desk, was a transmitter the size of a stamp. That probably explained the extra receiver. There was trouble in paradise. For some reason, Paula Derbin did not trust her own boss, the democratically elected president of the most important borough in the world.

By seven-forty, O'Connel had finished. Just as she had figured, Laura's, Pat's, and Jay's phones had been bugged, with no accompanying transmitter for each cubicle. Fortunately, Roy Watson's line and cubicle were both transmitter-free. O'Connel was now free herself. She wheeled her cart down the main hallway, back toward the north nineteenth-floor lobby from where she'd taken it. A few more steps and she'd be on her way out, where she could exhale and change into some decent clothes.

But well before she could exhale, she inhaled as heavily as she ever had. When the south middle elevator door opened, three important-looking people walked out. She didn't know the woman in the tight pinstripe suit or the man in the suspenders, but she recognized Art Shuler. That made the other two people Paula Derbin and Ned Richter.

O'Connel froze with the wastepaper cart firmly in her grip. The three hardly noticed her in her drab outfit and were too busy laughing. The sight of a sixty-year-old man in a hairpiece giving a high-five was pathetic but compelling. There was banter, but O'Connel focused in on what Ned Richter said: "Sensational. This is too good to be true."

Two minutes later Mercado heard a lock jiggle on 108.6 FM and then another lock. Next he heard the same gleeful noises that

O'Connel had heard moments earlier. He recognized Paula Derbin's voice from the answering machine tape Jon had removed from Naomi's machine. Paula's words cut through the rest. "Gentlemen, success feels good. The committee vote is next Wednesday and our number one problem is gone." An older, deeper voice now cut through.

"Teamwork, baby, teamwork."

Mercado now heard the muffled sound of a phone ringing, followed by Paula's shrill voice. "Oh, wait a minute. Jay Gonzalez is getting a phone call. Must be important." The voices settled down. The ring got louder and a male voice was now audible, but less clear than the live voices in Paula's office.

"Hello, this is Jay Gonzalez. Sorry I can't be here to take your call, but if you know me, you know I'll get back to you as soon as humanly possible." A distraught female voice spoke angrily into the machine. An engine and a babbling toddler could be heard in the background, but the female voice persevered.

"Jay, this is Elaine Kessler. My husband was killed today. I want to thank you from the bottom of my heart for doing nothing for him, with the possible exception of protecting your own ass."

"Yes! Yes!!" Paula screamed, loud, proud, and up close to Mercado's eardrum. "He's dead! Jon Kessler is dead!!"

Chapter 36

"It's me," Jon shouted into the intercom in the entranceway of Joel Haney's building.

"Me *who*?" came Mercado's voice.

"Me, Ben Franklin."

The intercom made no further noise. There was no buzz at the interior door to allow him to proceed. Jon buzzed up a few more times, the last time pleading: "I'm alive." He was alive, if not well. Stripped of so many things—family, home, car, employment—nothing seemed quite so bad right now as being stripped of keys. It was the penultimate form of nakedness. He looked down Nineteenth Street at a pay phone on the corner. At least he had some cash and some change to make a nasty phone call upstairs. It was a cool, dry night, just after eleven. As a dead man, he still had options. He could try the same routine with Keith. He could find a cheap hotel room, as if that were possible in New York.

Jon saw them coming down the stairs. Gibbs and Mercado took a few menacing steps toward him, the detective reaching for his pants as if to draw. Then, milliseconds apart, they froze and stared at Jon's weary frame, soiled clothes, and desperate eyes. Mercado ran toward the interior door, pushed it open, and patted Jon on the shoulders with two open palms.

"Oh my God," Mercado exclaimed, "he is risen!"

"And it didn't take three days," Jon said in droll fashion.

Gibbs and Mercado controlled themselves on the way up the stairs, and Jon was simply too drained to break their highly self-disciplined but temporary vow of silence. Once the apartment door shut behind them, it was a free-for-all.

"Half of New York thinks you're dead!" Mercado said. "The other half hasn't turned on the news yet."

"Include us in that first half," Gibbs said. "Shit, we were already looking for a new chief engineer. I guess I was next in line." Sharpe was standing in the living room near the foyer. Jon nodded as he pushed past him and took a seat on the couch. He stared at the phone sitting in front of him on the coffee table, as if figuring out exactly whom to call and what to say.

"Man," Sharpe said, "how the hell did you pull this off?"

"It pulled itself off," Jon said. "I just got lucky. Unfortunately, someone else got *unlucky*. That person was a friend of mine. Maybe that's why he left this earth. Took my keys with him too."

"I'll tell you this," Mercado said, beaming, "whatever you did or didn't do worked. The media practically forced the Suffolk County police into saying it was probably you who died in the explosion. And the morons at the borough president's office? They bought it lock, stock, and barrel. They're having a party over there. I was over there earlier wiring them up. They're popping open the champagne. Then your wife called and they picked that up. Did you put her up to that?"

"Yup," Jon replied. There was some good news. Elaine had proceeded on schedule—if anything, making her calls a bit early.

"That was the icing on the cake," Mercado said. "For me too."

"Obviously they figured out you weren't just calling in sick for a few days," Gibbs said. "But you nailed them right back and bought us some more time."

"Yeah and all it cost me was my house and my car and a friend's life," Jon said.

"I can't tell you how convinced I was," Mercado said. "First I heard your buddies over at the borough president's talking about it, and I started feeling sick to my stomach. But I had to keep doing what I was doing. Then when I got here and turned on the news—"

"It looked like Dresden," Gibbs said.

"I wouldn't go *that* far," Jon said.

"Then they said your keys—the keys that matched your minivan—were found in a severed hand."

"That part they got right," Jon said.

"Then when you rang up here," Sharpe said, "we thought one of the borough president's crew located us and was messing with us."

"There was a leak somewhere," Mercado said, "and we've been wracking our brains trying to figure out who it was. We thought it might be one of your friends at the office."

"No, no way," Jon said. "I've already sorted through all that. I got some pictures in the mail today of me and Naomi fooling around. They were taken off of a videotape. That same videotape had to reveal that I pulled that cassette tape out of her answering machine. But they didn't figure it out right away."

"So you really were living on borrowed time," Mercado said. "And once they did figure it out, they tried to call in the loan."

"Man," Gibbs said, "if anybody ever paid the price for half a blowjob—"

"What I can't quite figure out," Sharpe said, "is why they didn't include those photos you're talking about in the article."

"What article?" Jon asked.

"What article?" Mercado asked. "Maybe you really did travel to the next world for a while today. The article in the *Times* . . . about you. You had quite a day. You went from respectability, to infamy, to your Maker, and back again. I told you this was coming." Mercado pulled the *Times* off of the top of the TV set and dropped it into Jon's lap so the bottom of page one was faceup.

The headline was more upsetting to Jon than his own forthcoming obituary: RENEGADE CITY ENGINEER WAS HIRED GUN FOR ANTI-DEVELOPMENT GROUPS. Jon swallowed hard, tried to ignore the public destruction of a good name it had taken thirty-four years to build, and read on.

> Special to the *New York Times*, by Leonard Kretchner—A highly ranked city engineer, working in the Manhattan borough president's office and posing as a concerned environmentalist, was actually a paid consultant for a West Side antidevelopment coalition that had vowed to stop the popular Hudson City project at any cost.
>
> Jon Kessler, who had used his position in the past to speak out against the project, was within days of releasing a report on the North River Water Pollution Control Plant with the intention of blocking the Hudson City sewer hookup permit. That report, according to reliable sources, was based entirely on falsified data and used knowingly by Mr. Kessler. These revelations have not only shed new light on the merits of Hudson City, but have also called into question the standards to which engineers working for the city should—yet are often not—held accountable.

"Who is Leonard Kretchner?" Jon asked.

"Probably another guy on the Arlen payroll," Mercado said.

"I tell you," Jon said, "this little paid advertisement is not quite the hatchet job I expected. I mean, it's inventive—"

"Read on," Sharpe said, "it gets worse. It talks about how you slept in your office, how you sexually harassed your interns. It even says you detonated a charge to make that building on 110th Street collapse, to make yourself look good."

"I'm ruined," Jon said, "and I'm dead. And I'm broke. But at least I can tell you why those pictures of me and Naomi weren't in the paper."

"How do *you* see it?" Gibbs asked.

"This was a relatively highbrow piece," Jon said. "They had to show some sort of consistency. I'll show you the pictures later. They don't look like anybody's being harassed. No, those pictures were meant for Elaine, to mess my life up some more and maybe blackmail me, since it was obvious they have a whole video."

"The other thing that crossed my mind," Mercado said, "was that they might have not wanted to embarrass your intern."

"As if she's some kind of nun?" Jon said.

"Just a thought," Mercado said. "She may be in tighter than you think."

"Well here's a thought for you," Jon said. "While we bought ourselves some time, we lost credibility, because I've lost credibility. Their story makes a lot of sense. I was taking money, I was making mischief, and I pissed the wrong people off. Good riddance. Now I get to wander the streets of Manhattan like a ghost, looking for the reputation I once had."

"You'll get it back," Mercado said. "I told you, today was the day we wired them up. I got enough stuff on them in two hours to put them away for a hundred years each—Art Shuler, Paula Derbin, Ned Richter. They're all wired, and the tapes are gonna keep piling up."

"So are we just about done?" Jon asked.

"*I* think so," Mercado said.

"I thought Nagle was supposed to be here this week," Jon lamented. "Next week's June already. Laura told me he's sorry. He's a busy man. I'm a busy man too. I have to call a bunch of people and save them money on flowers."

"Not a good idea," Mercado said. "Your best bet is to treat that whole world as off-limits. You were bugged, Jon. Your little office and your phone."

"Good, I would have hated to waste your time."

"Your friends in that . . . Stink Tank," Mercado said, "they were under surveillance too. Just the phones, though. All three of them."

"I thought as much. I'm calling them at home."

"Why?"

"They're all invited to the funeral I'm not having," Jon said. He lifted the receiver off the hook and began punching in numbers. Mercado walked over quickly to the coffee table and used his index finger to disconnect the call. Jon looked up and scowled. "What are you doing?" he said under his breath.

"You need to describe to me a little more in depth just how you plan to blow our cover," Mercado said.

"With all due respect, Detective," Jon said, "these are my friends, and this is my call."

"Jon, what do we have to gain by letting these people know your status? And what do we have to lose?"

"They have their lives to lose," Jon said. "They put themselves on the line for us today from what I understand. At minimum, they deserve to know what kind of danger they're in."

"Okay," Mercado said, "but the complications multiply exponentially with every person you tell."

Jon sat back down and resumed dialing as Mercado backed off. Jon punched in Larry Golick's home number and heard Larry's groggy voice after the third ring.

"Yello . . . ?"

"Larry, it's me, Jon. I don't have a lot of time to explain—"

"King, it's you. You're alive! King! I was sitting here crying tonight—"

"Why, you missed the quinella?"

"That wasn't you in the explosion?"

"In a word, Larry, no, it wasn't. Listen, I'll be happy to tell you the whole story in a couple of days when I have the time. In the meantime, you've got to promise me two things."

"Anything, King."

"First, don't anyone know I'm alive. I'll take care of that. Just don't discuss it or even mention it."

"No problem, King."

"Second, I want you to go over to 40 Worth Street, on the eighth floor, and get me plans of the interceptor, the tide gate, and the regulator chamber at Eighteenth Street and Eleventh Avenue in Manhattan."

"Interceptor . . ."

"Write it down, Larry. All of it."

"You got it, King. When do you need this?"

"Yesterday," Jon said. "When you get them, leave them rolled up on your desk. Al will pick them up."

"Al Gibbs?"

"That's right," Jon said, "Al Gibbs."

On Friday morning, May 28, at ten-twenty, Jon awoke to the sound of the telephone ringing. "It's for you," came Mercado's voice from the bedroom.

"Got it," Jon said, picking up the receiver. "Hello?"

"Jon, it's Jay. I have some great news for you. You know who I have here with me? Janet Wong. Remember her?"

"Vividly," Jon said.

"I was at a C.B. Three meeting this morning," Jay said, "and Janet comes up to me and says: 'There's no way those things they said in the paper about Jon were true, right?' And I said, 'Janet, not only were they completely false, I've got an even bigger surprise for you.' When I told her you were alive, she almost passed out.'"

"Jay," Jon said, "Janet Wong's a nice girl and everything, but you can't go around letting everyone know I'm alive."

"Don't be stupid, Jon. I'm not. Do you know who Janet Wong's fiancé is? Dan Gianetta?"

"As in Mayor Gianetta?"

"That's right," Jay said. "Dan is the mayor's son. He works for his dad. Janet wants to help the good guys, Jon. I'm going to put her on."

"Okay."

"Jon, this is Janet. Janet Wong."

"Hi, Janet."

"It's good to hear your voice," Wong said. "The last time I saw you, you were falling through a floor. How many lives do you have left—seven?"

"Five, by my count," Jon said.

"Well, hang in there, because I think I have good news for you. You know, Dan's father hates Art Shuler."

"I was vaguely aware of that."

"Yes," Wong said, "and he's an admirer of yours, although he hasn't known about you that long. I told him all about you a couple of weeks ago, and he read those articles about the building on 110th Street. So last night at dinner we were talking about how you were killed, and he said that reporter from the *Times* was a weasel and he didn't believe a word of that stuff about you in the article. He said it was a sad, despicable thing to kill someone and then send them off with that kind of obituary."

"Especially when they're still around to read it," Jon said.

"That's what I'm saying, Jon. Dan's father said he wished you were still alive so he could step in and help you."

"Maybe he was just saying it out of respect."

"I doubt it," Wong said. "It's not just that he hates Art Shuler, it's that he feels partly responsible. He knows he's made too many compromises with people like Art. Now that he's made up his mind that he's not going to seek reelection again, I think he wants to leave a better legacy to the city than Art Shuler. I guess this is what happens when you get a little nearer to death."

"Hey, it worked for me."

"It's not a laughing matter," Wong said. "You don't really understand what you're up against."

"Okay, what's your point, Janet?" Jon said. "I woke up this morning scared shitless. Officially, I'm dead. Unofficially, I'm beginning to feel that way."

"I'm going to get Dan's father to help you," she replied. "You're on the right track with what you're doing. Keep doing it. Dan's father can do all sorts of things for you. He can give you the names of people inside DEP who will help you. He can give you information on people like Lee Sarnow. And once you reemerge with the evidence I hear is being gathered, he can throw his political weight behind you. That can go a long way."

"How 'bout giving me some police protection right now?" Jon asked.

"I don't think that's possible," Wong said. "Later, perhaps it will be. Your fake death provides you with better protection than they can ever offer anyway. I think you and I should meet."

"I'm free right now."

"No, that's no good," Wong said. "I need a little time. Dan's father is out of town for most of the weekend. I'm going to be seeing him at City Hall Monday morning. In the meantime, I have a bunch of calls to make. Can you meet me for lunch on Monday?"

"Sure," Jon said. "One o'clock. How about Ellen's, right across the street from City Hall, on Broadway and Chambers?"

"Perfect," Wong said. "I'll be a little early, in fact. Why don't I wait for you at a table for two in the back. You know what I look like."

"Of course," Jon said. "And I'll be in a beard, a Yankee cap, and dark glasses."

"You sure this isn't a problem for you, considering where it is?"

"No," Jon said. "I have something to do downtown anyway. And like you said, I'm already protected by being dead."

"Okay, thank you."

"No, thank *you*," Jon said.

"I'll call to confirm. 'Bye." By the time Jon had returned his own receiver to the hook, Mercado was staring down at him with a smirk.

"Well," Mercado said, "is she as good-looking as she sounds?"

"Better," Jon said.

"You're amazing. The mayor's people are calling you, and I can't get Internal Affairs to do shit for me." Mercado took a half-dozen steps toward the bedroom and turned once more toward Jon. "Can you do me a favor?"

"What?"

"Could you check with me before you leave for that meeting on Monday . . . or before you go anywhere else?"

"Sure, Mom."

By four in the afternoon that same Friday, after six failed attempts, Jon finally got ahold of Clarissa Marbles at her apartment in West Harlem.

"Clarissa? This is Jon . . . Jon Kessler."

"Well hello, Jon. I was going to call you tonight," Clarissa said, full of mirth.

"You were going to call me?" Jon said. "Haven't you heard? I'm dead."

"Laura straightened me out on that one," Clarissa said. "She called me yesterday."

"Laura Ober?" Jon said. "I thought the two of you didn't speak."

"I guess she finally realized we were on the same side," Clarissa said. "Or maybe she finally realized she needed me." Clarissa's laugh was hearty, profound, a thousand years old.

"*I* need you," Jon said. "That committee meeting is this coming Wednesday. You know they're gonna try to get their four-to-three vote right then and there and start building Hudson City the next day."

"You got *that* right," Clarissa said.

"My people over here are close to having all the evidence we need. But it's very important that that permit isn't issued and that Ronald Arlen doesn't break ground. Once he does, even if indictments are eventually handed down, it'll be very hard to stop them. They may have that monstrosity half built by the time this thing is resolved."

"You got that right *too*."

"So all I'm looking to do here, Clarissa, is buy a little more time. Even another week. Now, I know the vote is already fixed, you're in there as a gimme, and no matter what you do, you're going to lose. But if you could just do something . . . something to disrupt the first meeting."

"Already being taken care of," Clarissa said.

"You're kidding me."

"Already worked it out with Laura."

Chapter 37

It was twelve forty-eight on Monday afternoon, May 31. A light drizzle had just ended. Jon walked away from the locked doors of the Municipal Credit Union, kicking himself for not remembering it was Memorial Day. It was hardly a holiday for him. He stood at the corner of Reade and Chambers Streets for a moment to consider his options. He could always try the cash machine, but they usually had a daily $250 withdrawal limit.

He walked south along Centre, bought a paper, crossed to the northeast corner of City Hall Park, walked a few more feet and stopped. He still had a few minutes to kill. Janet Wong hadn't called to confirm their meeting, but she hadn't called to cancel it either. He turned over the *New York Times* and looked at the headline: RENEGADE CITY ENGINEER DID IT HIS WAY. He had to read this, and now was as good a time as any. He felt a bit queasy, but less so than when he'd read the first article. Each day, Leonard Kretchner buried him deeper and deeper, so that by now he was no longer sure if he even wanted a full resurrection.

Jon stuck his hand in his pocket and felt the comfort of his new set of keys to Haney's apartment. He also felt the two quarters he planned to use in a few minutes to buy the *Westsider*, which was sometimes available at the stand on the other side of the park. Mark Rosario was now in the loop and had promised him a fluff piece to offset the Kretchner series. There was a chance the *Westsider* would be running it in the latest issue. Thinking a pleasant dessert awaited would help him masticate and swallow a nasty main course.

But now as he looked up, he knew for sure he *had* taken an unnecessary chance, and it hadn't been at the bank. Paula Derbin was standing at the northeast corner of the park, less than a hundred feet from him. She was wearing a long black trench coat and turning to look south on Centre, then west along Chambers, using her slightly open cupped right hand to direct her vision, causing her brown handbag to whip around half a phase behind her. Though he was surprised for a moment, he recalled that the borough president's office was being used as mission control and that included holidays.

Paula, Jon, and the French pay toilet were almost perfectly collinear, the kiosk blocking out Paula when Jon shifted slightly to his left. He knew he could flee in a variety of directions, and that perhaps he wasn't immediately recognizable. But he also knew that the risk of moving in any of those directions simply was to call attention to himself. It seemed the safest place was right where he was.

Or perhaps the second safest. He pulled one of the two quarters from his right pocket and shoved past an elderly black gentleman waiting to get into the pay toilet. An obese middle-aged white man had just gotten out and the door had closed behind him. Jon shouldered his way past the black man, pushed in his quarter, and did his best to make peace with the black man as the door shut him out. "Colon problems," Jon said.

Inside, the suction fans couldn't work fast enough for Jon, who now needed the facility after all. He dropped his knapsack to the sterile floor and put his head in his hands. He felt his face with his fingers, kneading the skin in circles around his skull. He realized now that he was neither alive nor dead since he could enjoy the pleasures of neither state. Were he truly alive, he could spend his days freely with his family and friends. Were he truly dead, he wouldn't have any worries.

He had just under ten minutes left until the kiosk door would automatically open and expose him to the world in whatever condition he was at that moment. By then, Paula probably would have gone to wherever she was going, and he could do the same. In the meantime, he would read today's Kretchner article in the *Times*. He started at the top.

When a doctor tells you that you have cancer, you believe him. When a lawyer tells you that you indeed have a case, you believe him. When an environmental engineer tells you what you've been breathing could be toxic, you believe him as well. What these people have in common is a license to practice issued by the state. In return, they as professionals give an oath to be truthful and to protect the welfare of the people who hire them, and that of civilization as a whole. It is this oath which in the final days of his tragic life, Jon Kessler so shamelessly flouted in return for a quick fix of cash and cheap egoistic gratification.

According not only to the New York City Department of Environmental Protection, but several highly respected independent consulting environmental engineers as well, the readings used by Kessler in his study of the North River sewage treatment plant were multiplied by a factor of ten. By falsifying and distorting these data, Kessler was able to overstate the environmental risks associated with the plant and, as was his intent, nearly kill a multibillion-dollar development destined to bring thousands of new jobs to the city.

The significance of these revelations does not end with what some saw as Kessler's timely death. Rather, they have sparked a debate over the degree to which society can continue to have titanic decisions, with far-reaching economic impact, put into the hands of professionals regulated mostly by their own good faith.

Disgusted less by the further soiling of his name than by the bombast of the article itself, Jon skipped down to the juicy parts.

. . . She lived in a rent-stabilized apartment with a roommate and worked her way through college as a temp. She needed four more credits to get her masters in environmental policy and discovered that she could do it while working as an intern in the Manhattan borough president's office and even be paid a small stipend. Assigned to the borough engineer, she devoured maps, drawings, and legal documents in an effort to understand the city's infrastructure. What she did not understand, however, was the intention of her supervisor, who sought only to take advantage of his position and to denigrate hers. In the coming weeks, she would bear hours of relentless sexual harassment in the hopes that it would somehow disappear, only to be finally physically assaulted and molested in a locked office, far from the possibility of help.

Jon almost believed it himself. In the bright lights and confinement of the pay toilet, brainwashing had been accelerated. He was glad his quarter was up. Outside once more, he looked in all four directions and even considered looking up. Paula was long gone. It was 1:02 P.M. He walked briskly through the park toward the café. With the slander and the knowledge of all the people it reached clouding his vision of himself, he needed desperately to look into the eyes of someone who respected him.

Now, as he walked into Ellen's, he was only a few steps away from having it. There, at the table for two in the back, was Janet Wong's long, straight, shiny black hair, just as he remembered it. Her back was to him, and the shoulder straps of a floral print dress could barely be seen behind the hair. She waited patiently for him as if there was nothing more important in the world. He walked past her discreetly, planted himself in the empty seat, and looked across into the eyes of someone who could change his life. The eyes belonged to Paula Derbin.

Jon was motionless except for the involuntary shaking of his stiffened body. He could not exhale the lungful of air he had just sucked in like water. He saw now where Paula's wig failed to feather properly with the smaller, thinner hairs of her own scalp, but from the back it had all been the same. He was no longer in limbo. Rather, he was at once very alive and very dead. He looked around. From the walls, dozens of Miss Subways plaques hung and stared back at him from a simpler time. Miss Subways for June 1952 was Irene Scheidt. "Receptionist at New York Stock Exchange. Enjoys swimming. Her fondest hope: a trip to Bermuda." His too.

"Order something, Jon," Paula said calmly, coyly, with simmering malice. "You don't want to make big decisions on an empty stomach."

Jon slid his chair back as if to get up. Paula didn't miss a beat. "That's a decision to die. You may want to make a more informed decision. This restaurant is surrounded by sharpshooters from Hong Kong. The Sun Yee On. The most dangerous Triad society in the country. They're on the pavement, on roofs, in alleyways.

There's even one over there." Paula glanced at a well-dressed Asian man in his late forties sitting two aisles away. The man smiled at Jon and waved two fingers.

"They don't miss," Paula said, "and they don't care about your pathetic attempts to save the world. They only care about following orders, and right now, I'm giving them." Paula removed from her handbag a cellular phone slightly bigger than her palm and waved it in Jon's direction. "You want to try to bolt out of here? Great. Try it. One little phone call and I'll give them something to talk about tonight over spare ribs."

Jon slowly slid his chair back toward Paula and remained planted in it.

"Now you're going to do something for the first time in your life," Paula said. "Something it took a firing squad to get you to do—listen."

"Where's Janet Wong?" Jon said, seething.

"Somewhere," Paula said, "having a better time than you are."

"What did you do to her?"

"Nothing," Paula said, "*you* did. You faxed her a note this morning canceling. It seems you've found a way to make some serious money off of this whole thing and you're no longer interested in her help."

"You're disgusting."

"Guess what, Jon? I'm all you have. And here's a piece of advice. In the future, though it's doubtful whether you have one any longer, check your voice mail more often. Or tell your little friends not to confirm a secret lunch date on what is basically a public bulletin board."

Jon rubbed his eyes with his right thumb and two fingers. He'd had too much going on at once to be perfect. He had forgotten to tell Janet Wong to avoid using his voice mail for legitimate communication. Jay had apparently forgotten to explain to her the whole deal. Maybe Paula had intercepted Janet Wong leaving a message on Jay's voice mail as well. It was clear that expanding the circle of people "in the know" had meant more points of protocol might be overlooked, as Mercado had said, exponentially increasing the chances of getting into a situation like the one he was in now. A bluff was worth a try.

"Paula, your coming here was a desperate act. And you *should* be desperate. We're sitting on top of boxes of evidence implicating you, Art Shuler, and your little gofer, Ned. Tapes, documents, data—probably ten times what we need. And you know what else? You look like a skank in that wig."

"Now you shut up and listen, you self-righteous little piece of shit." Paula pounded her fist on the fragile café table, sending glasses of water hopping. Her face became a familiar beet red, though her wig prevented her real hair from flapping underneath. "It shouldn't matter to *you* if you have a videotape of Ronald Arlen dumping raw sewage into the Hudson himself. The important thing for *you*, personally, is that you have a simple choice: be shot trying to get off of this block or walk out of here with us and cooperate."

"I'll take what's behind door number three."

"*Shut up,*" Paula said, pounding her fist again and turning a few heads in the process. The well-dressed Asian man smiled and waved two fingers again. "You are worth nothing now, and your ideas are worth nothing. It is nothing for us to kill you, because you're already dead. Do you think that by trying to keep billions from flowing into this city you're doing someone a favor? Give me a fucking break. You don't know the first thing about how cities are run or about what's important to people. I do. That's why I'm going to be the deputy mayor of this city.

"You look down on someone like me for taking a tiny fraction of one percent of the wealth I'm bringing into this city. But you live in a fantasy. You and your self-indulgent friends can sit around dividing up nothing as many ways as you want. What did you expect? To ruin it for everybody and have people love you for it? I have news for you—if you've read the papers, people don't even *like* you very much anymore."

"Well, *you'd* better learn to like me, Paula," Jon said. "Because we're going to be right here all day and all night. Eventually, you and your toy soldiers are going to have to go home."

"Is that a fact?" Paula said. "Funny, I distinctly remember paying the owner of this fine establishment fifty thousand dollars in advance to let us close the place if we had to. Gee, do you think he'll let us?"

Jon's stomach now floated in his throat. He looked around and the walls seemed to be closing in on him. The people who walked along Chambers and Broadway, though only a few feet away through the plate-glass windows, appeared to exist in another world, a safe and sound one where life could be made up as you went along. Here, inside, within this jail, he would have to find a way to do the same thing. He felt nauseous, even more nauseous than when he'd thrown up behind the Municipal Building. This was his starting point.

"I . . . I don't feel well," he said. "I'm going to throw up." Jon stood up, letting the inside of his knees thrust his chair backward. "I'm going to the bathroom."

"There's no way out from there," Paula said. "And all the exits are covered."

Jon acted as if he could barely contain it. He'd had a lot of practice. Paula accidentally knocked a glass of water onto her lap in avoiding Jon's regurgitation. Instead, Jon lunged for the aisle before getting his hands over his mouth. Heads turned and chair legs vibrated all around him. Even the well-dressed Asian man lost his smile. At the end of the aisle a fresh-faced busboy pointed to Jon's right, apparently letting him know which way to the men's room.

The men's room was barely six by eight, with an enclosed stall inside. It was empty. Jon locked the main door behind him, then locked the stall door behind him as well. It was important to make people think that he was just getting started. He let out a credible forced groan from the bottom of his belly, meanwhile flushing the bowl continually. He pulled from his left pants pocket the cell phone Mercado had given him and punched in the number for Haney's apartment. After two rings, he heard Gibbs's voice.

"Yeah . . ."

"Al, it's Jon. Is Mercado there?"

"You know he's here, man," Gibbs said. "Everybody's here. We're about to get started. Where are you?"

"I'm in trouble. Put Mercado on."

"Where are you, with Janet Wong?" Gibbs asked. "I told you to try to push that up to eleven. What did she have to say about—"

"Goddamnit, put Mercado on now!"

"Okay, okay, Jeez . . . Detective, it's for you. Kessler." Jon waited a few seconds, continuing to pull toilet paper from the roll and catch his breath while he listened to the footsteps in the earpiece get louder.

"Jon?"

"Detective, I'm dead meat. I'm in the bathroom at Ellen's restaurant on Chambers and Broadway. Paula's waiting for me at a table in the back. She's says she's got the place surrounded with snipers. She's telling me I have to go with her calmly or be killed. She's got a Hong Kong hit man inside too. What the fuck am I gonna do?"

"Listen to me. Can you go back there and last ten minutes?" Mercado said.

"I . . . I think so."

"Do it then," Mercado ordered. "Ten minutes. Go back, sit there, and tell her whatever she wants to hear. Just don't leave your spot, do you understand?"

"Yeah, but—"

"Do it now, Jon."

Mercado was off the line. Jon closed his eyes and tried to focus his energy. He put away the cell phone, stood up, left the stall, and looked at his own terrified face in the mirror. He stared at it until it looked back at him with confidence. Then he smiled. It was forced at first, but then he grew into it. He washed his hands and resolved to continue giving the performance of his life. With the time he'd already killed, it would have to last only about six more minutes.

Fewer heads watched his return than had watched his exit. In New York, excitement was forgotten fast. As Jon took his seat again, the busboy had just finished wiping down Paula, who was still seething, redder than before, as if she'd added something to Jon's already enormous tab.

"I have something to confess," Jon said, outwardly maintaining utter seriousness. "This is the way I wanted it to happen."

"It is?" Paula said, her interest piqued.

"Paula, I don't give a crap about West Harlem either. The way this whole thing got started was that you challenged me instead of leveling with me."

"Well, you overreact to everything," she said.

"Maybe I do. When I feel someone's thrown down the gauntlet, I throw mine down too. I think we're pretty much the same that way. That's how I think things got out of hand. We exchanged blows, and it escalated. The shame is you never stopped the fight for a second to offer me a piece of the pie. I might have taken it."

"For Chrissakes, that's what I'm doing *now*," Paula said.

"Okay, good," Jon said. "Lay it on the table for me. I want to walk out that door with you, but I have to know exactly where I stand before I do. What do you need from me? And exactly what do I get in return?"

"First," she said, "you have to know you won't be coming back to this part of the world. Not for a while. You have to forget about your wife."

"That's not a problem," Jon said. "We're history anyway. She got the photos. Her friend picked up the mail the same day the house blew up. Elaine blew up worse. You nailed me. It's over. Anyway, she thinks I was killed. It feels bad but, you know, not as bad as I expected." Jon looked at the time on his beeper. Three minutes to go. Any more than that and he might have to throw up for real.

"Jon, get in that car with us and you can be having sex an hour from now. Naomi still wants you. And I know you want her."

"I'll admit that I do," Jon said. "But I don't know how I can trust her after what happened."

"She's the last person you have to worry about, Jon. She was your biggest advocate, even when we thought we had to get rid of you. She's crazy about you. I know my sister."

"Your sister?" Jon said. His head spun, but he tried to stay calm on the outside.

"My mother had us thirteen years apart," Paula said. "Our fathers were not the same. But Naomi and I are sisters in at least one sense. We decided we're going to get everything we can. I needed someone to work on you who I knew could handle it. True, she took a few liberties. That hurt us. In the end, it may not matter at all. In fact, it may work out for the best. I remember when I didn't make partner. I was devastated. But that worked out for the best too."

"Okay," Jon said, "I get Naomi. What else do I get?"

"First, you need to hear what *we* get. We get the names of all the people you're working with. Anyone in the NYPD, DEP, any other city agency. And that includes anyone in the borough president's office."

"The people in our office are chickenshit," Jon said. "A few went along with me a step or two, then bailed out on me."

"You'll have to do better than that."

"Well," Jon said, "there is someone. But—"

"But what?"

"But if I told you, you probably wouldn't believe me anyway."

"Try me."

"Okay—Art Shuler."

"Oh, really?" Paula forced a smile.

"Yeah, really," Jon said, "depending on how you look at it. Right after I fell through the floor at the Glass House and we were going to come out with my odor report, he called me into his office. Which surprised the hell out of me, to be honest. But he sat there and told me I should consider spending the rest of my life as an insider rather than an outsider and asked me how I'd feel about making a quarter of a million a year instead of fifty-two thousand. I told him I'd consider it, and then he told me if I took the offer, I wouldn't have to worry about working with the likes of you."

"Of me?"

"Yeah, you," Jon said. "He said, 'I know she's a royal pain in the ass, and she's about outlived her usefulness. I may be able to take her out of the ball game—permanently.' "

"Why should I believe you?" Paula said, lurching forward, her face turning a suffocated, purplish shade of red.

"Paula, I remember it like it was yesterday. He held his finger over his lips, letting me know not to talk. Then he reached under his desk, removed a little . . . I don't know, a listening bug, pulled out the battery and said: 'Okay, now we can talk.' "

"I knew I couldn't trust that son of a bitch," Paula said, pounding the table and jerking her head.

"I don't want him working with us either," Jon said. "It's gotta be you, me, and Naomi."

"That will be taken care of," Paula said, seething.

"I was seriously considering taking that offer," Jon said, "until I heard your voice on Naomi's answering machine. That threw me for a loop. I figured all bets were off, the offer was void, you and Art had worked it out. Paula, we could have settled this whole thing a lot sooner."

"Five million dollars, Jon," Paula said, the fire almost bursting through her corneas. "That's what *I* can offer you. You may have to have some plastic surgery . . . fix that nose. We need the names, and all of the evidence you've gathered. *All* of it."

"Fine," Jon said. "I can think of only one thing that might get in the way—" All heads in the restaurant now looked toward the front door and all conversation stopped, its sound replaced by the pounding, deliberate, resonant footsteps of a half-dozen uniformed police officers. They were coming down the aisle toward Jon, who looked at Paula for an instant, preparing for the fun of seeing her abused and cuffed. Instead, it was he who was abused.

One, two, three, four 9mm Glocks were pointed at his head as he fell backward in his chair, hitting the cool tile floor and trying to wriggle his way somewhere. But there wasn't a somewhere. The husky white officer who had led the charge forced the side of his face into the tiles, while another one cuffed him from behind. There was a heel in the small of his back, and he wasn't sure whose foot it belonged to. A loud female voice was now telling him about reality.

"Jon Kessler, you are under arrest for the murder of Charles Samuel Murdock."

"I didn't do it!" Jon cried out.

"Shut up," came a deep male voice from above. The heel in his back tightened and paralyzed him.

"You have the right to remain silent," the female voice said. "Anything you say can and will be used against you in a court of law."

He caught a glimpse of Paula's face as they dragged him out. The shock it expressed was not much more than that coming from the panorama of stunned faces around them. In a matter of seconds Jon's head was being pushed down into the backseat of an unmarked blue '87 Plymouth Fury. There had been at least four blue and white patrol vehicles parked out front and uniformed officers prompting onlookers back. But now the crowd, the officers, and the noise were shut out.

He was alone in the backseat. His knapsack had been thrown in the back with him, which he took as surprisingly courteous, considering the bruises now covering his body. In the front seat were a uniformed officer and the female officer, who was driving. She was wearing a black patrol sweater and a black baseball-style patrol cap. Jon's own baseball cap, like his sunglasses, hadn't made it to the car.

The car pulled away, immediately doing a U-turn on Broadway that only cops could get away with. While the other police vehicles proceeded in the downtown direction, Jon's car had turned left onto Chambers and soon made a right onto Hudson Street. Except for the rattle of the wheels against the partially stripped, still largely unpaved street, the car was silent. As they crossed Houston Street, Jon broke the silence.

"I'm glad you guys came. But there may have been some kind of mix-up."

"There's no mix-up," the woman said.

"I didn't kill Charlie Murdock," Jon said. "I was almost killed *with* him."

"Right now," the uniformed officer said, "we're really not interested."

"What the hell *are* you interested in then?" Jon said. "You got the wrong guy. The woman who killed Charlie Murdock and Fred Barrow and God knows how many other people is back in that restaurant. Why don't you go back and get her? I'm telling you, you got the wrong guy!"

"No," the woman said plainly, "we got the right guy."

Jon's head slumped down. He realized there was some swelling over his right eye. He began muttering to himself. "I'll call Mercado. There was a mistake. He'll straighten this shit out. I don't have to be treated like this." The car stopped at the southwest corner of Eighth Avenue and Nineteenth Street. The woman officer spoke.

"Think you can walk it from here, Mike?"

"Yeah, with a stop or two on the way," the male officer said. He reached for the handle, opened the door, and hopped out in one easy movement. "Call me at the Tenth." He closed the door firmly and stepped out onto the sidewalk. The woman now made a left and cut across Eighth and Ninth Avenues, along Nineteenth Street, and across Tenth Avenue past a DO NOT ENTER sign. A quarter block west, she found a parking spot that said TOW AWAY ZONE.

"Hold on," Jon said. "Do you know James Mercado?"

"Too well," the woman said, now turning to face Jon, removing her cap and running her left hand through her thick wavy orange hair. "I'm Janine O'Connel. I don't believe we've had the pleasure."

"Oh my God," Jon said, pushing his head against the back seat to prop himself up. "Mercado sent you?"

"That's right. Mercado sends me all over the place."

"Thank you a million times over," Jon said.

"I hope you didn't give us away."

"Not even close," Jon said. "Can I tell you how I handled the whole thing? You'll love it."

"On the way up," O'Connel said, pulling a handcuff key from her belt. "We're late for our meeting."

Chapter 38

Three minutes later, having explained to O'Connel how lucky he'd been that he started carrying Mercado's cell phone, how he'd used her discovery of a bug in Art Shuler's office, and how at first he was almost relieved to be headed off to jail, Jon slipped a fresh new key into the lower lock on the front door of apartment 4A. For the first time in a long time, he felt he was in no one's custody but his own, and it felt good.

Inside, there was a small conclave. Gibbs, Mercado, and Sharpe sat in the living room as George Nagle addressed them from a standing position. Laura Ober sat near Nagle. Nagle had an elongated, chiseled head, a squared jaw, tight, thin lips, and wide-set but undersized hazel eyes. Though he was somewhat pale, his six-foot-four frame, as well as a tailored black suit and a pair of wire-rimmed glasses, lent him stature. Jon remembered Laura mentioning Nagle had been valedictorian at Yale, and he now recalled the speech he and eight hundred graduating high school seniors heard sixteen years earlier at Avery Fisher Hall from another valedictorian. "Don't be afraid to take chances," they were told.

"Hey," Jon said, walking confidently into the living room with O'Connel alongside him, "you wouldn't believe what just happened to me."

"We know all about it," Nagle said. "Take a seat. We've started already."

"You told me three o'clock," Jon said. "What's the rush?"

"No, I have to be back in D.C. by five," Nagle said without affect. "We have a tight schedule. Just sit down."

Jon took a seat on the couch next to Gibbs. He looked at Mercado for a moment and mouthed the word *Thanks*.

"Please pay attention," Nagle said. "For all practical purposes, I am the President right now. Okay, we've got a variety of audiotapes. We've got testimony given to the detectives in conjunction with their murder investigation, we've got video surveillance of workers entering and exiting the regulator chamber at odd times, and we've got a statistical analysis of the flow data that demonstrates something is seriously amiss."

"So we're basically set," Mercado said.

"No, we're not," Nagle replied. "These things are fine as supporting evidence. But our primary evidence needs to be either a confession or videotaped evidence of the crime itself, which is illegal dumping of untreated sewage into a public waterway and the conspiracy to commit such acts."

"Those audiotapes are tantamount to confessions," Mercado said. "They reveal conspiracy too."

"Those tapes were illegally obtained," Nagle said.

"Not true," Mercado objected.

"Every audiotape but the ones Kessler and Ober made while using recorders on their person is inadmissible," Nagle said. "Allow me to cite Federal Law eighteen, paragraph two-five-one-one, which states: 'Interception and disclosure of wire or oral communication is prohibited for any person who willfully uses, endeavors to use, or procures any other person to use or endeavor to use any electronic, mechanical, or other device to intercept an oral communication . . .' Of course, the same section goes on to say: 'It shall not be unlawful under this chapter for a person acting under the color of law to intercept a wire or oral communication, where such person is a party to the communication or one of the parties to the communication has given prior consent to such interception.' Did you obtain such consent, Detective? Moreover, Detective, were you acting under color of law?"

"*She* was," Mercado said, pointing to O'Connel. "She had a court order. I was barely involved."

"Too close to call," Nagle said. "If you want the President to go to bat for you, the President has to be sure he's going to win the case."

"Okay," Jon said, "let's say we throw out every last one of the questionable audiotapes. What about the thirty-million-gallon drop in the flow and all the valid analysis?"

"This is not entirely a first for this plant," Nagle said. "I've been through the data. Remember, there have been other sudden drops in flow before."

"Yeah," Sharpe said, "every time someone wanted to build something big."

"What about the video surveillance we have right here?" O'Connel asked.

"There's a regulator chamber," Nagle said. "People go in, people come out. So what? What does it all mean? Remember, I'll be dealing with some federal judge, not an engineer. You have to make it simple for these bozos."

"So then let's make this perfectly understood," Jon said. "Virtually all of the evidence we've gathered so far can be construed in one way or another as admissible. You just don't like the idea of failing."

"Okay," Nagle said, "if it makes you happy to put it that way, fine. I'm afraid to take the chance."

"So now what?" Mercado asked.

"So go down there and get me what I need," Nagle said. "Get me a videotape of someone bypassing the regulator, inside. Get me a tape of some sewage coming out of the tide gate. Get me a tape of an empty interceptor. Get me a lab sample of that dirty water."

"I knew it," Jon said, rolling his eyes.

"Why do we need to send someone down there with a video camera?" Sharpe said. "What's wrong with photos?"

"With video we can tell the judge a story," Nagle said. "I want this thing narrated, clearly. Photos can be put out of sequence to tell a completely different story. Photos can't always show direction of flow."

"What you're talking about is very dangerous," Sharpe said. "I had a friend who died doing that. And you're afraid to take chances."

"Hey," Nagle said, "This is not about your friend. Look, I have a plane to catch. Are we going to do this or not?"

"I'm not going down there blind," Mercado said. "I need plans first."

"I know the damn regulator," Sharpe said.

"I need a map," Mercado said. "A good one."

"I have someone working on it right now," Jon said.

"You do?" Mercado said. "Is he any good?"

"Yeah," Jon said, "the best."

Larry Golick got off the elevator on the eighth floor of 40 Worth Street and walked briskly down the freshly painted bright white halls, toward the glass door at the north end that read, DEP——OFFICE OF RECORDS AND PLANS. He turned and pushed the doorknob and found himself in front of a large white Formica–covered counter.

In the approximately thirty-by-thirty-foot room of light-colored floor tiles, acoustic ceiling tiles, and hanging fluorescent lights, various green flat files and movable cubicles were scattered, as if they had not reestablished their turf since the big paint job. The smell of pipe smoke was just barely noticeable against the smell of drying latex. Only one of the cubicles appeared to be occupied. Larry saw him from the back. He had a big head of bright orange curly hair, was heavyset, and sat hunched over a book.

"Excuse me," Larry said, "I need a map of the interceptor and the regulator chamber at Eighteenth Street, on the west side of Manhattan."

The man wheeled his chair around slowly to face Larry from a distance of about fifteen feet behind the counter. The swivel rod squeaked ominously and the turn slowed even more as it reached completion, revealing the man's bushy orange beard, sallow complexion, smallish eyes amplified by massive unruly eyebrows, and a broad, slightly upturned nose. He was about Larry Golick's age, with a paunch to match, bulging through his short-sleeve button-down shirt. He puffed on a pipe and removed it with his right hand.

"You would like a what?" He had a thick English accent, as if he was eighteenth-century nobility. Wait a second, Larry thought. He had heard about this guy. Pipe, English accent. Oh, no—it was the Baron. He was in trouble.

"A map of the interceptor at Eighteenth Street," Larry said. "I came by here Friday, but a note on the door said you were on vacation."

"Do you have any idea precisely what you have interrupted?" the Baron said, indignant. "I happen to have been just about to read of the Battle of Crécy. Do you know anything at all about the Battle of Crécy?"

"Ah . . . no."

"Sir, that effectively marked the beginning of the Hundred Years War."

"How could a war last a hundred years?" Larry said. "That's stupid."

"Crécy, Crécy," the Baron said, now standing and flailing his pipe, "I remember it like it was yesterday. We, the king's yeomen, the loyal but free subjects of the king—King Edward the Third—crossed the Channel to fight the bloody Normans. Those feudal bastards! Those frogs! They fought high atop frightened horses, wearing useless armor so easily pierced by the arrow of the English longbow—"

"Look—"

"*Look,*" the Baron said, "at the well-aimed arrows raining down death on the hapless French, they without a king. What had defeated the English at Stirling Bridge and Bannockburn at the hands of the feisty Scots was now a means for victory at Crécy, then Poitiers, then Agincourt. This was more than a series of military victories, my good friend. This was the end of feudalism and the beginning of a true monarchy. The end of the Middle Ages and the beginning of the Renaissance!"

And the end of Larry Golick. He walked out the door and began to pace slowly down the hallway. He had seen the man somewhere before. It was coming back to him now. He'd heard someone talking about the Baron at a union meeting. No one knew much about the Baron except that he was born and raised in Brooklyn and had lost his high school teaching position many years earlier as the result of a suit over the corporal punishment he meted out regularly at Charles Evans Hughes High School. Larry knew he didn't have a prayer. The Baron hadn't given out a map in a decade. Once in a while an intern came in and tried to catch up on back orders, but that might take weeks to come through.

It serves me right, Larry thought. This is what it looked like and felt like from the other side. You become very polite, demure, and subservient when the one thing in the world you need most desperately is held by a single deluded moron with a gripe who couldn't give a damn about your meaningless plight. Larry considered sticking around to hear himself beg, but knew from experience what the result would be. Yes, this was exactly what he deserved.

But it wasn't what the King deserved. Larry did a 180, marched back down the hallway, whipped open the door, scurried around the counter, and approached the Baron from behind. He grabbed the Baron's collar with one hand, his right shoulder with the other hand, and whirled the Baron around to face him. He could see the whites of the Baron's eyes.

"You are gonna get me those plans in the next five minutes or I am gonna beat you into English pudding."

"But, sir—"

"The name's Larry. Don't you put on airs with me. I saw you at OTB last month."

"There must be some kind of mistake," the Baron pleaded.

"The only mistake here is if you don't follow the orders of the King."

"The King?"

"The King," Larry said, letting go of the Baron for a moment. "The King is a guy from Queens who is running for his life, being hunted down by criminals—by . . . robber barons. The King is a guy who tried to do the right thing for the city, for his *country*, and lost everything because of it. The King is a man full of problems and imperfections, but someone who is perfect when it comes to doing the best he can. The King was loyal to me, and I am loyal to him. Do you know who the King is?"

Fearfully, the Baron shook his head no.

"The King is Jon Kessler. And the King lives."

"All right, all right," the Baron said in his finest Brooklyn accent. "You'll have your maps in two minutes."

Chapter 39

Ted "Kill the Trees" Santorini clapped heartily as the governor spoke, then the mayor, then a few other dignitaries. When it was his turn, he kept it under a minute, just as the representative from the State Office of Parks had asked. At the podium, with the George Washington Bridge and the coast of Edgewater, New Jersey, visible behind him, he stood with the bright sun bouncing off his balding scalp and his suit jacket unbuttoned. In spite of a brisk wind, his girth and deep voice gave him presence.

"I am proud to have been a part of the council committee that made this park a reality. This park is a testament to the fact that economic growth and quality of life can walk hand in hand. So now I turn these facilities over to the children of West Harlem— the Ronald Arlens of tomorrow."

There was a smattering of applause and several boos and hisses from the crowd of about five hundred there to witness the official opening of Riverbank State Park. There, above the churning and bubbling of many millions of gallons of raw sewage in the plant below sat spanking-new tennis courts, an AstroTurf softball field, a soccer field with a quarter-mile track around it, an ice hockey rink, an amphitheater, and a restaurant. When the newly planted maple trees sent roots down to a depth of more than four feet, they would be turned away by reinforced concrete. But the trees weren't complaining any more than the local kids. To thrive in New York, you had to adapt to your environment and stand firm at the same time.

Today, however, Ted Santorini could not move quickly enough. The rotten egg smell was getting to him, so he lit a cigarette. It was already 11:30 A.M. on this Wednesday, June 2. He had to be at 250 Broadway by two o'clock to vote on the Hudson City sewer hookup. But squeezing in this little site visit was definitely worth it, even if it meant cutting things a little close.

Slightly out of breath, he now jogged across Marginal Street at St. Clair Place, a few blocks south of the North River plant and the park above it. To his surprise, here, out of the way of everything but a couple of lonely homeless fishermen, the rotten egg smell intensified. But it did not matter. The 46-foot cabin cruiser was moored to the wharf, and two men waved to him. The pilot was a tall black man in his late forties wearing an army shirt with the buttons all the way open and the sleeves cut off. The passenger was Gerald Grossberg, a stout mid-fiftyish white man with boyish blue eyes, thick wavy graying hair, and the beginnings of a double chin. Grossberg pulled his hand from the pocket of his windbreaker and, extending it to help Santorini aboard, gave the most chipper of welcomes.

"All aboard, Ted. Glad you could make it."

Grossberg had made a fortune over the last twenty years

purchasing run-down residential and commercial properties in Manhattan, refurbishing them, and reselling them at exactly the right time. In one notorious escapade, he had a rent-controlled tenement he owned torn down in the middle of the night. After testifying that the demolition was a total surprise to him, and then paying a two-million-dollar settlement of the city's civil suit, Grossberg wound up building a forty-story condo on the same spot, profiting to the tune of a hundred million dollars. He dabbled in a half-dozen other businesses as well, including the casino business. Though his Atlantic City casino, the Coral, was profitable, it was dwarfed both in size and in earnings by the casino right next door—Arlen's Armada. This paralleled Grossberg's experience in New York City, where his projects were rarely as high-profile as the Dodger's. If Ronald Arlen was the poor man's Donald Trump, Gerald Grossberg was the poor man's Harry Macklowe.

The boat motored south along the Hudson, whose waters were more choppy than usual on this day. As they passed a collection of solid and floating piers on their left, cluttered with houseboats, dinghies, and ketches, the black man pointed.

"That's home."

"Is it, Duane?" Grossberg said, smiling. "You're a resident of the esteemed Seventy-ninth Street boat basin."

"It's not too esteemed," Duane said, "but like I said, it is home. Got out of 'Nam in 'seventy-one, bounced around for a couple of years, then saved me some money to buy this boat and fix it up. The ultimate freedom, man. I got a Manhattan address, but I sail the whole house away anytime I please."

"I'd like to buy the basin and turn it into a yacht club," Grossberg said.

"Could we please step it up a notch," Santorini complained. "I have to be downtown at two."

"Relax, for Chrissakes, Ted," Grossberg said. "We already have that worked out. Getting to Hoffman Island takes a half hour, tops."

"Yeah," Duane said, "hang out there another half hour, then I'll turn around and drop you off at Pier Twenty-six downtown. You can walk to your meeting from there."

"Okay, okay," Santorini said. "I just want to check the place out and go."

"You won't be disappointed, Ted," Grossberg said, patting Santorini on the back. "Once the federal government turns it back over to the city and the city sells or leases it, the money-making potential is phenomenal."

"I believe it," Santorini said.

"Damn right," Grossberg said. "And Ted, I know you could be instrumental in getting the City Council to approve of a hotel and resort there. A casino is a possibility as well. The State's all ready to vote on it too. We can't let the Indians in Connecticut have all the fun."

"Sort of an offshore playland for the jet set," Santorini said.

Grossberg nodded. "You got that right, Ted. Long, long overdue for New York. And everyone will win. The gamblers, the investors, and the city will pick up a bundle in tax revenue. This is something you want to be on the ground floor of, Councilman."

"I got a couple of liberals in the council who want to put a university on the island," Santorini said.

"What a load of crap," Grossberg said. "And who's going to pay for that, the taxpayers? These assholes better get with it. The taxpayers want relief."

At 12:03 the cabin cruiser passed directly beneath the Verrazano Narrows Bridge, whose fantastic span overhead seemed like a thin walkway in the sky paralleling the curvature of the earth. Less than a mile south, the eleven-acre Hoffman Island poked its mound of green foliage through a mild mist. Hoffman Island was man-made and at one time the home of a quarantine station used to isolate new immigrants suspected of carrying infectious diseases. During World War II it was not only the anchorage of an antisubmarine net that extended across the entrance to the harbor, but also the site of a training facility for the U.S. Merchant Marine. Now, however, as part of Gateway National Park, it served as home only to colonies of seagulls.

"There she is, Duane," Grossberg said. But the sound of the motor disappeared.

"Oh, shit," Duane said.

"What, what?" Santorini exclaimed.

"Last time this happened was 'eighty-four," Duane said. "Electrical system cut out on me. We're gonna drift for a bit."

"Oh, crap," Grossberg said, "just my luck."

"Can't you do something?" Santorini said, barely a foot from Duane's face.

"I can call the Coast Guard," Duane said. "But first I gotta hook up the radio to the backup generator. That is, if that still works. Haven't tried it in years."

"Shit!" Santorini said, kicking the metal railing.

"Relax, man," Duane said. "You ain't gonna die."

"Ted," Grossberg said, smiling and shaking his head, "mea culpa. For a man with a half-billion dollars, I can be a schmuck sometimes. Can you believe I left my cell phone back in my limo?"

"Son of a bitch!" Santorini's shouts were lost at sea, reaching only his ears, Duane's, Grossberg's, and a few seagulls.

Grossberg tried to control his exuberance. Everything had gone as planned. They wouldn't be back until dinnertime. In time for him to catch the local news and have a laugh at Ronald Arlen's expense. Duane would take care of everything. Behind his placid, perhaps even worn appearance, he could be quite able and cunning—not unlike his sister-in-law, Clarissa Marbles.

Chapter 40

Duane Holland's forty-six-foot cabin cruiser pulled slowly away from the Seventy-ninth Street boat basin at 2:37 A.M., early Thursday morning, June 3. It was a warm night, but a steady breeze blew from the east, where ominous rain clouds were moving quickly toward the city. To the north, the Big Dipper could be still seen. The sounds of automobiles on the West Side of Manhattan were sporadic and faint. They were overpowered by the sounds of laughter and glasses clinking aboard one of the boats in the basin, the owner of which was throwing an all-hours party. Now, as Duane Holland throttled the engine, all of the sounds momentarily disappeared.

"Man, I'm going to have to sleep this off tomorrow," Holland said from behind the steering wheel.

"Hey," Charlie Sharpe said, "no reason you can't be in bed in an hour or two. You deserve it. Especially after pulling what you did with Santorini."

"Yeah, we didn't get his sorry ass back to Manhattan till five-thirty," Holland said. "They can't set up another meeting till Monday."

"But I'd love to get this over with tonight," Sharpe said. "I was never too crazy about doing it in the first place."

"Hey, no sweat," Holland said. "This baby moves. We'll beat that rain. It's a good night. You wanted low tide, and you got it."

"But I didn't ask for this smell," Charlie Sharpe said.

"Well," Holland said, "I'm really not much of a partier anymore. These days I'm usually in bed by midnight. But once in a while when I've been up late like this, that's the smell."

"Since when?" Sharpe asked.

"Last couple of months."

"Uh-huh, that's about when they started bypassing."

"People been complaining about it," Holland said. "Especially the partiers."

"Sure," Sharpe said. "You have an outfall right at Eighty-first Street. They've probably been bypassing right there. The current brings that sewage right down to you and your friends, man. Hardly diluted."

"They really do that?" Holland asked. "God, I take a swim now and again."

"I wouldn't do that for a while if I was you," Sharpe said.

"In the past," Holland said, "the only time we really got that smell was after a big storm."

"That's right," Sharpe said. "That's when the system bypasses automatically, so we don't have backups. Right now, they're bypassing because someone is messing with the system. So they can build a bunch of buildings over there." Sharpe pointed to the port side, toward the huge, vacant, weeded lot marked only by a few dilapidated piers and a long stretch of the elevated Henry Hudson Highway. But now, upon closer inspection, something else marked the property. "Could you pull up there for a minute?"

"No problem," Holland said. He steered the boat port side and motored toward land, aligning them almost perfectly with Seventy-second Street. Sharpe stepped onto the deck and aimed his five-hundred-thousand-candle-power quartz halogen lamp toward the shoreline from a distance of about a hundred feet. There, pouring forth from two five-by-four-foot holes in the concrete seawall, was a constant heavy flow of water filling up approximately the bottom half of each hole.

"Hey, there you go," Holland said, stepping out onto the deck and letting the engine idle.

"Yeah, there we go," Sharpe said. "Hold this."

He handed Holland the halogen lamp and steadied his Hitachi camcorder against his right shoulder. The camcorder, like the one in Haney's apartment, was equipped with an Astroscope, which at the moment it only marginally required. Sharpe focused, hit record, zoomed in, and narrated briefly. "Seventy-second Street and the west side of Manhattan. Sewer outfall in bypass position with heavy flow. No precipitation yet." Sharpe filmed for a minute more and stopped. He saw from the time code that it was already 2:48, and he had promised Mercado and Kessler that he'd be at Eighteenth Street by three.

"Okay?" Holland asked.

"Yeah," Sharpe said, "keep going. How's your electrical system?"

"Hasn't cut out on me since 'eighty-four." Holland smiled and pulled the throttle.

The outfall at Sixty-sixth Street was bypassing as well. It was like a medieval bloodletting ceremony for the island of Manhattan. As in virtually all such ceremonies, the patient was actually getting worse. Sharpe shot this one briefly too and asked Holland to go nonstop to Eighteenth Street.

"Now what's so special about Eighteenth Street?" Holland said.

"Nothing," Sharpe said. "Nothing except we know when we can get inside the regulator without getting killed. We've been watching the guys who do the bypass at Eighteenth Street every night. That's my old location. We know they leave the area almost every night between three and four A.M. They probably go up to Thirtieth Street to rig that one and come back down to check on Eighteenth Street. Whatever they do, we have lookouts. We ain't gonna proceed until we get clearance. That's why I got this." Sharpe pulled a 5-watt, 40-channel citizen's band walkie-talkie from the left pocket of his windbreaker.

"Okay, so you get to look inside the regulator," Holland said. "What's a regulator?"

"First of all," Sharpe said, "I'm gonna be right here on this boat. I'm not going in there. As far as what a regulator is—it's basically a concrete box about the size of a small house, maybe twenty-five feet by twenty, maybe fifteen feet deep. It's sitting right under the road, you know. Got a few manhole covers. Two separated rooms connected. One's the tide gate chamber. The other's the regulator chamber. Pull off a manhole cover, walk down a ladder, and you are inside the house of sewage."

"You drown in there?"

"Not normally," Sharpe said. "See, the old sewer comes in the back from the local trunk main, into the box. Then, inside the box, the water drops into a concrete hole called the diversion chamber and curves around to the right, like a little river. The water goes under a couple of sluice gates that are normally open, you see? If it's not flooded out, you can just stand there on the platform and look down at this shit like you're in a little cell block with a stream running through it. Then the water hooks around into the regulator chamber, which is just another little river in the next room. Then out the back of that into a five-foot pipe and into the interceptor. That's the main sewer that takes everything to the treatment plant uptown."

"So that's it?" Holland said. "What's being regulated?"

"Okay, my man, that's the question. Inside the regulator chamber room you got another little hole in the ground called the float well. That's just an offshoot of the main flow. If the interceptor gets too full, then the pipe feeding it gets too full and the float well gets too full. Once the float in there gets high enough, it triggers the sluice gates. One set closes and cuts off the flow to the interceptor. The other set opens the diversion chamber to the tide gate chamber, and out into the river it goes."

"A float, huh?" Holland said. "Sounds like a big toilet bowl tank."

"Yeah," Sharpe said, "but a damn toilet bowl hasn't got electronic wiring and hydraulic lifts. Those sluice gates are two-inch-thick cast-iron plates suspended from heavy chains. It takes a few seconds and a couple of tons of force to get those gates up."

"So you want to get this from every angle," Holland said.

"We hope," Sharpe said. "This son of a bitch from the Justice Department won't take anything else. So we got a guy down in the interceptor and another guy down in the regulator. The interceptor nearby has its own manhole. These two guys may be only forty feet away from each other underground, but they can't see each other unless they're both looking at the narrow pipe that connects the regulator to the interceptor. I told them exactly what to do, what to look for. I'll be taking video at the same time from the outfall."

"Wait a second," Holland said. "You're the man who's spent years down there, fixing that thing. But you're not going down."

"I ain't stupid," Sharpe said.

Jimmy Mercado was not thrilled about having Mark Rosario observing the operation from up in Haney's apartment. But with his latest article in the *Westsider*, Rosario had scored points with the allegedly deceased Jon Kessler by partially resurrecting his public image. In return, all Rosario wanted was a seat in mission control for the big launch. In turn, if things worked out, he would write the ultimate glorification piece for Kessler and company. Mercado warned Rosario not to distract Laura Ober, who had her hands full coordinating the surveillance team.

Now, at 3:04 A.M., Gibbs and Kessler, having just gotten clearance from Laura, fanned out at the intersection of Eighteenth Street and Eleventh Avenue, with Gibbs running almost completely across Eleventh. Just off the northeast corner, nearer to Mercado, Jon put down four yellow cones around the interceptor manhole and used a crowbar to lift the metal plate off its collar. He used brute force to slide it over fully to one side. He shined his halogen light down the narrow opening. Twenty feet straight down he saw a shallow stream of water moving north at about three feet per second.

This was the interceptor. It was like a long periscope, with a series of concrete pipes fitting into each other, each one slightly larger than the one immediately downtown and slightly smaller than the one immediately uptown. Here, the interceptor was seven feet in diameter, a far cry from the twenty-six feet to which it expanded down the line, but still large enough to walk through easily if you didn't play center for the Knicks, and to transport upward of forty thousand gallons per minute of raw sewage under extreme conditions.

Just to get to the top of it, Jon would have to slink down fourteen feet of manhole. Now was as good a time to start as any. Leaving the manhole cover open and with his light in his right hand and his equipment bag slung over his right shoulder, he began his descent, carefully placing each foot on its proper metal rung. As the rungs neared the bottom of the manhole shaft, Jon passed by a five-foot-high, egg-shaped opening in the shaft. He knew this was the branch connecting the interceptor to the regulator, where Al Gibbs was at this very moment getting oriented. Jon knew why nothing was coming out of this connecting pipe—the corresponding sluice gate was closed in the regulator.

Jon continued down the ladder and the space opened up around him. His head left the cramped manhole shaft just a moment before his knee-high boots hit the bottom, making a splash in less than a foot of flowing sewage. Now, in order to see the hole from the connecting branch, he had to crane his neck a bit. He stepped away and ran his left hand along the concrete ceiling of the interceptor. He had almost a foot of clearance above his head. Here, the interceptor was square, approximately seven feet wide as well as high. From here on in it was simple. He pulled his walkie-talkie from the bag, turned it on, tuned in to channel 22, whipped open the antenna, and heard Mercado's voice.

"Yeah, that's exciting, Laura. I'll tell Jon as soon as I have him. Over."

"You got me," Jon said, pushing his talk button. "I'm down here and I'm ready to start taping. Over."

"I read you loud and clear," Mercado's voice said. "How does it look down there? Over."

"It looks like a sewer," Jon said through mild static. "We're in business. Forty-nine square feet, and all I have is a trickle. I've got a branch coming in here and nothing coming out of it. A hundred thousand people in this neighborhood and not one toilet being flushed. Who would believe it? Over."

"Get it all on tape," Mercado's voice said. "And tell the judge what you're seeing. Over."

"Piece of cake," Jon said into the walkie-talkie. "Now what's so exciting? Over."

"Gibbs found the smoking gun," Mercado's voice said. "The float mechanism's tied with a chain in the up position. Over."

"Yes!" Jon shouted into the walkie-talkie. "We're golden. This shit is finally gonna be over. . . . Over."

"Okay, Jon," Mercado's voice said. "Get your tape and get back up here. It's starting to rain. Maybe we can all grab a beer. Over."

Gibbs had in fact struck gold. He now stood in the dry, isolated regulator chamber, about fifteen feet beneath the west side of Eleventh Avenue, his back grazing the ladder rungs he'd climbed down a few minutes earlier and his vision directed down toward the float mechanism, through the eyes of a camcorder. A metal chain was wrapped around the bar that held the float. The chain was hooked to a spike that had been driven into the concrete wall, about three feet above the top of the float well. Gibbs spoke to his future audience.

"No brain surgery here. We're in regulator N-50. Float from the float well has been tied in the up position. No water in the float well. Sluice gates closed. No water going to the interceptor. The weir is empty. Look at that, right there. There it is . . . nothing."

Mercado now had Sharpe on channel 23.

"When I worked down here," Sharpe said, "we called this failure. Right now, I have to call this a success. Over."

Leaning off the deck and filming from only ten feet offshore as Holland held the halogen lamp, Sharpe viewed the putrid man-made waterfall, with its crest just below his eye level and its bottom the Hudson's now turbulent surface. That surface was a good five feet below the daily high water mark, and that mark was plainly visible along the face of the concrete seawall.

The top four feet or so of the wall revealed decades-old concrete, with its typical yellowing, cracking, and spalling. Below that, demarcated with a surprisingly distinct line, was a thick covering of dark green algae continuing like ivy gone mad, all the way down. The lower visible portion of the concrete was largely rotted away, revealing steel reinforcement bars.

"Okay, real good," Mercado said into his walkie-talkie. "How's your footage? Over."

"Perfect," Sharpe replied. "And there's more. I got two other outfalls being bypassed uptown. This island looks like a sinking ship. And I got it all on tape. Over."

"Anything at Thirtieth Street?"

"No, nothing," Sharpe said, "and that's the first one I expected to see. McCord should be there right now. I don't know. But I do know this, Detective. The flow from this outfall just jumped way the hell up. It's this damn rain."

"Okay," Mercado said. "I'm getting soaked too. Start wrapping it up. Gibbs and Kessler are gonna wrap it up soon too. Head back to the boat basin, and we'll meet you up at the apartment. Over."

"No problemo," Sharpe said. "Over."

Mercado switched to channel 24 to get Gibbs. "How you doing?" he said. "Over."

"Few more minutes," Gibbs said. "How's Charlie? Over."

"A little wet, but better than the rest of us," Mercado said. "He's taking the Circle Line tour. Check that. Better than everyone but Rosario. He's up there having a sandwich. Over."

"Tell him to make one for me," Gibbs said. "Over."

Mercado jumped to channel 25 and got O'Connel, who was standing on the river side of Eleventh Avenue at Twenty-second Street and sweeping her head from north to south and back again. She brushed droplets from her eyes, as droplets danced off the asphalt on Eleventh Avenue.

"Any action over there?" Mercado said. "Over."

"Just a couple of drunks taking a leak," O'Connel said. "I did see a DEP van heading north. Same one I saw heading south two minutes ago. Keep an eye out. Over."

"Okay," Mercado said. "We're coming down the homestretch here. You hear from Laura? Over."

"Yeah," O'Connel said, "she tells me we're clear. You can check with her too, Jimmy. Over."

"That's what I'm gonna do," Mercado said. "We're gonna call it soon. Over."

Up on the fourth floor, overlooking the action, Laura Ober continued checking the surveillance camcorder, looking through a pair of binoculars with night vision, and flipping from channels 22 through 26 on the CB scanner Mercado had given her.

With alarm, she spotted two husky men dressed in gray work clothes running west on Eighteenth Street. They sprinted right past Mercado, through the rain and across Eleventh Avenue, dodging a white Ford Taurus heading north and a dark blue Jeep Cherokee heading south. Laura quickly turned her scanner to channel 26 and screamed into the microphone.

"They're headed for the regulator. The regulator."

Mercado heard her but did not respond. He'd already stuffed his walkie-talkie into the left pocket of his jacket and drawn his nine-millimeter pistol. When the words left his mouth, he was out on a limb in more ways than one:

"Freeze! New York City police!"

Both men were now safely within the confines of the traffic cones surrounding the regulator, protecting them from the intermittent traffic at the outer southbound lane. They both wheeled around, saw a soaking Mercado on the corner at Eighteenth Street across from them, and opened fire on him without hesitation. Through the rain, Mercado opened fire at virtually the same time, hitting the larger man with the black and gray goatee on the left, dead center in the chest and felling him. Mercado recognized him. It was McCord's partner, from the night he'd arrested McCord.

A stray bullet from the other gunman hit the windshield of the Toyota Cressida, which careened into a fire hydrant just down the block. In spite of the two cylindrical impact guards around it, the hydrant was instantly sheared off and spouted a sixty-foot geyser. A bullet from the other gunman had whistled by Mercado's head at the same time the hydrant was hit, and Mercado failed to hit the shooter with two more shots from his nine-millimeter.

A late-seventies Cadillac was breaking frantically, skidding north, crossing Mercado's vision. As if from the rear windshield of the Cadillac and through the stray mist of the fire hydrant, Mercado was hit by a bullet in his upper left thigh. It knocked him off his feet, sending him backward. He crawled toward the thin lamp post for marginal protection. In all his years as a cop, he had never been shot before. The pain he expected to feel had not set in. His pain at the moment came from his thoughts. His unwillingness to jeopardize innocent drivers on Eleventh Avenue had put him at a disadvantage. That was life. The walkie-talkie in his coat pocket continued to scream.

"We have a man down! Mercado is down at Eighteenth Street!"

From a prone position, the rain splashing off the sidewalk back up at his strained face, Mercado peered around the right side of the light pole and saw the shooter about to squeeze off another round. But an arm reached up from out of the ground, grabbed the shooter's left ankle, and pulled him backward. The shooter barked out a long, not entirely formed syllable as he disappeared. *"Wooooammm."* Mercado smiled. And then the real pain began to set in.

Up on the fourth floor, Laura flipped through the channels and continued to yell in panicked, upper-register tones that Mercado was down. Down in the interceptor, Jon heard this faintly on channel 22. But just as Mercado could not react immediately to his own wound, Jon's mind was already contending with the next set of decisions.

He had wandered about a hundred feet north of the manhole shaft from which he'd entered when he noticed a flash of light coming from perhaps a quarter mile north in the tunnel. By the time Jon understood that the echo came from the impact of heavy footsteps pounding wet concrete, he had begun a mad dash back toward the base of the manhole shaft, the nearest way out of the line of fire. Yet it was so far away. It was like the recurring nightmare he'd had of running from first base to second base but getting hung up indefinitely on a muddy base path.

It was clear, however, that the Thirtieth Street squad was returning early—both aboveground and below. Now, the light bounced off the concrete walls to his right, then his left. The sound of a bullet being fired ricocheted off a wall, followed by the sound of the bullet itself ricocheting off a wall. Another sequence just like it followed. Then he heard a third pop, but there was no ricochet.

He was facedown in the flow, coming to realize that *he* was the wall this time—that he'd been hit. His left shoulder was immobilized and he felt, more than he heard, a low-frequency hum. It would be easy to let this hum envelop him and take him away. But that next place could be anywhere. On the other hand, a few feet from his face, he saw the light bouncing off the metal rungs and knew exactly where they led.

He pulled himself up, gripping the second-lowest rung with his right hand, the hand he could still move. As another bullet ricocheted off the concrete wall behind him and the footsteps got to within a hundred yards, he thought better of feeling for the video camera or his lamp. Instead, using one good arm and two rubbery legs, he climbed steadily, desperately, up the first few rungs of the ladder, toward the dim light above.

His head now cleared the narrow, egg-shaped opening of the branch, but as his legs pushed him up two more rungs, he stopped. The hum got louder, his legs got more rubbery. He leaned against the damp concrete wall. He wasn't going to make it up the last ten feet, and even if he somehow managed, he would be shot up like ground beef as he crawled away from the opening at street level.

Below him, another shot whizzed by, and the beam of the shooter's flashlight danced momentarily off the surface of the stream. He had a few more seconds of safety, and after that it was over. The walkie-talkie, having survived in his jacket pocket, still barked on channel 22. "We have a man down at Eighteenth Street." Jon reached in with his right hand, flipped the dial at the top so that the illuminated digital channel indicator read 24, pressed Talk, and uttered the only thing that he could, the only thing that made sense to him.

"Al, unchain the float. Unchain the float. Please unchain the float."

The man in gray had fallen nine feet to the concrete platform in the regulator chamber room below and landed on his back and elbow. His pistol hit the concrete surface and skipped two feet toward the dry weir along the front wall. As the man in gray reached for the gun, Gibbs kicked it, sending it into the weir, falling three and a half feet to the bottom. The man in gray grabbed Gibbs's other leg and threw him to the ground. Gibbs landed across the back of the man in gray, who crawled toward the weir, dragging both himself and Gibbs. His eyes now peering over the edge of the weir, the man in gray saw the gun, reached for it with his left hand and grasped it.

He flipped over to aim the pistol at Gibbs's head, but Gibbs quickly grabbed the man's left wrist with his right hand. Now Gibbs tried to snatch the gun using his free left hand, but the man in gray rabbit-punched him with a series of rights to the face. Gibbs continued to hold the wrist with the gun, but now dropped to his left side in reaction to the blows.

They lay struggling in semidarkness, walled in by concrete, an empty weir to one side, an empty float well to the other. The man in gray, now on top of him, reached for Gibbs's neck with his free right hand. Gibbs kneed him in the groin and flipped him over once again, so that he was the one on top for a moment, still holding the gun hand at bay with both of his own. The man in gray squeezed off a shot, which hit the concrete roof. The shock jolted Gibbs back again. Gibbs lay sideways now, his back to the corner of a concrete wall, his legs extending out over the empty float well. He had never let go completely of his attacker's wrist.

Gibbs used his left hand to stop the right-handed punches thrown once again by the man in gray, while now only his right hand kept the gun barely at a distance. Gibbs looked straight into his attacker's eyes. They were gray as well, and there was nothing behind them but a thirst to kill. He was twenty years younger than Gibbs, who felt his own energy begin to drain from the back of his neck. Against the opposite wall, Gibbs saw the walkie-talkie he'd dropped moments earlier. Once he had pulled the man in gray down into the regulator, it seemed like more of a liability than a weapon. But now it spoke to him.

"Al, unchain the float. Unchain the float. Please, unchain the float."

Gibbs released the man in gray's right hand from his own left, took a blow to the solar plexus while attempting to sit upright, reached straight above his head, pulled the metal spike out of the wall, and plunged it straight down with an exhalation he doubted he'd ever replenish. The spike went cleanly through the front of the man's neck and out the back. As Gibbs's assailant went limp and his gray eyes surrendered what little life they still contained, the chain that had been wrapped around the spike unfurled and the float dropped to the bottom of the well. The sluice gates began to lift and water filled the weir almost instantly.

"Al, unchain the float. Unchain the float. Please unchain the float." He could not say it again. With his own last burst of adrenaline, Jon had climbed up two more rungs, so that only the bottom of his boots hung in front of the egg-shaped interceptor branch opening. Below, water had begun to trickle out of the branch opening and down the manhole shaft. Droplets of water landed on his boots as the flow quickly intensified. As he looked down, he saw the shadowy upright figure of the shooter, now at the base of the ladder. The flow now obscured the shadow, as the shooter tried to climb the rungs, one hand clutching a bar, the other attempting to fire.

"I'll kill you, you piece of shit!" he shouted.

"Look who's talking," Jon said.

The flow was now a thick, blinding, turbulent force—a tightly contained Niagara Falls that obliterated the presence below, swamping him, folding him, crushing him, and carrying him down a long tunnel not intended for life. There was a bellowing howl that receded and echoed, yet took what seemed like an hour to disappear. As much as Jon despised whoever had tried to end his life, he felt sickened by this howl, because he knew that anyone was capable of issuing it.

Mercado had already told the hysterical Laura to call the police. Now, lying on the damp sidewalk on his hip, clutching his soaked thigh with one hand to slow the blood, unsteadily holding his Glock with the other, Mercado found himself fading in and out of consciousness. What he saw now through the rain he feared was real.

On the sidewalk, halfway up the block, was another man in gray, this one with a shiny bald head, an earring like Mr. Clean, and a gun out in front, aimed at him. As Mercado tried in vain to steady his right hand, he heard rapidly approaching footsteps, even though Mr. Clean had stopped in his tracks. The walkie-talkie barked.

"Look out! Look out!"

A shot rang out and there was a thump. Mr. Clean dropped to the pavement, clearing Mercado's vision to see O'Connel, who was at the north end of the block, still looking down the barrel of her nine-millimeter, extended before her by both arms at full reach. Then Mercado blacked out.

As O'Connel's shot echoed from across the street, Gibbs now looked up at the square opening a few feet over his head. Within this crude frame, blocking out much of the street light, was a young white man with prominent gold fillings in gray and black work clothes. He had a crew cut and eyes of black tar that stared down at Gibbs along the barrel of a pistol. Another shot echoed, and the man dropped his gun down the shaft, then collapsed outside the frame, blood spouting from his left temple as he fell, splattering along the concrete walls just above Gibbs's head.

"Come on up," said a deep but excited male voice from somewhere overhead. "I got you covered." Gibbs slowly and carefully ascended the rungs. When his head cleared the opening, he looked to his right and saw Duane Holland standing atop the seawall, his gun still in the ready position.

"Just like 'Nam," Gibbs said, "huh?"

"Boy, if this was 'Nam," Holland said, "that son of a bitch would have rolled a grenade in first."

New York City blue and white police vehicles began to arrive and had already walled off the intersection of Eighteenth Street and Eleventh Avenue in all three directions. Gibbs and Holland, his gun now back in his belt, squatted around the interceptor manhole and pulled Jon up the last few rungs from beneath his armpits as the flow of sewage continued to rush by below at the rate of 3,500 gallons per minute. It was almost as wet aboveground.

"The camera got lost," Jon said, shivering and short of breath as his head poked through the surface.

"You can probably pick it up at North River," Gibbs said, "along with my walkie-talkie." The two laid Jon out on his back on the pavement, inside the yellow traffic cones. Gibbs looked down at Jon and shook his head gently. "Well, I actually killed a man. Put a spike through his neck."

Jon looked up at Gibbs's sullen eyes and replied, "How does it feel?"

"Terrible," Gibbs said, cracking a minute smile.

"Getting shot feels terrible too," Jon said.

"You were shot?" Holland said. "Where?"

"Back of this shoulder," Jon said with a grunt, pointing with his right hand. Holland reached under Jon's waist and rolled him slowly so that his left side came over the top. Jon was now prone on the pavement. Holland pulled down Jon's jacket halfway and through a torn sleeve spotted a small bloody hole at the fleshy part of the triceps, just below where it met the shoulder.

"Yup, you're shot," Holland said.

"Oh God," Jon said, "that's what I figured. I never had anything like this happen before. God, it hurts."

"Don't worry, my man," Holland said, "you gonna be all right."

"And I thought getting hit by a pitch was bad."

He had stopped howling a half hour ago. As frightened as he was, there was no place for howling anymore, and certainly no one to hear it. This was a different sort of prison and a different sort of torture. Though moving perhaps fifteen miles per hour, he had found a strange, desperate kind of equilibrium as he thrashed about in the reeking, flowing darkness. There was air to breath between the top of the sewage flow and the concrete ceiling of the interceptor. Though he'd bobbed down occasionally and sucked in a mouthful of rancid water, so long as he kept his head in the airspace, he could survive. He had stopped trying to claw the slippery walls. That was more trouble than it was worth. He shivered. His lungs pumped and his heart raced. It had to be over soon. He had a house and a pool and a boat. He had money in the bank.

He had a slender young woman to screw. The tube was widening. It had just taken a sharp left turn. This was good news. The end was near. There was light at the end of the tunnel.

He submerged completely for a moment, holding his breath as he whooshed through the final length. His body was banged around now against the concrete sides of a turbulent whirlpool, but he was almost free. His head was back out of the water, his diaphragm whacking the insides of his chest cavity, making up for lost time. He was in the wet well. He'd made it, and at the top of the shaft he saw the light. He swung like a drunken brawler and caught the bar screen. His fingers fit snugly into the one-inch openings between the bars and now his chest was flush against the screen. Panting, he began pulling himself up, toward the light, up toward salvation. Only six stories to go.

But emerging from the water, catching his feet like an alligator, was something. Something with teeth that climbed up both his legs simultaneously, shearing the flesh almost to the bone. Please, if he could only go back and drown. It took his groin and his buttocks. Then his abdomen, as the teeth cut through his innards like chicken fat. The teeth consumed his sternum next. The last thing he saw were his shredded boots falling to the turbulent water below.

Chapter 41

The same stubbornness that made James Mercado a first-rate detective, almost wrecked his marriage, and motivated him to solve the Hudson City mystery in plainclothes now had him standing in the front desk area of the Tenth Precinct at eight-ten in the morning, leaning on crutches, his left leg heavily bandaged. The doctors at St. Luke's-Roosevelt Hospital on Fifty-eighth Street had absolutely forbidden him to leave, but once the nurses made the mistake of giving him the crutches, it was all over.

Throughout the soggy night and early morning, arrests rained down throughout the borough of Manhattan, and as Carl Bowers, the short, stout, dapper NYC police commissioner, promised a throng of reporters outside the Tenth, more were on their way. As police escorted a pale, sullen, handcuffed, trench-coat-hooded Eugene Reinhart from the station, Bowers added: "There goes one now."

Bowers pushed his way past police guards, into the station, saying he had some business to take care of inside. He had only to walk a dozen steps to get to Mercado, who leaned on a crutch beneath his left armpit, and on the front desktop with his right. Before he had the chance to look up, Mercado saw his old badge appear faceup in his open right palm.

"You're gonna need that if you want to interrogate Paul Emrick," Bowers said. "He's over at Beth Israel."

"Thanks," Mercado said, squeezing the badge.

"You'll be getting another one in a couple of weeks," Bowers said. "A gold one."

"Thanks."

"No problem. I already talked to the chief of detectives."

"What about Reinhart?" Mercado said. "How did you even know about him?"

"The D.A. tipped us off three weeks ago," Bowers said. "We put the Joint Terrorist Task Force on this. We've been working with the Justice Department and the FBI for about two weeks. A guy named George Nagle tells me you made the best damn vacationing detective the city's ever seen."

"You knew what I was doing?" Mercado said, his eyes for a moment looking innocent, like those of a young boy. "Why didn't you reach out?"

"We had you covered. Look, we felt things would go smoother this way," Bowers said. "Internal Affairs agreed. But you didn't hear *me* say that."

"With all due respect, Commissioner," Mercado said, straightening up with the help of his crutches and looking Bowers directly in the eyes, "you and I have had exactly three five-minute conversations in the four years you've been on this job. You may think you know me, but you don't. Some people believe the ends always justify the means. I, however, do not."

"Okay, Jimmy," Bowers said, "I understand. Look, it's up to you. You can spend the next ten years bellyaching about our policy of cooperating with the feds at all costs, or you can start helping me change things around here."

Three officers were now dragging Lee Sarnow into the building. Having made it past the cameras, he dropped the newspaper from his face. He shook his head and grinned, not as if in profound trouble, but as if there had been some insane administrative error that would be cleared up in ten minutes with a phone call. As Mercado struggled to place the free crutch beneath his right armpit, Bowers placed his right hand flat and firmly against the center of Mercado's chest.

"Go to Beth Israel, Jimmy," Bowers said. "We're going to hold him for you till you get back."

Mercado pushed past Bowers's gate and hobbled up to Sarnow, who now continued to grin as he looked Mercado in the face. Mercado had but three words.

"Merry Christmas, Fuckface."

The remaining color left Sarnow's expression as his eyes darted about his head, searching frantically for some tiny crack in the walls or ceiling that represented an escape. But in Mercado's absence, they had finally repainted and retiled the precinct.

Police escorted Ronald Arlen from the penthouse suite of the Arlen Palace Hotel at 7:48 A.M. The officers met no resistance from Arlen's bodyguards and in return gave him time to make a couple of phone calls and pull himself together. Reggie Lang was on his way. At 8:35, Arlen's Armani suit looked *GQ*-perfect even though his eyes were somewhat bloodshot. He had partied till 4:00 A.M. at the Limelight, where he threw a blowout bash for three dozen models from the Ford Agency. Donna was nowhere to be found. Rumor had it she was spending time with a skier from the Norwegian Olympic team.

"Okay, boys," Arlen announced as he emerged from his dressing room, "should I call my driver, or are you going to bring me back yourselves?"

Art Shuler usually liked to start his day early, arriving at the Municipal Building by limousine and getting to his desk about seven-thirty to read all the major newspapers and determine whether he was closer to or further from becoming mayor than he was the day before. Since his secretary usually didn't get in till eight-thirty, he would sometimes surprise people by answering the phone himself, announcing: "Mayor Shuler's office."

This Thursday morning, the voice mail was catching calls from reporters, constituents, and other politicians. At eight-nineteen, when four officers from the First Precinct, the borough commander, and two armed members of the FBI walked past the empty but cluttered secretary's desk and around the tight left-hand corner into the thousand-square-foot, plush-carpeted borough president's office, they were routinely prepared for some resistance but did not really expect much.

They got less than they expected. All seven froze in their tracks, even the FBI agent who was a former Navy SEAL and had done reconnaissance work at Grenada in 1983. The youngest of the officers from the First dug his left knee into the seat of a pillowy, upholstered chair and braced his arms against the chair back for momentary support. Like the others, he could not look, but could not look away. In the final analysis, it simply was what it was.

Art Shuler sat still behind his large mahogany desk, leaning back in his chair, arms hanging straight down as if it had already been a long day. The day was indeed over. Sticking out of his chest was the seven-inch dagger his father gave him when he'd been elected to his first term as borough president. Only the bottom inch or so of the blade was visible—that and the gold-plated handle with the city seal and Shuler's name both engraved. Behind him, intact, was a large framed artist's rendering of Hudson City. On the desk before him was a blood-soaked Hudson City sewer hookup permit agreement, unsigned. The ex–Navy SEAL broke the silence when he pulled his cell phone from his pocket, punched in seven numbers, and asked to leave a message for George Nagle.

"Yeah. Tell him what we have here is a real bleeding heart liberal."

Inside, three uniformed officers guarded Paul Emrick, who was just coming to. He lay in a bed at a 30-degree angle of recline with a freshly stitched thorax and an IV tube coming out of his left arm. His size was still formidable, his shoulders almost filling the mattress from side to side, but his goatee seemed less intimidating when covered with drool. Outside, in the hallway of Beth Israel at First Avenue and Sixteenth Street, two more uniformed officers stood guard as O'Connel and Mercado chatted and waited.

George Nagle now approached them from down the hallway, wearing a bemused expression.

"You just get here?" Nagle asked Mercado.

"Yeah," Mercado said, jiggling his right crutch, "I ran."

"I just had a strange message relayed to me," Nagle said. "Borough President Shuler was found in his office, with a knife in his chest. Suicide."

"You're kidding me," O'Connel said.

"I don't kid," Nagle replied. "That's fine. That saves us time on the prosecution. They picked up Ronald Arlen. Alive. He's on his way to the Tenth Precinct. Your neck of the woods, I understand."

"Great," O'Connel said. "We just redecorated. Hey, Jimmy, you'll never believe this. You know who I was told is on the third floor in intensive care and under guard?"

"Who?"

"Bruce Gregory. His hepatitis took a turn for the worse."

"I hope he gets better," Mercado said. "I can't wait to get that dirtbag in a lineup."

"He's talking," a uniformed officer announced, poking his head into the hallway.

"Okay, let's go," Nagle said. He turned to Mercado for a moment. "Hey, no hard feelings about the way we handled things? Letting you run with the ball?"

"Tell you what," Mercado said, "I'm gonna run with it now."

Mercado stepped up to the sluggish Emrick's left side, and the others followed. "Do you remember me?" he asked.

"No," Emrick grunted. "No."

"I'm Detective James Mercado, New York City police, Tenth Precinct. I arrested your friend Max McCord a few weeks ago."

"Where's Reggie Lang?" Emrick moaned. "They promised me Reggie Lang."

"Forget about Reggie Lang," Mercado said. "He's with Ronald Arlen, holding his hand. After that, he has a date with Paula Derbin. You're last on the list. In fact, fat boy, you're not even on the list. They have a plan for you. You're gonna take the fall for everyone and get a lethal injection—as soon as they make it legal again."

"What did *I* do?" Emrick asked.

"You killed Joel Haney, for starters," Mercado said. "You know how I know that? Your friend Max McCord told me that a few minutes ago. Everyone backs him up. And you think they're gonna send Reggie Lang for you."

"It was an accident," Emrick said, raising his voice and then recoiling from the pain. "We got into a fight. He was filming me. I hit him with a wrench. I wasn't trying to kill him. McCord is the one who dumped him in the sewer, I'm tellin' ya."

"Yeah, you are telling me," Mercado said. "Tell you what, today's your lucky day, fat boy. First I shoot you and get your fat belly instead of your heart. Then a game show host walks into your hospital room and says, 'Let's make a deal.' Welcome to plea city. Every name you give me and what they did, I'll have the D.A. take five years off your life sentence. You just got your first five points. A few more and maybe we'll wind up sending you on a vacation in the Bahamas when this is all over. But damn it, do some sit-ups before you hit the beach."

"Fuckface ran the whole thing," Emrick said, an eager and willing contestant. "Lee Sarnow. I got five thousand bucks a week in cash to work in the sewer, just like everybody else. Except McCord. He got ten thou a week."

"Wonderful," Mercado said, "you're making us all very proud."

"Yeah, that Fuckface looks like a wuss, but he's a sick dude," Emrick said. "Like when he killed that whore, Barbara. No reason. She says something about how small his dick is, and he's already pissed off because he just found out he can't have kids. Choked her on the spot. Went crazy in his car. No reason."

"Barbara?" Mercado said, his composure broken. "You mean Barbara Sadowski?"

"Yeah, yeah, the hooker," Emrick said. "McCord's the one who dumped the body in the river. Then it came back up a week later."

"Oh, you just scored big, fat boy," Mercado said. "Get that suntan lotion ready. Tell you what—take five. We're going to videotape this whole thing, and you're gonna give the performance of your life, starting from the beginning."

"Fine," Emrick said. "I got plenty more."

"Good boy," Mercado said. Nagle and O'Connel followed Mercado back out to the hallway, where he began unfolding a tripod.

"Hook, line, and sinker on McCord, Jimmy," O'Connel said.

"McCord didn't give him up?" Nagle asked.

"McCord's dead," Mercado said. "North River. The treatment plant. The mechanical rake arm chewed him up. Carried his shredded body sixty feet straight up the bar screen."

"Bar screen," Nagle asked. "What's a bar screen?"

"It keeps the garbage out of North River," Mercado replied.

Mercado recalled what Jon Kessler had told him about Paula Derbin, how her demeanor could range from charming and vivacious to raging and vicious, depending upon the circumstance. Mercado himself had sampled both extremes during his brief stint subjecting her to electronic surveillance, and right now expected the worst. Instead, he got the best. Paula was bright, bubbly, professional, and cooperative, as if this was a job interview. It was one of the bigger surprises in a day filled with surprises.

Mercado was running out of adrenaline now and could barely steady himself on his crutches. The camera crews were still there when he got back to the Tenth. Since the media had learned where Ronald Arlen was booked, the outside of the Tenth put P. T. Barnum to shame. Now, a few minutes after noon, George Nagle looked in from the one-way glass outside the interrogation room, content to let Mercado handle it. Weakened, Mercado had already passed the torch to O'Connel.

"Go ahead," Paula said. "Ask away. I'm ready to make a statement. I waive my right to an attorney. I am an attorney. I passed the bar in three states."

"That's wonderful, dear," O'Connel said, "but we really don't give a shit. We just want testimony we can use to convict every person who had anything to do with this conspiracy."

"I think I can help you there," Paula said, looking over her hot pink polished fingernails. "Detectives, I'm going to deliver the big fish. But I need some assurance first that there's something in it for me."

"It's got to be good," O'Connel said. "Most of this stock has already been bought up. We could walk out of here right now and still get you and half the people you work with life."

"What would you do," Paula said, smiling coyly, "if I told you I could deliver Borough President Art Shuler?"

"Try again, honey," O'Connel said. "Already a done deal. He won't be doing much time."

"Well, good for you." Paula said. Mercado rolled his eyes and leaned against the wall.

"How about Ronald Arlen?" O'Connel said.

"Well, he's an ambitious man," Paula said, thinking it over. "Very good at financial matters, always looking ahead to building the next project. Good in bed too, which is more than I can say for that stiff they hooked me up with. But, of course, impotence and sterility are not crimes in the state of New York. Though they should be."

Mercado struggled to get his crutches into position and limped toward the door. He'd barely closed it behind him when Detective Jack Dunleavy passed him in the hallway.

"Jimmy, you don't look so good. You wanna lie down somewhere?"

"Yeah, the Bahamas."

"Can I get you anything?"

"Yeah, a stenographer. And a three-quarters disability."

"You're getting a statement from that lawyer chick?" Dunleavy asked.

"Jack, she's crazy," Mercado said. "Lost it. Gone, goodbye. Certifiably insane. I don't know what it is about working for the city."

"You wanna hear insane?" Dunleavy said.

"Yeah."

"Lee Sarnow just tried to jump out a window."

Friday, June 4, a few minutes after noon, against all sorts of medical advice, Detective James Mercado sat behind the desk in his new office and caught his breath. The bowling trophies, the *Hustler* magazines, the extra-large male girdle—as far as he could tell, all of Eugene Reinhart's stuff had been boxed. There was a knock on the door, and before he could reply, Detective O'Connel had taken a step into the room.

"Jimmy, I've got a young woman here to see you," O'Connel said, smiling herself. "I won't tell you any more."

"All right, send her in." Mercado didn't really want to do this. He had heard earlier in the day that one of the prostitutes who knew Barbara had some information for him. Maybe it was Tiffany Kline. Aside from the fact that he wanted finally to tie up and forget about that case and dozens more like it, he always had a problem dealing with the hookers. Uncharacteristically, he would fight to maintain his objectivity, his heart grieving over the fact that this was someone's daughter—perhaps not far removed from slumber parties and ballet lessons—being destroyed daily for pocket change. He had a daughter of his own.

Now, the young woman who stood before him only reinforced that grief. At about seventeen, she was—mercifully—not worn yet. But the other signs were present. The slim, fetching looks. The thin red halter top revealing bony shoulders. The painfully tight jeans. The pierced nose, and—oh, God, why did they do it— the pierced tongue. But as she spoke, the words were self-assured and well enunciated.

"I want to thank you for finding my father's killer. It means a lot to me."

"What?" Mercado said, refiguring everything.

"I'm Deena Haney. I had to come here to thank you. I already spoke to Miss O'Connel. My father was a wonderful man, and I miss him so much it hurts me every day. But yesterday was the first day I actually began to feel better. And the strange thing is, all I did was cry."

"Well . . . of course," Mercado said. "I lost my father when I was your age. Are you in school?"

"Senior, this fall," she replied. "I'm going to film school at NYU the following year. I can't wait."

"Good for you," Mercado said. "You know, let me tell you what I learned. Your father will always be alive as long as you live to honor him and speak to him in your heart."

"That's not easy," she said, "considering how they smeared him."

"Don't worry about it," Mercado said. "I know a very famous reporter. And he owes me one."

It was Wednesday, June 9, a few minutes before two in the afternoon. Jon had minutes earlier run up the double-curved stairway on the city hall rotunda. The stairway's keystone-cantilevered construction gave the illusion of weightlessness, contrasting with the heavy feeling in his head. Now it was just Jon and Mayor Vincent Gianetta in the mayor's office on the second floor. Jon studied the blue, white, and orange flag of the city of New York hanging from on high. The year on the city seal in the center was

1625. It depicted a colonial Dutchman and an Algonquin Indian chief in full regalia, perhaps coming to terms in the city's first real estate swindle. The fable of Peter Minuit buying Manhattan Island for twenty-four dollars in trinkets was as real as the agreement Jon had made two and a half years earlier to risk his life repeatedly for the city of New York. Jon sat down.

"It's official," the mayor said from behind his huge oak desk. "I'm going to run one more time. And I'm going to win."

"Congratulations," Jon said without affect.

"I'd like to do something for you, Jon," the mayor said.

"I'm not sure you *can* do anything for me," Jon said plainly.

"I feel I *need* to do something for you," the mayor said. "I gave your two friends early retirement."

"Yeah. They were thrilled," Jon said just as plainly. "I have a couple of friends who are dead. Can you do anything for them?"

"Jon, I wanted to bail you out when you were really snowed under, but I understand there was a mix-up between yourself and Janet. Well, at least you're alive now!"

"Reports of my resurrection are greatly exaggerated," Jon said.

"Well," the mayor said, "if you do wake up one morning and decide you are indeed alive, how would you like to be deputy mayor in charge of infrastructure?"

"Thank you . . . I think."

"There's a construction boom going on in this city. I need someone who's independent-minded."

"I'm flattered," Jon said, "but right now everything's a blur. A talent agency called yesterday. They said they can get me five thousand dollars per speaking engagement. Then they said something about getting my nose fixed."

"Okay, good for you, Jon. You think about it. My experience with that kind of thing is that it blows over rather quickly. But I understand why your thirst for a life in government isn't quite there now. That's the very reason I want you."

It was two-thirty. His meeting with the mayor had just ended and now Jon stood by a pay phone on the outskirts of City Hall Park. Things hadn't slowed down nearly enough for him, and he still saw the nightmare in the interceptor every time he tried to sleep. Strange people offered him all kinds of things for which he had no frame of reference. He was glad he didn't own a phone, though several vulturous types had made the ridiculous assumption that he still checked his voice mail at the borough president's office. Of course, he still did.

The *Daily News* had reported that there was already another group of investors, led by Gerald Grossberg, interested in financing an alternative development on the old West Side Rail Yard between Fifty-ninth Street and Seventy-second Street. No additional details were available yet. That story, of course, was a tiny piece of filler. It was buried by Mark Rosario's gargantuan article, which had been sold exclusively to the *Daily News*. Jon read the lead-in, appearing in eighteen-point bold type on the front page.

> One was a frustrated city engineer. Another was a renegade detective. Another was a sewer worker nearing retirement. Another was a civil servant long ago written off as mentally unfit. But they all had something in common—the desire for putting an end to business as usual in the game of politics and development in the city of New York.

Jon pulled from his knapsack the plain postcard Pat Truitt had found in his mailbox at the borough president's office the day before, and now read it again as well.

> Jon, there was something between us, and there's no use denying it. I want you to know that I didn't want to hurt you and in private always fought for your safety. I will always love you.
> —Naomi

Jon considered tearing it into a thousand pieces now, but stopped himself. It was postmarked Athens, Georgia. He'd give it to Mercado. It was worth a shot. Now, waking up from his revery, he remembered that he'd just used his calling card to dial Elaine down south.

"Hello?" she answered.

"Elaine, I'm sorry I was out of it last night when I called. I'm not getting enough sleep. But I feel a little better today."

"Good," Elaine said.

"Some money-making opportunities have come up, Elaine. Inside and outside of engineering."

"Good," Elaine said. "I think I'm pregnant."

"Oh my God."

"Yup," Elaine said. "I'm only a couple of days late, but I'm nauseous. You know—been there, done that."

"I guess if it's a girl, we'll name her Naomi."

"Not if you want her to have a father," Elaine said.

"Hey, look on the bright side," Jon said. "Now that you're pregnant, we don't have to worry about your getting pregnant. In our new life, I'd like to take out one day a week and just have wild, animalistic sex."

"I don't think so," Elaine said.

"What did I do now?"

"I'm almost thirty-five, Jon. Read *Cosmo*. I need it every day."

Acknowledgments

Acknowledging everyone who in some way helped me scale this mountain is something I dread, if only for the inevitable omissions and oversights. But the worst oversight of all would be to not make the attempt.

L. Ann Rocker of the North River Community Environmental Review Board showed me and thousands of others how knowledge is power. Madeleine Polayes, Batya Lewton, and Edgar Freud of the Coalition for a Livable West Side gave me not only a model for relentlessness in the name of justice but the chance to fight the good fight.

Tim Forker of the Manhattan Borough President's Office displayed courage and honesty I will not soon forget. Marty Kotin, Ken Nemchin, and Molly Liu are true friends who always kept the door open. Mariet Morgan, Angela Dews, Judy McClain, and many others proved to me on a daily basis that committed government service is a kind of nobility.

Wayne Barrett and Denise Kiernan must be thanked for inadvertently starting me along this path. Tom Castronuova of the Easton Bureau of Engineering is acknowledged for taking the time to help out a stranger.

Without the encouragement of friends like Jim Craner and Peggy Clark Craner, the only things I'd be writing these days are shopping lists and my signature on building inspection reports. Rick Spear has been there for me from day one, and Ellen Zimmerman Spear is his perfect complement. Marc Landis, Matt Selton, Hunter Gordon, Carol Novak Gordon—your boost while I was in midstream kept me from drowning. Elliot Berkowitz, Abram Hall, Peter Robbins—you are top-notch folks and great shoulders to lean on.

I have been blessed with the world's greatest family, one that holds supreme the dreams of its sons and daughters. Jack and Judy Herschlag and Charles and Marianne Mann are rocks who anchor those around them. My mother Harriet is always still with me. Sue and Rachel have the hardest lot. They have to hear my unedited diatribes in the kitchen. Jane and Herb Herschlag gave me a second home for about half my adult life. Irwin, Sandra, Danny and Anju, Yonason and Sarah, David and Sheila, Megan and Nick, Alex, Josh, Vivian, Jobette, Greg, Barbara, David, John, Lois, the rest of your ever-growing clans, and everyone else who cared— *muchas gracias* a hundred times over.

Around now, a drum roll should be heard in the distance, ending with a deafening cymbal crash.

I thank Detective John M. Gaspar (NYPD, ret.) for his tremendously valuable technical assistance and frank discussions regarding real police work.

I thank Donald Warnett, P.E., for helping to build the real interceptor as well as this book.

I thank Jonathan Ridgeway, NYCDEP, for opening the vault and showing me the underground.

I thank my agent, John Ware, for his professional guidance and his priceless friendship.

Last, and as it turns out, foremost, my editor, Doug Grad. Doug, you have vision, dedication, and talent that are rare in any walk of life. You used them keenly and generously to shepherd my work, and for that you have my most profound thanks.

About the Author

Richard Herschlag was born and raised in New York City. He is a graduate of Princeton University (BSE, 1984), where he studied civil engineering. After college, he worked as an engineer for the New York City Department of Sanitation, the New York City Parks Department, and the consulting firm of Syska & Hennessy. He received his full New York State license as a professional civil engineer in 1991. From 1991 to 1995 he served as Chief Borough Engineer for the Office of the Manhattan Borough President, where he focused on policy issues relating to building safety, municipal sewage treatment, roadway reconstruction, park design, and environmental regulation.

In 1993 he foretold the collapse of the building at 350 West 110th Street in Manhattan, as reported by the *Westsider*. His various professional achievements have been reported on by publications including the *New York Post*, the *New York Daily News*, *Newsday*, the *Westsider*, the *Amsterdam News*, the *Sun*, and the *Village Voice*.

Since leaving the Borough President's Office in January 1995, he has performed extensive research on behalf of the Coalition for a Livable West Side, which is suing New York City for violation of the federal Clean Water Act, specifically for understating by approximately thirty million gallons per day the flow to the North River Water Pollution Control Plant. The litigation is now pending a decision in federal court. As a private consulting engineer, Mr. Herschlag also performs a variety of services for his clients, including residential and commercial property inspection and structural design.

He lives in Easton, Pennsylvania—just across the Delaware River and about an hour outside New York City—with Susan, his wife of ten years, and their five-year-old daughter, Rachel.

THE
ANGEL OF
DARKNESS
by Caleb Carr

In *The Angel of Darkness*, Caleb Carr brings back the vivid world of his bestselling *The Alienist* and once again proves his brilliant ability to re-create the past.

It is June 1897. A year has passed since Dr. Kreizler and his team of trusted companions tracked down a brutal serial killer. But another series of deaths pits Kreizler and his colleagues against a murderer as evil as the darkest night. . . .

Published by Ballantine Books.
Available in your local bookstore.